No Place Like You
Christina A. Bennett

As Written Books

For my parents, who have the ultimate Love Story.

Soundtrack

Music was instrumental in creating this story. I revisited the songs on this playlist so many times, trying to recapture the moment, mood, or feeling that I needed to get down on the page. I hope you will listen along for an immersive reading experience that evokes the soul of this love story.

Scan the QR Code for Spotify Link.

Prologue

Perry

P erry blinked awake, his tired eyes coming into focus on an unfamiliar room. Sunlight streamed in through unfamiliar curtains. He lay
still, listening to the quiet as his bearings slowly came back to him. For
a moment, he'd forgotten where he was, and that he'd spent the night
with the girl of his dreams sleeping away soundly on his chest.

He stretched an arm out, palm grazing the sheets where her sleeping
form should've been, finding it empty. Cold. No soft skin tucked against
him, no sleepy murmur in his ear, no trace of the girl he'd finally had a
real moment alone with.

"Lauryn?" He sat up to look around the now recognizable hotel
room. His eyes scanned the space, confirming what he already knew.

Her heels and purse were missing from the nearby console.

Her overnight bag that had been open on the luggage stand was gone.
And so was she.

Perry eased off the bed and checked the time. Barely nine in the
morning. She wouldn't have checked out already, would she? And if
so, why hadn't she woken him?

He wracked his brain trying to remember anything he might have
done to put her off. Had he managed to ruin things before they'd even
gotten started? After she'd kissed him so softly in the dark the night
before, her soft pink dress shimmering in the dim light from the lanterns
along Wacker Drive.

Perry stared at the swirls in the sheets where she'd been curled into his side just a few hours ago. She'd been warm, soft, impossibly close after six years of never being able to tell her how he really felt.

They hadn't slept together–not fully. Just kisses that somehow felt like confessions, their fingers wandering, both of them laughing and whispering in each other's ears. She'd pressed so close he'd been convinced she felt the same way.

Did I move too fast?

Perry's jaw worked as he considered it, finding his dress shirt and shrugging into it. He buttoned it up slowly, wondering if he should have declined when she'd invited him to stay and get some sleep before he got on the road. It'd been late when he'd walked her to her hotel last night, and even later when they closed out at the hotel bar. He'd been headed toward the hotel lobby doors, but upon her asking, had escorted her upstairs instead. And couldn't believe when she'd invited him in. He'd been telling himself all evening that if she asked him to stay, he would.

Maybe he'd read the moments all wrong, misjudged the shift in her eyes, and the way her laugh softened around him. Or worse, had he inadvertently said or *done* something that made her uncomfortable?

No. Perry crossed the room again in long strides to retrieve his phone from beside the bed. His battery was dying, but he swiped his thumb across the screen to call her anyway, setting it to speaker phone.

It rang once. Twice. Three times.

"Lo. At least let me know that you're alright, girl," he grumbled into the phone, starting to pace.

Maybe she wouldn't. "Hey," her voice came through, faint, a little breathless, the muffled clang of a train announcement breaking through in the background. "Sorry... hold on."

He stopped pacing. "Lauryn?"

"Yeah...sorry, I'm on the train. Headed back."

Back? "You're on your way home?"

"Yeah, back to the burbs." The pitch in her voice tipped higher, airy in a way that sounded like she'd practiced exactly what to say to him. As if there was any possible way they could skip over the awkwardness of her disappearing at the crack of dawn.

Perry listened for her to continue, the clamoring sounds of the train sounding a lot like all the questions banging around in his mind. "You good?"

She hesitated just long enough to make him doubt everything, before rushing in, "Yeah I'm good. I meant to text, I'm sorry. I had something early that I totally forgot. Didn't wanna wake you."

"I wish you had." And he did. At least then he wouldn't feel like he'd imagined their closeness. "I would've made sure you got home, or at least given you a ride to the train."

"No! I just got a cab. You enjoy the room. It's already paid for and one of us should be able to sleep in," her laugh was unlike the laughter he'd heard last night, missing the ease with which she'd rolled him onto his back, her dense straightened hair falling around them like a curtain as she kissed him.

She paused, softer now, like she was smiling on the other end of the line. "But... last night was good. It was really great to see you.'

Great to see me? Perry exhaled, stepping forward and switched off the speaker phone. He held the phone to his ear with one hand, while the other wound in the air as if it might help him form his next question. "Lo, did something happen that you didn't want to happen? Did I–did I say something?"

"No, Perry." Her voice was clearer this time, firm and warm. "No, you were a gentleman, as always."

"Then what?"

"It was just... the drinks hit kinda hard, I think?" She exhaled with another laugh as if she was trying to keep it light. "And maybe the whole romantic *wedding* reception vibe and all. But it was really, really nice to hang. I promise."

Perry swallowed and his jaw loosened, but the knot in his chest remained.

She continued, gentle but final. "Thank you for being my unofficial wedding date."

He closed his eyes, anchoring himself in her warming tone. "Any time. You know that."

Her breath caught, like maybe she wanted to say more, but then the loudspeaker cut through, her voice rushing out, "I gotta go, the train is almost at my stop."

"Lauryn-" he started, but heard the triple dial tone of the call dropping. He held the phone out, finding the screen black and the device completely dead.

Perry cursed. He had no charger, no way to call her back until he got back to his car. And even then... would it matter?

He could chase her, maybe. Call her once his phone was charged. However, something about the way she'd slipped out, quiet and careful like it was safer to leave it all unsaid, made him hesitate.

Perry sank down onto the hard couch near the windows. From where he sat, he could see Wacker and the Chicago River that was already sparkling in the morning light on its way out to Lake Michigan. He wasn't supposed to have last night. Not the way she'd felt in his arms, or how her laugh sounded when she finally let it spill out unguarded. He wasn't supposed to have the weight of her thigh draped over his, or the quiet little gasp when his fingers traced down her stomach. He wasn't supposed to have any of it, but it had happened.

He'd finally had her close, and she still chose to go. Still chose distance. Maybe it was the drinks, or just every damn thing he'd never said out loud.

It really didn't matter now.

She was gone. And he didn't know what hurt more: the fact that she left, or how right it had felt before she did.

He sat there in the stillness, her absence loud and pressing on him. Now there was only air. Just questions and the imprint of something real she hadn't stayed long enough for them to claim.

Chapter 1

Winter 2022

Lauryn

"T his mother fu-" Lauryn grumbled under her breath as she adjusted a sticky silicone nipple cover over her left breast for the third time in a row.

It was bad enough she was running late, and for a party with people she hadn't seen in over a decade. The last thing she needed was to add a stray nipple in the mix. After a few more minutes tugging, carefully peeling, only to reapply again, she gave up on the pasties completely. Exasperated and increasingly annoyed, she tossed both of them, one after the other into an empty shoe box lying nearby. Each landed with a slap against the crisp tissue paper. She decided to simply raise the straps of the chocolate brown slip dress she'd chosen to wear because putting on a dress was easier than trying to figure out a whole outfit when she was anxious enough already.

She plucked at the delicate straps until the right amount of cleavage had been concealed.

In about thirty minutes she was due to appear at a holiday-slash-birthday party for a high school friend she had not laid eyes on since they were barely old enough to drink. Suddenly, it struck her just how much time had passed. Enough time for history to turn over: the first Black president, a once-in-a-century pandemic, wars and recessions, hashtags that became movements, and a whole new generation raised online. Kids born after her college graduation, now running the internet like it was theirs all along. And just enough time for her to lose herself completely in a relationship, only for that same relationship to detonate in her face. After twelve years with the same man, she had nothing to show for it.

She'd spent the whole day debating whether to go to the party at all, her imagination running wild with the questions people might ask. Eventually, Lauryn realized she didn't owe anyone the whole story. She could reveal as much or as little as she wanted. Over the years, she'd lost touch with this particular crowd and whatever glimpses they'd caught of her life were filtered through the careful lens of social media: bright smiles, fashionable moments and curated captions, the sheen of having it all the way together. None of it hinted at how restless she'd felt these last few years. How unhappy she'd been.

Though she'd decided to go to the party, the thought of facing old acquaintances made her feel jittery and uneasy.

She shook her head, best not to psych herself out and guarantee a terrible evening. She made up her mind to just go as-is: bad breakup, unruly nipples, and all. Pretense required energy Lauryn didn't have. There would be no crafted backstory tonight, no carefully constructed explanations about where she'd been or why she was suddenly back in Chicago.

A moment later, her phone buzzed on the dresser, and she didn't need to look to know it was her friend Deonna. Probably calling to confirm Lauryn was still coming. Lauryn let it ring, apologizing out loud to the room as the call went to voicemail, "Sorry, girl." She would call Deonna back from the car. Right now, she needed to maintain the fragile aura of calm before this party.

Standing before the sink, she sized herself up in the mirror, not so much inspecting, but accepting the reflection before her. She pulled her mass of thick hair to the side and rubbed a vanilla musk oil behind her ears.

Just three weeks before, she'd been minding her business, picking up a few things for her new place when she heard someone call her entire government name across the mall plaza.

"Lauryn Michelle Lindsey!"

Deonna Abernathy, weighed down with Sephora and Nordstrom bags, had been craning her neck to see Lauryn past one of the frozen fountains. The comfort of seeing a familiar face caught Lauryn off guard. She'd been so focused on starting over without distraction, but putting one's life back together during the holiday season was none too easy. It was wonderful to reconnect with someone.

Deonna had been more of an acquaintance in high school, but they'd reconnected once or twice after undergrad and Lauryn remembered how cool she was. She liked to be on the scene, have a good time, and didn't judge. They had fallen out of touch over the years, Deonna moving to Miami for a while and Lauryn getting caught up in her ex's whirlwind, but it seemed their friendship would be reborn in a new light. And for the past couple of weeks, Deonna had been exceedingly thoughtful, inviting her out for coffee and gifting her a welcome-home basket of candles and sage. "Clear that old energy out of your new space, girl."

Lauryn, unsure of whether she believed in the cleansing powers of sage, had nearly burned down her new kitchen trying to light it. She'd ended up leaving the charred little bundle outside in the snow on her balcony. Remembering it now, she quickly blew out all the candles around her bathroom.

The vanity was as cluttered as Lauryn's thoughts, with bits of jewelry, eye shadows and a make-up-stained towel hanging over the edge of the sink. Her dress with its silky length and lace trimmed neckline, might have been a little too much for the evening, but it made her *feel* good. And that, she desperately needed to quell her anxiety. Turning to examine her back side in the mirror, she tried to channel Whitney Houston in the opening scene of the film, *Waiting to Exhale*.

Of course, she was nowhere near as long and lean as Ms. Houston was. The dress cascaded over Lauryn's hourglass figure without tugging. She had a short torso, like her mother and aunties, but long legs for a woman less than five-foot-five inches. Still, Lauryn started to feel just as good as she'd felt watching that scene for the first time as a young girl. Even if she'd had no business watching it.

With a final turn in the mirror, Lauryn decided the dress was getting worn no matter what and pressed a pair of diamond studs into her ears. She tried to pick up the pace. If Deonna was calling, she was probably running a lot later than she thought she was.

Padding into her bedroom, past stacks of moving boxes, she tiptoed across the newly installed cream carpet. Most of her furniture had yet to be delivered, but she was almost tempted to stay home, turn on her music and finish unpacking. "Too late to cancel," she said aloud and reached for a pair of knee-high, pointed-toe snakeskin boots. They were her favorite pair and just pulling them out of the box improved her mood tenfold.

The boots were a splurge from a ski trip with her ex for his fortieth birthday. He'd pissed her off so badly, she bought the boots as a reward for tolerating a weekend of his theatrics and obnoxious ego.

In the last few years Joseph Gray, her ex, had gone from being the man she loved most in the world to a person she hardly recognized. To the point where six weeks ago, she'd walked out on him and a near twelve-year relationship. She'd left behind their life in Memphis; a completely decorated home, friends, her job–everything.

Joe had been impossible in the end, taking all the pain and disappointment of their break up for himself. After months of being distant and refusing to communicate, he was suddenly so devastated at how their relationship had unraveled. He claimed the situation had been affecting him more than he realized, and he "just didn't know how to fix them".

Lauryn ground her teeth, grimacing as some of their last conversations replayed in her mind. Like many narcissistic men, Joseph took up all the space in the room, if you let him. What's more, he was an artist, with a fully loaded arsenal of passions, eccentricities and self-inflicted wounds.

Now, back in her hometown, Lauryn was determined to get back to herself. Detox from all of Joe's erratic emotions and manipulation. She pulled on a full-length chocolate brown suede coat, feeling fortified as she locked her front door.

"That's the last time we're thinking about him tonight," she muttered to herself, dropping her keys into a furry Brandon Blackwood clutch that matched the trim on her coat sleeves, then headed down to her car.

It was unseasonably warm in Illinois, far warmer than she ever remembered December to be while she was growing up. Whatever snow had fallen was completely melted and swaths of soggy brown grass were everywhere. Still, the wind coming off of Lake Michigan would be whipping through the skyscrapers downtown and she was glad for the gloves stuck down in her coat pockets.

She sped down streets she knew well, avoiding traffic on her way toward the highway. However, after so long away, her hometown felt foreign. Rather, she felt like a stranger in a place that should have been familiar. And now, after painstakingly planning her new life she was getting derailed already. Her first ninety days were meant to be quiet and undisturbed. When she stepped off the plane at O'Hare Airport four weeks before, she'd been eager for the space to process somewhere neutral. She feared this party might leave her a little more exposed than she wanted to be.

Her phone buzzed again, this time a text message from Deonna.

> Girl, where are you?

Lauryn bit her lip, she'd meant to call back. Instead, she typed a quick, *OMW,* before dropping her phone into the cup holder.

"Siri, play afro beats," she said aloud, and one of her favorite tracks sounded. She turned up the volume just as the Chicago skyline came into view. It was a sight she had seriously missed, the twinkling lights standing tall against the deepening evening. It was the first place she'd come to know herself, where she hoped to find herself again after so much time betraying her dreams for someone else's.

As she exited onto Ohio Street and maneuvered her car past the familiar buildings, memories flooded back. Old haunts, summer festivals, and tucked off places that had shaped her after college.

She found parking just across the street from the party and couldn't help how sexy she felt crossing South Michigan Avenue for the first time in so long. The knee-high boots did exactly what they were supposed to–lengthening her legs, adding sway in her step that masked her misgivings about this party. The doorman practically jumped when he saw her, springing up to greet her with a grin and guiding her toward the gilded elevator doors.

On the top floor, the elevator chimed and the doors slid open–TLC's *Sleigh Ride* sounding all the way down the hallway. She couldn't help but follow the beat, grinning as it pulled her straight to the right apartment.

Lauryn stepped in slowly, taking in the entryway with its oversized concrete console tables, decked out with succulents, spotted orchids, and glossy satin Christmas ornaments in blush and gold. Voices mingled in the background, but it wasn't until she heard a familiar laugh that she moved deeper into the space.

Deonna spotted her first, her whole face lighting up as she waved. "Ah! You made it!" she called, loud enough to turn a few heads.

Lauryn felt the eyes on her as she walked over, but she stayed calm, steady.

"Sorry I'm late," she said once she reached her friend, admiring the waist-length, Sade-inspired braid that swung every time Deonna moved. When they embraced, Lauryn noticed her perfume, something sultry and sweet, like cocoa laced with tonka. Leave it to Deonna to find a fragrance that matched her energy exactly.

"You're right on time. To new beginnings?" Deonna said, her up-turned eyes sparkling as she handed Lauryn a glass of wine.

Lauryn accepted the glass, clinking it gently against Deonna's.

"To new beginnings."

Chapter 2

Lauryn

"Girl, you look amazing. I didn't know you were comin' with all of that!" Deonna took a step back to admire Lauryn's outfit.

"Thank you girl. And my bad, running late. In my own head," She exhaled, rolling her eyes and pointing to her temple.

Deonna nodded and linked arms with her, leading her through the living area–a stunning mix of white, cream, black, brown, and rust. Lauryn was still taking it all in when Deonna steered them straight into an adjoining, equally impressive room.

"Come on," she said over her shoulder. "The grown folks are in here."

"I'm sorry, grown folks?" Lauryn's delicate eyebrows drew together in her confusion.

"*Our* people!" she emphasized. "Everyone else here are Nathan's NBA friends, hence the excessive height and all the groupies standing around with blank expressions."

"Not blank expressions," Lauryn stifled a laugh. She remembered Nathan and that he'd gone pro after high school, but she'd forgotten how ruthless, and hilarious, Deonna's mouth could be. "Groupies? Wait, who's here that I would know?"

"People from high school, people from U of I. A ton of folks you probably know, girl, they're going to be shook when they see you."

Lauryn smiled weakly, a little shook herself. She was learning fast that Deonna enjoyed bringing everyone together. As the queen of calendar invites and candor, the woman kept a running Pinterest page of restaurant openings, poetry readings, and brunch hot spots. And although she always extended an invite to Lauryn, she managed to maintain a friendly distance. In the past few weeks, whenever they met for breakfast or furniture shopping, Deonna had never once asked about Joe. She kept it all above board, asking about her career, her family, where all she had been traveling all these years.

Feeling a warm appreciation for Deonna, Lauryn leaned into her a little more as they shimmied past more party guests and high boy tables.

"Hey ya'll," Deonna announced when they reached a tight circle of people talking.

Lauryn was bringing up the rear, moving slowly as she marveled at the expansive apartment. She thought about her own condo. This place felt stylish and intimate, with custom cabinetry and lighting. Where her new place, by comparison, felt a little stark and prefabricated. When she finally caught up to Deonna again, she immediately recognized several faces.

One of the guys was joking with Deonna, making the entire group laugh. He nodded toward her in acknowledgement but soon doubled back in recognition. "Lauryn Lindsey? Oh, shit!"

He immediately engulfed her in a warm hug.

"Well, hello, Michael!" she laughed into his shoulder, suddenly remembering the very last class, on their very last day of high school. He'd worn Sean Jean from head to toe, including a hat and matching backpack. The outfit had been huge on him—had practically swallowed him whole. However, he was not to be out done on the last day of school.

She saw all of them this way, as they had been the last time she saw them, whether high school or college. Slowly, as the 'welcome homes' settled down, their faces began to morph and she could see them as they were now. Faces were fuller or slightly thinner. The guys she remembered from football practice were a little rounder than they had been doing burpees in the grass. The women too, were all grown up, clutching their designer handbags and cocktails where there had once been textbooks and Vitamin Water. She was grateful the group was small, knowing there might be several waves of this.

"Are you back in Chicago or just visiting?" another classmate, Jeremy Gaines, asked her.

"I just moved back," Lauryn confirmed, surprising herself. Did she want anyone to know she was back?

"Ah—going against the grain! Seems like everyone we know is moving south now. Change of scene I guess, better cost of living. I get it."

"Better weather," Lauryn added, laughing.

Jeremy's wife, Sasha Gaines, who'd graduated a year before them, whooped and raised her glass to toast Lauryn on that point, then realized her wine glass was empty. "Do you need another drink?"

"I'm good, Sasha, thanks," Lauryn smiled warmly, intent to keep a level head tonight. Years before she'd attended their wedding, as well as several other couples in the room.

She thought back to the year she finished grad school, when it felt like every week brought another wedding invitation. For four straight months, her inbox filled with e-invites and cheerful texts asking for her mailing address. Many of those couples had children now, most were close in age, and the couples who'd stayed in Illinois still managed to see each other often.

"You missed Friendsgiving at Anthony's house. Such a good time!"

Lauryn turned to see a woman she recognized but whose name she couldn't immediately place. She pictured her as a girl sitting in science class—then it clicked. Fallon. She'd always had the prettiest braids, but the short natural cut she wore now was absolutely stunning.

"His brisket is good," another friend chimed in.

"Fire! I told him I'm putting my order in for Christmas." They were all laughing, reminiscing about times that Lauryn hadn't been present for and she took the opportunity to step away. Somewhere in the last twenty minutes, Deonna had disappeared, but her infectious laugh could still be heard over the music.

Lauryn wandered through the rooms, taking in the scene. She thought back to industry events she'd gone to with Joe, the way she used to walk in beside him like she belonged there. Back then, he was still finding his footing—on the cusp, not quite known. The artists and celebrities in the room didn't rattle her then, mostly because they didn't know her. Honestly, they barely knew Joe.

Slowly, he started to break through, beginning to move in those circles for real. But somehow, *this*—being alone in a room full of familiar faces from a past life—felt more unsettling than those early red carpet walks ever had. Joe's people didn't know her backstory, and weren't measuring her against who she used to be. As Joe's band gained more clout, people barely engaged her, speaking only to Joe or stealing him away completely. Somehow, that anonymity felt safer than the recognition she was feeling now.

She'd been at the party for close to an hour, catching up with more people than she could count, when the DJ finally arrived. The R&B holiday mix was abruptly switched for a Kanye classic that took them all back to freshman year. The energy of the crowd shifted and people's arms went up as they caught the beat and started dancing. She marveled at the power of music, that a single song could have her smiling and tracing her lips with a single manicured finger as if she was right back on campus; belted jeans, graphic tee and all.

Still mouthing the words and sashaying in time with the song, Lauryn made her way out onto the terrace. Heat lamps and a quartz fire pit glowed, warming the space comfortably. She scanned the lounge areas, hoping for an open spot. Most of the couches were taken by groups of women engaged in either flirtation or gossip. She was enjoying the air, but standing awkwardly in the center of the terrace was not the ideal perch. Moving to the edge of the terrace, she gazed out at the skyline where a half-million windows glinted back at her. Until this moment she hadn't quite realized how much she missed this city. It startled her how much it felt like home, even after so many years.

She spotted Deonna across the room, seated at a table with several women Lauryn had met for the first time that night—wives of their old high school friends. Deonna waved, a quick flicker of recognition, but seemed to understand that Lauryn had no plans to join them.

The scene was very familiar. Back when she used to travel with Joe, she'd often found herself in the *Wives Circle;* never a wife herself, but an "honorary member," as they used to say, because she and Joe had been together so long. Lauryn had always known better. The invitation wasn't about inclusion. It was about surveillance.

Lauryn wrestled with the memories, anger rising over all the things she should've said, the things she should've done differently. She thought about how much of it had been self-inflicted, how long she'd lingered under the pretense of success and happiness, convincing herself it was enough. Before applying for her new job, she'd considered moving away to some small place where no one knew her. A true fresh start–she fantasized about a peaceful house that she'd fix up and the contentment that would come with a small-town routine.

Something like the rom-com movies that always ended on a high note, with the heroine making more of an impact on the town than she thinks she will.

"All the skinny chicks took all the seats," Lauryn turned to find Kayla Jones, another alum from the University of Illinois, stepping up beside her.

"Yeah, it seems that way," Lauryn let out a slow, surprised laugh.

Kayla looked exactly the same as she had in school, save for a few more piercings. They'd lived in the same dorm and had more than a few classes together, but Lauryn had never been sure Kayla liked her. Something about a guy sophomore year? She couldn't really remember. "How are you, Kayla?"

"Doin' alright, girl," Kayla's tone was pleasant enough, and Lauryn felt a little silly for assuming there might still be tension after all this time.

But several minutes passed without Kayla saying another word.

Lauryn blinked, unsure whether to linger or drift away. She already felt awkward standing alone, but now it felt even more ridiculous to be standing this close to someone in complete silence. Maybe time hadn't erased the tension after all.

She pressed her lips together, slowly winding her hands as she tried to think of something to say.

She nodded toward Kayla's red Solo cup. "So, what are you drinking?"

"The sangria. I don't usually drink, but I was at my social limit. If I didn't have something soon, the introvert in me was going to start shutting down my organs," she cracked up, the corners of her eyes crinkling with joy.

Lauryn laughed hard—she understood very well what it felt like to endure a crowd for too long.

Over the years, her roles at work—and being with Joe—had conditioned her for endless small talk. She'd built up a tolerance, learned how to pace herself, how to preserve energy between mingling and making conversation with total strangers.

She also knew when to make a graceful exit.

"I think I'm going to get some of that sangria," she announced smoothly.

"It's strong as hell, girl," Kayla called over her shoulder as Lauryn inched back toward the door. It might have been Lauryn's own nerves that made the moment uncomfortable. As she pressed back indoors, shouldering her way through the party crowd, she realized Kayla was fine.

The apartment was full of more people than she would've ever imagined could fit without scarring the beautiful walls. She shouldered her way through until she finally reached the kitchen.

Sangria in hand, she took a slow sip, letting the sweetness settle on her tongue as her gaze swept the room.

She was mapping the best route of escape when something seized her attention—a face that seemed to leap out from the crowd. A split second of strong recognition that made her double back in search of it. The party brimmed with old friends and acquaintances from nearly every chapter of her young life, but something about this face was different. She was taken aback by her own urgency and the sudden need to find the face again.

Minutes stretched and she pressed further into the crowd. Her mind pooled with curiosity, but even as she searched she started to lock in on who she might have seen. And just as she traced that face to a memory, there he was.

Delight bloomed in her chest as she fully recognized a very old friend.

Their eyes met and the ruckus of the party around them instantly subsided. She was, admittedly, a little stunned to see him again after so long.

The man took a moment to send her a knowing smile before taking the first step towards her. The noise around them dulled and receded, as if the two of them had slipped beneath a tide, watching everyone through the foaming waves above.

As he closed the gap between them, Lauryn's eyes tried to catch up.

Who was this grown man approaching her? She took in his tall, now muscular frame, his chiseled, groomed features, and the beard that had never been there before.

Lauryn pursed her lips, noting his style that was so meticulous and considered. He wore a cream-colored sweater that lit up his skin. It looked expensive and effortless, the warm tone glowing against his complexion like candlelight on velvet.

It was something he never would have worn back in the day. Although his walk was familiar, it seemed so much more confident than she remembered, with heavier, unhurried foot falls.

All at once it struck her, how much older they both were and the years since they last saw each other. They were finally standing face to face but Lauryn could only smile.

"Lauryn Lindsey," he greeted her with a familiar voice that resonated deep, landing heavily like an old song.

She let out a breath she hadn't realized she'd been holding, and replied, "Perry Mitchell."

Chapter 3

Perry

P erry couldn't believe his eyes, even as he watched her moving through the crowd. For a moment, the air in the room seemed heavier, charged even. What cosmic event had pulled Lauryn Lindsey out of the ether?

He hadn't planned on staying long at the party and had he spent just two seconds longer catching up with the guys, he might have missed seeing her completely. He felt a faint stir of dread at the thought, and it surprised him.

He watched the puzzled expression that claimed her face. She'd lost him in the crowd, and like him, seemed to be questioning the moment.

She hadn't recognized him. Using this to his advantage, he allowed the passage of time to conceal him just a little while longer. When Perry last laid eyes on this woman, she'd been just twenty-four years old. She looked different now, familiar, but refined. Her hair was fuller than he remembered, and her silky dress traced fuller curves with an ease that shouldn't have been allowed.

The corners of his mouth drew up into a wry smile, realizing she'd always had this effect on him. On everyone really. He noted the attention she was getting, the glances that fixed on her whenever some of the fellas realized who was passing next to them.

A moment later Lauryn turned, her eyes still scanning the crowd until they found him.

He watched as her face brightened with a growing smile, like she was still processing whom she was seeing. Perry straightened, fighting the grin tugging at his mouth. His heart thudded in his chest, the ache of old wounds mixing with the undeniable warmth of seeing her again.

The one who got away– and now she's back.

"Lauryn Lindsey." He spoke her name calmly, but his smile widened as they drew closer to one another. She spoke his name in response, looking up at him with dazzling eyes and a very familiar smile. Of all the witty greetings that formed in his mind as he walked over, he couldn't remember a single one. He felt himself smiling at her like an idiot, but was quite unable to do anything about it.

As he looked down at her, Perry thought back to the last time he saw her. He remembered a summer weekend years ago when he was broke as hell but the weather was perfect, and true adulting still seemed a ways away. He had started to believe she was becoming his. Then, without warning, she'd disappeared and left him hanging. Wondering.

Standing before her now, more than a ten years later, he recalled how it felt to lose her. He remembered the pain of it just as vividly as the taste of her lips.

The two met at college, brushing arms at a student union booth on Quad Day. She'd been a cutie pie then, with all that hair braided and pulled back off of her face. In that moment she'd been one of an overwhelming number of pretty girls he'd been exposed to during his first month of college. However, over time, she was the one who made the rest of the world drop away, and it never quite returned.

He didn't see her again until second semester, standing at the steps of Foellinger Hall, watching one of the fraternities bring in a new line. He hadn't even been sure she remembered him until they made eye contact from opposite sides of the crowd. Her expression had warmed in recognition and beamed at him through the spectacle of young men shouting their founder's history, ready to officially receive their line names and letters.

They'd seen each other more often after that, running into each other in the dining hall and on game days. Freshman year was a blur of lecture halls, work, late night dining hall binges, and studying. Working two jobs and managing a full class schedule, he missed many of the best parties, only attending whenever his shifts ended for the night. When he saw Lauryn again the following year, her braids were gone, her long hair was pressed, coal black and gleaming in the fall sunshine. He'd wasted fifteen minutes trying to find the right time to approach her, the right thing to say, just to see someone else drape an arm over her shoulders and kiss her. A moment that pretty much set the tone for the next four years.

However, the second his eyes met hers across this party, the years between them burned away like fog under the sun.

He was much too glad to see her to dwell on how things had ended. He'd done plenty of reconciling since his younger days. Pushing the thoughts aside, he opened his arms, carefully bending to embrace her. She was just as stunning as he remembered and her scent... he made a point not to hold onto her too long. "How you been, girl?" He spoke the words into her hair so she could hear him over the music.

"I'm good! How are you?" Her hands slid from his shoulders and came to rest in his hands. He felt her lightly squeeze her fingers around his as she asked.

"I can't complain, but man, Lo, when did you-"

Before he could finish, his long-time friend Rashad appeared out of nowhere, shouting Lauryn's name as he barreled between them. "Hey-hey, what's good girl! I heard you were here. You move back or just here for the holidays?" Rashad hollered at her all at once.

Perry couldn't help the annoyance that came over him. It was just like old times, always trying to get five minutes with this woman. Rashad always found new ways to be *extra* and oblivious at the same time, at exactly the wrong time. Then again, Rashad had saved him from having to ask the question Perry was sure Lauryn had been answering all night.

He was surprised when Lauryn confirmed she was back for good, but this stirred more questions in his mind. She'd been gone so long, why return now? He tried not to seem eager to hear her response as Rashad continued railing her with questions. "That man Joe here?"

"Nope," Lauryn replied. Her expression was pleasant, but revealed nothing further. She raised an eyebrow, clearly daring Rashad to press any further. Perry drew a fist up to his mouth to disguise a smirk.

Rashad nodded while taking a long drink from his cup. "Tell me it's none of my business without telling me it's none of my business." He flashed a charming smile at her and laughed it off. "Hint taken. Good to see you too! Still looking fine as always."

Perry watched as Rashad leaned in to hug her and noted how his friend held on a little longer than he needed to. Lauryn made eye contact with him over Rashad's shoulder, looking more humored than annoyed.

"He hasn't changed at all," Lauryn laughed when Rashad disappeared into the crowd.

"Not even a little," Perry agreed, his slight annoyance with Rashad quickly subsiding, and he refocused his attention on her.

He still had questions. He mainly wanted to make sure she was ok. Something about the circumstances of her reappearance felt off somehow. After the way things ended between them, she hadn't kept in touch. Over the years, he'd seen things on social media, and even though she rarely posted, that was how he finally learned she moved to California after she disappeared. With a boyfriend he hadn't even known she had.

After that, he'd stopped torturing himself over her. He'd *invented* the social media hiatus–cleanse or whatever they were calling it now days. He pushed her and the hope from his mind, accepting that, whether he liked it or not, Lauryn would always be the one that got away.

"This party is insane. I've seen so many people from school. Hella nostalgia right now."

"Yeah, it's good to see everyone." He bit his tongue for a few moments. "How long have you been in town?"

"Just a few weeks."

"How'd you hear about all this?" He whirled two fingers in the air, indicating the party that was still swirling around them.

"Ran into Deonna at the mall, maybe... a week after I got back. She's been really sweet about including me in things, connecting me with some of her girls."

Perry nodded, although he didn't remember Deonna well. Still, he was already thinking of a way to thank her for bringing Lauryn Lindsey out tonight. He marveled at her discreetly, watching the way her hands moved as she told him about everyone she'd run into tonight. Her espresso-colored eyes glittered with the same sweetness he remembered, though her voice was calmer, more measured than the excitable tone she had in their college days.

The lip color she wore was subtle, but still amplified how appealing her mouth had always been to him. He'd worked hard to forget that.

In that first year after she left, he spent a long time wondering why the hell he'd revealed his hand. How he could've been so gullible in believing she shared his feelings. Maybe he'd done too good a job pushing her from his mind, from his heart. So much so that now he was hesitant to ask anything more. A familiar thudding had already started in his chest and he wasn't sure he wanted to know the circumstances of her being thrown back into his life either.

"Do you still live in the city?" she asked, oblivious to his thoughts.

"I do. Bought a place two years ago. I'm still renovating." He volunteered the information without fully knowing why.

Her face lit up in that way he remembered from undergrad. "Congratulations, that's great! I'm still in the damn burbs, renting, but Skokie isn't too far from downtown."

"Yeah, that's not a bad drive." Skokie was close, very close and it suddenly felt surreal that they were even standing here making small talk. Especially when so much had been left unsaid. Explanations that should've taken place, instead scattered over a decade of absence. "Listen, I double booked myself tonight. I promised a friend I would make it to his exhibition before midnight. I gotta head out if I want to make it on time."

"Oh, ok. Well, it was really great to see you!" Lauryn's voice lifted and she grinned up at him, but Perry could have sworn he saw some weight behind her dark eyes. "Hope you and your family enjoy the holidays."

"You too. Seriously," he assured her, realizing he didn't know whether he would see her again. "Have a good time tonight." He was already pulling away as he said it, taken off guard by a sudden desire to stay. He didn't dare hug her again, worried he wouldn't be able to let go.

Determined not to lose his nerve, he quickly turned away and pushed back into the crowd. He made a beeline for the door, stopping only to say a quick goodbye to Nathan. He was grateful the party was so crowded, less chance of him glimpsing her on his way out.

Making his way outside, Perry was greeted by the cool night air, a stark contrast to the heat and noise of the party. He inhaled deeply, letting the crispness of it settle in his lungs as if it might clear the fog that had formed in his mind. His footsteps echoed faintly as he made his way back to his car, but his thoughts were miles away, still back in that hotel room with Lauryn eleven years ago.

Seeing Lauryn again had thrown him. Completely.

Of all the things he thought might shake up his day, running into her hadn't exactly been on the list. She was the absolute *last* person he expected to see. And yet, there she was, looking damn near the same, and somehow nothing like she used to.

He'd believed he was over everything that had happened. Over her. Convinced that whatever they'd had during grad school, whatever connection had once sparked between them that last summer, was ancient history.

They'd both lived entire lives since then, years passing without so much as a second thought from her direction. However, seeing Lauryn tonight stirred a mix of emotions he hadn't been prepared for and couldn't deny. Meanwhile, she'd smiled, laughed, and made chit chat as if it was the easiest thing in the world. Everything was, after all, water under the bridge, right?

They were grown now.

But if it was all of that, why the hell did he still feel so drawn to her? How could he be so conflicted when it was clear she'd never been worried about the way she'd left things?

Perry started his car and began to pull off from the curb, glimpsing the balcony far above where he could just make out the glowing DJ booth and wriggling crowd. The distant hum of music was just enough to remind him he wasn't that far away from her. And maybe that was the problem.

He drove off, heading north to the exhibition he promised he would attend. As he turned onto the entrance ramp there was one thing he couldn't shake. That look. The flicker in her eyes and faintest trace of sadness. It was enough to make him keep wondering why she was back, solo, and without the man she'd disappeared with all those years ago.

He blew out a breath, tightening his grip on the steering wheel, surprised with himself for even thinking back that far. Curiosity had edged its way in. Quiet and unwelcome, leaving him off balance in a way he hadn't been in years. He'd built his life around knowing where things stood. Now he wasn't so sure.

Chapter 4

Lauryn

The next day, Lauryn was rocking back on her heels as she waited in line at the grocery store. She clutched a bouquet of flowers, sparkling wine and a bright red shopping basket. Peering over the flowers and cellophane, she could see a tense conversation starting between the cashier and the two customers ahead of her. Some heated discussion about lamb chops. Any other day, she might have been annoyed, but today she appreciated the delay. Despite waking up early, she'd been procrastinating all day about making the trip to see her parents, who lived just east of her place, in one of the most beautiful neighborhoods of Chicago's North Shore.

At best, it was a twenty-minute ride, barely enough time to figure out how much she would tell them about why she'd moved back.

Lauryn shifted the plastic basket in her hand, heavy and weighed down by deli made pasta and chicken, an assortment of cheeses, fig jam, crackers, and a chocolate mousse cake she knew her father would love. Still, she regretted not grabbing a cart when she had the chance. Her intention was just to pick up flowers and dessert, but every moment she lingered in the store was another moment to get her story straight. Lauryn's mother, Francine, had a special talent for making her regret telling them anything. The last thing she wanted to do was volunteer too much of her business. Especially as she was still trying to figure it all out.

As the cash registers beeped around her, Lauryn's mind drifted. She thought about the last time she had a real conversation with her mother. It'd been over a decade now; on the day she'd left home for good. Lauryn could still remember how warm the house had been that morning as she

packed her bags. After months of him asking, Lauryn had finally agreed
to leave with Joseph Gray.

Like some nineties love song, he was on his way back to LA and had
been doing everything he could to convince Lauryn to go with him.
Flowers delivered to her job, insisting she study at the studio while he
recorded, even a few weekend trips to Miami and New York. The two
of them had been completely smitten and finally, she agreed to fly away
with him. She'd packed her best things and tiptoed downstairs in her
socks, trying not to wake her parents. Stumbling like a child, eager to
play outside, Lauryn stood on one foot pulling her Timberland boots
on. And despite all of her tip-toeing around, her mother caught her.

"You have everything?" Francine had been sipping her coffee and
waiting in the dim morning light. With the shutters drawn, she hadn't
noticed her mother's form seated in the dining room. The middle-aged
woman seemed to appear out of nowhere, silhouetted as she rose from
the table, a halo of shining particles floating around her.

Francine sauntered her way into the kitchen, her silk robe gliding
behind her as she went. Her short hair had been wrapped elegantly in
a sage green and cream-colored scarf. Lauryn could recall the pattern
exactly, along with her mother's fragrance as she'd approached her that
day and set her coffee cup down on the counter.

Lauryn had been unsure of what to expect. Would she try to keep her
from leaving? Lauryn had been nearly twenty-four at the time. She'd
thought the decision was her own, but found herself unable to move as
her mother examined her with an expression she'd never seen before.

Her mother had smiled suddenly, posting up against the counter, and
that smile turned into a smirk. "You found a talented one." A puzzling
observation at the time. "Come here," she summoned without extending
a hand.

Lauryn had obeyed, padding across the kitchen to stand in front of
her mother. Francine had reached out to fix her hair, turning Lauryn
around by her shoulders and fluffing her coils. When she was satisfied,
she turned her daughter around to face her again. With elegant fingers,
she fished Lauryn's necklace from beneath her sweatshirt. The jade and
gold pendant was unlike any other gift her mother had ever given her.

It was a keepsake, given in one of those rare moments when her
mother was present, seemingly proud. As the years passed, Lauryn had
worn it less and less. By the time she and Joe had moved to Memphis,
Lauryn had stopped wearing it completely.

Lauryn allowed the memory to play on in her mind. The way her mother had hugged and kissed her cheeks hard. Francine had never been one for unprompted affection and Lauryn, despite the strange farewell, realized her mother was not going to tell her to stay.

She remembered her mother opening her purse and retrieving a credit card. "Remember to call when you settle in."

She'd handed it over like one doles out of a bag of chips. Lauryn had accepted the card, her voice soft as she spoke, "I will."

"Go out of the front door so the garage doesn't wake your father," Francine had instructed, shepherding her towards the front door.

She'd been surprised to find her mother not just following but ushering her out, clutching her robe tight against the morning chill. She'd looked past Lauryn, waving at Joe whose Ford Expedition sat idling at the end of the driveway. He'd gotten out, returning the wave as he moved to open the trunk.

In her mind, she saw her mother at the top of the driveway, silent and steady, as Lauryn reached Joe. She remembered pausing then, caught by the thought that this might not be the right step. She'd done her best not to look back, handing her bag over to Joe. He'd greeted her so sweetly, his fingertips brushing hers as he took her suitcase and set it into the truck next to his guitar case. Francine still waited, hugging herself against the cold, but watching intently as the sun rose.

A mist had lingered that morning, hanging over the lawn and shrouding the house, giving it a dream-like appearance as Lauryn stared at it from the passenger seat.

For the first time since being a little girl, Lauryn wanted to run back to her mother. She'd known that once the car pulled off, there would be no going back. At that moment, she had more than her mother's blessing. Francine was seeing her off, almost ensuring she committed to her decision to run away with Joe. She'd still been gazing at her mother when Joe grasped her hand.

"You ready, babe?" His expression had been soft, his hazel eyes joyful and full of excitement.

Lauryn had reassured him with a smile, even though she no longer knew if she was ready. Her seatbelt hadn't even been fastened when he shifted the SUV out of park and started to pull away. Lauryn had snapped her head back to see her mother once more, but she'd been gone. Already back in the house. The front door closed.

"*Paper or plastic*?" Lauryn was jarred out of the memory by the cashier repeating the question, her irritation clear even behind her face mask. "Ma'am?"

Lauryn tried not to frown at the young girl as she answered, "Paper."

Her mind still reeling, she tried to not to remember the months after leaving her parents' home that day. How naive she'd been in love back then, trying to make a home with a man for the first time.

The mental door she'd shut on those memories was splintering, and seeing Perry Mitchell last night had blown it wide open. She'd known she would have to face pieces of her past, coming back to Chicago, but he wasn't one she'd prepared for. She had a game face for everyone else, but not him. She hadn't planned on how it would feel to look at him and remember the way she left, or how quickly the regret would press in. The ache of it was sharply familiar and entirely hers to carry.

Lauryn sighed. Today would be challenging enough, no sense in going any further down memory lane. After paying and carting the groceries back to her car, she set off towards her parents' home. A house she'd helped maintain from a distance, but hadn't been back to in years. The cape cod style home was her mother's dream house and quite a departure from all the places they'd lived in while she was growing up. With its covered porch, columns, and sloping drive where her mother had stood watching as Joe had carried her daughter away, it held as much memory as it did charm.

All too soon, Lauryn found herself pulling into their paved driveway. She took a moment to rally herself mentally, but realized her parents could probably see her through the window.

The large flower pots out front were winterized with burlap and last year's potting soil. One of her mother's pastimes was interviewing and firing landscapers, just to take the whole thing over herself. In another month she'd be outside in her baseball cap and flared yoga pants setting out new blooms. Lauryn fiddled with her keychain, trying to identify the key she hadn't used in years, all while juggling the fudge cake.

"Hi!" she called out when she finally managed to budge the door open. She hurried to the entryway table, sliding the cake onto it to save herself from losing her grip on it completely and ruining the rug beneath her. She called again, "Dad?"

Slipping her heels off, she padded through the main living room and into the kitchen. She could see the backyard through the back windows.

The trees and pots were naked back there too and a few mounds of snow were still holding on.

The expansive kitchen was bright despite an overcast sky outside. "Mom?" She called again, crash landing with the groceries onto the island countertop. There was still no reply even as she washed her hands and searched for her mother's serving ware. After a few minutes of opening and closing the crisp white cabinets, and finding everything but what she needed, she gave up. Far too much time had passed since she'd been in this kitchen. If her mother had any organization system Lauryn had no idea what it was.

The silence of the house drew her back into the living room, where she scrunched her toes into the thickly woven rug, the botanical Japanese design fanning out towards the fireplace. She bent down to inspect a photo of herself as a kid. Box braids and a linen short set that her mother purchased from Marshall Field's department store, her skin a deep cacao from riding her bike in the summer sun, and a pleasant expression on her little face. Staring at the fourteen-year-old version of herself, Lauryn's jaw worked, recalling her blissful state of mind that summer. The vast optimism that hadn't been clouded by doubt. How little she knew of what was to come.

Turning away, she inspected more family photos, huge oversized prints of her parents' wedding and her father just before his first deployment. All of them professionally matted and framed in chrome. She gazed at her father's handsome face, at the determination and certainty in his eyes that were fixed somewhere passed the camera.

"Hey there!" Lauryn whirled around to see her father making his way down the staircase. Her eyes settled on the mature version of him in his suede house shoes, slacks and a navy zip front sweater.

"Well, hello. I was starting to think you forgot I was coming." Her laugh was stifled by her father's embrace.

"No, I was in the back reading." He pulled back to get a better look at her. "How are you, sweetheart?"

"I'm good," she fibbed, not even sure about how she felt.

"Well, you look good! How was the move and the new house?" he asked jubilantly, walking her back towards the living room.

"The condo is great," she corrected gently. "Furniture is taking forever, but other than that-"

"Ah yes well," her father nodded empathetically as if he was all too familiar with such matters. Lauryn resisted the urge to laugh aloud. In all of her thirty-five years, she'd never known her father to buy a coffee mug for the house, let alone a piece of furniture. That was strictly her mother's domain, and Lauryn was pretty sure he liked it that way.

As they settled into the living room, her father's initial excitement at seeing her seemed to stall. Before too long the air between them tightened, old tensions settling in as they always did. Lauryn remembered calling for the holidays, her parents' anniversary, or simply to check in and the conversations being so strained she'd invent some excuse to get off the phone. Put them all out of their misery. It seemed they were destined to have the same problem today.

Less than ten minutes and they were already running out of things to say to each other.

The first year they dated, Joe had come to visit her parents several times. Still, her father had never been thrilled about his youngest daughter running off with a singer. However, her father had never actually said anything against them either. In the two years that followed, he seemed indifferent, talking to Lauryn as if her relationship with Joe was just another course, another internship she was finishing up and would soon be onto the next thing. Then, in recent years, it became apparent her father had expected her to move on long before now, his disappointment leaking into every phone call. No matter how he tried to conceal it.

Lauryn took a seat in one of the matching arm chairs. "Where's mom?"

"Oh, she's just taking a nap. She'll be down after a while." Lauryn nodded, accepting this and looking at her feet. She couldn't believe it, they'd planned to have dinner together nearly two weeks before, she'd spent almost two hundred dollars on groceries and her mother wasn't even awake.

"It's good to see you," her father offered when their conversation hadn't continued on its own.

"It's good to see you too," she smiled affectionately at him. It'd been five years since she'd last seen him in person, but he looked much the same. In his late sixties, Neal Lindsey was still fit and stood just as tall as when he was in command on base. Lauryn could tell his sweet tooth was beginning to get the better of that belly. Her mother must be taking it easy on him. "You all getting ready for Aunt Mary's?" she inquired about their most recent trip. Her parents were always traveling, especially in the winter months and usually took advantage of her aunt's ranch in Georgia.

"You know, we're not going this year. Some things came up last minute so your mother and I decided to stay home."

Lauryn frowned inwardly. After grinding for nearly 40 years, her parents had officially made it to snowbird status—it was unusual for them to be home this time of year anyway, but to cancel their annual trip to see Aunt Mary seemed particularly odd. "How have you all been?"

"We're good!" Her father smiled wide, standing in the doorframe with his hands in his pockets. "I'm enjoying my retirement, you know, but I stay busy. Your mother, she-" he stopped short and Lauryn looked over at him. He was absentmindedly turning the wedding band on his finger. "There's always lunch or a committee meeting, you know your mother."

"I do." Lauryn watched him, but did not immediately press, despite the distinct feeling her father wasn't sharing something. No sooner did she open her mouth to ask, she caught the sight of her mother at the top of the stairs.

"What about me?" The stunning petite woman made her way down the grand staircase, taking her time as she always did, pulling up her knit trousers as she went. Lauryn couldn't help smiling, watching her mother glide into the living room. She wore a mint-colored lounge set with matching velvet slippers. With all the drama of a woman used to being watched, Francine Lindsey smirked at her husband before clutching Lauryn's arms and leaning in to kiss her on the cheek.

"Well, hello, nice to see you, Lauryn," she cooed, her tone excessively formal.

"Hello Mother," Lauryn's lips curved as she echoed her mother's tone, but still took a moment to breathe in her scent. The jasmine and rose fragrance were unmistakable and she knew at once her mother had just finished a bath. Daily bubble baths were one of the only habits Lauryn adopted from her mother. And one of few affectionate pastimes.

Years before, at the tail-end of Lauryn's senior year of high school, after getting her hair done up in a nineties updo with tendrils and curls, her mother had drawn her a bath, squeezing in swirls of shimmering bath soap. For the first and only time, her mother took a seat on the edge of the tub, talking to her about life and her own girlhood. She remembered her mother reaching a manicured hand around her shoulders with a soft wash cloth and washing her back as she told stories about the other women in their family.

That fragrance was lodged in her memory, like cut grass in summer, like smelling the ocean before you arrive at the beach. The way it wafted through her parent's bedroom and down the hall and she knew not to bother her mother until she emerged.

Just as soon as she'd embraced Lauryn, her mother was already floating away, fixing and adjusting decor that was already perfectly placed. "You're here early. We're not making anything fancy for dinner. We weren't sure if you would be able to stay through the evening."

"How can I be early to my parent's home? And, we made plans for dinner. I brought food," she countered her mother's statements in sequence, wondering if they should have just met at a restaurant.

Or better yet, scratched the whole damn thing.

Just then she remembered the bouquet of flowers she'd brought in anticipation of her mother's fickleness. A peace offering that was probably wilting. "Besides, I wanted to see how you both were," she called over her shoulder as she moved to put them in water.

When her parents didn't answer immediately, Lauryn craned her neck to see them, still standing rigid in the middle of the living room. She caught her father staring at a pile of magazines on the coffee table, seemingly unsure of what to say.

Her mother spoke for them, "We're good! Keeping busy, you know, with your father's retirement our schedules are much more flexible now. We're mostly interested to hear what's new with you!"

Lauryn was filling a vase with cool water. She stared intently at the gurgling water rising in the crystal vase, running a full risk analysis in her mind. She could keep things light, avoid the obvious and say nothing about why she was suddenly back living in Illinois. Then again, she could dive right in, rip the proverbial Band-Aid off and get it over with. Chances are, her parents already had an idea of what had finally brought their daughter back home after all this time. Still, she didn't feel like volunteering any information she didn't have to. "Oh, settling in!"

Her father, bless him, took the opportunity to steer the conversation in a lighter direction. "Where is your new place again?"

"Right off of Old Orchard Road, the glass building with the trees on the terraces?"

"Now where is that?" her mother asked airily, fiddling with the hem of her top.

"Oh—that's not far at all!" Neal exclaimed at the same time. "Nice building?"

"It is! Great amenities, amazing view. There's even an indoor pool."
Lauryn set the flower arrangement down on the island and slid it toward
the center where she knew her mother preferred it.

"A pool huh? I don't expect you'll be getting in there," her father said
as if he still knew her well, taking a seat on the couch. He seemed to be
breathing easy for the first time since Lauryn arrived.

What is up with them? She wondered, but dismissed the odd vibe between them, remembering how easily her mother could turn her father's
mood. Anyone's mood, really.

"I think I'll try a lap from time to time." As a young girl, Lauryn
avoided swimming. Getting in the water meant a whole afternoon stuck
sitting in a hard kitchen chair with her mother sectioning, braiding or
pressing her hair. And that was after washing and conditioning. However, she'd grown out of that phase in her teens. Before she'd even moved
out of the house, really. Her father was so determined to remember her
in a particular way, frozen at a particular age. "There's a preserve across
the street with trails and bike paths too. When the weather gets warmer,
I'll check it out."

"You just be careful," Francine finally spoke up again, looking directly
at Lauryn this time. "Come all the way back here just to end up kid-
napped or worse. These people out here are crazy." The older woman
leaned across the island and scooted the bouquet of flowers over a few
inches.

Lauryn said nothing, estimating how much more tedious the evening
might get. She attempted to serve food, but without an inkling of how
her mother's kitchen was organized, she ended up needing help. Even
as her mother pulled down the daytime dishes and set the table, she
couldn't shake the feeling that something odd was going on between her
parents.

Did they really not know how to be a family anymore?

The three of them sat at the 10-seat dining room table passing bowls
and chewing. No matter how Lauryn tried to steer the conversation
elsewhere, it kept drifting back to how good the food was. Her father
kept asking "Where'd you get this again? Mariano's?"

"Sunset Foods," she'd answer, picking at her plate and watching her
parents munch and discuss the weather as if they were all strangers and
not parents and child. Unwilling to sit through more contrived conversation over dessert, Lauryn excused herself from the table to prepare the
cake. She unwrapped the thawing chocolate confection and slid it onto

one of her mother's many cake stands. Carefully, she set the glass cover over it and wiped her hands. "Alright, you two enjoy the cake."

"Oh, you're headed home?" Her father seemed disappointed.

"Yeah, Dad, I have an early morning unfortunately."

"Okay. Well, thank you so much for bringing dinner. It hit the spot." He stood and followed as Lauryn made a beeline to gather her purse. When they reached the door, he pulled Lauryn into another hug. He held her tighter and longer this time and she found herself squeezing him a little more because of it. It felt good to get one of his real hugs again, she couldn't remember how long it'd been.

"Maybe I'll stop by next weekend?" she offered when he finally released her.

"Do that," he was smiling at the idea when her mother cut in.

"That's really nice, sweetheart, but we know you're busy unpacking and figuring things out. You come when you can. If not, we understand." Her mother was perched against the stair railing, the same way she'd stood by when Joe had come to carry her off, all those years ago.

Unsure of how to take this, Lauryn looked from her mother to her father. Suddenly, they both looked so much older, crowded around her at the door like the first day of school. Something was definitely off, but she knew they wouldn't be revealing anything tonight. She leaned over to kiss her mother's cheek before pulling her purse over shoulder. "Night, Mom."

"Good to have you home," her father added when it was just the two of them on the porch. Her mother had already disappeared up the stairs.

"Thanks Dad. I'll text you when I get home."

"You do that." He nodded at her, in his Colonel way. She pictured him in uniform then. As she closed the door to her SUV and turned the ignition, she could barely keep from smiling, her head suddenly swimming with memories of the army bases they'd lived on, her father, looking brave and pristine. And her mother, always radiant, looking every bit like the colonel's wife.

She would have to look in on her parents regularly now. At least until she could suss out the root of all the evasiveness she was feeling from them. She breathed out an abrupt laugh at the thought. Leave it to her to come home to figure out her own life, just to end up volunteering as the family therapist.

Chapter 5

Lauryn

The next two weeks passed quickly and quietly. Lauryn spent the rest of the holidays alone, content to ring in the new year by organizing her tea collection into a single drawer. Something she'd seen on Pinterest and was eager to try now that she had a kitchen all to herself. None of Joe's antique pots and pans lying all over the place.

Her parents hadn't called since her visit and secretly she was grateful to have had such a long, uninterrupted stretch of solitude.

Each day she fixed herself a pot or a cup of tea as she unpacked and watched movies. Then she'd top off the evening with a single glass of prosecco or sparkling rosé while sitting on her living room floor. De-onna had posted a few pictures from the holiday party, tagging Lauryn's instagram account, inadvertently causing a stream of notifications and a few insistent calls from friends in Memphis who had no idea Lauryn was even in Chicago. Instead of responding, she'd set her phone on *Do Not Disturb* for a week straight. It was glorious to be alone, in this new-old place. She ventured out only when she absolutely felt like it, getting lost in gourmet markets and furniture stores. In the days after New Year's, the store window displays, lights and decorations started to look stale in the grey overcast.

When she'd first moved into her new apartment, she thought her mornings would be slow, affording her time to take advantage of the solitude, to meditate and heal. However, she found herself waking at nearly 5AM each day. Somewhere in the night, when her dreams were just getting going, she would feel herself drawn back to consciousness. Once awake, her mind would start going and all her regrets would stream in, playing on a loop until she couldn't stand to lie still anymore. No matter how comfortable her new bed was, she'd throw the covers off, pull on a pair of joggers and head two floors down to her building's gym.

She ran on the treadmill and did squats until she was exhausted, working hard not to think of her old life, of Joe and all the holidays spent together.

Although she did not regret leaving him, it felt surreal to stand alone in her kitchen, making stir fry for herself as the snow fell outside.

This time of year usually involved rushing to put on some sort of cele- bration for Joe, his birthday falling just two days after Christmas. Unless he was working, they usually spent the end of the year on a beach or in a cabin somewhere. With his parents often traveling during the holidays and her own family living overseas until recently, family gatherings had never been part of their rhythm. And after the performance her parents had put on at the house, she wasn't the least bit surprised she hadn't heard from them.

And now Lauryn folded her laundry, standing peacefully in her un- derwear and a chunky cardigan. She relished the time she had to ease into her new life: sleeping in, reading, shopping or curling up in her robe whenever she wanted. She built playlists in her music app, adding dreamy tracks with heavy beats that suited her mood, and lost herself in a book or movie.

Being alone now didn't feel all that different from how she'd been feel- ing the past two years. The only real change was that she wasn't counting down the days until Joe came back, no wondering if he'd keep his word or disappear into another delay. Even when Joe wasn't traveling, he was barely present. And after many years of holding space and *trying harder*, she'd stopped looking forward to him returning home; stopped planning special meals or strapping on pretty lace lingerie under her clothes. The whole *clean-the-house-and-wax-yourself-from-head-to-toe thing* was done.

Still, hearing the splash of water as she bathed that night conjured up a memory.

It was one of their last happy days together. They'd spent time in Bali to celebrate Joe being featured on a major artist's new album. It was his first real feature, and even though things had really started to take off for the band, the industry was starting to single Joe out. Like so many front men before him, he was getting opportunities to collaborate and appear on his own.

As she laid back in the tub she pictured him on that trip, hoisting himself out of the pool, water streaming down the muscles of his torso. She recalled the sound of his wet footsteps as he joined her on the lounge chairs that looked out onto the Bali Sea. His brown curls had been dripping and slick and he'd smelled of Chanel and chlorine when he leaned in to kiss her. She could still taste him. How could it all be ancient history now? Lauryn traced a wet finger back and forth along the back of her neck, taking a moment to process the mix of her emotions.

When, exactly, had she stopped loving him? After giving him so many chances over the years, she couldn't recall.

When Joe was at his worst, playing the martyr or complaining, she would escape to the bathroom. Even in their very first apartment, where the bathroom was barely large enough to wash her face, she would spend an hour or more in the tub. Sitting there until the suds ran thin, turning her decisions over in her mind and decompressing. Joe resented it. Anything that steadied her only seemed to grate on him.

Now she didn't have to hide to avoid conflict, but she still enjoyed her baths. This was her last weekend before starting her new position and she was eager for the distraction of getting into something new, where no one knew her. However, as her first Monday back to work loomed closer, she was already looking forward to being done with it.

Truthfully, she was ready to be done with the whole year. Lauryn had a one-year plan to regroup and find herself. Although she couldn't quite envision what the tail-end of that plan looked like, she prayed the emotion deep seeded in her chest would be lighter by then.

The most difficult part about the heartache she felt was the shame that came along with it. However, she approached it in her mind, she couldn't escape the shame of having walked through life for so long with a single person, just to come out of it empty handed. The hollowness was deep and she resented herself for not having the sense to leave him sooner.

Lauryn finished her bath and got dressed before realizing she didn't have a thing to do that night. No errands, no phone calls that she actually wanted to return, certainly no Thursday night plans to speak of. She peered down out of her window, following the moonlit mounds of snow still hugging the edges of each lawn around her building. Perhaps she would order in tonight.

As she waited for her food delivery, Lauryn unpacked the last of her moving boxes. Pretty soon she was standing in a pile of tissue paper, prying open a keepsake box she'd packed away long before she even decided to leave Memphis.

"Ah!" She squealed happily, lifting out an old university sweatshirt. She stroked the blue vinyl lettering that wasn't as faded as she might have expected. She set it aside gently and dug deeper through the box of memories.

Two heavily wrapped bundles caught her eye and she smiled when she finally got through all the bubble wrap and recognized what they were. Two small brass elephants she'd had since middle school. One of the many gifts her father brought home from his posts overseas. Thinking of him, she smiled, looking for a new place to display them. Since visiting her parents, she kept wondered where her jade necklace might be. It was possible it was lost, left behind in one of her and Joe's first apartments or lodged somewhere in the Memphis house. As she emptied the last box, with no sign of it, she let herself admit that it was definitely gone.

Lauryn was breaking down the moving boxes when her phone rang. The harsh tone jarred her out of what had been a peaceful few days. Realizing her delivery guy must be trying to get upstairs, she jogged into the kitchen and slowed when she caught a glimpse of the name on the screen.

P-e-r-r-y-M-i-t-c-h-e-l-l scrolled from right to left and her hand froze midair as she puzzled over whether to answer.

With all the trepidation in the world, she swiped the Accept button. "Hello?" She listened, but the line was quiet. She checked the screen to make sure the call hadn't dropped. "Hello?" She called again.

"Ms. Lindsey. It's Perry, how are you?" His voice came across the line, deep and familiar.

"Perry? Hey," she laughed lightly. "How are you?"

He laughed too. "I'm good, I'm good. I know you're wondering how I got your number."

"I am." She wasn't. Lauryn hadn't had a chance to wonder anything, still stunned that he was calling. They hadn't had a real opportunity to talk at the party, let alone exchange phone numbers.

"I hope you don't mind. I saw I still had you in my phone's contacts. I took a chance."

"Yeah! Your name popped up too–and how is it possible that you also have the same phone number? People call me crazy for keeping mine."

"Creature of habit. Verizon and I go way back. They take care of me."

"They should! I remember all the events you missed, opening the store practically *every* weekend of junior year."

"Man!" He howled. It seemed she'd caught him off guard with that memory, but relished in his laughter. It was like scoring first in their particular game. "Young man had no life."

"Not that year," she added, leaning down onto the kitchen island, phone cradled between her ear and shoulder. One minute into the conversation and their banter was flowing like they hadn't missed a beat. She grinned as he went on a little longer about Verizon.

"So how does it feel to be home?" he asked after their giggling had subsided.

"A mind trip," she admitted it more quickly than she meant to, revealing more than she meant to. "But, it's good. It's been good." She prayed he wouldn't press.

"That's good. Are you working or taking some time?"

"Yeah, no I found a gig before I came back. I start next week. Mostly I've been getting this house together, unpacking, checking on my folks."

"Your folks are back too?" he asked, surprised. She raised her eyebrows, just as surprised that he remembered anything about her parents.

"Yeah, they moved back from Italy two years ago. You remember that? It's been forever."

She could feel him waving it off through the phone. "Naw, I remember you saying your dad had another assignment, then when they were getting ready to leave. They sat you down for the whole living-will, estate conversation. Put the trust in your name..."

"Oh my god, yes! That was such an odd time," Lauryn said, as the memories came rushing back. Just before she finished grad school, her father had taken a final assignment that sent her parents to Vicenza, Italy–a move her mother had dreamed of. Neal Lindsey had three other daughters from previous relationships, but as the only daughter he had a relationship with, he'd brought Lauryn in on his accounts, investments and the home warranty, trusting her to manage everything while they were away.

One day, he'd surprised her with a very grown-up father-daughter lunch at a beautiful restaurant downtown. Standing at her kitchen counter now, Lauryn remembered how excited she'd been to spend time with him without her mother. She loved her mother, but conversation was just easier when it was just the two of them. She'd worn her best black dress and a little white blazer she'd found on sale. When they arrived, the host had seated them practically dead-center in the restaurant, concealed only by a giant floral arrangement. She had barely taken a sip of her water, when Neal had begun offloading information to her and stressed the importance of having a plan. So many Black families didn't.

Her mind had been swimming when they finally stepped out of the restaurant. She'd barely eaten, but the two of them had finished the lunch with a cognac, their shared drink of choice. She understood the importance of the conversation they'd just had. With her parents moving overseas again, someone would have to hold down the fort at home. They'd just purchased a new home and renovated. Her mother, "spending a fortune like they had it like that," as her father would say, but the result was beautiful. And her father was so close to retirement, it would be nice to have somewhere to land after this last round abroad.

Lauryn hadn't known how to feel about her parents packing up to move away without her. It was her duty of course, to honor her father's wishes and take care of the family home. She hadn't been afraid to be alone. By the time she was twelve, and her family returned to the US, she'd lived in three different countries. She was used to goodbyes, losing friends, making new ones, coordinating family phone calls at just the right time of day.

In the end, it was all for nothing. Lauryn had moved away before they did. The handshake she'd made with her father had gone up in smoke, the moment she agreed to go to California with Joe. By the time her parents had left for Italy, she'd been living her new adventure, still smitten with Joe and the warm weather. It wasn't like she'd been a child watching them leave her behind, but it had left her feeling adrift, like a boat cut loose from its dock.

Perry asked something else then. Lauryn had nearly forgotten she was on the phone. "Sorry, what?"

"How are they doing?"

"My folks? Oh, yes, they're doing well. Easing into retirement. Dad anyway."

"Glad to hear it. Welcome home, girl." The warmth in his voice made her smile.

Since running into Deonna, she felt better about being back home. For all her efforts to isolate herself, there had been moments of loneliness. Doubt was most likely what was waking her up at the crack of dawn every day. And then Joe had not called. Out of everyone that was blowing up her phone, she had not heard from him once since she left him standing in the driveway. She knew the day would come when she wouldn't be worried about it anymore. In the meantime, she could grab a few extra pillows on those lonely nights. A false sense of security as she slept with her back against them, she admitted to herself silently.

Fuck Joe. For now, those pillows were a necessary means to a good night's sleep.

Lauryn chewed the inside of her cheek. She needed to change the subject before Perry asked anything more about the past. "How was your second party?" she asked incredulously, perking up at having initiated the perfect conversation change. "Couldn't hang with the old heads? Had to invent a whole second party so you could leave and go home early?"

And there was his laugh again, contagious like it always was, but suddenly rather sexy. "I am a grown-up," he asserted. "I don't need to invent an imaginary party to excuse myself. I have zero problem telling those negroes I'm not coming. Especially after Covid! I've been very selective with my attendance."

"Is that right? So, then I suppose we should all be grateful that you showed up?"

"Man," he crooned in agreement. "Wouldn't have caught you other-wise."

He said the five words and left them hanging in the air. Neither of them laughed or spoke right away and just as Lauryn was thinking of a response, a timely knock sounded at her door. "Can you hang on one minute?"

She waited for Perry's reply before setting the phone face down on the counter, grateful for the brief pause to collect herself. She answered the door, took the double-bagged Thai food without really looking at the driver, murmured a thank you, and shut it again. All while his words lingered in her head. *Wouldn't have caught you.* The phrase wrapped around her, unsettling and sweet at the same time. Her brain worked, trying to decide how she felt about the statement, but her mind was foggy and she couldn't dismiss the delight of hearing his voice again. One thing was clear, she needed to maintain control of the conversation.

"So, what's going on your way?" she asked, snatching the phone back up.

"At the airport, waiting on this plane."

"Oh? Where you headed?"

"Charlotte to see family. I'm meeting my folks and everyone there, but the flight's delayed, of course." He sighed and she could hear him moving around. She pictured him, all six-plus feet of him, trying to lounge on the uncomfortable airport chairs. Then without meaning to, she pictured him as he'd been at the party, emerging from the crowd, his gaze taking all of her in.

"Yeah, holiday travel is the worst," she said quietly, still recovering from the image of him.

"All good. Plus, you and I are getting a chance to catch up. Long overdue, don't you think?"

By the time Lauryn hung up, she and Perry had been on the phone for nearly two hours. In that time, Perry's flight was delayed again and she was surprised to find herself content to keep him company. The conversation flowed, meandering between undergrad memories, music, and work. He'd kept her laughing for nearly thirty minutes straight in the end, filling her in on one of the crazy trips he'd been on with their mutual guy friends to Lagos. While he recalled the details, she tucked herself into the corner of her couch, put the phone on speaker, pulling her feet up under herself and listening comfortably. They exchanged photos and Lauryn found herself scrolling a lot longer than necessary to find just the right photo. After all these years, she wanted to make an impression. She sent it before she could change her mind.

"Oh, Lauryn Lindsey," he said and she could practically hear him zooming in. She smiled, feeling a little victorious.

The phone buzzed in her hands and she looked down, seeing a photo of him with the guys, all in mauve and burgundy suits. He was cracking up in the photo, his white teeth contrasting beautifully with his beard.

A second photo appeared, this one of just him standing chest deep in an infinity pool facing a sea and mountain view. Lauryn bit her lip, letting her gaze roll over his bare shoulders and the gold chain that rested at the base of his neck. He looked impossibly handsome, the water dazzling on his skin, and his expression pensive. Lauryn wondered who the hell had taken the photo; certainly not one of the guys. Laughing to herself, she recognized he was countering her photo with his own *thirst trap photo*.

"And where is this?" she asked, keeping her voice even so as not to betray anything.

"St. Lucia. Crazy view."

"It is." She couldn't even pretend to be talking about the view. With one last look, she closed the message app. Somehow, her nerdy ever-responsible friend had become a man's man. She could hardly believe it, remembering times when he showed up at parties with his work shirt still on—rarely having time to run home and change. She grimaced, remembering how the same guys used to clown him.

"That's great that all of you are still close. I couldn't believe how many people I knew at that party."

"It's kinda like that. We see each other often. Someone is always having a birthday party, getting married, having a baby, moving away..." his voice trailed off and she wondered if he was alluding to the way she'd left. Lauryn was struggling to find something to say when she heard his flight being called.

"Boarding time?"

"Yeah, that's my flight. Well, Miss. Lindsey, it great to catch up with you," he said her last name again and Lauryn felt a surprising wave of disappointment at their impending farewell.

"Yes, this was a nice surprise." She was going to have a hard time carrying on her evening of solitude after this. "I hope you have a good flight and enjoy your family."

"You too. Have a good evening, Lauryn. Congrats again on the gig."

She hung up, but couldn't shake the smile that tugged at the corners of her mouth. Talking with Perry had comforted her somehow. Catching up with him felt like stepping back inside after a long day battling the chill and snow. It was remarkable how much he'd changed since their college days. Evolving from the reserved, studious sweetheart into a confident, adventurous man who seemed to be living his best life.

Images of their shared memories played in her mind like an old film reel—the late-night study sessions at the library, carpooling back and forth from campus, and then there was that last summer. The summer before she left for California with Joe. She and Perry had spent nearly every weekend together that June and July. Even then, many of their friends were getting married so it was impossible not to run into one another. Lauryn felt the pang of nostalgia for those days. The two of them, laughing until their stomachs hurt, attending every festival, and sharing their hopes and dreams for the future.

Back in her kitchen now, Lauryn unpacked the food she hadn't yet eaten. The thought of how optimistic she'd been that summer damn near paralyzed her. Sitting in this new place, right now, back in her hometown, she was that young girl's future. She wondered what she'd tell her younger self if they could sit together for a while. How would she explain all the choices and the detours? Crossing the line with Perry and then running before she could face what it meant. Losing herself in Joe's dreams, calling it love, and staying way too long.

Lauryn's movement slowed and she stared down at her food. Just like that, the peace she found in talking with Perry started to erode.

Electing not to eat dinner, she stashed the metal trays in the refrigerator and turned off every light on the way to her bedroom. It all felt like a lifetime ago. So much had happened and yet Perry was still steady, grounded in the best way. "How is he still so cool after all these years?" she asked aloud.

How is he so damn fine after all these years?

Chapter 6

Lauryn

*S*o much for being early.

Lauryn's reward for showing up ahead of schedule on her first day was a windshield full of frost and a parking lot that was already full. "Typical Monday," she murmured, tugging on her lined gloves and hitting it across the parking lot to the main entrance.

It was her first day at her new office and she prayed to God this was the correct door. Memphis wasn't exactly tropical and it certainly had its rough winters, but this Chicago hawk was something else entirely.

Finally, inside, safe from the wind, she loosened the belt on her long white parka. The matching wool skirt and sweater should have been enough insulation, but she was grateful for the parka. The reception desk loomed ahead of her and she smoothed her hair as she approached it. She had the job, but she didn't want to look completely disheveled on her first day. An old man took his time identifying her, but soon positioned a small camera to take her new employee photo.

After receiving a parking pass and a hot-pressed badge she was on her way up the escalator. At the top, air hit her, clean and powdery like some of her favorite stores. Lauryn checked in with the receptionist and examined her surroundings.

The company name and logo gleamed in chrome above the main reception desk. Amara Beauty & Co. was now Amara Labs, a recent name change to usher in a new era for the near sixty year old company. Lauryn could just barely make out where the chrome lettering had been switched out. She shed her coat and took a seat in a boucle arm chair. She'd be walking in these doors every day for the next twelve months. Just enough time for her to figure out her next move, leave the relationship drama behind and figure out what the hell was going on with her parents.

The stone walls around her held fragments that glinted despite the lack of sunshine. There were fresh floral arrangements tucked into alcoves around the lobby. *I should've asked for more money.* She raised an eyebrow at a nearby bouquet of white amaryllis, anemones, and magnolia leaves set into a brass vessel.

"Lauryn?" She turned at the sound of her name and was pleased to see a familiar face. "Hema Nair. It's nice to finally meet you in person."

Her new boss, Hema Nair, was the company's VP of Digital Transformation. Before applying, Lauryn read up on Hema in an article about STEM programs and sponsorship in Chicago. Lauryn hadn't even realized there was a minority owned, woman-led beauty brand this size still operating out of its original site before reading about this woman. Then, in one of those serendipitous turns, a recruiter had reached out about an acting director role covering a leader on extended leave. She'd typed her reply in the blue light of her laptop while Joe snored beside her.

The job description had felt like a calling, even reminding her of a brand idea she'd been daydreaming about for two years, but hadn't moved on yet. A luxury bath care line, something she would build and launch on her own one day—when the time was right. And although the position at Amara Labs was meant to be temporary, it was a clear opportunity for her footing in the beauty industry. It wasn't just a way out of Memphis. It was a step toward a life that was her own.

She'd interviewed with Hema and a panel of other department heads, delighted to find most of the panel were women. Hema was just one of six powerhouse women who were leading the charge for a company that was still holding its own after more than half a century.

"It's wonderful to meet you too. I'm glad to be here." They shook hands and Lauryn remembered being twenty years old when her father taught her the right type of handshake. He told her to give a quick, but firm squeeze, like she meant it. Nothing flimsy. He told her this was how to make your intentions known.

Hema led her through the glass doors and into her office, offering her a cup of coffee from her personal cappuccino machine. "So how goes the move from Memphis go?"

"Surprisingly smooth," Lauryn was pleased to report and took a seat in front of Hema's desk. She took in the expanse of windows and the chicly decorated seating area. This was like the pilot episode of a Netflix series–meeting the big boss in her very big office.

"I should say so, considering the moving stipend we offered."

Lauryn smiled knowingly, but kept an even professional tone. "I appreciate the opportunity."

Hema smiled, leaning back in her chair slightly as he sipped her espresso. "Decent commute?"

"Not bad."

"Don't worry. Our hybrid model is still in place. It's a ghost town here on Fridays, but I encourage you to be in on Mondays."

"Not a problem."

Hema set her gold espresso cup down for a moment and folded her hands together. "I spoke to your mentor. Roman Stevens."

Lauryn frowned, hearing the name. Roman was not a mentor at all so she was surprised to hear Hema mention him. Careful not to appear as bewildered as she felt she lifted her chin. "And how's Mr. Stevens?" she asked, keeping her tone even.

"Preparing to start another company, so I expect he's well. Anyway, he couldn't say enough good things about you." She waited a moment, but sensing Lauryn's confusion she continued. "Roman and I went to university together. We've remained close friends. When he saw your LinkedIn post about joining the team, he reached out to me and congratulated *me* on hiring you."

Lauryn wasn't sure how to respond to Hema. She wasn't sure what crazy six-degrees-of separation was involved, but his was not a name she'd expected to hear in Chicago, let alone at her new job.

Five years before, when Lauryn & Joe were still in California she'd met Roman across a conference table. She'd been a data analyst then and Roman, the front man for one of her company's top clients. While things with Joe were fraying at the edges, Lauryn's career had started to bloom. She became known for speaking up in meetings, giving input, rather than just doing the work. Her eagerness and creativity landed her a seat on the project team working on Roman's account.

Throughout the project, Roman took an interest in her perspective, he said she was sharp and far too underutilized.

What started as friendly banter at the end of each meeting turned into the occasional LinkedIn message. Then more frequent check-ins from him to her personal email. Career advice. Article links. Lunch invitations. Flattering compliments that walked the line.

When her company's contract with Roman's firm ended, they stayed in touch. And for a while, his guidance was harmless and she welcomed it. Especially in the moments when Joe was on the road and she was questioning everything. Six years into their relationship, and any mention of marriage came only in the form of hypotheticals that never amounted to anything. So, she'd indulged Roman, to a point.

But eventually, the tone between them shifted. Roman's interest turned personal, and when he invited her out of town "just to talk, uninterrupted," she knew exactly what he was asking for.

She'd never responded and had not heard anything more from or about him until coming into Hema's office. However, she had felt guilty for entertaining it, for accepting the lunch invites–for pretending. For considering a different life with a different man. The guilt settled deep, and in its wake, she'd thrown herself back into Joe, determined to be more patient and more loving. For a while, it even seemed to work.

Hearing Roman's name now caught her off guard, but he was just another piece of her past she had no desire to revisit. *Mentor? Hilarious.*

"Small world," she said, her annoyance smoothing any initial panic. Roman, as his name suggested, was ancient history. A professional acquaintance and any praise he'd given was inconsequential. She already had the job.

"Indeed," Hema picked up her espresso again and knocked it back. "You're an Illini aren't you?"

"I am," Lauryn replied wondering why she was speaking in two-word sentences.

"We have an intern partnership with UIUC. We're snapping together a team for a forum in the spring. Our Diversity Coordinator and Head of Recruiting will be leading the project. I'd like to see you lean in as well. As a University of Illinois alum and your experience in predictive modeling, I think you bring impressive representation."

"That would be amazing," Lauryn's heart lifted, and she had to adjust her seat. This was exactly the type of forum that would have impressed her as a young student on campus. It was exactly the type of work she'd longed to do, but hadn't yet worked for a company that saw the value in this kind of initiative. She had not expected to be included in anything like this. This was just a fortunate connection and a perfectly timed job opportunity. "I would love to contribute to the program."

Hema seemed pleased to hear this, but soon whisked her out of her office and onto the main floor. She walked her through the rows of desks set up in pods, pointing out the location of each team and introducing her to the administrative assistants. Lauryn found it odd that Hema, not a junior associate, was showing her around, even taking the time to let her know which was the "good" break room.

"And here you are." Hema leaned against the glass of an empty office, smiling and waiting for Lauryn's reaction.

She had not expected an office. "Hema, I thought-"

"So many people are grandfathered into working remotely we've been moving department heads into their own offices. Not all meetings should be held on the main floor."

Lauryn eyed the sleek corporate furnishings, but turned to smile warmly back at Hema. "This is great. Thank you."

Hema nodded sharply. "Mary should be by shortly to get your laptop and printer setup. See you at ten for our leadership call."

Lauryn returned the same nod, realizing she was inadvertently mirroring Hema's boss-ass energy. "See you then."

Alone in her office, Lauryn draped her coat over the back of one of the chrome and black chairs that sat in front of her new desk. She wondered what meetings she'd be having that she needed to have reception chairs and a small conference table in the corner. She could barely stop the smile that began to spread across her face. Every position before this had just been a job. This was supposed to just be a job, a way to gain some chops as a director and rebuild her savings so she could branch out on her own. However, everything about this place was already feeling different.

After finishing undergrad in central Illinois, Lauryn moved back north to stay with her parents and started graduate school in the city. With classes and an internship downtown, commuting back and forth from the suburbs, her two-year program flew by, and she earned her master's in marketing Analytics. Even with the economy tanking and jobs scarce, she felt a quiet thrill of her accomplishments. The sense of arrival.

Her goals had been soft around the edges then. When asked, she'd talked about joining a small consultancy and somehow landing a seat abroad, preferably in Milan or London. However, in practice she'd just kept obediently moving forward on autopilot, following the path laid out for her, and making good in a field that suited her.

The summer her degree posted felt like a deep exhale. Six years of classes, case studies and late nights ceased and she could just breathe.

That was also the summer where everyone seemed to be getting married. Lauryn damn near went broke purchasing wedding gifts for people she hardly spoke to now. For three months straight, their undergrad friend group was seeing each other nearly every other weekend. Starting in May with classmates Jalissa and James, followed by Paris and George. Then in June, Dawn and Malcom, Leah and Isaac, then Marissa and Michael all exchanged vows. It was a whirlwind of venues and guest-books with the previous bride and groom shuffling to the back of the line and showing up as guests at the very next wedding.

That was the same summer she and Perry had gotten really close. It seemed they were seeing each other all the time and usually seated at the same "Singles" table.

By that time, she and Joe had been dating for nearly a year, sneaking in time between her studies and his shows. She'd been completely smitten and completely overwhelmed by the dreams he had for his music career. Even as he courted her, she was never sure if she would see him again or if he would simply disappear into the industry. Cautiously, she'd kept the relationship to herself, barely sharing any details with anyone. As far as everyone knew, she'd been single since undergrad, so she accepted the wedding invitations and arrived solo. She'd spent time with her girlfriends from school who were often invited, taking advantage of the open bars, glamorous locations, and enjoying the romance of it all.

They all carpooled in those days and even started sharing hotel rooms to save money as the invites kept coming. At the last wedding she attended, her friends had all been fixed on partying all night. They'd been blowing up her phone, but Lauryn had been overlooking the riverwalk with Perry. The two of them had escaped the reception and set off down Wacker Drive to the hotel where she was staying. And then, after two generously poured glasses of Scotch whisky, she'd asked him to walk her back to her room.

Lauryn jumped out of her desk chair, sending it spinning behind her. There was no way she was going to baptize her office in a wave of *those* memories.

She was grateful when the support tech, Mary, appeared with her new laptop. Soon, Lauryn was saving her email signatures, reviewing her calendar and pushing those memories back to where they came from.

Her first meeting was an avalanche of information, there was no time to be thinking about that night or Perry. Lauryn listened intently, taking notes as each department head gave their updates. She was impressed by how fluidly they seemed to work together, practically finishing each other's sentences and nodding in agreement as they shared action items and talked through roadblocks. *Honeymoon phase*, she thought, knowing things wouldn't always be this smooth.

In another conference room, Lauryn was finally introduced to her own team and she was grateful when Hema stepped out, giving her the space to get acquainted on her own terms. There was Sophia Roberts, her senior project manager and David Moss, the manager presiding over the company's data science team. Sophia was startlingly pretty, with a dark brown pixie haircut that stood out against her alabaster skin. Before starting, Lauryn had looked them up on LinkedIn and both had impressive experience. Now to put a personality with those profiles.

Sophia was stoic and Lauryn could tell her smiles would be rare, but she seemed amicable to the idea of working together. David, who'd been hired only a few months before Lauryn seemed pleased to have a completed team, and perhaps a boss that was a bit more approachable than Hema.

They each took turns introducing themselves, sharing details about their respective work, their teams, and experiences at the company so far. Sophia and David were older than her, and both married with children. Lauryn nodded along, making mental notes of their children's ages. Sophia mentioned almost four years married, less than half the time Lauryn had been with Joe. When the conversation slid to daycare and after school pick-ups, Lauryn had nothing to add. They seemed disappointed for her. *Funny.*

Lauryn got another breather in her office around noon. She was familiarizing herself with the employee portal when her cellphone rang. Absently, she reached for it and swiped her phone to answer, realizing too late who was calling. "Hi, Dad?"

"Hey darling, why do you sound like you didn't know it was me. You don't have my number anymore?" he questioned.

"No, I do. I just wasn't..." Lauryn exhaled, shaking her head. "How are you?"

"Doing well, on my way to the pool." She nearly forgot. In an effort to stay nimble in his retirement, her father swam three days a week at an indoor pool a few towns over. "I wanted to call and see how your first day was."

Lauryn paused, unable to stop the smile that was tugged at the corners of her mouth. He'd remembered. "It's going really well,"

"That's wonderful. I'm glad for you, honey." He was pleased–she could almost feel him beaming through the phone. "Do you like your boss?"

"I do. She's amazing. A powerhouse, really, I think I'll learn a lot from her."

"Ah. Boss lady?"

Lauryn laughed, "Yes. This isn't nineteen-seventy. There are women who run whole companies now."

Her father chuckled. "With your field, Lauryn, I'm just surprised. All your previous managers have been men."

Lauryn paused for a moment, recalling her previous roles. "You know, you're right."

"Still, I'm sure it's nice to have a diverse workplace. Any other black folks?"

"Uh, a few-"

"Delivering packages or running the marketing department?"

"Goodness, this isn't Boomerang!" She snatched up her phone and took him off of the speakerphone as they both laughed. "Is that your only basis for corporate America?"

So much time had passed since they spoke like this, and she regretted all the long-distance phone conversations that felt so strained. There were times in the past when she hadn't written or called. And they hadn't either. There was a knock at her door and she looked up to see one of her new colleagues, leaning in the doorway.

"We're headed to Capital Grill for your welcome lunch. Would you like a ride?" Paris asked, her coat in hand.

Lauryn dropped the phone from her ear. "Yes, that would be great. I'll grab my coat."

"See you in the lobby." Paris smiled and dipped off toward the elevators.

Lauryn put the phone back to her ear, "Dad?"

"You gotta go?"

Poor timing, she'd been enjoying their conversation. "I do. They're taking me for a welcome lunch."

"That's really good, honey. I'm glad it's working out."

"Thanks Dad. And, thanks for checking on me."

"Of course." He was beaming again. "Have a good day. Handle your business."

She was giggling when she hung up the phone. Her father always said that when he felt he was interrupting. Hearing from him had lifted her spirit. The universe seemed to keep telling her that moving back home had been the right move. She lifted her coat from a stand in the corner of her new office and thought, maybe this would be good for her and her folks. They could smooth things over and start behaving like a family again. Grabbing her purse, she strode off toward the elevator, her teammates smiling genuinely when she met them in the lobby.

That evening Lauryn made a beeline for her bathtub when she got home. Her first day back in the office had been exciting, but exhausting, and she couldn't wait to put a hydrating mask on her face and slather herself in shea body butter. With the temperature so icy outside, she'd have to start taking more honey with her tea.

"Well, that's done!" She announced to her closet as she hung her wool skirt and sweater back up and sifted through for something to wear the next day. Just two days before she'd been standing in the same spot wishing she could fast forward through everything. There were only 365 more evenings like this—260 if she considered holidays and time off. After laying out her clothes, she headed into the kitchen to pour herself a glass of crisp prosecco.

She raised her glass to the skyline glinting through her living room windows, and prayed the days would pass quickly.

Chapter 7

Lauryn

The rest of the week passed by in a blur, with Lauryn working hard to master a new schedule juggling the gym, unreliable furniture deliveries, and an actual commute. Her previous job had remained remote, even when larger companies announced their *return-to-office* plans. And although her new job wasn't far from her condo, getting fully dressed every morning to go into the office was a serious adjustment.

Once at work, Hema brought her in on one channel initiative after another, and she was already booked for a leadership retreat in May. By Thursday afternoon, her thighs were sore from Monday and Wednesday leg days, and all she could think about was slipping into another hot bath when she got home.

Still, she leaned into the pace, knowing that if she kept moving, there wouldn't be enough time for her to second-guess the fresh start she'd embarked on. She could simply focus on what was in front of her.

"Working from home tomorrow?" Sophia asked after they wrapped their last meeting that afternoon.

"I may," Lauryn was still typing notes so she wouldn't lose her thoughts.

"It's typically pretty dead in the office and the café doesn't open," Matt added, holding the glass conference room door open for them.

Lauryn gathered her laptop and the paper cup filled with terrible green tea she'd gotten from the "good" breakroom. She'd have to bring in her own tea and a mug from now on. Create another tea drawer in her desk like the one she had at home. She thought of Hema's personal espresso machine, the chrome finish reflecting everything happening in her office.

"Any plans for the weekend?" Sophia asked as the three of them walked down the hall in stride.

"No. Just waiting on my furniture to deliver. If it actually shows up this time." Lauryn waved as they all parted ways at the corner of a pod of cubicles, Lauryn stepping into her office, while Matt and Sophia headed back to their desks.

Her first week was nearly done. *Two-hundred and fifty-six days to go,* she thought to herself as she sank into her desk chair, slipping her laptop onto its docking station. She clicked through a few emails, the business correspondence resonating with her now that she had more context.

A violent thudding pulled Lauryn from her thoughts and she turned, frowning at her vibrating phone. A wave of déjà vu passed through her, seeing the phone laying in a familiar position and the same name lit up on the screen.

"Do you always answer the phone so suspiciously?" a familiar voice greeted her when she answered.

Her lips parted, but nothing came. They'd done the full catch-up just a few nights before. She tried to think of what reason he'd be calling her back. "No! I just wasn't expecting to hear from you again so soon."

"Should I call back in another ten years?"

Lauryn paused, unsure whether she found that funny. His tone was playful enough, but something about his question was telling. *Alright. Touché, my brother.* She recovered, leaning back in her chair. "What can I do for you, Mr. Mitchell?"

He let out a low, easy laugh. "Wow—Mr. Mitchell? I just wanted to see if you had plans this weekend. Tomorrow, actually."

"Tomorrow?" Lauryn blanked. "I hadn't decided," she lied, knowing damn well her only plans including reading and dodging other invites out from Deonna. "Just a few errands and setting up new furniture. Why, what's up?"

"Have you been to The Hoxton since you've been back?"

"Perry, I haven't been anywhere since I've been back." She'd have laughed harder if it wasn't so true.

"Come to Cira. We can grab dinner then go to Lazy Bird. Really nice speakeasy that's right downstairs. My guy's little brother will be performing that night. It'll be the perfect way to get you reacquainted with the city." She could hear his steps through the phone and what sounded like a crowd around him. "Seven o'clock, alright?"

"Seven o'clock," Lauryn echoed, surprising herself. "Perry, where are you?"

"Toronto," he breathed and she could practically hear him navigating through the crowds. "It's a hike to get to any connections here."

"It is," She remembered her last few trips through that airport. Joe did a few shows a year in Toronto or Montreal. "So, when does your flight get in?"

"Tonight. No delays today. So, I'll see you tomorrow?"

"Yes, you'll see me tomorrow." She was still smiling as they said their goodbyes and before she hung up, she heard the gate agent wishing Perry a good flight. She wondered if he always called old friends while he traveled. When the call dropped, she sat up in her chair frowning.

Had she just agreed to a date with Perry Mitchell? Had she even told him she was single? *Am I single?* She wondered, then reasoned that it was way too soon for labels of any kind.

"Here you go," she said aloud, acknowledging she might be making too much of it. Her mind had already begun to whir like an engine turning over–full analysis mode in progress. There was enough for her to think about: with her new job, furniture delays, and now she would have to wash and style her hair tonight. No way was she going to see him again with a week's worth of edge control on her temples.

She made it home at a decent hour that evening, but the winter sun had already set. Within thirty seconds of dropping her purse and keys down on the kitchen counter, she started the bath water running and squeezed in a shimmering glob of orange blossom bubble bath. She really should shower to wash her hair, but she couldn't resist the thought of slipping into hot water after the freezing weather outside.

As the tub filled, she sauntered into her bedroom, stripping off a pair of thick black slacks and a favorite oversized sweater that always made her feel sexy, despite its size. She ran her long nails through her hair, detangling it and giving her scalp a scratch so good it made her eyes roll back and flutter closed. Her home was quiet, nothing but the muted roar of the bath running and the scrunch of her stocking feet on the carpet.

In the old days, after a grueling day of back-to-back conference calls, she would come out of her home office to a brooding Joe, frustrated by his recent writer's block or scheduling conflicts. She'd find him standing in the kitchen grumbling about upcoming travels or a song he and the rest of his band couldn't agree on.

But then other days, she got glimpses of the early Joe, the amazingly talented, generous, romantic man who'd swept her off her feet when she was twenty-three years old. On those good days, she'd come to a clean house, candles lit, and an elaborate dinner in the works. When he wasn't being self-absorbed, Joe was a pretty outstanding cook. He was particularly good with Italian, mastering risotto in the first two years they lived together. She remembered when his bandmate Rob, had come by. After looking in their refrigerator he said "You have some real fancy taste to be a struggling musician. There's goat cheese in your fridge, but literally nothing else."

Lauryn shook her head, hearing Rob's voice as clearly as if he was standing in front of her now.

When Joe was into something, he went all in and that meant the best ingredients, whether they could afford them or not. She could distinctly remember the buttery rosemary aroma of the lamb chops he made on special occasions. He would come fetch her from her computer or out of the bathtub, guiding her into the dining room where the table was set for two. He'd serve her and pour wine like they had nowhere to be the next day. And when the weather was nice, they'd sit outside and he would play his guitar, trying out new songs on her while she sipped or cleaned the kitchen.

Then the music and drink would get him feeling passionate and he'd be on his knees in front of her, running his hands up her thighs and placing kisses between the buttons of her blouse. Lauryn's stomach flipped, recalling how connected they'd once been. How much they used to crave each other. Over the years, they'd experimented and explored each other, becoming more and more knowledgeable of what it took to please the other. Then becoming very efficient about it until there was absolutely no mystery to how a night of lovemaking would go.

He'd lay her down or lean her against the nearest surface and it all became pretty routine. At least until they stopped all together and she was pretty sure he was exploring with someone else.

It wasn't so much the cheating that bothered her. It was the lying and the uneasiness it created in their household. She started to look forward to his travels out of town and attended fewer and fewer of his shows. She preferred solitude, being able to move as she wanted without his incredible ego to maintain. Then a year before, it all started to feel pointless.

Unhooking her bra, Lauryn did the math in her head. It had been nearly seven months since the last time she'd graced Joe with anything more than a goodnight kiss. And things had been chilly between them long before that.

With her breasts free, she turned on her favorite playlists and waited for her phone's Bluetooth to pick up her speakers.

Regardless of her situation with Joe, she missed the rush that came when she was about to kiss him. The way her stomach somersaulted whenever he pulled her close at parties to whisper something torrid in her ear. Dreamily, her thoughts shifted to how long it'd been since she wanted to reach out and touch someone, to claim their mouth with hers. How lovely it had been to be scooped up and carried off to the bedroom, kissed until the world melted away.

Perry had certainly scooped her up at that party last month. He'd practically picked her up off the ground. She remembered her chin being forced up by his broad chest and shapely shoulders. Not to mention how incredible he smelled–smoky and grounded. The scent lingering long after he'd let her go.

Lauryn felt a shiver pass over breasts and it wasn't because of the cold. *Oh, no.* She shook her head, wrapping a forearm around herself. *Not tonight.*

She set her phone face down on her dresser like it had caught her doing something she shouldn't. Perry was just nostalgia with great timing. That was all. A familiar face in a season of unfamiliar territory.

She exhaled, heading back into the bathroom to turn off the water and light a few candles. The truth was, she felt lost. She'd led an entire life being composed, reliable, and accommodating to those around her. Now in her mid-thirties, newly single, newly arrived in a city that was just starting to feel like home again, she was mapping a new path forward. Considering only herself and no one else.

The bath water rippled softly as she got in and she leaned back, thinking how nice it would be to navigate with only her voice in her head.

Even so, she still hadn't told her old friends about leaving Memphis. She'd barely stopped for snacks on her way through the terminal at

Memphis International; just strutted straight onto the plane. She hadn't been interested in a round of goodbyes.

Nearly two months since she left and she still wasn't interested. But the guilt weighed-in anyway. Several text messages were piling up:

> *When did you move?*

> *L, You good?*

> *Just heard you're in Chicago? Since when??*

She sighed, conflicted about whether to respond. Some of those people meant well. Her old co-workers, her hairstylist, and her personal trainer. However, others were just trying to get whatever information they could to gossip about her, run back to Joe with an update he didn't deserve. And why was she expected to explain this decision? This attempt at starting over might have been clumsy, but it was hers to make.

Lauryn sank down into the tub, soaking her hair in the steaming water. She didn't have the energy to decide how to deal with Memphis tonight.

Outside her bathroom window, tiny snowflakes fell slowly outside her bathroom window, each illuminated by the highway lights below. Tomorrow, she'd go out. She'd get dressed up and head downtown to meet Perry at Cira. She would try to enjoy herself, even if she still wasn't sure what she was doing opening that box again when there were so many other unresolved aspects of her life.

Perry didn't appear to have any hang-ups about the way things between them had gone before. In fact, he seemed intent on being the master of ceremonies in welcoming her home.

Lauryn rolled her head from side to side, saturating her hair until her scalp hummed with pleasure.

"I really hope this is the part where it starts to get better," she said to the ceiling above her.

And for a second, she believed it might be.

Chapter 8

Lauryn

Balling her hands into fists and plunging them deep into the pockets of her coat, Lauryn high-tailed it across the street. If there was one thing she hadn't missed about the night scene in Chicago, it was the choice one had to make between a sensibly warm but cumbersome coat or a lighter, stylish option that was easy to tuck under an arm but offered absolutely no protection against the cold.

"Dress for the worst-case scenario," her father had often said when she was heading out to the mall or movies in her school days. *"Trying to be cute. Let's see how cute you are when one of your friends' raggedy car breaks down and it's negative-two degrees outside."*

After a lengthy deliberation in front of her closet earlier that evening, Lauryn chose a full-length olive wool overcoat that fell somewhere between fly-as-fuck and cozy. With the collar turned up and the wide belt tight around her waist, she could almost tolerate the disrespectful wind that barreled down Green Street as she made her way toward the Hoxton.

Why did I move back here? She blew her warm breath into the wool of scarf, careful not to smear her lip stick. Wiggling her toes inside the points of her smooth leather boots, she navigated around the Uber drivers coming and going, looking for their passengers and barely watching for pedestrians. Barely missing a patch of ice, she vaulted into the revolving doors, taking baby steps and pushing forward until she was let out into the hotel's lobby.

It was warm and fragrant, like cloves and bitters.

"Do you have a reservation?" a young woman asked when she reached the hostess stand.

"Perry Mitchell?" Lauryn's mouth quirked at the feel of his name in her mouth.

The hostess, a slight and pretty young woman, with a floral maxi skirt, an immaculate white blazer and converse sneakers, bounced excitedly, having found the name on the screen. "You're the first to arrive," she smiled pleasantly.

Lauryn just nodded, equally disappointed and impressed with herself that she'd arrived on time. The hostess escorted her to a low table with mid-century leather chairs. She floated across the adjacent lounge like a fairy, her converse sneakers kicking up the gauzy edges of her skirt. Lauryn took her seat when she stopped at a table near the windows. She set two drink menus down in front of her before floating away.

Lauryn tried not to appear as awkward as she felt, practiced looking at ease at the tiny table that was set for three. The hotel lobby was packed, with people crowded around the bar and clustered around the potted birds of paradise. The lobby felt like a velvet lined jewelry box.

She was contemplating buying her own drink when Perry finally arrived. "Lauryn."

At the warm sound of his voice behind her name, she turned. She could actually feel her smile growing too broad, seeing his tall frame above her. "Hi," she stood to hug him.

It seemed she'd caught him off guard with her embrace. She found him stiff at first, before his hands found their way politely around her waist. She felt a rush of self-consciousness. Was it silly to hop up and hug him like this, as if they'd been cool all this time? Although he'd hugged her at the holiday party, part of her still felt Perry wasn't hers to touch anymore, that she hadn't earned that kind of closeness back. After the way she'd left things, maybe she never would. Still, he had called. The only reason she was even here was because he'd reached out. Beneath the swirl of doubt and embarrassment, she was glad to see him again. Grateful that fate had given them such an easy chance to reconnect, to finally sit across from each other and catch up without all the weight of before.

He took a seat, settling comfortably into the mid-century chair. His edges were softer than when she first saw him. "I'm glad you made it."

"Yes, thank you for inviting me. This place is great."

He nodded, reaching for one of the two glasses of water. "Crowd can be a little weird sometimes, but most of the time it's cool. Parking is always crazy though–have you been waiting long?"

"No, just a few minutes. I can't believe how early I was."

"I wasn't going to say anything. When I saw you sitting at the table, I thought to myself, who is this person? This cannot be Lauryn Lindsey-"

"Hey-hey, I wasn't that bad," she said, rolling her eyes.

He continued, "The girl who all through undergrad consistently ran between thirty and ninety minutes late."

"How is that consistent? There's so much time between thirty and ninety minutes."

"Your consistency was in your lateness, in general." He grinned and herself doubt began to fade.

"I'll own that," she shrugged, smiling back at him. It was a miracle she hadn't been late tonight, puzzling over what to wear when she knew damn well this wasn't a date.

"I'm just glad you're allowing me to give you a proper welcome home. It's good to see you." He zeroed in on her for just a moment before his gaze began darting around the lobby again. He seemed so distracted. "Did you order?"

"Uh, no," she said, smiling a small smile. She'd just told him she'd only been there a few minutes before he'd arrived. Between getting her bearings there wasn't enough time to cross her legs, let alone fight all the people surrounding the enormous bar. He spent some time adjusting his jacket, but then seemed to finally settle in his chair. "So, how have you been?"

"I'm well." *Is he nervous?* Lauryn speculated, feeling as though their conversation had begun all over again. "You?"

"I'm good, I'm good," he assured her, though his body language said otherwise. She watched him hunch awkwardly over the table to scan a tiny framed QR code for the drink menu. He wasn't disheveled. Far from it, every detail about him was deliberate, down to the burgundy leather gloves that completed his ensemble. Maybe she wasn't the only one unsettled by their reunion. He looked up from scrolling through the menu on his phone, "What can I get for you?"

She hesitated, not about to wrestle with that QR code, then offered, "Gin martini. Dry."

His eyebrow raised and he paused, blinking at her in surprise. "Well, alright."

"Hey, its fucking cold outside and this was my first week back at work-"

He brought a finger to his lips to silently assure her there was no need for explanations, and then he held a hand out to her. "Come with me."

She trailed him through the crush of bodies until they reached the bar. While he leaned in to order their drinks, she kept her eyes on the crowd, people watching, pretending not to study him. Then, as if the universe conspired in their favor, the press of the crowd shifted and a single barstool opened up. Perry pulled it out for her, and though she tried for poise, her leather pants met the leather seat, catching just enough to turn her slide into an awkward scoot before she finally settled in.

"You're looking very sharp tonight Miss. Lindsey," he said without looking at her. Instead, he watched as their drinks were prepared.

"I can say the same for you. What is this, suede?" She reached to stroke his jacket, which she could see now was much finer than wool. Even with that light touch, she could feel the solidness of his muscles beneath.

He slid her drink over to her, careful not to spill a drop and she held her breath as he drew closer. "For the lady." He lifted his own drink to his lips, but seemed to watch until Lauryn tasted hers.

She eyed the drink, mixed so well she could see straight through the glass. Gingerly, she brought the delicate chilled glass to her mouth and let the familiar liquid meet her tongue. She sipped until she was satisfied the drink had been prepared well before setting it down. "Bomb."

He was pleased, smiling as he finally took a long sip of his own drink. For a few minutes, they sipped in silence, with Lauryn concentrating on not drinking her cocktail too fast.

Over the rim of her glass, she caught Perry observing the bar tenders as they crafted drinks for the mob encircling the bar. She noted his hand, the drink nestled securely between his fingers. He seemed to be looking everywhere but at her. On the phone, he'd been easy. Present. But now, face to face, it felt like they were both figuring out how to translate that version of themselves into real life.

She set her glass down. "How was your trip?"

Perry looked over, his expression softening. "Good. It was only a couple days, but always good to see the fam."

She nodded, the crowd around them growing louder.

"Yea, thanks again for keeping me company the other night. I won't be flying that airline again any time soon." He leaned a little closer, raising his glass to her. Then he finished the last of his drink. "Shall we go down?"

Lauryn paused, confused at what he was asking. "To LazyBird. The speakeasy is in the basement of the hotel."

She'd forgotten. "Oh! Yes, let's go. I want to see this place." She set her own half-empty glass down and hopped off the barstool to follow him. She was delighted to find him waiting and holding an arm out to her, making space for her to escape the crowd. He guided her through, parting the crowd of people waiting for drinks. *He smells good*, Lauryn thought to herself as they finally passed the hostess booth and headed toward the elevators. It was cooler on this side of the room and he led her to an inconspicuous door with the name "LazyBird" seemingly scribbled across the frosted glass.

Behind the door—a plain and inconspicuous concrete stairwell. Perry led the way down, Lauryn following close behind curiously. The stairwell spilled out into an opulent hallway.

"This way," Perry smiled over his shoulder as he started down the long hallway.

She could hear jazzy hip hop echoing from somewhere at the end and a short line of folks slowly disappearing through a door she couldn't see.

Perry was already bumping his head to the beat, but he was focused on his phone, clearly texting someone. Lauryn hung back, allowing the scene to reveal itself slowly to her. Her heels clicked as she found herself also sauntering to the relaxed beat. Watching Perry from behind, she wondered if the whole night would be this odd. If the comfortable familiarity and ease of their conversation had been exhausted over their two calls.

But just as she got close enough to recognize the music, Perry slowed and turned to reach for her. "Here we are."

Weaving his hand behind her, he corralled her toward the end of the line, and Lauryn peeked around to take in the scene.

LazyBird was intimate, luxurious, and just a little surreal. Wide, rounded booths in navy velvet curved elegantly beneath the glow of gold sconces. The tables were topped with black marquina marble, sleek and cool, and the backlit bar glowed in amber light like a ramen shop at midnight. The space buzzed with energy, stylish guests and the clink of highball glasses.

Lauryn's eyes widened as she took it all in. She followed Perry toward a curved loveseat just in front of the small stage, where a trio of musicians tuned their instruments and tested their mics. A server appeared almost immediately, taking their second drink orders with the smooth rhythm of someone who'd done it a hundred times before.

She grinned and leaned back, letting herself melt into the cushion as the ambient music gave way to a live set. The band launched into a jazzed-up cover of *We've Got the Jazz* by A Tribe Called Quest.

Without realizing, Lauryn mouthed the lyrics, amused by how easily the 90s classic pulled her in. She glanced at Perry. He seemed more relaxed now, settled into his seat, watching the performance.

She marveled at the masterful way time had refined this man. Even in the dark, she could spot the greys coming in around his hairline and beard. The years had worked on him so elegantly.

He rested against the arm of the couch with an easy confidence, one hand gripping the rocks glass and the other resting casually on his thigh. He seemed at ease, yet commanding, as if the years had gifted him not only wisdom, but an assurance that made him feel at home wherever he was.

"Aye! Look at y'all, early and everything!"

Startled, Lauryn turned at the sound of a very familiar Yoruba accent, booming and impossible to miss. It had been years since she'd seen Dayo Ajayi, maybe since her campus days or some long-forgotten game night. He seemed unchanged with the same bright smile, fresh fade, and a voice that could cut through a thunderstorm.

He wasn't alone. A whole crew came in behind him, people Lauryn didn't recognize. There were two women in fur coats and bone straight hair, men laughing loudly with drinks already in hand. Clearly Perry had invited a *group* of folks out tonight.

Dayo moved in towards Perry and pulled him up into a shake-up like they also hadn't seen each other in years. "My guy!" he said, already laughing. "You always find the best spots. And look at this. How'd you manage to find *this* one?"

He turned to Lauryn, grinning. "I haven't seen this pretty woman in a *very* long time."

Lauryn smiled reflexively, standing to hug him. "It's good to see you too, Dayo."

But even as she said it, the energy was shifting fast. The private moment she and Perry had slipped into was gone. Poof! He was already leaning in to talk to someone else from the group, nodding along to plans for where they'd go next, what the drink rounds would look like, who was coming late.

Lauryn blinked, trying to catch up.

She hadn't known exactly what to expect when he invited her out, but she'd assumed it would be just the two of them. A proper catch-up. Something like old times and hopefully a continuation of what had started on the phone the other night.

As she watched the others talking, she traced the years back in her mind, to the moment she'd started to see Perry differently. The reserved, driven guy she used to study with had somehow become the one she searched for at all of their friend's events, hoping he'd be there. Behind all that work ethic, she'd found a playfulness and charm, a quiet strength, and a sense of knowing that drew her in before she realized it. They became more than old classmates, lulled by an ease that felt so much like intimacy. They spent the that entire summer hovering somewhere between friendship and something more, walking that line without crossing it.

That is, until the night she'd let things get out of hand.

Lauryn took her seat on the couch again. Maybe it was best they weren't alone. History had proven their chemistry wasn't exactly manageable. That one night still lingered between them, unspoken and unresolved.

She crossed her legs and reached for her fresh martini that had appeared out of nowhere. Everyone else was laughing, crowding around the little couch, already deep into club energy. Perry caught her eye, sending her a reassuring smile, but his attention was split now, and she wasn't sure how she felt about it.

Returning his smile, she mentally checked herself. They weren't in their twenties any more and this wasn't some romantic reunion that needed to spiral into mixed signals and more regret. They were adults with full calendars, boundaries, and better judgment. Supposedly.

So why was she so disappointed?

Chapter 9

Lauryn

"Lo!" Dayo called from the corner of the bar, using her nickname from college. "What would you like?"

He motioned toward the bartender, who was busy pouring a generous amount of whiskey into a glass. No guessing who that was for. After catching their friend's set, the group wandered up the block to Blind Barber, a moody cocktail lounge hidden behind a barbershop. It was the kind of spot you'd never know about if someone didn't tell you. Out on the street, the West Loop was alive despite the cold; people spilled out of ride shares, their laughter rising in cloudy burts as they power walked toward the next warm doorway.

Leaning into the bar, Lauryn had to shout over the music, "I'm alright, thanks, Dayo!"

He frowned slightly and shook his head. "We have to welcome you home properly." His lips popped beautifully as he exaggerated his accent on the word *properly*. "Seriously, whatever you like."

Lauryn thought for a moment, eyeing the backlit shelves behind the bartender. Her eyes passed over the various bottles as she debated on what type of morning she wanted to have

She turned back to Dayo. "Johnny Walker."

Dayo's face lit up and he nodded in approval before waving down the bartender.

He was ordering her drink when Perry slid in beside her. "So it's going to be that kind of night?"

She burst out laughing. They'd all gone through a bit of a Scotch whisky phase post-undergrad, but after one-and-a-half martini's, Lauryn was regretting her choice already. "Apparently! I'm going to regret this in the morning."

He laughed too. "We'll keep you hydrated. And I know you've got some ginger-tea–mint-detox thing that fixes everything by morning."

He remembered, she thought, beaming at him. "I've got a tea for everything!"

The bartender set a lowball glass on the counter in front of her and started to pour. She accepted the drink cautiously before catching Dayo's eye. He raised his glass to her, his voice carrying over the music, "Welcome home!"

In perfect sync, they tapped their glasses against the bar before downing their shots. The taste was so familiar it carried her back to a moment in time, and she couldn't help but smile.

They made their way to the dance floor, where it was still crowded but several degrees cooler than the stifling crowd around the bar. She'd started to truly enjoy herself, winding her body in place when one of Dayo's friends, Alexandria, joined her on the dance floor.

Younger women, barely in their twenties, danced all around them, adorable and petite in their fuzzy matching sets and fitted knit dresses. They bobbed, weaved, and twerked effortlessly as they fed off each other's energy and caught the eye of shy young men holding up the wall nearby.

Lauryn felt relaxed and confident despite the obvious age gaps with the surrounding company. The two of them started to grind with an expertise that could only have been refined with age. Alexandria caught Lauryn's exact rhythm and the two rocked, mouthing the words "*Is it hot in here or is it just me...*" as Jhene Aiko's *Sativa* sounded.

Before too long, they were actually giggling and feeling beautiful as the music got better and better and Alexandria linked arms with Lauryn. Not two hours before, they hadn't even known each other. The South African beauty had smiled at Lauryn politely when she first arrived with Dayo, but had spent most of the evening scrolling through her phone. Now, Alexandria's cool demeanor was beginning to thaw, and Lauryn leaned into her affectionately. She remembered this–the sudden affinity and ease that blossoms between women when the vibe is just right. It was a temporary state, born of a few key ingredients: good music, a hint of admiration. And liquor. Always the liquor.

Lauryn let the ice melt a little more in the rest of her drink. She was having a great time. *This* was what it used to feel like when parties were actually fun. Not like the events Joe had taken her to over the years, where she had to stay on guard in case someone wanted a piece of her. Or a piece of Joe. He could be so naive in his earnestness. In the beginning, he'd just been trying to get anyone to listen. But over time, his ego had gotten them into more mess than she cared to remember.

It felt incredible to be somewhere she didn't have to worry and could just enjoy herself.

The DJ blended in a Mary J. Blige track, and all the older folks in the crowd who hadn't already been dancing suddenly made their way to the floor. Alexandria pulled away, fully consumed by the music, swaying on her own like she couldn't help it. The lyrics flowed effortlessly, and Lauryn found herself lip-singing again. She was in the middle of Lil' Kim's verse when she spotted Perry. She was mouthing the words in perfect time just as he eased through the crowd. His movement was cool and unhurried, just like at the holiday party.

You work more body than Jane Fonda
Physical fitness, Mary Blige be my witness
Under pressure, I lie for ya, die for ya
Ruger by the thigh for ya, right hand high for ya...

She delivered the verse like she was in the music video, patting her chest and lifting her lip in her best *uhn*-face. It was all for fun, until she realized how closely Perry was watching her. He paused for a moment to catch her "performance," his smile broad and amusement in his eyes. He stepped close as she finished mouthing the verse and she found herself singing the damn adlibs to him.

Catching herself, she moved away, playing it off as if she was just too into the music. Missing nothing, Alexandria smirked knowingly in her direction before turning her attention back to Dayo. Ordinarily, Lauryn might have been embarrassed, but she was having too much fun. After weeks of planning and uprooting her life, she needed this.

When she turned back, Perry was doing his best impression of Mary J. Blige's signature two-step. Lauryn covered her mouth, trying to control her laughter. It was amazing to catch a glimpse of the guy she'd first met on Quad Day so many years before.

He transitioned smoothly to bobbing his head, and they began moving together, the distance between them shrinking again. She couldn't tell if it was her drink or his proximity, but her face started to warm. In a flash, she recalled all the times she saw him in school. Always running late to a party or missing them completely because of his work schedule.

For four years he was either closing down that store for the night or getting up early to go open it.

"You seem very at ease for a man who barely made it to a house party in his life."

He chuckled lightly, "You're not wrong."

She smiled up at him, something playful stirring beneath the surface. "You come here often?"

He bent his head toward her. "No, but I have had a life since the last time you saw me."

Lauryn touched her chest. "Excuse *me.*"

He laughed again, "Now, now you're not completely wrong. I used to be a fly-on-the-wall kinda guy. Kinda like these muthafuckers in here." He glanced around them, noting the perimeter of young men dotted along the walls, watching with drinks in hand as the women danced and enjoyed themselves.

"Yeah, why don't they just ask a girl to dance?"

"Because these kids are different."

"They are. We were not like this."

"Nope—oh, shit." Another throwback sounded and suddenly he was really dancing. Lauryn watched, impressed as Perry and Dayo started motioning to each other across the crowd. The song was clearly their jam. She watched him moving and enjoying himself, unwittingly catching the attention of all the women within ten feet. They were intrigued and she didn't have to wonder why.

There was certainly something magnetic about Mr. Mitchell. For a second, she caught herself wondering if the women were wondering about *her*; if they thought she and Perry were together. They had been dancing together, sort of. Close enough to look like it.

Lauryn swayed on her own, reminding herself it wasn't that deep. Just a night out. Just Perry looking entirely too good under soft lights. As if on cue, the song changed and Perry immediately turned back to her, pursing his lips in approval of the song. It was a very familiar track, an anthem from their senior year of college. No matter how many parties he'd missed, there was no avoiding this one.

"OK, *who the fuck is this DJ?*" she asked aloud, standing on her tip-toes trying to see.

"Right?" Perry laughed in agreement. He was dancing more with arms now than anything. Heaven-forbid he get too caught up in the moment. Still, his body language was open, as if he was inviting her to reminisce with him. Lauryn edged toward him, stepping to the beat of the song and reaching him just in time for them both to sing, "Radio Killa!" with the rest of the crowd. It was so much like old times, Lauryn was almost afraid to blink, afraid the moment might disappear.

They grinned at each other, miming their favorite parts of the song and danced around each other. How could he have known she needed this? Then she remembered, he'd always seemed to know what she needed. As the DJ seamlessly transitioned from T-Pain to Twista, Jamie Foxx to Kanye, and Lil' Wayne, the memories came flooding back. How had she forgotten how easy it was to be with him? During that last summer, they'd never had a bad time together.

At some point, the music slowed. The DJ had shifted into something softer, moodier, yet still threaded with memory. Lauryn's body followed without thought, her rhythm changing before her mind could catch up. She was just working up the nerve to close the space between them when he touched her elbow, light and deliberate. He leaned in, and his cologne rose to meet her. It was a warm amber scent, with a trace of patchouli, something clean beneath it Lauryn couldn't figure out. He smelled good, so good that it made her forget herself for a second.

Her breath caught as she realized how easy it would be to let this moment turn into something else entirely. As he leaned in, it seemed he had already made that decision. His mouth brushed near her ear, and she went still.

"Let me know when you're ready to call it a night."

Then he was gone, releasing her elbow and slipping back through the crowd. The noise of the club swelled around her again, as if it had been waiting to reclaim her. Lauryn blinked, trying to hide her reaction, nodding as if she hadn't been anticipating something else. Perry's voice echoed in her ear.

Let me know when you're ready to call it a night.

It was nearly 2:00AM when they all surfaced, stepping out into the brisk night air. Dayo hugged everyone like he'd never see them again. Alexandria kissed her on the cheek, her lip gloss leaving a little mark Lauryn didn't bother to wipe away. As much as she'd enjoyed the night, she still had a thirty-minute ride home, and her feet were starting to protest in her boots.

Perry walked her to the curb, the group trailing behind in pairs, their laughter echoing down the street behind them. Her Uber was one minute away.

"Really good to have you home," Perry said, his voice low, breath curling in the cold. "Felt like old times tonight."

"Old times indeed," she echoed, smiling at him. She meant it. The night had been exactly what she needed. A proper welcome home if there ever was one. Still, the words "*old times*" landed with a weight she couldn't dismiss.

When her Uber pulled up she turned and hugged him without hesitation. She took in the smell of his wool scarf and cologne, lingering for just a moment longer than necessary.

"Is that the right plate?" He asked, eyeing the back end of the car, when she finally pulled away.

She laughed and checked her phone. "Yep, all good."

She reached for the car door just as Perry stepped forward, his hand brushing past hers to open it first.

"Oh. Thank you," she looked back at him over her shoulder.

"Goodnight, Lauryn."

"Goodnight, P."

She sank into the seat as he closed the door, the warmth of the car rushing around her. Outside, the city blurred under the glow of streetlights and passing headlights. As the car passed beneath the L tracks and merged toward the highway, she exhaled deeply.

She was going to be so hungover; the first real one in years.

And somehow, she didn't mind at all.

Chapter 10

Lauryn

"Alright, I'm headed out. I need to stop by and check on my ungrateful children before tonight." Lauryn glanced up from her laptop, catching the flick of Hema's olive blazer as she gathered her things from the conference room table. One thing about Hema–she never missed. Not with clothes, not with strategy.

"You're coming, right?" Hema pressed, enunciating in her beautiful accent.

Lauryn smiled, closing her laptop with a soft click. "I'll be there." Hema was on her way to the company's fiscal-year-end celebration. Lauryn couldn't promise she wouldn't slip out of that evening's work event early, but as the newest director, it would be foolish not to make an appearance.

Hema's grin was quick and knowing. "Good. Maybe I'll get something interesting out of you over a cocktail."

As she swept out of the conference room, her elegant fragrance wisping behind her, Lauryn leaned back in her chair, letting out a slow breath.

Outside, winter was just starting to give up the fight. Everything was thawing, streets less icy, skies less gray, and some of that shift was happening for Lauryn too. The frantic pace of the last few months had started to ease and her days settled into a rhythm that felt manageable. Familiar even. She was adjusting to her new role well, already making an impact, and living up to the reputation Hema had been counting on. Slowly, she was learning who to trust, who to avoid, and how to navigate yet another corporate dance.

But after-work events? She still felt some reluctance. Lauryn knew the game well enough: smile enough, drink just enough, reveal nothing.

People didn't need to know the details of her life to respect her work. That rule had served her well before, and she had no plans to break it now.

Back in her own office, she collected her things. She could feel the jubilance around the office as everyone packed up their things early to head over to the key supplier dinner that the rest of Hema's team had been planning for weeks.

By the time she reached the restaurant where their fiscal close outing was being held, the lot was packed. A quick hike from a side street, and she was stepping into soft lighting, fresh flowers, and the hum of early arrivals. She'd barely shrugged out of her coat when a familiar voice called her name.

"Lauryn!"

Her co-worker Vivienne was in front of her before she could blink, weaving through the crowd with a champagne glass in one hand and that wide, unforgettable grin.

Lauryn couldn't help but smile back. Vivienne Moore had a presence that filled the room before she even got to you. She was on the marketing team, and everything about her hit a little louder–full '90s blowout folding over one eye like a Dark & Lovely ad, skin the color of Japanese milk tea, a petite frame but an enormous smile. And her mouth was always moving. Hands flying, words spilling out in quick rhythm, her facial expressions finishing half her sentences before she could.

"Glad you made it," Vivienne said, pulling Lauryn into a warm half-hug. "I refuse to be bored tonight. Especially not during my farewell run."

Lauryn leaned back. "Wait–farewell?"

Vivienne's grin stretched wider, her dark eyes flashing. "Yup. Two more weeks and I'm out. Launching my own brand strategy studio. Podcast coming. Probably a workshop or two. I'm doing all of it." She took a sip, that confidence radiating off her like heat. "Life's too short to build someone else's dream."

Lauryn let out a quiet laugh, watching her. *That* was the energy she'd been trying to find again. "So, you're about to leave the company and I'll be wandering these work events by myself. "

"Girl, yes, this is my last hurrah."

Side by side they ventured further into the restaurant, taking note of who'd arrived and who hadn't. Vivienne even stopped to point out the co-workers who'd embarrassed themselves at last fiscal year-end party, having had one too many.

"Well, unfortunately I'm probably going to miss anyone getting wasted at this party. I'm only staying until Hema gets here.

"Still making a good impression?"

Lauryn rolled her eyes and laughed, "Some of us are planning to stay with the company a *bit* longer."

Vivienne smirked. "And on that note, I'm going to start my farewells now. You'll be alright?"

Lauryn nodded, lifting a glass of champagne from a passing tray and let her eyes sweep across the room as Vivienne disappeared. She was acutely aware of being the new girl, and some of the curious expressions she caught from people she had not been introduced to yet. However, she planned to conceal any weariness behind her finely honed professionalism.

The dynamics of her job were things she could easily manage, even if her personal life was a mess. At past jobs, she'd learned how to compartmentalize, navigate people's intrusive curiosity, even their indifference. A skillset she'd picked up from her professors and mentors, not from her father who had been in the Army since before he could legally drink. He'd taught her plenty, but civilian corporate life was not his lane.

Her mother, who had bounced from banking to Mary Kay, to event planning and finally real estate, was a woman full of reinvention but had never been especially open, and certainly not the person Lauryn could turn to for career advice. Then there was Joe, who tried, but could never relate. His advice always fell a little flat or oversimplified in a way that made Lauryn feel silly for consulting him in the first place.

And yet tonight's work event was not unlike her mother's sorority functions. After years of watching Francine at those fundraisers and luncheons, it was no wonder she mastered the art of small talk and diversion. Her gaze drifted to her team gathered over by the bar, their energy easy, welcoming. She smiled to herself, making her way over. This time, things felt different. She was building something that was hers.

Even as she sat there laughing with them, she longed for the moment she would step off of the elevator, walk the long hallway to her front door, turn the key in the lock and step back into her place.

Lauryn glanced over her shoulder, looking for Hema somewhere in the growing crowd. No sign of her or the fabulous olive blazer she'd been rocking earlier.

She sipped her champagne, realizing she might have to stay longer than she planned. With the slender glass in hand, she excused herself and slowly made her way toward the hors d'oeuvres table. It was a long table, piled high and decorated in a woodland spring theme with little florets of salami, various cheeses, seafood, fruit and crudités. If she had to stay, she might as well have snacks.

She was happily building her plate when one of the guys from marketing moseyed in next to her, reaching for the next set of tongs. "Pretty nice spread, huh?"

Lauryn smiled politely, trying hard to remember his name as he helped himself to the salmon she was just reaching for. "Yes, it is." She hoped the small talk would stop there, but no.

"So, how are you settling into the new role?"

She'd just presented a new reporting suite to him and his team earlier that morning—he knew *exactly* how she was settling in. "Great," she responded politely, focusing on the bunch of beautiful dark grapes lining a platter of cheeses. "The team has been amazing; I've been able to jump right in."

"That's excellent," he stood, seeming to appraise her for a moment. He hovered as Lauryn finally had a chance to lift a few delicate pieces of salmon onto her plate.

"And how are you?"

"Doing well, looking forward to the long weekend you know?"

"Yes, absolutely. Long weekends are the best." He hadn't added anything onto his plate, but instead was continuing to prolong the conversation. Lauryn decided to pass on the salad she'd been hoping to sample. Perhaps if she ventured away from the table she could lose him.

"So, you recently moved here, right?" he asked as soon as she took a step away.

"Yes." At this point she was looking for a place or person for refuge. She scanned the room as casually as she could, looking for anyone she knew. As much as she wanted to duck from this man, she would just have to see him again on Monday. And he was a department head after all, there would be no avoiding him in future.

Lauryn tugged a salmon free with her small silver fork. The tender fish came away easily and she scooped a few capers before taking a bite. Perhaps if she didn't volunteer anything else he would move on.

"Hema mentioned you're originally from Illinois?" He trailed off, trying to prompt her into filling in the blanks.

"Yes, I grew up here."

"Nice!" He seemed overly delighted with this tiny piece of information she'd confirmed. "How is it being back home then?"

Lauryn tried not to sigh and walked a few more steps to a highboy table that was free. "It's great. Especially now that the weather is breaking." Setting her plate and champagne glass down, she looked back up and offered him a little eye contact and a manufactured smile. She knew how to turn the charm on when she wanted to.

He laughed pleasantly, seemingly even more delighted now that they'd successfully made it to the height of small talk–the weather. "I'll bet. Every winter I ask myself why I still live here. Then spring comes and I forget what I was complaining about."

They stood awkwardly for a moment, Lauryn nibbling politely. At least the plate of crudités gave her something to hold, something to focus on so she didn't feel quite so exposed.

"Well, enjoy the party."

"Thank you," she said, offering a warm smile.

As he walked away, she felt a flicker of guilt. He was just trying to be nice. She was mid-grimace, already overthinking the whole exchange, when Vivienne appeared out of nowhere.

"I was on my way to save you, but got held up talking with Christian. You good? Did Matt talk your ear off?"

"No, he was fine. Just inquisitive."

"Aren't they though. They love trying to unpack the single people. Wait? Are you actually single?"

Lauryn realized this was the first time she'd be answering the question since leaving Memphis, since leaving Joe.

"Yeah," she volunteered, feeling more at ease with Vivienne than she had just a few seconds before.

"Yeah, it's always twenty questions. Especially coming up on long weekends–they always want to know what your plans are, who you're going to see, where you're traveling to. They're like lifestyle vampires. It's ridiculous."

Lauryn laughed hard because it was true. "So, you're single too?"

"Yeah girl, but I have someone to call on when I need him. You know as needed," she pursed her lips in a telling smirk.

Lauryn nodded as Vivienne continued, nodding her head impressed. She tried to imagine having someone on an *as-needed* basis. How one might negotiate something like that. And what exactly did *as-needed* entail?

"But I remember how they were when I first started and there was no ring on my finger. Every Friday they were like, 'Got any fun plans for the weekend?' And I was like, 'No, I'm actually going to finish working on my business plan so I can get the hell up out of here!'"

It was unfortunate that Vivienne was leaving. Lauryn was really enjoying getting to know her. She seemed so sure of herself–adamant about going after her dream. How fortunate it was that they'd crossed paths at this exact moment: Vivienne on her way out, Lauryn just getting started.

She admired her resolve, the way she seemed entirely at ease with herself. Vivienne had the kind of ambition Lauryn longed for–making decisions for her life with the same clarity she used at work. Moving through life with less hesitations and fewer calculations.

The two of them chatted a while longer, finding themselves on the opposite side of the restaurant. The work crowd had dropped off, with most people heading home once the free drinks stopped circulating. Lauryn and Vivienne were tucked away in a booth across from the bar. They'd switched from champagne to gin and tonics and the conversation had shifted with it.

"I'm telling you that man was ready to risk it all!" Vivienne was teasing her about Matt.

"Stop! I have a meeting with this man on Monday. And you making jokes is not helping."

"I'm just reporting what I saw. He saw all his chocolate girl fantasies coming true," Vivienne sipped her cocktail pointedly, smirking all the while.

"You are terrible"

"While we're on the topic. What's your situation, have you dabbled in the Chicago dating scene yet?"

"I have no dating situation. I just ended something pretty messy. It was the closest I suppose I will ever get to marriage and it ended in the closest any unmarried person has ever gotten to divorce."

"Woa, it's like that? How long were you together?"

"Twelve years."

Drunkenly, Vivienne swallowed and sat up a little straighter. "Why'd you stay?"

Lauryn, rubbing her arms, sobering a little at the question. "When it was good it was good. By the time it started to unravel, I was too deep to see what it was. There was always something I thought was missing or would fix it. For a while I thought maybe when his career took off. Then I thought, maybe a baby-" she turned her drink in her hand, watching the lime pulp settle.

"Oh, girl, I've been there. Not the baby thing, but thinking it would get better if I just tried a little harder? Never again. I deal with these men on a transaction basis only. Tit for tat. What are you doing for me? And sex is no longer going to cut it."

Lauryn nodded, a quiet laugh catching in her throat. She felt a little foolish being the one who'd kept trying. Waiting for things to get better–hoping.

Something in Vivienne's blatant honesty loosened her own.

"So how is work?" Vivienne asked, tilting her head with a knowing look. "How's it really going?"

"I do like it! Hema is amazing and I love the direction the Marketing team is taking. It's as close to *feel-good* work as I'm going to get working for this size company.."

"That's probably true. And I have to admit," she sat back against the booth. "I love to see a black woman running the numbers. There's plenty of us in the creative spaces, but data science? Now *that's* inclusion."

"Yeah I am proud of that, and so far the team doesn't appear to have any issues like I've seen at other companies I've contracted for."

"Oh, you're a contractor?"

Lauryn nodded, taking a sip of her drink. "Standing in for twelve months."

"Oh wow. How do you like it?"

"It serves the purpose and it's flexible. I've only done it the last few years, but it allowed me to pick up and move when my ex needed to be somewhere new."

"Oh yeah, I see what you mean. So, what are your plans? You going to keep going like this, or consult?"

"Funny you ask, I've been thinking a lot about next steps. There's a lot of money in consulting, but it's a grind. I'm not sure I could sustain that."

"But what would you like to do if you could be anywhere? What's your endgame?"

Lauryn shrugged, too tipsy to be ashamed. "I don't really have one yet. I'm supposed to be figuring that out right now. My jobs have always just been a means to an end, you know? Plus, I happen to be very good at what I do so before I know it, I'm wrapped up in it and another year flies by. I have some ideas, but haven't gotten very far."

"But you're a STEM Bae! You could do consulting, mentorship, support startups, hell you've got all the makings of an influencer. Data science boss meets lifestyle. Boom." She waved her hands, like she was framing it out in the air.

Lauryn nearly choked on her drink. "Who's going to watch that?"

"Lauryn there is an audience for everything and you are really bringing something to the table. An independent black woman, working in big data, consulting top brands. You're smart as hell, fly as fuck..."

Lauryn bit her lip even though she was touched by her words. "First, I love you for saying all of that. I just don't know, I haven't been dreaming for so long, it's hard for me to actually *see* it. That's probably why I ended up in the relationship that I was in. I didn't have to dream; his dreams were big enough for the both of us." The gin had her confessing more than she meant to, and she tried to pull back. "I was content for a long time. And I can't blame him for that."

Vivienne didn't miss a beat, "That could be part of your influencer story. Everyone loves a redemption story and a fresh start! Coupled with you being Black female excellence? Girl, say less, let's do this! If you don't hurry up and sign this contract with me..." she took another long sip from her drink and set it down, punctuating her statement.

"I don't think influencer life is for me, but there is an idea I've been playing with for a few years now. It's less boss-bae and more *home-baddie*?"

"Ha! I love that, homebaddie, homebody," she giggled, repeating it a few more times. "Well, nurture that dream girl. Check out Pinterest and Youtube for inspiration. It'll help you stay excited and get that business plan going!"

When Lauryn got home that night, she did feel energized about her future. Until now, it had been about getting out of her fruitless relationship. After that, her focus had been all about making a home for herself and starting anew. She hadn't considered anything more yet. The panic she often felt, like she'd wasted so much time and now there wasn't enough time to course correct, still had her reeling.

After a steaming eucalyptus bath, she settled against her pillows in bed with her laptop, a saucer of butter cookies, and ginger tea. Nibbling carefully on the crumbling cookies, she clicked through Google and Youtube. She typed in a few keywords, checking to see if anyone had beat her to market with the same concept.

The idea had come to her two years earlier, during one of the strangest, stillest times of her life. Memphis was under a "Safer at Home" order, and the weight of the pandemic hung heavy over everything–sirens in the distance, grocery shelves cleared, and headlines that became worse and worse each day.

At home, she found herself reaching for comfort wherever she could. When she ran out of bath salts and her favorite soaps, it hit her harder than she expected. Those evening baths had become a ritual–one of the few things that helped her feel human, steady, safe. That's when the idea hit her: a subscription service for bath kits. Thoughtfully made; delivered with care. Not just salts, but bath teas, oils, body brushes, candles or incense...everything you needed to tend to yourself.

While Joe had gone stir crazy, she tried to anchor herself in the small moments, trying her hand at baking to stave off her sweet tooth and soaking in the tub until the water went cold.

Now, sitting cross-legged on her new bed, in her new condo, Lauryn excitedly made notes on her favorite fragrances and skincare brands. Vivienne hadn't even officially launched her consultancy yet, and here Lauryn was pinning ideas and rereading the draft of a business plan she thought she'd deleted.

Maybe she was getting ahead of herself. But after nearly a decade of only thinking in two-year increments, always adjusting to someone else's life, it felt good to dream again.

To imagine something that was only hers.

Chapter 11

Lauryn

Lauryn woke early the next morning feeling energized, despite the gin she and Vivienne enjoyed the night before. She was up and headed for the gym by seven, then back downstairs sipping black coffee at the table with her laptop. Her morning run had started more ideas flowing and she was eager to get her thoughts down.

An hour ticked by and she felt a little silly, scribbling notes of things to research. She questioned whether she was ready for a real career change. She thought about the realities of entrepreneurship, and her typing slowed as her confidence wavered. Lauryn had daydreamed about this concept for years but never pushed past the fantasy. Finishing her business plan would have meant tuning out whatever Joe had going on, but she'd been wrapped up in their lives together. Plus, she'd allowed his questions and skepticism to seed doubt in her mind.

It was time to take a page out of his book. Be selfish and make her own damn dreams come true.

She spent the rest of the morning multi-tasking, searching for perfume and candle making workshops in between work emails. Her thoughts drifted back to Joe. His ambition had always been relentless. Over the years, she'd watched him pour everything into his music, chasing the next opportunity with tunnel vision. Then, five years ago after a handful of his songs blew up on a popular Netflix series, things had started to take off. Everyone wanted to know more about him and his band, *No Saints Left*.

Lauryn remembered smiling as she read the *NYLON Magazine* feature, especially the part about the woman on the cover of their first album.

"Yes, that's my girlfriend, Lauryn," Joe had said. "She's amazing. She's been so supportive to me and the guys. And I mean, look at her, she's a knock-out. Not a bad idea to put her on the cover, right?"

She remembered the photoshoot. Two hours in a hot warehouse with funny smelling vintage furniture. The resulting photos had been epic, but that was the last record she'd posed for.

And now she was studying luxury beauty brands and their websites, making note of elements she would include when she built something of her own.

At noon she signed off, logging out of her work laptop and shirking off any remaining work for Amara Labs until Sunday. She was lost in a website building app, playing around with templates when her father called. "Hey Dad, what's up?"

"Hello there. Are you home?"

"I am!" she said delightedly, wondering why he was asking.

I'm at old orchard mall, thought I could stop by and see your new place?"

"Yeah, that would be great. Right now?"

"Yes, I'm wrapping up, just picking up a few things for your mother. You know she's always shopping, engraving or monogramming something."

Lauryn laughed. "Oh yes, well that's great. Do you need the address?"

"No, no. I know where you are. The doggone building is practically hanging over the highway!"

Lauryn laughed. Her condominium *was* large, with two massive towers glazed in tinted windows that reflected the clouds and sky. The garden level wrapped around the south tower and jutted out like a concrete diving board topped with trees.

"Alright, I'll see you soon."

"See you soon." Lauryn straightened a little, wishing she'd gotten some fresh flowers, or at least some fresh fruit. This would be her first-time hosting anyone in her new place. And the first time hosting her father in longer than she could remember.

She hurried around, making sure to hide anything that might prompt any questions she wasn't ready to answer or fuss about. Her father, Colonel Lindsey, could be very inquisitive, even when he didn't mean to be. And there were some conversations Lauryn just didn't want to have right now.

Her phone rang again, "Where is the elevator in this place? I'm so lost my voice is echoing. Am I going the right way?" After some direction, she finally heard him knock at the door and checked herself in the mirror before answering.

"Hey, Dad!"

"Hey-hey. " He was weighed down in bags so she could barely hug him.

"What's all this?" she asked, reaching over to help.

"I made some short ribs the other day. We're not going to finish it all so I thought I'd bring some by." She ushered him into the kitchen. "Oh, and your moms friend, Ms. Grace–you remember Grace?"

"I remember her caramel cake–Dad, is there caramel cake in those bags?" She was trying to peek into the tote that looked like it could have a cake box in it.

"Well, yeah, we told her you moved back and she insisted-"

"She always was my favorite of mom's friends," Lauryn whisked him over to the kitchen island, unloading the bags from his fingers and taking his coat.

"Well, this is a nice surprise." She remembered this heavy coat of his, and had to dig around for a hanger sturdy enough to hold it. It smelled like him and she smiled, hanging it next to her parka.

"The cake or me?" He teased.

Lauryn squinted at him, "Both."

Well, I figure you're up the road now, and we still haven't seen your new place. This is nice, Lauryn, bigger than I thought. Good lord girl, you got a view."

"I do!" She was pleased because he was. "That's what sold me, honestly. When it's really clear, I can see the whole city skyline."

"Yeah, this is quite nice. You bought it?" He was standing like he did on the base, surveying in his Colonel stance.

"No, just renting," she admitted without thinking. That was certainly going to prompt some questions down the road. The truth was, she wasn't even sure she was staying in Illinois. Although she was loving her new space, this was supposed to be temporary. A one-year plan to get her bearings and figure out her next move.

"May I have the tour?"

"Of course," she'd been so busy anticipating his next question she hadn't noticed him starting to peek down the hall. She showed him around, careful to position herself in front of a pile of unfolded clothes on her couch.

"This is really nice, honey." He took a seat on one of her barstools. "I think it's time for tea and cake though. How about you?"

"Oh yes, I think so." She was pulling out saucers and forks when she asked. "So what else is new? How's Mom?"

She caught his expression and could've sworn she saw him frown. "She's good. Running all of her events and trying to run me too. You know how she gets."

"I do," she observed her father a little while. Normally, he was so lighthearted about her mother. The woman's antics just never seemed to put him off. No matter the fuss or entitled comment she made–he just let it roll right off his back like water. Laughing it off and puffing away at his cigars.

Lauryn cut two perfect slices of caramel cake and handed a slice to her father. Looking at him now, seated across the kitchen island, she could tell something was bothering him. A new frown line was etched deep between his brows. "Dad, what's up? You and Mom seem off. I've felt it since I got back. What's going on?"

"Your mom is just in one of her moods." He did not elaborate, just took a few bites of the cake. "Grace will talk your ear off, but that woman can bake a cake now."

"Man! I am telling you," Lauryn and her father laughed, digging into their cake a little more.

"Have you heard from your sister?"

By sister, he meant Alicia–Lauryn's third eldest sibling and the only one close to her in age. She had two older half-sisters from her father's first marriage, but they were almost always mentioned as a unit, distant and tightly knit in a way Lauryn had never been part of.

"Assuming you mean Alicia? No, we don't really talk, Dad."

They didn't talk at all. In the thirty or so years since Lauryn learned of her big sister's existence, they'd never had a real relationship. Her father had an entire life before meeting Lauryn's mother and moving to Illinois.

Neal's first wife, Lenora, had been his high school sweetheart. And he was just joining the army when they found themselves pregnant. He did the right thing, marrying Lenora and soon a second daughter was born. Kelly and Tasha were nearly twenty years older than Lauryn and lived in California somewhere. Neal and Lenora divorced after 7 years.

From what little Lauryn had been told, Lenora had not been a kind woman and did her best to demonstrate how much she didn't need Neal.

Alicia was daughter number three, but Neal had never married her mother, Pat. Lauryn knew even less about Ms. Pat and Alicia although she'd written a few letters to her sister as a child. Two letters on her favorite bumblebee stationary. Lauryn could remember using *White-out* for the first time and trying to be extra careful with her penmanship. She hadn't wanted her big sister to think she couldn't write well. She'd rewritten the whole first letter three times before handing the final draft over to her father to mail.

She'd been so excited to share all the details about summer camp with her sister, even inviting Alicia and her mom to come visit in the second letter she wrote. She never received a response to either letter.

Lauryn shook her head at the memory, "Mm," was all she could really manage to say. "And how is she?" she added out of politeness.

"She's alright, but you know her mom has been real sick."

"No, I didn't know that. I'm sorry to hear it."

"I called last year after my retirement. I hadn't spoken to her in a few years. I used to hear from her when she was in school, but-" He trailed off. "Anyway, we've been talking regularly now and getting to know each other."

"That's good." Lauryn offered, unsure of what to make of this conversation. Had he come all the way over here, bribed her with caramel cake just to talk about a daughter that had never seemed to care about either one of them? "Are they still in California?"

"Oh yes, her mother stayed in the same house. And Alicia married a nice fellow and they're closer to Long Beach now. She has two girls. Your nieces."

Lauryn considered that for a moment. How could she have nieces when she didn't really have a sister? "How old are they?"

"Thirteen and four. Zora and Angela. Alicia says she's keeping them busy." Lauryn didn't know if she wanted to hear more, but she smiled despite herself. It was a lovely thought, being an auntie. And yet, she couldn't shake the feeling that her father was sharing all of this to avoid talking about the issue between him and her mother. "I've been trying to reconnect with all my girls. Tasha and Kelly too, but they don't seem too keen on talking'. And your mother-"

"Well Dad, it's been what, twenty years since you've seen them?"

"No! Not that long. I went to Tasha's wedding and flew in when Kelly got her masters."

"Yes, but do you really have a connection with them anymore?"

"I don't. And that's what I'm aiming to fix. I'm retired now, I'm still healthy. And I want to know my grandchildren. And try to make amends for some of the selfish decisions I made. Your mother doesn't see the point and I'm tired of talking to her about it."

Lauryn stayed quiet, mulling that last piece over. Was their family, she and her mother, one of those selfish decisions? It made sense, he was getting older and she wasn't popping out any grandbabies anytime soon. Lauryn thought of her mother, running off for some convention or planning another sorority event. Her mother always seemed to have everything she wanted out of life. Perhaps he needed more. She wondered why her mother wouldn't be more supportive. She watched him, looking a little weary suddenly as he stroked his own head, deep in thought. "I think you need more cake. And some tea."

He exhaled a soft laugh and slid his saucer across to Lauryn. "I agree."

Chapter 12

Perry

"Ladies and gentlemen, welcome to Chicago where the local time is six-thirty-two p.m. The weather is seventy degrees. Please remain seated as we taxi toward our gate. Baggage can be retrieved at carousel seven. On behalf of the entire crew, we'd like to thank you for flying United."

Perry exhaled a long, steady breath into his face mask, bracing for the moment the plane slowed and the aisles filled with passengers scrambling for a two-second head start. He knew better than to join them, especially with no connection to catch. After a long week on the road, he was finally home.

The plane slowed to halt, and a cacophony of seat buckles sounded as everyone wrenched themselves free of their seats and threw open the overhead bins. He couldn't understand it. Where did they expect to go with the plane door still closed? Shifting his focus from the chaos of the aisle, he pulled out his phone, and swiped off the Airplane mode. The screen brightened, glowing a little stronger as the rest of his apps came back to life.

Text messages began flooding in, including one from his father, saying:

> *Love you too, Son. Have a safe flight.*

Patiently, he flipped through the other messages, finding one from his little sister, the tiny icon of her baby picture hovered next to her words:

> *Running Late. You landed early.*

He smirked. She was always running late unless it had something to do with a party. He shook his head, cradling the phone in his hands as he typed back.

> No problem, we're still on the plane.

Simone was picking him up, as she'd started to do now that she was home from school. With her recent graduation from Northwestern and Perry finally completing renovations on his second floor, his sister found excuses to house-sit. This, of course, was less of a favor to Perry and more one way to extend her solo living after college. Like most post grads, Simone was grinding to afford a place of her own. She was eager to leave home again and despite Perry's advice, couldn't yet see the benefit of staying home and saving money with their parents.

> OK good because I literally just left Sorry P! See you soon!

Of course. It would be another thirty minutes, at least, before Simone was even close to the airport and that was only if traffic held up. Perry shifted in his seat and settled in. Between his sister's punctuality and the amount of people on this plane, he wouldn't be getting off any time soon. He considered sending another message back, telling her to stop texting and driving, but figured that would defeat the purpose of warning her. God willing, she'd get to the airport when she got there.

Simone was right at that age where everything seemed possible, running around the city playing adult. She was slightly spoiled, but only because she was the baby. The one who completed their family. It'd been a mind-trip to see her walk across the stage at her graduation, the kente cloth stole in vibrant color around her neck.

Without warning his mind immediately called up an image of Lauryn, standing under the trees in her graduation regalia, what felt like a lifetime ago, looking like the odd-man-out amongst her own family. He recalled how preoccupied she looked as she posed for pictures, then the shift in her expression when she saw him walking over. Her dark eyes had been warm and full of appreciation.

The memory blurred into another, meeting her at the entrance of a summer festival on the North Side. The two of them hanging out all day, running into other friends from school before ending up in Greektown for gyros and chicken wings. Then at the end of the night, Perry would head south while Lauryn made her way back north to her parents' place in the suburbs.

He tried to shut down the memories, mentally flicking the switch on every image of her in his mind. However, thinking about his sister, where she was in life, pulled him back to his first few years after undergrad. He remembered the phase clearly, trying to find his footing after four years of classes and structure. After college, most of his classmates had packed up and headed back north. A handful of them took opportunities out of state, while the rest of them circled back to Chicago, struggling to find decent gigs in a challenging market.

It had been a rough time, but Perry landed on his feet getting a job right away as a general analyst. It was challenging work, but compared to retail it built his expertise, gave him a steady check, and weekends that were his own. His car was paid off, Obama was in office, and for the first time he was stacking real money. He started venturing out, reconnecting with Rashad. Before long, the two of them had moved in together, splitting rent on a place in the South Loop. He shook his head, remembering all the women he'd found tiptoeing around their bathroom while Rashad snored off the night before.

A temperature shift in the cabin air tugged Perry from his memories and he looked up to find the row ahead was already on their feet, moving into the aisle. The front of the plane was clear, just the clean crew racing to wipe everything down before the next flight. He slipped his phone into his pocket, lifted his carry-on from the overhead, and stepped off the plane. In the terminal, he pulled off his mask and shoved it into his pocket, inhaling the familiar scent of roasted nuts and Garrett's Popcorn welcoming him home.

Simone was still a few minutes away when he rolled his carry-on towards the passenger pick up lane, but he was grateful for the cool air. His next vacation was too far away and even though it was Friday, he was already considering taking Monday off.

"P!" Perry snapped his head around at the sound of his nickname, finding Simone standing half-in and half-out of his BMW, waving at him. He frowned as he made his way over.

"And why, pray tell, are you in my car?"

"I thought you might want the comfort of your own vehicle after such a long flight," she cooed, lifting the trunk open for him.

Perry narrowed his eyes on her, "The flight was two hours. You've been driving this since I left, huh?"

"My car's in the shop! I'm not even sure I should pay to get it fixed. I'm so close to a down payment for a new one."

He slid his bag into the trunk, shutting it with one hand as Simone bumped him on the way toward the driver's side. "Cute, but I'm driving home." Once Perry settled behind the wheel, he glanced over, his voice easy but edged with that older-brother weight. "I keep telling you to keep that car running. The way you like to shop and eat out... You do not want a car note."

Simone nodded, fastening her seatbelt, "I know but, I'm just so tired of fixing this thing."

"Simone cars require maintenance. Getting your tires replaced is not *fixing*, it's maintenance. Just the-"

"Cost of independence?" Simone finished for him, lifting a brow at him. "Did you turn into our father while you were gone? What's in the water in Denver, because you sound a whole lot like your daddy."

They hit traffic on the way back, but eventually made it back to Perry's place.

Simone had at least left the house clean and neat, the dishwasher blinking away with freshly cleaned dishes. It felt good to be home, he thought, and parked his carry-on and shoes near the back door before heading into the kitchen. At the counter, he scooped up a stack of mail, thumbing through it, setting bills to the side and tossing the junk straight into the recycling bin. He looked up to where Simone was walking and scrolling through her phone at the same time. If she wasn't careful, she was going to run right into a box of leftover subway tile Perry hadn't quite gotten around to storing.

"You planning on staying tonight too," he asked, just barely saving her from stubbing the heck out of her toes. "Should I order for both of us?"

She pursed her lips like she was trying to figure out how to let him down, "I actually have plans. But, we can do brunch on Sunday!"

"Wait, brunch or *brunch*-brunch?" Perry asked, the first option meant breakfast cooked up in his kitchen, while the second meant thirty minutes trying to find parking or waiting for a table, and a hefty bill that would most likely be his to pay. Simone had loved breakfast food since childhood, and the only thing that had changed was her preference for French Toast over pancakes.

"Brunch-brunch?" She actually poked her lip out and Perry sighed, unable to say no.

"Yeah, we can do that. Let's go early though so we can get in before the crowds." He sent her an easy smile across the kitchen and her toffee-brown eyes sparkled as she nodded in agreement. With that, she disappeared upstairs to get ready for whatever event she had that night.

Perry finished ordering dinner and set his phone down, stepping over to the sink to wash his hands. After patting them dry, he shuffled over to the bar cabinet in his living room. He reached for a decanter and poured himself a drink, the smooth dark liquid instantly recognizable and fragrant.

With his pointer finger, he tipped one of many records forward and slipped it from the shelf. Carefully, he slid the vinyl record from its sleeve and palmed the edges as he set it onto his record player. He eased down onto a chrome and leather lounge chair as the first few crackles sounded and Curtis Mayfield filled the room.

Perry raised his glass, the first sip of bourbon hitting hot before melting into dark sweetness, caramel and oak lingering at the back of his throat. The warmth spread slow, easing his shoulders as the music carried through the room, but his mind was already back on Lauryn. She'd been slipping into his mind more and more since the party, uninvited but relentless, the thought of her trailing him through the most ordinary parts of his day. Packing his gym bag. Unlocking his front door. Driving down Lake Shore. All it took was a pause and there she was again–her face, her voice, the reminder that she was back. And somehow, his world tilted differently with her in it.

He remembered the night in the airport when the urge to call her had caught him sideways. He'd been sitting by the windows, watching planes taxi under the lights, his own flight still delayed. At first, he'd only wondered if her number was still saved in his phone. Slowly, he had scrolled through his contacts, finding it right where he'd left it. His thumb had hovered for a while, logic and curiosity fighting for control. After all this time, would she even have the same number? He did.

When she answered and that voice filled his ear, it had thrown him back to when things were good between them–simpler. He hadn't had a reason to call, at least not one he could name. Although part of him had wanted to call and check, make sure she was really back and not his memory playing with him. He would've felt more like a fool if the conversation hadn't flowed so easily.

Perry leaned back in his chair, the leather creaking as he swirled the amber in his glass. He thought about how easily they had slipped into laughter that night, her words tumbling into that breathy little giggle he realized he missed. After they hung up that night and his flight finally boarded, he accepted things would end there. One call, a catch up, nothing more.

Then, on his last trip, he got it in his head to invite her out, the younger version of himself getting the better of him. He knew he should have left it alone, let the past stay where Lauryn had dropped it. Because she had dropped it, and him, without warning. He had carried that silently for years. However, he'd felt that familiar yolk between them, even over the phone, and he hadn't been able to resist the chance to spend time with her again. Find out who she was after all this time. Had she found everything she wanted with Joe? And if so, where was he?

She hadn't outright said she and Joe were done, but everything in her voice had hinted at a clean slate. Lauryn was starting over. Despite the way she'd left Perry hanging, he was starting to understand her panic. Though she hadn't asked for forgiveness, he found himself giving it anyway, or at least inching toward it. That night years ago, after the wedding, when he walked with her past the Riverwalk to the hotel, when she'd kissed him, Lauryn had already been spoken for. She had already chosen Joe.

Perry let the thought settle. He knew better than to open this box and yet, but the more he tried to shut her out, the more memories and questions pulled at him like there was more to their story.

He lifted his glass, let the bourbon burn into sweetness, and honed in on the record playing. If he was honest with himself, he didn't want Lauryn gone from his head. Not when he could still see her as she'd been waiting for him at Cira. He'd been distracted as hell when he sat down at that table—her legs crossed, the black leather of her boots climbing all the way to her knees, melting into those insane leather pants that fit her like a fucking glove. Her mass of thick hair had been swept back over one shoulder, catching the light as her gaze floated over the crowd. The picture of her lingered in his mind, slow and vivid.

When they'd danced together later that night, laughing and lip-singing to nineties classics, the air between them had been playful and electric. Perry took another slow sip, knowing damn well that no matter how much his pride was fighting it, he wanted to feel that charge again.

Chapter 13

Spring

Lauryn

S pring in the Midwest is never promised. Snow could still blow in as late as April, cold and unrelenting, as the winter season refused to let go. However, for the past two weeks, spring had started showing out. Seventy degrees arrived just in time for Lauryn's thirty-sixth birthday, warm enough to feel like summer but fleeting enough that everyone still kept their coats hanging by the door. Even though everyone knew it wouldn't last, people wasted no time indulging in the weather. Patios filled. Parks brimmed with near-festival crowds, and every restaurant downtown had flung its doors open like an invitation.

Tulips bloomed all across the city, in planters and along medians, standing tall against the Chicago architecture. Little bursts of color insisting that maybe, just maybe, the season had turned for good. The air felt lighter and sweeter, tempting Lauryn to walk a little slower every time she found herself in the new sunshine. She had been waiting for the perfect day to wear her vintage off-the-shoulder top, and today finally felt like it. Deonna—more reliable than any weatherman—had brunch booked before Lauryn even heard the weather would be warm.

January and February had been long, and Lauryn's early morning commute hadn't helped. Once she'd learned the ropes, things really took off at the office, the pace picked up and she found herself lingering, answering emails and running reports while traffic died down.

Her mother had started emailing her at work now, finding it easier to communicate through daughter to-do lists and the occasional article about the best cities to find a husband. Lauryn would roll her eyes, delete the article, then write back agreeing to help in the garden or tackle some other chore.

She'd been hearing from Perry too. Not every day, but enough to feel like they were developing a thing. His texts always popped up when she needed it. The occasional Tik Tok video that had her crying with laughter at her desk or just the simplest, *How are you today?* always sent at the perfect time.

When he wasn't traveling, their work hours were similar, and in the past two few weeks a rhythm had formed. He'd tell her to log off and go home, calling her "Superstar" or "CEO of Doing Too Much," though he clearly never followed his own advice. Still, she liked it. Liked that he understood the corporate grind and could relate to the demands of the job. She appreciated how easily he seemed to read her moods, knowing exactly when to make her laugh and when to leave her be. And on the days they didn't chat, she caught herself missing his messages.

"This is like the third time she walked by without my drink. I'm trying to understand what the problem is," Deonna said that Saturday when they met for their brunch date. She lounged so coolly in the bistro armchair; one would never suspect their tip was starting to disappear. She watched their server floating obliviously around tables, pausing to check on other patrons.

"Probably because she can feel you staring, girl." Brittney Hartwell, Deonna's cousin, teased from the opposite side of the table. In the few months Lauryn had gotten to know Brittney, she found her to be tenacious, but a girly girl through-and-through. Her pale-yellow skirt suit and matching nails hinted at her sweetness, but Brittney could sniff out gossip the way most people caught a scent of perfume. She was lovable, if a little much at times.

Lauryn laughed, catching the eye of Esme Martin, the fourth member of their party and a long-time friend of Deonna's. Esme returned a knowing smile, her beauty striking and effortless. Gold dotted the curve of her ears–studs and small hoops that caught the light as she turned. Esme had the ease of a woman who knew herself, a quality amplified by her recent marriage. She enjoyed being the fly on the wall, chiming in only when she had something sharp or witty to add, her calm presence grounding the group. She was a perfect balance to the lively energy of the others, and Lauryn was always glad when Esme attended. Her steadiness was a vibe all its own.

Lauryn was becoming very fond of these monthly brunches and the small friend group that was forming. There was a ritual brewing through all their outings and when Lauryn had casually mentioned dreading her own birthday, Deonna had sprung into action, making reservations at not one, but two of the most beautiful restaurants in the city. Lauryn glanced around the table, feeling a warmth that had little to do with the spring sun and everything to do with the company she found herself in.

Deonna gave up looking for the server, "So, I rewatched the last season of Insecure to get ready for this spring and summer. I plan to be in these streets, I plan to be flirting, I plan to slay and ya'll will be getting these looks."

"I second that motion! I steamed my entire summer wardrobe during that blizzard a couple weeks ago," Brittney was taking a selfie.

"Deonna, when is your trip anyway?" Lauryn asked when their server finally appeared with Deonna's drink and their appetizers.

"In a fortnight." Deonna leaned in to grab her drink. "Ladies, can we talk about these swimsuits that I found? I'm gonna fuck this man's whole life up."

"Well, damn." Lauryn shook her head, taking a sip of her own drink. She thought back on her trips with Joe. The excitement and flirtation around planning the trip, squeezing in a few date nights or excursions in between Joe's studio time and appearances. The two other members of his band usually came too, with their wives, girlfriends and other acquaintances. Beautiful beach homes with too little privacy, stunning sunsets, and Joe so inebriated she could barely stand him. She sighed quietly, remembering.

"So, what about you, birthday girl? Do you have any steamy birthday trips planned?" Brittney asked, turning to her.

Lauryn laughed as the memory of Joe faded, "A few steamy shopping trips, yes."

Although both Deonna and Esme raised their glasses and nodded in agreement, Brittney narrowed her eyes at Lauryn, "You know what I mean."

Suddenly it felt like all three women leaned in to hear her response. Until now, Lauryn hadn't had to share. Skillfully, she'd sat back and allowed the other ladies to spill all of their tea, without divulging any of hers. In all these months, Deonna hadn't pressed, but sitting in mixed company now, she too seemed eager to hear Lauryn's response.

"What? I'm not seeing anyone, and I don't feel like going to some romantic resort right now. I'm keeping the romance noise to a minimum." That much was true, but she saw their expressions. If she appeared to be open to the idea of dating, they might start asking her about the past. And *that*, Lauryn definitely did not want to discuss. "Although, it would be nice to just flirt with someone sometime."

"Mm! I remember flirting," Esme beamed at her cheekily and she raised her glass. Her wedding rings shone brightly from across the table.

Lauryn continued, pleased she'd thrown them off the scent of her actual life. "I have been seeing this app called Crown Match-"

"No!"

"Girl, do not download that shit."

"Sweetie, what!" All three women sounded off at once.

Lauryn instantly started laughing, "I sense strong feelings here."

"L, don't even waste your time with that," Brittney touched her hand to the table near Lauryn's, clearly prepared to save her from a terrible mistake.

"Well, I haven't yet," Lauryn countered, laughing. "I just keep seeing the ads on Youtube and the 'gram and it looked a little more sophisticated than other apps I've seen. No good, huh?"

"Girl, trash! The men on these apps are all married or still living with their exes."

"Or their mommas," Deonna added without looking up from the menu she was reviewing for the third time.

"And that's not what we're doing in 2023." They all laughed and raised a glass to Brittney's statement. "Plus, you need someone awesome for when that hammer comes down. I know you're in relationship detox mode, but girl when you need some, you need some. And you want it to be quality."

Lauryn shook her head. Truthfully, she hadn't given the app a second thought, but Brittney had a point. The next man she decided to talk to would have to be some kind of wonderful.

Shrugging, she said, "I don't know, by the time I get ready to meet somebody, they won't be interested. I think about all the years I was in a relationship and all the men that were playing in my face."

"Exactly. No respect!" Esme sat up in her seat, this particular point clearly hitting a nerve. "It's like they can smell when you're unavailable."

Deonna quipped again, "Or happy."

"Right. Asking me out when my guy is literally standing right next to me. Now, I'm single and wouldn't mind some *single-person* attention and I can't tell you the last time a man approached me."

Deonna shook her head sharply, sending her perfect bob flowing back and forth around her face. "OK, that's not true at all. You're just oblivious, girl."

"What do you mean?" Lauryn was really curious. What had she missed?

"Lauryn, every time we go out you turn heads." She clapped her hands together with every word, before crossing her legs and leaning back in her chair. "I've even seen a few women looking at you like they want to risk it all."

Lauryn laughed hard, "I don't know what you're talking about. I promise it is not like that."

"Certainly, seemed that way at Nathan's holiday party! I saw the hugs you were getting. These men were excited to see you." Esme sipped her drink, smirking playfully. "I don't know who that chocolate man was that was chatting you up, but he was nineties-fine! *That* is the type of guy you need to be detoxing with."

Lauryn tempered her reaction. She knew Esme was talking about Perry, but was not about to confirm anything. She chanced a look over at Deonna who also had a poker face. She watched as her friend set her menu down and asked the table, "Wait–are we ordering or are we going to that other spot?"

Brittney was only distracted for a moment. "Let's order, we've already parked and I want to hear more about this chocolate man."

"I don't even remember who you're talking about! I saw so many old friends that night." Lauryn picked up her own menu pretending to be engrossed as she responded. After so many years dealing with Joe's delicate ego, she was a master of tiptoeing around a conversation. "But chocolate does sound good. I'm looking at these beignets with the chocolate bourbon sauce..."

That did it. Brittney snatched up her own menu and frowned, exclaiming, "Where are those? I didn't see them." Lauryn and Deonna exchanged a quick glance, enough for Lauryn to show her appreciation for trying to change the subject. She wasn't sure how much Deonna knew about Perry. She'd casually mentioned that he'd taken her out back in January, but had not elaborated. She appreciated how intuitively

Deonna recognized she needed a lifeline. Even when she did not know the full story herself. What a novelty, to have a new friend who not only respected her privacy, defended it too.

The girls were less inquisitive for the rest of brunch and Lauryn took every opportunity to keep the conversation flowing in another direction. Asking Brittney questions about the wedding planning was easy enough, and soon the chatter drifted to bridesmaids dresses, signature cocktails, and whether a live band could really pull off Lucky Daye.

Lauryn let Brittney's excitement wash over her, grateful that the hunt for menus and venues kept the spotlight far from her own tangled love life. When their plates were cleared and the check was settled the sun was still burning high in the sky. The ladies rose from the table as one, closing up purses and trading long hugs.

"Brunch at the Duplex next month, same time," Brittney announced, wagging a manicured finger. "Bring updates! Preferably messy ones."

"We'll see what the season delivers," Deonna laughed, and they scattered toward awaiting Ubers and side-street parking spots. "Bye, ladies!"

Halfway to her car, Lauryn's phone buzzed:

> Hope you're enjoying your birthday. Plans tomorrow?

A slow smile captured her face and she typed back.

> I am thank you :). No plans except dinner with my folks.

She bit back another smile, watching the three dots as she eased into her car. So, he remembered her birthday. Thinking back to the last time he'd taken her out on the town, she wondered what he had in mind.

> Mind if I treat you to brunch? I know a great place. Plus, it's supposed to be warm again tomorrow. Perfect sundress weather.

Lauryn raised an eyebrow at that. Sundress weather, huh? She considered the blatantly flirtatious text. She had no intention of wearing one, but that didn't stop her from cataloging the sundresses in her closet at his suggestion. She imagined a gauzy one with straps that never stayed put, and Perry's gaze, rolling over her shoulders. Down the center of her bare back. His huge hands caressing her through the thin fabric.

Lauryn slapped at the console, turning the air to its highest setting, as a rush of heat rippled up through her chest. "What the hell...?" she chided herself quietly.

It must be the heat. Or the cocktails? She rolled her eyes, remembering Esme's insinuations. Absolutely, no good would come from fantasizing if she was going to meet Perry tomorrow. She typed back:

> Lunch sounds great. I'll let you surprise me with the place.

> I plan to.

Her grin returned. Perry didn't even have to try, and somehow he still managed to disarm her. Though she was enjoying their growing flirtation, the idea worried her. Lately, things between them had started to feel like grad school days again. Playful jokes, helping to keep each other motivated. She'd almost ruined their friendship once and she was not eager to risk that again.

Lauryn made her way north on Lake Shore Drive, the lake shimmering in the distance. She had dinner plans with her parents, but fortunately she had a couple hours to build her appetite back up. She settled in the driver's seat, feeling grateful for the day's events. She hadn't known how she'd feel—another year older, starting over again, but brunch with the girls had lifted her spirits. However, her mind kept drifting, picturing everything about Perry that she'd tried to forget. The night at the hotel all those years ago. Then dancing with him all damn night just a few weeks ago.

Pressing down on the gas pedal, she told herself not to read into it, not to make it more of a thing than it actually was. And yet, the little flip in her stomach at the thought of seeing him again told a very different story.

Chapter 14

Lauryn

The next morning was just as beautiful, with a bright cloudless sky. A cooler breeze was starting to whip its way through the half-bloomed trees, a reminder that true summer was still a ways off. The same breeze ruffled Lauryn's hair as she made her way down Cottage Grove Avenue. Bronzeville Winery, the spot Perry chose, gleamed in the sunset up ahead, its flower boxes spilling over with red and white petunias that seemed to reach for her as she passed by, headed for the door.

Inside, the restaurant was alive, already humming with an early morning crowd and busy staff. The scent of something savory and sweet wafted from the kitchen and her empty stomach responded. She made a point to arrive early and give herself a chance to observe Perry's entrance for once. So far he always seemed to appear out of nowhere, as if he'd been waiting for the perfect moment to catch her off guard.

She was grateful when the host seated her at a table with a perfect view of the door, windows and the street beyond. Sliding into the banquette, she fidgeted, smoothing her pants and twisting her bangles until they sat just right. Despite Perry's text message, she had not worn a sundress. Instead, she aired on the safe side, opting for a loose pleated button front and matching pants. She'd pulled a blazer over her shoulders just in case the weather turned cool then made it more interesting with layers of gold jewelry.

Standing in her closet that morning, she resisted the stream of thoughts and memories that had stirred the day before. In this outfit, she was practically covered head to toe. Not an inch of exposed skin to imagine Perry looking at or doing anything with. She recalled her daydreaming, the idea of Perry's hands on her, and though she still couldn't say where they'd come from, it still pulled at her. With a quick breath, she snatched up the menu, determined to distract herself before they took hold again.

The brioche French toast sounded amazing, then again so did the shrimp and grits. She deliberated, considering which one would satiate her more, knowing full well she would go with the sweet option.

She angled her menu up to study the other options, stealing another glance toward the door just as Perry walked in. And–*Oh my goodness.*

Perry stood in the doorframe, holding the door open for an older couple that was leaving. In the morning light, his dark hair and full beard gleamed with hints of copper, and a breeze caught his jacket as he stepped through.

She watched as he pulled his phone out and started scrolling, undoubtedly getting ready to text her to let her know he arrived.

She was no more than ten feet away, so close that she heard the *swoosh* sound of him sending the text. And when her phone pinged half a second later, his head snapped up. He clocked her immediately, his mouth curving into that slow, familiar smile, and she felt the years collapse in on themselves.

It hit her, just then, the way he used to find her in the library back in their undergrad days, sliding a coffee or snack across the table before dropping into the seat across from her.

He was wearing that same easy grin as he wove his way across the restaurant and suddenly it felt like no time had passed. His buttery yellow denim fit looked so good against his complexion, she was ready to post a memo. All dark skin men should wear this color. It was good for the community.

She tried not to visibly shift in her seat, noting the long strides as he moved down the line of tables towards her, his walk and manner catching the attention of quite a few women in the room.

When he reached the table, he leaned in, dropping his voice just for her.

"You know," he started. "You look *exactly* the way you used to when we studied at Club U-G-L."

He used the nickname for the undergraduate library on campus where, ironically, hardly any studying could be done.

Lauryn's lips parted in surprise, a laugh slipping out before she could help herself. "I was literally just thinking the same thing as you came in," she admitted, shaking her head, feeling lighter already. He laughed, that quiet, rich sound she realized she was really starting to like.

"Some things don't change," he said, easing into the seat across from her. "Except maybe the coffee. That mess we used to get out of those vending machines..."

Lauryn crossed her legs beneath the table, "Hey, those vending machine cappuccinos had their charm."

Perry grinned and added, "Only when paired with a Honey Bun."

"Microwaved!" She laughed, feeling less tense now that she was just trading memories with her old friend, even if he was the most attractive man in the room.

His smile remained. "Glad you made it, Lo. Happy Birthday."

"Thank you," she beamed at him as he leaned back, getting comfortable. He caught sight of her blazer draped over the chair beside him. Carefully, he adjusted it so it wouldn't slip to the floor.

"Oh, this is very nice," he said, teasing lightly, smoothing the fabric back into place. "Nice spring ensemble you've got going here."

Lauryn laughed under her breath, watching him. "What color would you say this is?" he asked, glancing at her, eyebrows lifted.

"Um..." she inspected her own blazer before turning back to him. "Stone, I think it's called?" Perry deadpanned, staring at her like she'd just spoken a foreign language and then cracked up quietly, shaking his head.

"You're gonna have to help me out," he said, still grinning. "I only had the basic colors in my crayon box growing up."

"Shut. Up." Lauryn laughed, enunciating playfully.

"So, what's going on Miss. Lindsey, how was the birthday? How's life?"

"Really nice. Deonna chose a great place. My folks chose a great cake... No complaints."

He leaned in, "So how's thirty-six feel?

"You'll find out soon enough," she eyed him playfully. "But no, things are good. Getting used to the gig."

"Ah yes, sounds like you're liking director life! You'll be running circles around everyone soon."

She waved off the compliment. "It does seem like a good fit. Challenging. I'm learning a lot and actually interested in what we're working on. We'll see how long that lasts."

"Yeah I know what you mean, my travel schedule is picking up a bit more now that companies are returning back to the office. I fly out again this week. But no matter, we're still going to celebrate."

Realizing, Lauryn shook her head. "Oh no."

"Oh yes," he confirmed, craning his neck to get one of the staff's attention. An extremely tall man walking towards the bar did an about face and made his way over to their table. Perry asked, "My man. How you doing today?"

"I'm very well sir, how are you both this afternoon?"

"Fantastic actually. Can we get a flight going here?" Perry held his hand a couple feet above the table, as if suggesting the height of something. Lauryn's brow furrowed, curious.

"Of course, the wine flights are an excellent way to experience our collection. And which flight were you interested in? We have the *Sweet Flight,* the *Women in Wine* flight or you may enjoy the *Black on Black Flight.*"

"Oh, that *Black on Black* might have to happen one day, but let's go with the *Women in Wine flight.* We're celebrating a birthday and a new job here." He nodded in Lauryn's direction.

Lauryn resisted the urge to squirm while he made a spectacle of her. The tall man's expression lit up as he turned fully to face Lauryn and congratulated her warmly. "I'm Mason, the manager here. I'm going to have the bar get started on your flight. If there is anything we can do to make your celebration more special, just ask for me."

They both thanked him as he turned on a dime, heading back to the bar as smoothly as he'd appeared. Lauryn leaned over the table to whisper-shout at Perry, "This was supposed to be brunch! I came prepared. That being, on an empty stomach!"

"Ah, you'll be fine," he waved her off playfully.

When another staff member appeared, Lauryn blinked, her eyes widening as a tower of crystal wine glasses was placed in the center of the table. Four, very full looking, glasses of wine dangled from the tower, glinting in the sunlight, and she hadn't even had a piece of toast yet.

She felt a warm touch on her hands that rested on the table. "Hey," Perry had lightly laid his hand over hers, "better this than tequila right?"

She smiled, but cut her eyes at him as she did. Her last taste of tequila had been in Cabo, more than a year before–a completely impromptu trip she'd taken alone when things at work got overwhelming. She'd spent the first night sipping mezcal on her little private terrace, letting the sound of the waves drown out everything.

The next morning, hungover but deeply content, Lauryn had cracked open the wooden passthrough in her suite and found a tray waiting with warm pastries, fresh papaya, and a tiny carafe of espresso. She'd carried it to the balcony and sat cross-legged in the sun, chewing contentedly as the tide rolled in and out. Joe had shown up unannounced the next day, torpedoed her solo trip by booking a larger suite at the same resort and insisting they needed the quality time.

Lauryn hated that every memory from the last ten years somehow involved Joe. Had she really had so little life without him? Intently, she reached across the table for the glass of rosé, suspended from the highest tier of the tower.

Taking her queue, Perry reached for the South African red blend. His smile widened and he raised his glass to her. "To *Growth*."

Seeing that smile and his dimples sent another ripple of heat over Lauryn's shoulders, down her chest, all the way to the tips of breasts. She exhaled, masking it with a laugh. That smirk did something to her. It was easy and self-assured, the kind of look that made her body tense without permission.

Lauryn shifted again, trying to play it cool as she lifted her own glass. "To *Better Choices*."

They clinked glasses, and she held his gaze as she took a sip.

While they sampled the rest of their wine, they traded stories about their favorite trips: Mexico City, Port of Spain, Bridgetown. Twice, they'd nearly overlapped. Same cities, same weeks, just missing each other by a day or two. Lauryn couldn't help but sit with that for a moment. The thought that they might've passed each other on some cobblestone side street, skin deepening brown in the sun, brushing shoulders at Carnival, oblivious to one another at an airport gate. It pulled at something in her.

Then again, timing had never been on their side.

She didn't dare imagine what might have happened if they had ever run into each other.

Their server returned to take their order, fully supportive of Lauryn's choice of French toast. When she left them again, a quiet energy settled between Lauryn and Perry, as if they were both waiting for something unspoken to surface.

She lifted her gaze to see Perry–leaned back in his seat, eyes scanning the restaurant like he had all the time in the world–and wondered if the universe had been nudging them toward each other all along. Just a little off tempo.

They'd been orbiting the same places for years, first college then grad school, then random travels and now, only now, choosing to see each other again.

The arrival of their food was a welcome distraction–plated like art, each dish almost too pretty to touch. But the wine had loosened them, and within moments they were leaning in, forks cutting through the beauty without hesitation. For a few minutes, conversation thinned to quiet murmurs and the occasional, "How's yours?"

Perry dabbed his beard with his napkin, "So... what made you come home?"

Lauryn blinked. She had known it might come up, and was surprised that it hadn't already. But hearing the question aloud, she could tell he'd been wondering.

She didn't answer right away. Instead, just stared out at the street and the sunlight bouncing off the hood of a passing car. As she watched a woman pushing a stroller while sipping an iced matcha, she puzzled over how to explain.

"I didn't even know what I wanted anymore," she spoke finally. "It's like I woke up one day and realized my life wasn't something *I* built. I'd just been moving through it, accommodating, adjusting, following *Joe's* path without ever stopping to ask myself where mine was going."

She paused, fingertips tracing the edge of her water glass. "I thought I had a plan after school, but that just went away. After a while I didn't recognize myself. I was ashamed that I kept staying. That I stayed for so long," Lauryn swallowed, shocked at herself for revealing so much. Even so, it felt good to speak it aloud instead of parsing it out in her mind.

Perry nodded, but didn't interrupt.

Lauryn clasped her hands together as she continued, "Once I made up my mind about leaving, it was actually easy. I didn't say goodbye to many people, I just got on the plane. Because it meant I didn't have to explain anything. Didn't have to see everyone who knew that bland-ass version of me. I could just disappear for a while and try to put myself back together without the commentary, you know."

She laughed it off, even though the same line of thought had her crying in the tub not a month before.

"You know you don't owe anyone an explanation right?"

Lauryn nodded quickly, although she appreciated him saying it. "I'm just hoping for clarity now," she said. "Just space and peace," she exhaled the last word out and threw her head back. "I want to get back to myself and feel that I'm not just surviving my own life. That I'm choosing. Every part of it."

Perry's gaze softened. "That sounds reasonable. How long were y'all together, in the end?"

Lauryn hesitated for a moment, feeling like he already knew the answer. Did he already know the whole reason why she'd moved to California? She'd never exactly told Perry about Joe. She'd just left him wondering. "Twelve years," she confessed finally, watching him run the math in his head.

Perry leaned his head back, then zoomed forward again in mock amazement. "Shit! That's a long time."

Lauryn smiled. So, he'd decided to take the high road. Perhaps after everything, he had forgiven her.

"Good thing I didn't plan on keeping you here all afternoon crying into your plate."

Lauryn's laugh burst out before she could stop it, light and unguarded, and she felt the knot in her chest ease just a little. "Yes! Can we *please* change the subject?"

"Of course. You ready for the next spot?" He made eye contact with the server.

Lauryn side eyed him as their check appeared, "You haven't told me where we're going."

"You'll see, you'll see" he said smoothly, as he pulled his wallet out to pay. "But I will say this, it involves an uber and possibly a bit more reckless nostalgia."

"Because we need more of that?"

"You'll love it," he promised. "Trust me."

She appreciated him. The way he hadn't pushed her to keep unraveling the mess of her time away from Chicago, the thoughtful way he shifted the mood, and the hint of mischief in his eyes as he described their next destination. "I do," she said softly, surprising herself.

Perry held her gaze then, "Well then," he said, signing the receipt when the server brought his card back. "Let's disappear for a while."

Just as he said it, the past loosened its grip on her. Lauryn stood, following him into the bright, open air of the afternoon, wondering what the night would bring.

Chapter 15

Lauryn

Lauryn marveled at the city blocks passing by as their uber whipped them uptown. She'd never lived in this part of town, but it still felt special. She could almost see her twenty-something self-running these same streets to find some blues spot or to attend someone's party.

It felt like they hadn't hit a single light since leaving the winery and the breeze was helping to wake her up after a generous plate of brioche French toast she'd barely been able to finish. *At least it soaked up the wine*, she thought to herself and glanced over at Perry.

Perhaps the wine had calmed her nerves about him and she observed her friend without fantasizing.

He too was engrossed in the cityscape whizzing by. He appeared to be just as relaxed as she, despite scrunching his tail frame into the miniscule Hyundai they were riding in. His long legs and knees stood high above hers and she caught a better glimpse at his sneakers. Immaculate as usual. She resisted the urge to tease him, to inquire about this new found fashion sense.

Does this man have a stylist? And almost as soon as she thought it, Lauryn mentally checked herself. Quite some time had passed since she'd shared a back seat with this man. Years, in fact. There was likely nothing "new" about him, it was just new to her. In fact, everything about Perry felt cultivated and intentional. There was a certain way about him, and it was effortless. Genuine as he had always been.

When their uber driver asked to drop them off a block away they agreed. The afternoon air was warm and they walked side by side, passing ramen shops and Irish pubs as they went.

"The last time I was here, they demanded to see vaccination cards," Perry started. "Got all the way out here, right? It was freezing rain, and then I remembered the damn card was on my dresser."

"Oh no, did they let you in?"

"They did not," he confirmed, pausing for effect before holding out a hand. "Fortunately, I'd taken a picture right, and creepy-ass Google photos was able to bring that shit up when I typed 'vaccination' in the search. Brought it right up."

Lauryn giggled "Creepy, yes, but it's just so damn convenient–"

"Convenient!" he echoed at the same time.

He grinned, slowing to a stop in the middle of the sidewalk. The rush of traffic and laughter from nearby restaurants as he stepped around her to open a very ordinary-looking door, the kind you might miss if you weren't paying attention.

Apparently, they'd arrived. Lauryn eyed the building, but the facade was so narrow she'd have to step off the curb to get a real look. Perry simply held the door, that small, knowing smile on his face.

Inside, the brightness hit first–fluorescent white walls, two over-sized globe lights casting a clean, almost clinical glow. Black-and-white chevron tile stretched under their feet, toward a small back room.

It took a few more steps for her to realize they were in a record store. Built-in bins hugged the walls, and a massive counter dominated the far end. Empty. Not a single person in sight.

She pivoted on one heel, her brow lifted. "Are we buying records? *Are they even selling records?* Because no one's here." With a flick of her wrist, she spun her purse in a lazy circle.

"Not tonight." Perry gave her an easy smile and nodded in the direction behind her.

Lauryn turned to find an open doorway behind her, with a white backlit sign above that read "Listening Booth". She frowned again.

"A listening booth, huh?" She wasn't entirely disappointed at the idea of being squeezed into a soundproof booth with Perry. Pushing the thought aside, she stepped through the doorway into an all-white room where colorful record covers hung like paintings. A slim white desk held a translucent record player with a single pair of headphones beside it. One vinyl chair sat in the corner, leaving barely any space to move.

"Where are we going? I feel like we're in a sophisticated funhouse. This is giving me anxiety," she laughed.

"I'm going to need you to take some deep breaths. Relax, relate, release, Whitley Gilbert." No sooner had he said this, a hidden pocket door suddenly slid open.

Lauryn watched, as the shape of an afro emerged, followed by a smiling face attached to a long lean body in a full Puma outfit "Hey, welcome to Dorians."

"Oh!" Lauryn's eyes need a moment to adjust from the bright white room. Behind the doorwoman, a deep room cloaked in inky blue and purple darkness. And for the first time Lauryn could hear music. Excitedly, she stepped down into the speakeasy with a long bar and enormous booths and tables. She smiled, recognizing the cool keyboard and brassy trumpet of a classic Fela Kuti song.

They wandered deeper into the lounge, where the low lighting cast long shadows over a row of empty booths. Early evening left most of the tables empty, and Perry claimed the center booth for them, pulling off his jacket and folding it beside him.

Lauryn slid into the booth, her eyes drifting over the space. A massive wall of records stretched from corner to corner, extending high up toward the ceiling. She tried to guess how many there were, thousands probably, slotted together in an endless archive. She was still taking it in when Perry leaned down close to her ear. "What are we drinking?"

His voice was smooth and molten, as if it could slip into every corner of her being. She tried not to visibly grip her purse. Exhaling, she took her time considering their options. "Well, we started the afternoon with wine. But I'm good on that."

"Smokey? Sweet?"

What exactly were they talking about now? Still drinks? "Um, smoke. Do they have mezcal?"

"They should," he was nodding to the beat of the song now that the saxophone solo had started. "I'll be back."

She watched him venture off, down the short flight of stairs towards the bar. She pulled her hair to one side of her neck, feeling a warm rush. He'd chosen the perfect spot, the right atmosphere, and just dark enough to conceal the effect Perry was having on her.

Steadying herself, she mentally examined the moment. Since they'd left the winery there'd been a hum moving through her limbs. Likely the wine, but she knew better. It was the catch up. There was something in their exchange that called for caution.

She stole a glance at Perry, seeing him move with an ease that almost mocked her memory of him. The guy who once lingered on the sidelines had become a grown ass man who owned every inch of space he entered. He wasn't just the friend she remembered, not anymore. Not with the way his shirt caught against the breadth of his shoulders, not with the warmth in his voice when he asked about things she hadn't thought anyone remembered. With every laugh and memory, he was slipping past the guard she'd been working so hard to build up these last few months.

It felt natural to sit across from him and be seen.

Mental examination done, she let the music seep in and soon she was dancing in her seat.

A moment later, Perry returned, setting an impressive looking cocktail down in front of her. "Let me know if you like it."

Lauryn mouthed a 'thank you' as the music grew louder. With her thumb and middle finger, she twisted the frozen stem of the glass to get a better look. She took a sip and the smoke flavor unfurled in her mouth, starting behind her teeth and working its way back.

She eyed Perry and pursed her lips–impressed with his selection for her. "Well done."

His smile was all teeth then and he clapped his hands together. "Yes, I thought you'd like it. It's a Mezcal Manhattan."

Whatever kind of Manhattan it was, it was certainly strong. Lauryn made a mental note to *nurse* it.

The two of them sat like that for a while, sipping and enjoying the music. It wasn't too long before more people began to arrive. A couple here, a group there, easing in slowly from that blinding white room into this insulated den. She recognized at once why Perry had chosen this booth–they could see everything from this spot. She looked over at her friend. Perry was lounging, an arm stretched along the back of the booth, one hand on his drink. Something neat, like the one he'd had when they saw each other last. She realized with a start that he'd spent the entire afternoon asking about her. Panicking slightly, she said a silent prayer that she hadn't already overshared, and wouldn't before the night was over.

"Mr. Mitchell?" she called over the Ghanaian jazz that was playing now.

"Yes, Ma'am." He looked straight at her and she felt the sudden urge to sit up straight.

"Tell me more about what you do."

"You mean my job?"

"Yes."

"I'm a consultant."

"I know that," She rolled her eyes playfully. "What do you consult on?"

"Ah-mostly strategy. I work with a team, we go in, conduct market analysis, help create market entry plans, growth strategies, and branding. We walk our clients through risk and change management..."

Lauryn nodded, thinking of Roman. In her past few roles, she'd worked with many consultants over the years. "The dream team."

"Exactly."

"Do you like it?"

He thought for a moment and finally nodded. "Yes. I actually do."

Somehow she could hear him over the music now, the curved leather booth insulating them from the brunt of the music. "Is your company based in Chicago?"

"San Francisco. We have a few offices, one in London actually, but we function like different businesses so we don't get out there much- Hey, did you ever get to London? I remember that was part of your plan."

Lauryn traced the rim of her glass, taking a moment to swallow the swell of disappointment she felt in herself. That version of herself–the one that dreamed of one day finding a place at a boutique firm abroad–felt very far away now. Things had turned out very different, and though she was starting to make peace with herself, the question still stung. He seemed to remember everything. "No, I didn't."

If Perry noticed her pause, he didn't address it. "I went a couple years ago. Cool to visit, don't know if I could live there though."

"Oh, so you're not going to get big and leave us like Common, Kanye... Hebru? Become an LA dude," she teased him.

"Says the girl who just landed back in the Midwest," he teased right back. "Naw, I'm staying put. I belong here. I like what I do. Shaping strategy, steering companies through their mess, deciding which challenges are worth my time. There's more I want to build in this space. Not sure how much longer I'll stay with my current company, but there's more I want to do."

Lauryn smiled, proud of him, impressed that he spoke with the kind of conviction she wished she carried herself. Perry had always known where he was headed, even in school. Listening to him now, she noted the contrast–how clear and fulfilled Perry sounded, while she still wrestled with a future that refused to take shape. Work was one thing. Focused ambition was another. She thought of Vivienne, sharp as glass in her pursuit of success. Joe, who had always known he wanted the stage. And her father, who had carved out a decorated Army career, using it as a vehicle to get where he wanted to be, to see what he wanted to see. They all followed some inner call, some definition of purpose they'd chosen for themselves.

Lauryn knew, she just didn't have that. Not yet anyway.

"How long have you been there?" She sipped her drink again, forgetting all about nursing it.

"Going on seven years. I felt like a fish out of water that first year, but now business is booming, we're traveling all the time, hitting all the major conferences. We were at C2E2 last year."

"Where?"

"C2E2. The Comic Expo!"

"You got paid to go to Comic-con?"

"No. I got paid to go to C2E2. VIP package." He started dancing again and slid closer to her in the booth, purposely rubbing shoulders with her and continuing to celebrate his all-expenses paid chance to nerd out.

"You always were a nerd."

"I recall you started to get into comics too."

"Some of the graphic novels you shared were amazing," she acknowledged, swirling her drink. "I had no idea."

"I have never steered you wrong." He stated, noticeably leaning into that 'never'.

Lauryn had to admit it was true. Another wave of nostalgia hit as she thought back to their first class together—a grueling econometrics course junior year. They became regular study partners, and through the demanding coursework, went from two Black students who only knew of each other to true friends.

And in grad school, when she'd been commuting back and forth from her folk's place, he'd given her a ride more times than she could count. Dropping her off at the Metra station just in time to catch a late train home.

She smiled to herself, "Do you remember that semester we had Dr. Phillips?"

"What! Are you kidding, it's still too fucking soon to talk about *that* class."

Lauryn giggled, her eyes brimming with tears. The feeling was mutual. Dr. Phillips did not play and although neither of them had a life that semester, they'd both gotten A's in that class. Twenty years later, they'd escaped to this secret spot, surrounded by records instead of books.

They kept reminiscing, cracking up laughing about more of their school years, each of them calling up a memory that would top the last one.

"Damn, I did not know they hooked up!" Lauryn whisper-shouted in awe as Perry spilled the tea on two mutual friends that everyone believed couldn't stand each other.

"I'm telling you, they were carrying on like I wasn't even there." Perry took a sip of his drink for effect.

"I had no idea you were such a gossip, P! My goodness, men chit chat worse than women!" she playfully poked his arm as she teased him.

"My goodness," he repeated her words, turning his whole body toward her. Somewhere in the last few minutes, his eye contact had begun to linger and now their shoulders were touching.

She didn't remember when they'd gotten so close to each other in the enormous booth. She could smell his cologne, woodsy and clean. They were definitely closer than they had been. Perhaps he was feeling it too–either the liquor or the charged air between them.

"How are you feelin'?" he asked.

His question was timely and Lauryn sat up a little straighter, resting her elbows on the table before answering. She turned to look at him over her shoulder. "I feel good," she confessed, holding his gaze again, letting her eyes reveal all that she'd been thinking today.

He smiled and turned away in response, his jaw working like he was deciding what to say next.

Interesting, Lauryn noted.

The way he looked at her now, like she had gotten under his skin. Like he'd just remembered who he was dealing with, and Lauryn was remembering too. She let the moment stretch, savoring it until he leaned in again.

"Ready for another?" His voice was rougher now, and so low she felt it before she heard him.

"I got this round." Lauryn slipped from the booth, putting some distance between them. After a few steps she turned back to him, "Same thing?"

She saw him lean back, arms stretching along the back of the booth. His t-shirt pulled, hinting at the muscular shape beneath. His chain winked at her in the darkness and the weight of his gaze held her in place. "Surprise me."

Chapter 16

Perry

"Why is it that every time we hang out, we go to multiple places? Help me understand why you can't end an evening at a decent hour." Lauryn was tiptoeing around the edge of the indoor pool on her building's seventh level, light bouncing from the water's surface onto her bare feet.

Perry stood at a safe distance, shoes still on and hands in his pockets. He laughed in response. "You said you needed to be reacquainted with your city. I'd say you are successfully reacquainted."

"Yes, but *I'm going to be weak in the morning*," Lauryn said in a sing-song voice. Perry watched her, pulling her flowy pants up so they wouldn't get wet. Without realizing it, he'd been admiring her painted toes, the jewel red polish a sharp contrast to the endless shades of white he'd seen on his last vacation.

He watched as she found a dry place along the edge of the pool and pulled her pants up even higher. She slipped each leg into the water slowly, carefully like one presses a knife into a cake to see if ready. The water barely rippled as she did this and he remembered she'd always been graceful.

It was one of the first things he'd noticed about her, the delicate, but intentional way she reached for things or set them down on a table. And that walk, her walk was like nothing else he'd ever seen on any woman anywhere. He thought back to a few hours earlier when she'd left to buy them a second round of drinks. He'd barely been able to take his eyes off of her as she moved down the stairs and across the lounge. And the way she'd looked at him, over her shoulder when he'd asked her how she was feeling. "I feel good," she'd said with those dark almond eyes on him, her mane of coils shrouding her face.

The same way she was looking at him now, "Getting in?"

He ventured a little closer to her, but shook his head. He was enjoying watching her play and remembering her splashing through the tide one weekend at Montrose Beach. Somehow, even in the silky matching pants set she wore, she seemed just as at ease as she had in shorts and bikini. Even now, she'd piled her hair on top of her head in an expert bun.

He didn't know the man, but he didn't have to. The carelessness said enough. Only a man who didn't know what he had could lose her like that.

Perry mulled it over, trying to square it in his mind. He couldn't. Lauryn had that rare mix of beauty, grace, and a mind that made you want to step up your game. He decided it was better not to try to figure out someone else's relationship, especially not theirs. Things were always more complicated than they looked. Not to mention, Lauryn had disappeared on him. He too knew what it felt like to have her walk out of his life.

She was out of the pool now, padding back towards him with her shoes and purse and their left-overs in one hand, her pant legs bunched up in the other. "You know this is my first time down here?"

"Oh yeah?"

"Well, second time if you count the virtual walk through they gave me when I first rented the place."

"You never saw it in person before you rented it?"

"Nope."

"Yeah, you meant business. You happy with your place?"

"I am. I used to drive past this building all the time and wondered what it was like to live inside. Kinda full circle if I think about it." She was beaming up at him and he thought, for the first time, the shadows in her expression were finally clearing. She wasn't thinking about her old life, she was excited about the new. He was pleased for her and grateful that he might have had something to do with her new outlook. The day had gone better than he expected. He hadn't thought they'd be out quite so late either, but the evening had slipped by so quickly. They'd finally gotten to do the real catch up and after more than a decade, there was plenty to talk about. "I'm hungry again. I'm about to bang the rest of those fries. Want me to warm your food up?"

"Naw, actually I'm about to head out. I just wanted to see this pool and make sure you're good."

"Make sure I'm good?"

"Had to make sure you found your sea legs. Those mezcal Manhattans are nothing to play with."

"Are you insinuating I cannot hold my liquor?" she waved a finger at him, her lace-up heels dangling from the same hand.

"Nothing wrong with being a lightweight." He held his arms up in mock defense. She slid her shoes back on and waved him over as she made her way toward the pool entrance. He caught up to her at the elevator, and offered her an arm to steady herself as she laced her shoes back up.

Something about standing in front of an elevator with her again was unsettling, like time had folded back on itself and took them back to where everything had started. When the elevator doors open, he hung back to let her enter first, then took his place opposite her and leaned back against the railing. The doors closed.

"You didn't have to come all the way up, I know its late," Lauryn said as the elevator hummed past the third floor. She started digging around in her purse, turning it back and forth and peering inside like she was trying to find her keys.

"It is late. That's why I'm walking you up," he said, crossing his arms. "Here you are digging in this itty-bitty purse, so small it don't make any sense, and you still can't find your keys? All I need is for somebody to kidnap you because your hand was stuck in your damn bag and you weren't paying attention."

Lauryn stared at him, mouth agape, but burst out laughing. "First off, don't come for my bag! I have everything I need in this bag."

Perry said nothing, just smirked at her because she was still struggling to pull her keys out of the unreasonably small opening.

The key ring was hooked on something. She caught him watching and laughing at her. "Hold this." She cut her eyes at him playfully, her nostrils flaring as she handed him the greasy paper bag of left over polish sausages and fries. He could tell she was trying not to laugh. By the time she retrieved her keys, they'd reached her floor and the elevator doors were opening.

"After you-" he waved his hand out toward the hallway.

"Hush!" She said, laughing. "Talking shit about my bag."

"The bag is nice!" he said, defensively. "It's a look, Lo. You nailed the look." And she certainly had. Even now, he watched the way the silken fabric of her outfit floated over her curves. She was completely covered from her neck to her ankles and somehow still enticing as hell.

They reached her door and she turned to face him. "Thanks," she said softly, snatching the greasy paper bag back. "I'm keeping your fries."

He nodded. "You get one petty pass."

"Petty?" she exclaimed, laughing "Boy, get away from my door. As you can see, I am safe, you may go." She unlocked the door, stepped inside and pretended to close the door in his face. They were both laughing by then, and she stepped back into the hall, stepping right up to him so that she had to turn her face up to look at him. "You're terrible."

He smiled down into her pretty face. "Thanks for coming out. Happy Birthday."

"Thanks for a wonderful day. Seriously, I had such a good time."

It seemed like the evening had flown by and just as she was softening into the girl he remembered, it was time to say goodnight. "I'm glad. See you know all the spots now."

"I do!" As they came down from their laughter, the air thickened between them. The scene was too familiar–Lauryn standing in the hotel room doorway and Perry in the hall about to say goodnight.

"You good to drive? I can make coffee–" Lauryn asked, practically echoing her words from eleven years ago.

Perry leaned down to hug her, effectively stopping her mid-sentence. He wasn't presumptuous enough to think that she was inviting him in for any other reason than she wasn't ready for the night to end. Truthfully, he wasn't either. He was enjoying her, the way he always had, and quickly realizing how much he'd missed her since she'd left. Watching her tonight as her eyes lit up at their old jokes and the gossip he had no business sharing had stirred old feelings. Feelings he hadn't tended to in some time.

Her invite was tempting. He could easily spend the next few hours with this woman, reminiscing and laughing, tip-toeing around their history until the sun came up. However, Perry was in no way ready for another sleepover with Lauryn Lindsey. The last time had not turned out the way he'd hoped. Still, he had to admit how good she felt in his arms. Somehow, he pulled away, releasing her from his embrace. "Thank you for the offer. I'm good, though. We'll catch up soon."

After a moment she smiled, nodding as she stepped back across her threshold. "Goodnight, Perry."

"Goodnight." Perry turned to head back to the elevators, still concerned that something between them had shifted in the last few minutes. The day had gone perfectly, without much effort, but now it seemed he was leaving on an odd note.

He took his time returning to his car, retracing their steps back through the lobby and into the parking garage. Part of him was yelling for him to turn around, go straight back up there but his pride wouldn't allow it. As he eased back into his car, he caught a whiff of her perfume. The warm, deep cherry fragrance lingered, mingling with the scent of the leather interior. He sat for a moment, car door open, one foot still on the garage floor as he thought about all she had revealed today.

Everything that Perry knew about Lauryn's relationship was through social platforms and the rumor mill of their friend group. It was weeks after the hotel incident when he learned that Lauryn had not only moved to California, but that she had a whole-ass man she'd never mentioned. A single post told him everything he needed to know. Perry had stopped following her after that. For a while, her page would occasionally pop up as a suggested connection. Then there'd been the little matter of her face on Joe's second album cover. He'd keep right on scrolling, unwilling to have another post catch him off guard again. He'd wanted to move on.

Sitting in the car now, Perry's thoughts shifted to the last summer they'd spent together. Sushi happy-hours, scorching days at the beach, house parties, seeing each other at a wedding every other weekend, and still she'd never mentioned Joe.

After what she'd described today at brunch, it was like the man had done no wrong. Lauryn seemed to be taking accountability for how everything went between them. She'd hardly said one disparaging thing about him, but Perry had heard the weariness and regret in her voice. He'd seen the embarrassed way her eyes flicked away from him as she shared her truth.

As he rolled out of the parking garage, Perry speculated just how badly you'd have to hurt someone to make them leave you after staying for twelve years. He might not be sure he'd forgiven Lauryn yet, but he hated the idea of her being hurt by Joe.

By anyone.

Chapter 17

Lauryn

J ust six hours later, Lauryn's alarm went off. She kept her eyes squeezed shut as she palmed around the bedside table until she found her phone and silenced it.

She exhaled when the quiet rushed back in, sinking into the center of the mattress. Eyes still closed, she tried to coax herself back to sleep, but the damage was already done. Her mind was already calling up images–first of Joe, sleeping soundly on the other side of the bed as he'd done for so many years. Then, just as quickly, melting into an image of Perry, his deep complexion looking infinite in the dark of the lounge last night.

With a sleepy groan, she crossed her arms over her face, as if she could physically block out the images of both men.

It was regrettable, losing all sense last night, inviting Perry in. She wasn't even sure what she'd thought would happen. A slight jab of regret, coupled with embarrassment, almost made her wish their whole day away. But truthfully her abs were still sore from all their laughing and reminiscing. And she'd already added some of the songs they'd heard at the speakeasy to her playlist. Fela Kuti, Miles Davis, A Tribe Called Quest, tracks that would probably always remind her of last night.

She moved slowly getting out of the bed, swinging her legs to the edge of the bed and rolling her neck before pushing off into the bathroom. Her makeup and hair products were scattered across the bathroom vanity. Exhaling, she reached for a rat tail comb, parted her hair and styled it into a reliable flat twist style that made her look more together than she felt.

Was she upset because he'd declined? Or because she'd offered at all? The question turned itself over and over in her mind. She'd felt ridiculous after, leaning against her front door as Perry walked back to the elevator. Her entire body had started to vibrate when they walked back from the pool. His closeness, and his scent pressing on her as he'd scolded her about her tiny purse.

When she thought about it long enough, she could make her skin prickle on cue, almost recreating the effect he'd had on her from memory.

Turning to and fro in the mirror as she slicked her edges, she tried to concentrate on the work week ahead. Every time she tried to focus, blending her foundation or stepping into her heels, her mind slipped right back to Perry. She recalled him in the doorway, awkward and hesitant, his voice low as he said, *"Perhaps another night?"*

None of this – not the embarrassment, or gallivanting all over the city with Perry – was part of her plan. Lauryn longed to travel back in time to those first few days after she'd landed back in Chicago. Before she'd run into Deonna and certainly before she'd locked eyes with Perry across that damned party. She yearned for the anonymity that had once given her space to breathe and heal in private, to focus, instead of stumbling into situations she wasn't ready for. She carried so many regrets already; so why was she setting herself up for another?

Determined to shift her mood, she arrived at the office early to review a presentation her team was putting together. She'd dressed for confidence, rocking a slate blue maxi dress and long matching duster that swept behind her like a cape. The fabric was soft and warm, but snatched her figure perfectly. The perfect armor for what was sure to be a very long day.

> Happy Belated! Working through lunch again?

A ping from her phone caught her attention a few hours later and she was delighted to find a message from Vivienne, her vibrant profile picture standing out against the blurred background. A welcome distraction, she snatched up the phone, typing out a response.

> You know I am. Hoping to get out of here a little early today.

> Believe it or not, it's supposed to snow.

See, that's why I'm in Dallas. I need some consistency in my weather. How was your birthday? Did you get out?

Lauryn pursed her lips, recalling.

Yeah, I made it out.

Any cutiepies?

No one that held my attention.

She grimaced as she typed out the lie. Perry had all of her attention last night and might have gotten a lot more of it had he'd actually stepped across her threshold. "Oh, my goodness, Lauryn. Focus," she chastised herself out loud then remembered her office door was wide open.

Annoyed, she snatched up her phone to type another message to Vivienne.

When are you back in town?

Would love to schedule a consult with you. Discuss working together on my brand idea.

She was desperate to refocus, and her luxury brand idea was exactly where her attention should be.

Lauryn stared at the three galloping dots as Vivienne typed in response. Another image of Perry sipping his drink last night pressed in on her thoughts–the way he'd licked the citrusy liquor from his lips.

Suddenly her phone was ringing, vibrating so violently she nearly dropped it. "Hello?" she answered.

"I figured it was easier for us to talk instead of texting. I'll be home Thursday so yes we can definitely meet. I can make reservations for us unless you prefer to do something virtual? How are you doing, girl? I cannot wait to hear about this brand idea!"

Lauryn laughed at the speed with which Vivienne relayed information, "I'm alright, how's Dallas?"

'Warm," she snorted. "Really though, it's been great. Did you know there are more people from Chicago down here than folks that are actually from Dallas?"

"I've heard that."

"Yeah, it's almost *too* small of a world. I'm pretty sure I gave my number to a nigga I already dated."

Lauryn's eyes closed with the threat of a belly laugh. "Vivienne! I thought you were talking to someone."

"Yeah, whatever, he's not here. We talk when we talk, and right now we're not talking, so I'm checking for other options. There is no ring on my finger."

After comparing schedules, they made arrangements for the same day Vivienne was due into town. "Bring your laptop–oh and dress cute! I'm filming everything these days for content. Plus, the vibe at this place is crazy good. Perfect date spot–speaking of which!"

The escalation in Vivienne's voice caught Lauryn off guard. She'd lost track of how they'd gone from business planning to date spots, but she caught on fast enough to stop Vivienne in her tracks, "No."

"No? Lauryn, come on. I think I have someone for you."

"Is this part of your contract deliverables?"

"Yes–you can lump this under 'Resources provided'."

Lauryn nearly coughed with laughter, "Wow, you are full service aren't you?"

"Bet! He's a friend from college who just moved here from DC last summer. This is actually perfect, you both can get to know the city together, see how things are looking before summer…" she was speaking to Lauryn in a sing-song voice as if that would help to convince her.

This is exactly what Lauryn didn't need. "Just think about it. He's very cool and he's not looking for anything too heavy. He's a workaholic like you, but looking to spend time with someone. I believe the word he used was *companionship*."

"Did you interview this man or something?"

"Yes, of course, he's one of my clients."

"Stop. This has to be a conflict of interest."

"How? You're *both* my clients now. If you both end up knocking boots and combining your personal brands in some Ciara and Russel shit, that only benefits me."

Lauryn gazed up at the ceiling as she considered the nonsense. It might get her mind off Perry.

"Lauryn, let this man take you out. If you don't like him, you don't like him." Vivienne went into a bit of a monologue on how Lauryn deserved to be wined and dined and how it was an opportunity to flirt with someone new, shake off the cobwebs of her previous relationship. "Get into your lovergirl bag. Flex a little bit, shit use him to network for investors. You don't have to stay with him forever. He fine though."

Lauryn laughed, "You just have this planned all the way out."

"Sis, this is what I do. I'm a planner. I make dreams come true. Speaking of which, I'm inviting you to my brand re-launch."

A welcome change of subject. "Vivienne–that's amazing. When is it?"

"Five weeks! I can't wait. I'm inviting a few of my legacy clients and some new. And as my newest client, I would love for you to be there. You're pretty much a walking vision board for my target client in 2023."

Lauryn wasn't sure whether she could truly be flattered. Part of her did wonder whether Vivienne's enthusiasm had anything to do with her affiliation with Joe. "Celebrity adjacent", as Deonna sometimes teased her. The residual perks of breaking up with a rising star.

Lauryn sighed inaudibly, "Send me the details. I'll be there."

"Great," Vivienne responded slowly. She was obviously typing or working on something on her phone. "So, I'll see you Thursday!"

"Yes, you will."

"Perfect. Bye, Love." The call dropped before Lauryn could say goodbye.

There was something intimidating about the pace Vivienne kept, but Lauryn couldn't help admiring her ambition. She set her phone down and tried to find her place in her stream of emails in her inbox. Vivienne's affirmations, however genuine they may or may not have been, were starting to work their magic. Since hanging up, Lauryn already felt lighter and excited to share her idea, to start bringing it to life.

She'd have to make some time to work on her mood board and round out her brand story. Something she'd seen a thousand times while working as an analyst, but shaping a vision for herself? This was new territory. A yawn forced her into a back stretch and she promised herself an early night to bed that evening. She'd had quite the birthday weekend and was ready for some much-needed rest.

Great. She'd managed a whole *five* minutes without thinking of Perry.

Chapter 18

Lauryn

Lauryn's dining table looked like her thoughts spilled out in color. Magazines lay open and sliced through with scissors, color swatches overlapped like flower petals, while a Youtube video played silently on her laptop. Sunlight poured in through the windows, catching the rounded edge of the table and glinting against the perfume and oil bottles Lauryn had pulled for inspiration.

A half empty teacup was balanced in her right hand, and a full pot sat at the center of the table, still warm and fragrant. She'd been at it since sunrise, shuffling images of amber glass, muslin towels, natural sponges, and rippling bathwater into some kind of mood board. She took a moment to sip her green tea and tilted her head, wondering if she was getting any closer to a brand story that made any sense.

It had been a few weeks since Lauryn's last check-in with Vivienne. They managed to connect over dinner and go over her brand concept. Vivienne, as direct as ever, had given Lauryn homework, challenging her to define her target customer, brand story, and most importantly, come up with a name.

Now, on a rare Saturday morning to herself, with no requests from her mother or spontaneous brunch invites from Deonna, Lauryn was trying to bring it all to life. Her phone sounded abruptly, the vibration, jarring her from her thoughts.

Frowning, she turned her phone over, surprised to see a missed call and a message from one of her old co-workers. After five months, she thought she'd heard the last from people wondering why she'd left, but it seemed Memphis was intent to hold on. Lauryn, equally intent to stay focused, set the phone and her tea on the table

"Please keep me from getting distracted," she prayed aloud.

Her gaze moved over the table, the magazine clippings and fragrance bottles becoming less inspiring and more overwhelming by the minute. Her brand was meant to stand for something. Ritual. Presence and wholeness as luxuries that come from self-care. Too bad she hadn't even thought of a name yet.

Lauryn reached for one of the small vials of oil and uncapped it, lifting it to her nose. The scent bloomed dark and honeyed. *Oud.* One of the notes in Perry's cologne.

She rolled her eyes. It was ridiculous how quickly he came to mind. They still hadn't spoken since that odd exchange through her front door, but she could still see his kilowatt smile as he sipped his drink. She envisioned him relaxed; his muscular arms stretched wide along the back of the speakeasy booth. Then there was the way he'd looked at her from the other side of the pool, amusement flickering in his gaze, shadowed by something quieter.

Lauryn touched the oil to her wrist and inhaled, the scent deepening with the heat of her skin. An idea came to her suddenly, and she leaned across the table, snatching up pen and paper. A *scent that lingers*, she thought, imagining a bath set of golden bath oil, salts infused with amber and cardamom, and the perfect candle to set it all off.

She sat back down to jot a few more notes, the inspiration just starting to return when her phone chimed again. "You've got to be kidding me," she muttered, flipping the phone over, prepared to dismiss whoever was calling.

However, the location of the number made her pause. *San Bernardino, CA* appeared in small print below a number she did not recognize. San Bernardino—the same place she'd addressed the letters all those years ago. It was probably a sales call, but something about the recent conversation with her father compelled her to answer. "Hello?"

"Hello," the voice was light, inquisitive, but strangely sounded a lot like her own "Is this Lauryn?"

"Yes," she held her breath wondering if the voice on the other end was who she thought it was.

"This is Alicia. Your Dad... our dad gave me your number. He and I have been talking lately. "

Lauryn took a breath. *OK Dad, what are you trying to accomplish here?* "Yes, he shared that your mother hasn't been well. How are you?"

"We're doing alright. Mom is getting the care she needs. We're all just adjusting."

"What can I do for you, Alicia?" Lauryn asked carefully.

A long pause and her sister finally spoke again, "I thought we might talk. We've never known each other. I heard you moved back to Chicago recently?"

"I did. Just this past winter."

"You were in LA?"

Lauryn raised an eyebrow. Alicia knew full well she'd been in LA. Twelve years before, when she and Joe were just settling out there, she'd reached out to her sister on Facebook. Unlike with the three childhood letters, Alicia had finally answered. She'd even accepted a friend request, but when Lauryn attempted to meet in person or keep in touch, there had been no further response.

She'd had better luck connecting with her eldest sisters. Tasha and Kelly had responded right away, posting on their pages excitedly *"Our little sister is in LA!"* with all the exclamation points and heart emojis. They'd started chatting over the phone almost immediately and made plans for Lauryn to visit. Kelly worked long hours for the postal service, but Tasha was a real estate agent and had an incredible place in Burbank.

Lauryn had been so excited to finally meet them in person. She remembered packing her favorite jumpsuit and heels for the occasion.

"Oh, you're wearing that? Perhaps I should go with you." Joe had teased, pulling the jumpsuit out again and dangling it from his forefingers. She'd ignored him and carried on packing. "So, it's a party or you're staying the weekend?"

"Both. My oldest sister Tasha just got her broker's license and a new place, so she's having a house warming."

"I wish I didn't have to work."

"Me too," she'd said, putting her arms around his neck and kissing him sweetly. "Do you think you can take off?"

"No, I need to save my time. I barely have days as it is, honey. We don't all have great benefits, my dear." And although she'd have preferred for him to come with her, she'd taken their Ford explorer up into the hills alone. She should have never gone without him.

Standing in her kitchen now, Lauryn went a little numb as she remembered that weekend.

So many years had passed, but she easily recalled the scent of gardenia and grilled shrimp as if she was still there. The drive into Burbank had been dreamy, sunlight flickering through the palm trees as she wound her way up into the hills, her heart fluttering at the idea of finally meeting her sisters.

Tasha's house was covered in bright pink bougainvillea with an enormous palm tree commanding the yard. She'd opened the door in a white jumpsuit, gold bangles gleaming, greeting Lauryn with warmth that had felt overwhelming. They'd stayed up late eating shrimp tacos and flipping through photo albums, and for a moment Lauryn believed it might be the start of something healing.

Tasha's party the next day had been surreal, like something out of a nineties romcom. That's when she met Kelly, her second eldest sister, the one who looked most like their father. She'd squealed and hugged Lauryn so tight they'd almost fallen over. "You look just like our cousin Janae! Same cheekbones and everything." Lauryn remembered her sisters insisting on a sibling picture and introducing her to everyone. She'd felt the promise of belonging.

However, once the drinks started flowing, all that warm excitement cooled. Walking around the party, she started to feel uneasy and unwelcome. Little things throughout the day that she'd known she wasn't imagining, started happening. Her purse had been moved and the small gift bag she'd brought for Tasha suddenly went missing. Then there were the backhanded compliments.

"You're so worldly," Tasha had said, when Lauryn joined in with Tasha's friends swapping travel stories.

"I love this natural on you," Kelly exclaimed later, motioning around Lauryn's hair. "I love how you didn't even bother smoothing it down, it's very free."

Then later, Tasha had actually rolled her eyes as she advised Kelly not to bother sharing certain things with Lauryn. "She's the officer's daughter. You know she don't know nothin' about that?"

Lauryn's first mind had been to clap back, but the reality was she was in a house full of strangers. Her sisters were, in fact, strangers and the energy shift was enough to make her wary. She'd decided to go home, instead of staying another night.

In Tasha's guest room, she'd shoved everything into her duffle bag, realizing she should never have come. Lauryn felt badly that Tasha and Kelly had grown up without their father. Regretted that they'd never experienced his warmth and didn't seem to know him at all. His divorce from their mother wasn't their fault, but it wasn't hers either.

She was so busy gathering her things, so set on leaving, that she missed the knock at the door. If there'd been a knock at all. When she'd turned to get her toiletries from the bathroom, she'd found a man, standing in the middle of the room between her and the door.

"Sam?"

The man Tasha had introduced as her boyfriend had just smiled. "I know you're not leaving already?"

"I am." Lauryn had zipped her bag closed so hard she almost ripped it off. At that point she was ready to leave behind anything that wasn't already in that bag. "Excuse me."

She'd moved to pass him, but he blocked her path.

"What are you doing?" Lauryn had pulled away, anger rising with every second.

"I wanted to talk to you about the Chi. I've never been, thought you could help me plan my next trip."

Lauryn had watched him carefully. "Shouldn't you be downstairs with Tasha?"

"She's not paying attention to me."

"I can't imagine why–can you get out of my way?"

"Woah, woah! Why are you in such a hurry? Now, I know your sisters upset you. They're just jealous. Daddy issues. Both of them." He'd pressed in so close and all Lauryn could think about was using her full weight, and the weight of her over packed duffle, to body slam him into the nearby wall.

Tasha had appeared in the doorway then, peering at the both of them like she'd been expecting to find them there. Instead of checking Sam, she'd fixated on Lauryn. "You know I had a feeling, but I welcomed your little entitled ass into my home anyway. Just for you to slink up here with my man on day two!"

Lauryn had squinted at her sister in disbelief, trying to make sense of the turn of events before brushing passed both of them on her way out the door. By the time she reached her car, Tasha was cutting across her lawn, hurling every insult she'd probably been wanting to say all along.

Lauryn had barely slowed her pace as she reached her car, yanking open the door. "Your man is a fucking creep, Tasha. Trust me, I don't want him." She'd thrown her bag into the passenger seat, slammed the door, and peeled down the hill with her windows down and her anger so deep she had to fight back tears.

She hadn't spoken to either of her eldest sisters since.

"*Lauryn?*" Alicia's voice sounded loudly on the other end of the phone, bringing her back to the present.

Lauryn blinked away the memory. "Sorry, yes we were in LA until 2018. We stayed in Atlanta for a while, but we've been in Memphis the last few years. That's where I just left." She wanted to say so much more, wanted to ask why Alicia hadn't responded back then or warned her about her sisters. "Hey Alicia, did you and Tasha ever-"

"I've never met them. My mom was really overprotective anyway, but I don't think she was a big fan of their mom, you know?" Alicia let out a soft laugh.

"Yeah, I can understand that." The air went out of Lauryn's anger like a popped balloon. Of course, Alicia hadn't warned her. She hadn't known any more about their sisters than Lauryn had when she hit Tasha's front stoop. All these years, Lauryn had assumed that because they were all in California, that they must all know each other somehow.

"How'd you like Memphis?"

"Well, it's not LA. And it's not Chicago!"

Alicia hummed in agreement, "How'd you convince Joseph to move back?

Lauryn answered slowly, "Uh, Joe's still in Memphis. We're not together anymore. How did you know?"

"Confession time. I read a few things online. When his first album dropped, I recognized you on the cover. I thought you had started modeling like everyone tries to when they move to LA, but then I saw you in a magazine, that ya'll were together."

"Is this why you're reaching out-" She couldn't help the resentment in her voice, the memory of Tasha and Kelly exceedingly fresh in her mind.

"No! No, I just thought it was cool how you two were living your dream life. You both always look so beautiful and happy together."

"Yeah well, it was his dream. Not mine."

Alicia hummed again, "I get that."

"Are you married?" Lauryn asked, hearing some solidarity in her sister's tone.

"Yes," she responded quickly. "My husband and I have our challenges too. He's wonderful, but sometimes he forgets I have more on my plate than supporting his ambition."

"Oh, I get that." Lauryn echoed her sister's earlier statement. They talked a while longer. Alicia was an only child too; her mother had never married. And when she spoke about her, there was such softness in her voice, a kind of reverence that told Lauryn everything she needed to know about their bond. Underneath it, Lauryn could hear the fear in Alicia's voice whenever she mentioned her mother's illness, as if saying it out loud made it more real.

"But she's fighting, you know? We're renting a house in Malibu for Mother's Day. She wants to be on the beach in her mesh Rihanna dress."

"That sounds wonderful," Lauryn struggled to find her next words. They were, after all, sisters with thirty years of catching up to do. And as the younger, she knew she should be the bigger person. That it would be easier for her to forgive the resentment. "Alicia," she started. "You all should bring your girls to visit. I know you have so much happening with your mom, but maybe-?"

She was truly surprised when her sister agreed, "Yes, that would be lovely. We've never been to Chicago."

Probably avoided it at all cost because this was the city where her absent father lived. To them, Chicago, Lauryn and her mother all personified his absence. "Really? Well, we have to make sure you get the full experience."

"I'll call in a few weeks from the beach? You can meet the girls on Facetime?"

"I would absolutely love that."

They said their goodbyes, and Lauryn listened until the call disconnected. She set her phone down, staring at it like it might light up again, then reached for her tea instead. The heat was gone, but she took a sip anyway before whispering into the quiet, "Well... that's new."

Chapter 19

Lauryn

There was too much to unpack for just one phone call and Lauryn was reeling from the effort of trying to figure out what to say. She blew out a slow breath, her eyes darting across the dining table, still scattered with all her ideas and research. The conversation with Alicia had stirred more than expected and all her inspiration seemed to slip away with it.

Some memories were best left undisturbed.

Outside, plump rain drops clung to the windows. The sky was hazy, but she could just make out the city skyline in the distance. Stopping the video on her laptop she made a beeline into her bedroom. Rather than sit there and spiral, she decided to take herself out, spend the day preoccupied by something other than the Lindsey Family saga.

She dressed and did her makeup quickly, smoothing her hair back into a fluffy ponytail at the nape of her neck. After stepping into a pair of burgundy, square-toed boots, she stopped at her front closet to grab her trench coat. Even as she pulled on her coat and reached for her purse, she had no destination in mind. All Lauryn really wanted was to think about something else for a while.

A small pile of mail sat unopened on her new entryway table and her eyes caught sight of a swirling blue and green image. She reached for it, tugging the envelope out from the rest. Claude Monet's *Water Lilies* graced the cover of the Art Institute of Chicago's ad for its Monet exhibition, which was closing later that month.

Perfect, she decided silently and headed out the door.

Before she could overthink it, she was already on her way downtown. Traffic moved easily, and she sped toward the museum, barely stopping until she parked her car. The rain fell soft and steady as she passed the Symphony center, heading toward Adams Street. The bronze lions guarding the museum entrance loomed ahead, their green patina striking against the creamy limestone of the building's exterior. She glanced up at the south lion, something easing in her mind as she jogged up the steps.

Inside, Lauryn treated herself to two special exhibitions and a steaming cup of lavender earl grey.

"You've got about thirty minutes before the next Monet tour starts," the museum guide scanned her pass and pointed her in the direction of the exhibit. She barely heard him, seeing the Grand Staircase before her. The marble shone brightly under the skylight above and Lauryn felt herself drawn in, her mood lifting completely as she passed under the filtered light.

Wandering and sipping her tea, she lost herself in the galleries. The restful pace of the Monet tour quickly dissolved any remaining tension she felt. For the moment, her estrangement from her siblings felt very far away.

Lauryn hung back behind the crowd, staring at the enormous canvases, most of them taller and wider than she ever imagined. Around her, every sound softened—the shuffle of footsteps, the low hum of conversation—until even the air seemed to slow. The muted colors and even the texture of each canvas set her at ease and she felt her inspiration stirring again. Ideas for her brand began to surface like ripples in her mind.

Hurrying so she wouldn't lose the idea, she snapped a few selfies in front of another canvas, then zoomed in on the plaque: *Branch of the Seine near Giverny (Mist)*.

"I can take your picture, if you like?" A young woman nearby offered.

Smiling, Lauryn handed her phone over. "That's kind of you, thank you." Shoving her hands down into her coat pockets, she stood in profile next to the canvas. She was feeling a little shy, posing there, but realized the woman had taken several pictures, managing to capture a great candid as Lauryn had been getting into position. She liked it better than any of the poses she'd tried and decided to post it.

If peace had a color palette. She typed the caption out, making her way down the grand staircase. Then she doubled back, taking the long way through the Japanese exhibits toward the museum cafe. She ordered a matcha latte and avocado toast before settling in to eat at one of the small tables that overlooked the modern wing.

The toast was good, bits of Everything seasoning and sprout greens falling back down onto her plate as she took her first bite. She watched the people around her as she chewed, her gaze settling on a family of four. The father, wrangling the kids while the mother arranged their food and drinks.

The conversation with her sister had triggered way too many memories for one day. Despite the warmness she'd felt at the end of the call, she wasn't sure what Alicia was expecting–or if they'd even speak again. Her father would be pleased to know they'd talked, and would probably see it as a sign of progress. But Lauryn wasn't ready to get his hopes up. She wasn't ready to get her own up, either.

It was nearing closing time when she finally stepped out of the museum with a new tote bag loaded down with goodies and books from the gift shop. She'd just reached the base of the steps when her phone sounded.

Fishing it out of her deep coat pockets, she glimpsed a text message from Perry hovering on the screen.

> You in the city?

Nearly a month had passed since he'd taken her out for her birthday. She still felt a little foolish about their last exchange, but she couldn't deny how nice it was to hear from him. She typed a response:

> Yeah. Museum day.

Adding a little painting emoji, she pressed send before taking off down the street. The rain had thinned to a mist, leaving the city slick and shining. Her boots sloshed through shallow puddles as she wandered towards her car, not quite ready to call it a day. If the weather had been any nicer, she would've taken a walk through the nearby Millennium Park or found a place to jot down more ideas. Her phone chimed again:

> Meet me at The Gwen? I'm here early for Ricki's "pre" bachelor thing.

> We can grab a drink before you head back?

She slowed to read the message a second time. It was warm, casual, and low pressure, as if the last time they saw each other hadn't ended with her inviting him in for a nightcap that he'd politely refused.

Still if he was texting now, then perhaps things weren't as weird as she imagined. She pursed her lips, realizing she was probably the only one still dwelling on it. If he could get past her ghosting him a decade before, then she could get past an awkward moment.

Besides, she hadn't carved out this lovely–albeit damp–afternoon just to spiral back into uncertainty. She'd been hoping for some excuse to linger downtown, but after the last two times, another round of drinks with Perry might not be the best idea.

She held up her phone, thumbs hovering as she considered her response. All the while suppressing the flutter in her stomach. She typed:

> You have perfect timing, I was just leaving.

The sun had finally made its full appearance by the time Lauryn stepped onto the top floor at The Gwen. Its golden rays stretched across the skyline, bouncing off mirrored windows and purple tinged clouds, casting the entire city in a wet honeyed glow. The air conditioning skimmed past her trench coat as she stepped into the lounge, where the lighting was already warm and low, the buzz of conversation mingling with the steady beat of lo-fi playing.

She spotted Perry near the bar, shoulders relaxed, turning his glass around on its napkin. Something she noticed he always did before taking a sip, like he was looking for the best place to taste from. His outfit was monochrome olive, pants that were clearly tailored, and a fine button-down polo that fit in a way that held her attention. He looked composed, effortless as usual, and she caught a shift in him. The way his posture straightened, his focus narrowing as if he could feel her coming before he saw her.

He met her with his dazzling smile, stepping off from the bar. "Hey, you found me."

"I did," she said, smoothing a hand over the front of her coat as he pulled out the empty stool beside him.

"Good. Would you like something?" He was already half-turned toward the bar, giving her space to settle in before even really looking at her.

She shrugged off her coat and slid onto the stool, catching his scent in the process. It was different from the last time, something fresh and clean but grown, like vetiver with a little smoke behind it. She dismissed another flutter in her stomach, "Just water for me."

He raised two fingers to the bartender without missing a beat. Only after she was seated and the bartender had set a glass in front of her did he really look at her. His gaze lingered, searing into her before he spoke again.

Finally, his lips quirked into another smile and he said, "Hi."

Lauryn blinked, caught slightly off guard by the quiet heat behind the simple greeting. "Hi, Perry," she laughed.

"You look good, friend," he added, calm as ever. "I see the artsy museum vibes."

She gave him a small smile, head tilted. "Thank you, so do you. You always do."

Perry smirked just enough to make her wonder if he was about to deflect the compliment, but he didn't.

Instead, he shrugged it off humbly. "Thanks for making time to swing by. I know this is a little random, but figured I'd try my luck before all the guys get here."

"Well," she said, feeling brave enough to nudge him with her elbow, "I appreciate the invite. But you still haven't explained. What even *is* a pre-bachelor party?"

He rolled his eyes, also laughing, "It's for the guys who can't make the real one," he said. "Destination trip next month. Dominican Republic. Some of the guys couldn't swing the travel, so tonight's the hometown edition."

Lauryn nodded slowly, amused. "Ah. So, this is like... The Chicago chapter?"

"Exactly. No passports needed."

Lauryn sipped her water, "Are you looking forward to going to the DR? I'm sure it'll be nice to get some consistent sunshine."

"I am! It should be a good time." He looked over at her again, a little more serious now. "How's work been? Still running the world?"

"Oh yeah," she said with a small laugh. "It's been busy. Actually, it's never not busy, but I kind of like it for that reason."

"Yeah, being busy can be a good thing. No time to sweat the small stuff. It heightens your decision making" he said, leaning back a little. "Sounds like you're finding your rhythm though."

Lauryn looked down at the glass in her hand, the ice clinking softly as it dawned on her. She looked up, meeting his gaze with quiet certainty. "I think I am."

For a while they just looked at one another, Lauryn feeling a sudden desire to keep looking.

Perry broke first, averting his eyes and focusing back on his drink. "But seriously, it's good to see you."

Why does that sound like a confession? She wondered and set her drink back down onto the mirrored bar. "And you? Promotion right around the corner?"

His mouth lifted in that way she was really beginning to like, "We'll see. They seem pleased with me."

Like always, they slid into easy conversation, catching up more on the weeks since they'd last seen each other. She asked about his house renovations, and he moaned about his mom dropping off décor she swore "fit his vibe". Velvet ottomans, gold-accented artwork, a decorative tray that read *Boss Energy* in looped cursive. Lauryn laughed, shaking her head as he deadpanned, "I think she thinks I'm still in my twenties."

"Eh, let her decorate. It clearly makes her happy. Just rotate out the things you don't like when she comes to visit."

He stilled mid-sip and raised his eyebrows, "Lauryn Lindsey. Are you suggesting I pull the wool over my momma's eyes?"

"If it makes you both happy? Then yes."

He laughed before taking a sip. "Not sustainable."

Perry spoke about his younger sister, Simone, how she'd been campaigning for him to turn his unfinished attic into her post-graduate studio. Lauryn had forgotten he even had a younger sister, but she found herself smiling, enjoying the way he spoke about her with such easy affection. It was grounding. Sweet. With a pinch she remembered the conversation with Alicia. It didn't even feel like the same day anymore, but Lauryn was still a bit stunned by the random reconnection.

Random reconnection is apparently a theme this year, she thought to herself, looking up at Perry. A year ago, she would have never imagined running into him again. Yet, here they were, back to their old banter. She was relieved to find no awkwardness since inviting him in for a night cap. Apparently it had all been in her head and they were still comfortably set in the friend zone.

Slowly they were approaching the closeness they had in the last months before she moved away. Standing beside him now, playing grown up at a rooftop bar, she realized how much she'd missed him. She was attracted to him too–a fact she was still grappling with, but behind all that, she missed him. Somehow, they always found their way back to this, picking up from wherever they'd left off. First junior year in undergrad, after grad school, and now.

She found herself thinking about their last summer, all the epic times they shared in just a few months, and all of it, behind Joe's back.

In a split second, Lauryn remembered the beginning of everything with that man. The first time she'd ever seen Joe had been on stage. A show her colleagues had dragged her to go see, insisting she needed a night out. Lauryn had hung back in the crowd, amused when they tried to get closer to the stage. Joe had looked good under those lights, commanding the small stage like he was playing an entire stadium. His voice was deep, textured beyond his age, and threaded with the influence of the blues, country and soul. Lauryn had just started to sway to the melody when his eyes found hers. Through the lights he'd held her gaze and plucked a few womb-stirring notes on his guitar. He'd leaned into the microphone until his lips nearly brushed it, closing his eyes he demonstrated his full range with each lyric. Then he'd grinned at her, as if they were sharing something private in a room full of people.

Lauryn had played along, smiling skeptically at him over the rim of her glass. She'd been convinced it was all part of the performance, a tactic to draw the audience in. However, when he'd come to find her after his set she'd had a tough time remaining unaffected. Even now, she could still see him rushing through the club door after her to ask for her number one last time. She'd finally agreed.

A fateful decision if there ever was one.

In the beginning Joe was thoughtful, intensely romantic, and intoxicating in a way that left her dizzy. Their connection had been instant, blinding. Despite her schedule, he found ways to see her. Video chats after her study sessions, meeting her at the train station with coffee, and whisking her to private events and shows. She'd started spending more time at his place than at home. It had felt like love, but over the years she'd learned to see it for what it was—love bombing disguised as devotion. However foolish it might have been, she'd been swept away by it. Swept away by him

So much so that the morning of her graduate school commencement, she spent more energy justifying his absence than enjoying the ceremony. Joe had an "opportunity he couldn't pass up."

But Perry had been there, solid as ever in a trim navy-blue suit. She'd been so preoccupied with Joe's absence and her family's antics that she hadn't noticed Perry walking over. He'd been there to celebrate someone– a cousin, maybe a friend–Lauryn couldn't remember now. She just remembered how glad she'd been to see him. The sight of his kind smile and crinkled eyes set in the face of a boy then.

"I thought I heard them call your name–congratulations!" He'd pulled her into a tight hug, his joy for her so genuine and warm, it had stirred her own.

That moment was the beginning of what would become *that* summer–their summer. Long, golden days filled with festivals and weddings, nights that ended in laughter and the smell of grilled onions from their favorite late-night Polish stand. In Perry's easy presence, she'd fallen in love with the city, its rhythm, and its promise. For the first time, she'd begun to imagine a future rooted in Chicago instead of chasing something uncertain in London or some faraway place where she knew no one.

Her actual choice hadn't been much better, running off to California, where the only person she truly knew was Joe. She felt a ripple of guilt remembering, but thinking about what might have happened if she'd stayed only made her head ache.

Anchoring herself back in the present, Lauryn swallowed, her throat suddenly dry. She smiled up at Perry to conceal her thoughts.

"Well, if your style is any indication," she said, reaching for her purse and coat, "I know your place is going to turn out amazing." Perry stood when she did, hands in his pockets, watching her with that same quiet attentiveness. She slipped on her coat. "I better let you get back to the guys before they think I've stolen you."

He didn't move right away. "Oh, wow yeah. Time is flying."

"It is." she said, reaching for her coat.

He stood up with her, finishing his drink in one slow sip, then gestured toward the elevators. "At least let me walk you this time?"

She followed him through the lounge, but before they reached the elevators, he hesitated, touching her elbow with the lightest touch.

"They're just upstairs on the terrace," he said. "You wanna say hi to these Negroes real quick? You know most of them anyway, from back in the day."

Lauryn paused, halfway into her coat. A part of her wanted to decline, to keep the moment light and end it right here, on a high note. She leaned back on her heel to side-eye him, "Aren't there dancers up there? Pre or post–it's still a bachelor party."

"The entertainment," he emphasized, licking his full lips. "Won't be here for another couple hours."

"Alright," she laughed, shaking her head. "But only for a minute."

Perry grinned like he was genuinely pleased, and they headed into the elevator. She followed Perry down the carpeted hall, shifting in her heels as he pressed his keycard to unlock the door. The suite was opulent, with oversized couches and velvet pillows. She could already hear the ruckus of men joking and laughing as they rounded the living area of the suite and steeped through the open terrace doors. The air on the terrace was damp but fresh, the rain having passed, leaving a soft sheen on the patio furniture and low glass railings. An outdoor fireplace was going and the guys were spread out, sipping from heavy rocks glasses and passing around a Bluetooth speaker someone had finally synced.

The music was low, the energy just starting to pick up.

"Yo, look who it is!" someone called when they walked in, and a few heads turned with easy smiles.

She smiled, cheeks warming at the welcome as a few of them raised their glasses in her direction. One of them, Tony, who she vaguely remembered from college grinned and nudged Perry as they approached.

"Man, you've been keepin' the fairer company all to yourself, huh?" he teased.

Perry gave a shrug, but Lauryn noticed the subtle flicker of a smile tugging at his mouth. "Yeah, I convinced her to stop by for a minute."

"Mmmhmm," Tony said, exaggerated, nodding like he didn't believe a word. "Is this the reason you are late for the opening ceremonies, P?

"Opening ceremonies? Please don't act like ya'll didn't just get here." They bickered playfully, debating on which of them was responsible for kicking things off.

It was strange in a sweet way, seeing how much some of them had changed. Their "dad bods" settling in, and hairlines retreating, while others still looked the same. But all in all, it felt good to be seen like this. No explanations needed. Just history and laughter and familiarity.

Ricki, the groom, made his way over with a drink in hand and a broad smile. "Lauryn! You look good. Brittney's gonna be mad she missed you."

"Truth be told, I'm surprised she's not here." Lauryn observed, genuinely surprised. From the way Britney had been planning every detail of their wedding, it was a wonder she let him have a bachelor party on his own.

"Nah, we finally decided on the whole split thing. She's got her girls in Miami this weekend."

"Ah, that's right! Esme did mention that."

"Yeah, she's been texting me since they landed," he laughed. "Tell me, has she mentioned anything about a second dress? I overheard her say 'reception reveal' the other day and now I'm sweatin'."

Lauryn sucked in a breath playfully, "You might be in trouble."

Ricky dropped his head, shaking it slowly for dramatics. "She's got me scared to check the credit card statements," he added, half-joking. "She smiles every time I open a delivery box and says, 'Oh, that's for the wedding.'"

"She's got vision," Lauryn teased. "You're in good hands."

Ricky raised his glass with a grin. "That's what I keep telling myself."

They kept chatting for a few more minutes, catching up on mutual friends and career updates, until Lauryn's phone buzzed in her coat pocket. She pulled it out, seeing a text from Deonna with a single line:

Girl... is this *now*?

Beneath it was a screenshot of an Instagram story. A selfie from one of the guys she didn't know as well as the others. Somebody standing just a few feet away. In the background: Lauryn, unmistakably visible, laughing mid-conversation with Perry, Ricky and a few others.

The caption read: *How you gonna bring your girl to the bachelor party? She strippin' or no?*

Everything inside her went still.

The blood in her ears, the low music, the conversation around her all muted. Lauryn blinked, steadying herself, then slipped her phone back into her purse and quietly made her way back inside.

Why hadn't she trusted her first mind, she was shaking her head as she stalked toward the elevators. She'd made it halfway through the suite when Perry caught up to her.

"Lauryn! Lauryn–what's wrong?"

"I'm going home," she said, barely looking at him.

"You alright?"

"I'm fine. Apparently ruining the vibe," she said flatly, shrugging her shoulders.

"What do you mean?"

She shook her head trying to dismiss it, her jaw tight. "It was good to see you, Perry. Have a good time." She didn't mean to let it sound so sharp. But it was already out there.

He stepped in front of her, his brow furrowing. "Did somebody say something to you?"

"No." She exhaled, keeping her voice flat. "Nobody *said* anything to me."

He looked like he didn't believe her, already scanning the terrace behind them and squaring his shoulders like he was two seconds from going back to check.

She pulled open the door and stepped through, hearing him follow close behind.

"You don't have to walk me down," she added quietly.

"Lauryn, what happened?" He asked more sternly, his tone laced with concern. "We were chillin'. I looked away for a second, and now you're leaving?"

She paused at the elevator, reached out and touched his arm. His skin was warm despite the early evening air, the muscle underneath firm and familiar. It disarmed her for a second.

"I wasn't planning on staying," she said with a weak smile. "It *is* a bachelor party, after all."

She'd forced a tone that was breezy and designed to throw him off. Because he might not let her leave if he thought something was genuinely wrong.

The elevator bell sounded and she stepped inside, keeping her chin lifted just enough. Dignified. Untouched.

"Have a good time," she said again before the doors closed.

Perry didn't move and didn't press further. He just stood there; his eyebrows drawn together in concern. Or maybe frustration.

"Get back safe," he said quietly and the doors slid shut between them.

It took over an hour for Lauryn to get home that night, the improved weather bringing more people out onto the roads. Lauryn started undressing as soon as she walked through the door. Her earrings hit the counter and her phone landed face-down beside them. She tried not to be so sore about the stupid Instagram post, but it stuck with her.

Deonna had called her not long after she left. The post had been deleted, apparently just twenty minutes after he'd originally shared it.

"That nigga is just mad ain't nobody trying to dance on him unless he's paying," Deonna tried to console her.

Lauryn exhaled slowly, unfastening her pants and shifting until they slid to the floor.

"Thanks, Dee. I'm gonna go, girl."

"Oh shit, you're blown, aren't you?" Deonna asked, clearly picking up on the tone in her voice.

"I am. I can't even lie. I was having a perfectly pleasant evening and this just killed it."

"Ugh—I can't believe you didn't say anything to him. I would've knocked that man out his chair." Deonna continued on, clapping between every word, walking Lauryn through her imagined retaliation with full dramatic flair.

Lauryn opened the refrigerator, staring inside for something—anything—to take the edge off. She frowned, realizing she'd had nothing sweet in the house. And tea just wasn't going to cut it after the day she'd had.

"You in for the night?" Deonna asked.

"I am most certainly in for the night." Lauryn flicked her hand to close the fridge door.

"I hear you, girl. I have a new pajama set and a rose clay mask calling my name. I'm about to find something to watch."

Rubbing her face, Lauryn muttered, "That sounds lovely. I'll let you go."

"Alright, boo, forget about that dumbass."

"Just—" Lauryn started. "Thank you for letting me know, girl."

"Of course! Can't have these vagabonds out here posting unauthorized images."

They both laughed and said goodnight.

Her mood lifted slightly, knowing the post was gone, but something about the moment lingered. It poked at an old ache. Memories of other times, quiet humiliations, small betrayals in her past. The gnawing uncertainty of not being seen clearly or respected fully. Eerily similar moments with Joe where she'd swallowed her discomfort and convinced herself it wasn't that deep. Then she felt ashamed for tolerating it all for so long.

Lauryn shook her head, as if the motion might finally dislodge the thoughts. She rolled her eyes and walked straight to the bathroom for a bath.

All the recent encounters had unearthed too many memories, and just as many regrets. Every run-in with Perry resulted in an avalanche of memories, or left her cross examining herself. Combined with Alicia's call, it was more feeling than she knew how to function under right now. She needed a break from it.

Though she didn't blame him, she needed a break from Perry too.

Chapter 20

Lauryn

"Yeah, that's the dataset you want to reference. You can re-run your query now." Lauryn smiled warmly at Sophia before sliding back in front of her own laptop.

"Thank you, I have submitted this report twice and Finance keeps rejecting it, saying it's not right, but couldn't specify why. I can't believe I didn't catch that, and you look at it for two minutes and save the day."

"To be fair, Finance didn't catch it either," she raised a playful eyebrow over the back of her laptop, typing out the last of an email. "We're just all moving fast. Easy to miss things."

"True, but you're like *on it* lately," Sophia's cropped hair swung forward as she said it. "Not that you're not always! But for the last few weeks you're here early, you just brought in a new third party, and you're taking time to help me and Matt? You are killing every presentation and your complexion is clearer than the models in our product photos."

"Sophia!" Lauryn laughed.

"I'm serious. Please tell me what it is that you're doing at home. Please write it down." Sophia so normally so stoic that Lauryn wasn't sure whether or not to laugh.

Still, she wasn't wrong. For the past few weeks, Lauryn had been feeling sharper. Dialed in at the office and staying late to compile her notes for the next day. She'd ordered more furniture for her place, and she was keeping up with her gym schedule, even cutting back on her Saturday morning pastries.

Lauryn exhaled a laugh, tapping the side panel of Sophia's desk, "Just energized and focused, you know."

She would've given herself more credit, if the catalyst for her recent hyperfocus hadn't been that spectacle of a bachelor party. It'd been weeks since the incident at the hotel, spring was in full swing, but she still winced whenever she thought about it. She'd stopped caring what the others thought, but the look on Perry's face, part confusion, part concern, stayed with her. The way he kept his eyes on hers until the elevator doors closed... yeah, that was still bothering her.

Well, you did act like it was his fault. She'd tormented herself about this a handful of times already.

"I need some of that energy," Sophia mumbled, already engrossed in the data tables on her screen again. Lauryn took the opportunity to step away, reflecting as she headed to the ladies room.

Things–*people* were getting in the way. Six months had already passed since she'd moved back. And that stupid bachelor scene was just a reminder she needed to keep her priorities straight.

As she washed her hands, she cringed again and nearly groaned aloud as Perry's worried expression formed in her mind again. Why hadn't she just gone home after their drink instead of going upstairs?

Everything had been perfect at the bar, just the two of them. For a while, she forgot about the family drama and the quiet insecurity she still carried about blowing up her life to start over back home. Perry's easy manner soothed her, going all the way back to their last year of undergrad. While she ran herself ragged working part time in the residence halls and cramming for exams, he'd always been right on time, pulling up in front of her apartment to treat her to a late-night gyro. A vivid memory of the two of them in his car laughing over French fries, the windows fogged the heat turned up too high. That warmth had stayed with her, tucked into some corner she hadn't touched in years.

Now, he was back in her life again, making her head hurt every time they crossed paths, but looking like the main love interest in an HBO series. She'd wanted to reach up and rake through his beard with both hands, rise onto the tips of her toes until she was close enough to kiss and suck on his bottom lip.

The hiss of the faucet still running over her hands pulled her from her thoughts. Remembering where she was, she glanced back at the stalls behind her to ensure she was alone. Her intrusive thoughts were more colorful these days and that was exactly the distraction she did not need. Every move she'd made toward Perry ended in some sort of embarrassment. Basically, the universe reminding her to stick to her damn plan.

Still, she should at least call him and clear the air, let him know she wasn't upset with him. She'd just needed some time. A few days had turned into weeks, she thought, biting her lip as she scrolled through her phone to the last message from Perry. He'd reached out to make sure she was okay after leaving the hotel. Her last response had been short:

> I'm good P, thanks

Lauryn grimaced, regretting being so short in her response. She typed out a few characters, trying to piece together the right thing to say.

> Hey Perry, what's going on? It's been a whi–

She deleted it, realizing the gap in their communication was solely her fault. Still the right words refused to come. Her phone buzzed in her hands, jolting her out of her thoughts–a FaceTime call from Vivienne.

Lauryn answered the call quickly, grinning as her friend's face filled the screen, "Hey!"

"Hey, hon, oh you look cute. You must be excited about tonight!"

Frowning, Lauryn asked, "What's tonight?"

Vivienne blinked twice, "Tonight, as in the night you're meeting Terrance at the Alcove."

Lauryn was drawing a blank. "I'm sorry, who?"

Vivienne brought her hands together in a praying motion, "If I have to come back up to this job, where I no longer work, and get you–"

"Vivienne, I have no idea what you're talking about."

"You remember! Last month, I was telling you about my friend from DC who just moved here. Sexy as fuck, no kids, looking for some grown up sophisticated companionship. I sent you a picture!"

"Yeah, yeah I remember the picture now. What I do not remember is agreeing to *meet* this person. Let alone tonight!"

Vivienne stared at the camera so long, Lauryn wondered if she'd frozen. Finally, she pointed at the camera with a bright pink manicured finger. "I might have planned it with him and forgotten to tell you."

Lauryn let her head fall back in exasperation, "What the hell Vivienne!"

"I know, I know. I switched up my sleep meds and I've been forgetting shit. But this is a non-issue, you look incredible, girl. He made reservations for like six-thirty; you can meet him after work."

"Is that right? So, you just know my schedule."

"I kinda do. You've been moving in a triangle lately. Home, work, your parents, Gym. Home, work, your parents, gym-."

"That's four corners–that's a square, friend."

"Isn't your gym in your building? Honey, don't play me."

"Why are you playing with me! You're sending me on a blind date that you forgot to tell me about."

"It's lunch time. Consider this your notice. I know Hema! If she knew you were going out to meet a man this fine, she would have no problem with you leaving early."

Lauryn shook her head unwittingly, tempted to simply hang up.

"Okay, okay," Vivienne continued. "I'm sorry, I meant to call you right after I confirmed with him, but I must've just forgotten in all the excitement. I really think you two will hit it off. Honestly, he's cool as fuck, I would not bother you otherwise. Plus, if you need to knock Joe's dick print out of your–"

"Hush!" Lauryn whisper-shouted and ended the call.

Six hours later, after a speeding across town, Lauryn pulled up to The Alcove.

"I don't even know why I'm doing this", she grumbled, slamming her car door closed with her hip. But the idea of ghosting someone, just felt wrong. Even if she hadn't agreed to meeting in the first place. The restaurant was narrow, with a stunning illuminated bar running down the one side. Vivienne had shared another photo of Terrance Boyd as Lauryn drove across town and she tiptoed past the host's stand, scanning for him.

A figure towards the back stood, waving to her. *Definitely good looking*, Lauryn admitted, venturing past the bar, towards the table where he stood. He was caramel brown with locs intricately twisted to the back. A small candle in an amber votive flickered on the table, casting a soft light onto his handsome face. "Terrance?"

"Yes," he drew the word out softly and his mouth curled into a smile. "It's nice to meet you, Lauryn." He stepped from behind the table, caught somewhere between a hug and a handshake.

Lauryn offered her hand, "You too. Sorry I'm late."

"You're right on time." He pulled her chair out for her and then took his seat across from her. "Hope the drive wasn't too bad?"

"No, I don't work far from here. How about you?" After all the rushing to get here, she'd forgotten everything that came next– small talk.

"My office is downtown, but I had client meetings near here this week, so I thought it would be more convenient."

"Oh, well thank you for that. This is a great neighborhood, too," she said warmly, lifting the single page menu. He mirrored her movements, peering at his menu like he hadn't already had time with it before she arrived. It seemed they both needed a moment to regroup before the next round of polite conversation. "Have you been here before?"

"I haven't, but, uh, highly recommended on Open Table." He waved his phone, chuckling lightly. "I'm still getting to know the area."

"That's right! You just moved here last year?"

"Yes. I was presented with an opportunity I couldn't pass up."

She nodded. "And how is our fair city treating you?"

"*Very* well." He smiled at her politely. It was clear he was pleased that she was the other participant on this blind date. He laughed, admitting he'd done every corny tourist thing just to feel out the city–boat tours, selfies by the Bean, all of it–and still hadn't recovered from the shock of his first Midwest winter. Terrance was an attorney who'd traded the courtroom for construction sites, channeling his ambition into restoring some of Chicago's historic Black spaces. Vivienne was helping him refine *Boyd Heritage*, a cultural restoration and design firm he'd started in his twenties. "So, I hear you're a data alchemist and you run your own luxury brand?"

Lauryn nearly spilled the water she'd been sipping. "What–no! Well, yes, I do work in data science, but no I don't have a luxury brand. Not yet anyway."

"Yet?"

Motioning with her hand, she explained, "Vivienne is helping me."

He nodded. "How'd you two meet?"

"At work, we connected right away and started sharing Black lady tales of corporate America. You know how it goes." He gave a knowing nod as she continued. "Anyway, I shared that I want to start a self-care subscription service and she constructed this entire brand scheme for me in about fifteen minutes."

"That sounds like Viv," He lifted his own water and sipped. "She's got a great eye for spotting others' potential, even if we can't see it yet. But big data, that's pretty cool."

"I like finding patterns. Making sense out of tons of information, finding an answer that no one else could see."

"Mm, you manage to make it sound poetic. I see you're beautiful as well as brilliant," he said, and actually licked his lips.

Lauryn resisted the urge to roll her eyes, wondering if her flirtations would be any better after so many years "off the market". Despite his corniness, she thought how nice it was to connect with someone new who didn't have eons of mutual history and regrets attached to them. She thought back to her first date with Joe. He'd tried so hard, asking question after question about her studies and pretending to be fascinated. Even if he hadn't dropped out of college to pursue his music career, he would have steered clear of the sciences. Joe's magic lay in his intuition, his timing, the way he could seduce a room or pull a song out of thin air. She read somewhere once that for however many years you were in a relationship, you needed half that time to get over it. And while she was pretty sure she was over Joe; she was less certain about dating again.

Their server appeared, making a few suggestions before taking their orders and disappearing behind the bar.

"You know," she started, smiling before she could even finish her sentence. "Vivienne forgot to tell me about this date."

Terrance stilled, "Naw, seriously?

"Yep. Called me earlier today and realized she'd made all the arrangements with you and didn't tell me."

"Wow, I didn't realize." Puzzled he set his drink down, his eyes squinting at the table like he was trying to remember. "She said she told you about me."

"Oh, she did a couple weeks back! Just forgot to tell me you were taking me out today."

"And yet, you came anyway." He watched, smiling pleasantly as he examined her, like the reason she'd showed up might appear somewhere on her face.

She found him disarming and with a slow exhale, Lauryn decided to be honest. "Terrance, I just got out of something. A very *long* something and although I'm enjoying your company, I'm not one hundred percent ready for whatever Vivienne may have... suggested."

He broke, chuckling until his shoulders bounced. "I like your word choice, there."

"You like that?" Lauryn leaned back in her chair, stroking her chin.

"I do." There was a lot going on behind the way he said the two words.

Lauryn averted his gaze, focusing on the candle between them. She was finding conversation with Terrance easier than expected. He was refreshingly unknown, but interesting enough that she was glad their food had yet to arrive. Still, she questioned how much harmless flirting she was willing to do.

"Look," he continued. "You seem like exactly the type of woman I'd like to spend more time with. We can just get to know each other. If things keep going as well as they are now, we can *keep* getting to know each other. If anything changes, we just say it. No hard feelings."

Vivienne had not exaggerated in her description of this guy. He was all of the things: successful, good looking, focused. Reasonable. She speared a piece of the grilled octopus they'd ordered, meeting his eyes.

"No hard feelings," she echoed. "I can handle that."

Chapter 21

Lauryn shouldered her parent's front door open with her hip; another paper grocery bag tucked into the crook of her arm. The smell of sawdust and fresh wood stain met her at the threshold and a chorus of power tools screamed from the back of the house. As she ventured further into the house, she noticed movement in the back yard through the far paned windows; men in safety glasses, carrying lumber and saws.

She found her father in the kitchen. Neal stood by the coffee maker in a long sleeve polo and trousers, glasses low on his nose, a James Patterson book open in one hand like he'd been pretending to read for the past hour. His expression was hard as he peered over the magazine.

"Hey, Dad," Lauryn leaned up to kiss him on the cheek, then followed his line of sight toward the dining room. Where a set of sliding doors and her mother's framed Bisa Butler prints had once been, there was now a gaping opening at least fifteen feet across. A team of men in matching blue T-shirts worked in sync, sawing and ripping apart what used to be her parents' back deck. "What is all this?" she asked, half-laughing as another metallic screech sounded.

Neal closed his book with a finger keeping his place. "Your mother and one of her projects again," he said, dryly. "It wasn't enough that the deck needed refinishing. She insisted on replacing it *and* adding French doors to the backyard."

From the dining room, a voice called, "Watch your step!" followed by the thud of lumber. Another whining grind made both of them wince.

"Apparently," Neal went on, "two French doors are not enough. We need four. So, she can-" he lifted his brows and did his best Francine impression, "'bring the outside in.'"

Lauryn breathed out a laugh. *That sounds like Mom.* "You have to admit it's going to be beautiful," she said, glancing back at the opening.

Through the plastic sheeting and green tape, she could see the frame of the new opening and, and beyond that, the blur of her mother's garden, hostas fanning out in the sun, hydrangeas just about to bloom, everything trimmed and waiting for true spring. However, the breeze coming off the lake made it clear spring was still a ways off, spilling sharply through the opening and into the house. Lauryn's skin prickled as the chill threaded through her light coat and cardigan.

"I can imagine it," he said, pouring hot water over the grounds like he was punishing them. "I can also imagine finishing this chapter without a circular saw serenade."

Another shriek and they both winced at the same time. Neal caught her eye and mouthed soundlessly: *Would you like some coffee?*

Lauryn shaped her mouth around a single word. "Tea."

He nodded, turning on the tea kettle. After fixing their steaming cups, they made a retreat into the basement, stepping around a stack of matte black door hardware her mother had probably picked out after five nights of "research."

The basement was warm, quiet and familiar. Her father's office still smelled faintly like cedar and old papers, with a hint of the cologne he wore every day. The walls were covered in framed commendations, a flag in a triangular box, photos of his golf crew and family members Lauryn hadn't met. On one shelf, her graduation smile beamed back at her. On his desk, square and shining in a little silver frame, was a photo she hadn't seen in years.

Lauryn reached for it, her breath catching a little in her chest. In the photo, she was five or six, hair in a high puff, cheeks and forehead glossy, clutching a plastic tea set like it was the crown jewels. Early nineties. The colors had that soft, sun-faded look. She remembered it being pressed into an old photo album with sticky clear pages, the plastic curling up at the corners. Now, it was neatly matted and on prominent display.

"Haven't seen this in a while?" she said.

Her father, seated in his mid-century armchair, looked up from his coffee and smiled. "Found it last week." A soft chuckle rippled from him, "You looked like you owned the whole world."

"I did," she said matter-of-factly, and he laughed a little harder. She remembered that tea set and the gallons of invisible tea she'd served to Addy, her American Girl doll. Just then the ceiling rattled with the heavy thunk of something being set in place overhead.

Neal sighed through his nose, bringing his mug and taking an irritated sip.

"You know you could leave," Lauryn offered, perching on the arm of the leather chair he never let anyone sit in. "Go...run errands or something."

His brow furrowed like didn't know what she meant, then gave himself away with a half shrug. Errands, for him, consisted of visits to the cigar shop where they greeted him by name, his morning swim, the record store where he almost always found something, or nine holes if the weather was kind. "I just don't understand. She's barely speaking to me lately and out of nowhere she insists we need a whole new deck and new doors. It's ridiculous–I don't know who she's doing this for. We're not even here half the year."

It was true, with the exception of this year, her parents were snow-birds, spending the cold months visiting her mother's sister or back traveling in Asia or Europe. Lauryn's mind ticked. First, they hadn't gone to Aunt Mary's for the holidays and now her mother was icing out her father and tearing up the whole house. Something was definitely off between them, but after three months Lauryn hadn't uncovered the cause. Speculating, she turned the picture frame in her hands before asking, "Why isn't she talking to you?"

Her father shrugged, and cut his eyes, "I have no idea. I only get reminder notes from her now. Or emails."

Lauryn nodded at that, laughing inwardly. "Yes, I'm familiar with the emails." She set the little silver frame back exactly where it had been. She looked around, her gaze falling onto her father's bookcases, the top shelves filled with biographies and histories, while the lower shelves were packed with albums–many of them older than she was. "Hey, Dad?"

"Hm?"

"Do you think you could find me a record for someone? Something kinda rare?" Lauryn spoke absentmindedly, crouching to examine the album spines. They hadn't spoken, but she had Perry on her mind and something about her father's vinyl collection had her thinking about their night at the speakeasy. The wall of albums and the way her abs hurt the next day from all the laughing they'd done. She wanted to gift him something, say thank you for her reintroduction to their beloved city. Perhaps smooth things over since the bachelor party. She rolled her eyes, remembering.

"Genre?" her father asked.

"Soul. Chicago based if possible." She stroked the spine of an Otis Redding album.

Neal nodded, "I think I can help with that. When do you need it?"

"Whenever." No telling when she'd see Perry again.

"Alright, I'll keep an eye out." Her father looked toward the stairs like a man considering escape, then back at her. "What'd your mother have you bring anyway?" he asked, clearly remembering the bag.

"Some fancy olive oil and something sweet for you," Lauryn said. "I got a tiramisu cake." She turned the frame in her hand, catching the light.

"That sounds good, but all I really needed was some peace," he said, smiling. "Which apparently has a four-door minimum."

The house vibrated with another long, timely grinding sound. Neal set his coffee mug down, a little less than half of its contents gone. "I'm going to take your advice," he said, rising to his feet. "Tell your mother I'll be back before dinner."

He kissed the top of her head, squeezed her shoulder, and went upstairs, calling out something pleasant and polite toward the construction crew as he passed. Lauryn waited until the garage door went up before setting the little silver frame back exactly where it had been.

She climbed the stairs slowly, her undrunk tea warming her hands, as she whisked through the kitchen and up the second stairwell to the second floor. The master bedroom was empty, the bed tightly made like a hotel, pillows doubled, their cases pressed. She padded down the hall toward the room that used to be hers.

It took her a second. The bones were the same–the window bay, the spot on the wall where she'd tacked up posters–but everything else now looked like a magazine spread. Crisp black-and-cream velvet accents, two-tiered glass side tables with stacks of vintage Condé Nast on the bottom shelves, the spines slightly yellowed with time. She was even more surprised by the leopard print rug beneath her feet, big and unapologetic, anchoring the monochromatic room.

"Mom?" Lauryn called, wondering if she'd missed her.

"Yes?" The answer floated from the walk-in closet, softened by hat boxes and garment bags.

Lauryn found her mother in the walk-in, balanced on the third step of a step stool. Francine wore a black tank dress that looked a lot like something in Lauryn's own closet, her silver silk-pressed hair gleaming and smoothed into a high, ballerina bun. Her arms were defined, honed, like she might drop into a plank at any moment.

She glanced down at Lauryn, "Hi, baby. Reach up here and see if you can pull that red shoe box down for me."

Lauryn set her tea on the dresser nearby and shuffled past her mother, their booties brushing, as Lauryn moved toward the step stool. She stretched, fingers grazing cardboard, the box just an inch out of reach.

"How did you even get this back here?" she asked, her laugh rising into the ceiling.

"It fell when I was rearranging," Francine said, clearly annoyed by gravity. "You sure you can't reach it with your long arms?"

"Mom, we're the same height with the same arm length." Lauryn stepped back down. "Why don't you ask Dad?"

Her mother's mouth flattened, "I'm not asking your father to do anything. Anytime I say something, he acts like I've ruined his entire day."

Lauryn let the comment sit in the air. Her parents had their own tides; she'd learned early on not to wade too far out when she couldn't see the bottom. *So, Dad thinks she's not speaking to him, and Mom thinks he just has an attitude.* She speculated further as another power tool wailed somewhere beneath them. She slid the stool closer, climbed up, and this time the box gave with a dusty sigh.

"Here." She passed it down, careful of the edges.

"Thank you," Francine said, as if Lauryn had performed minor surgery. They spent a few minutes tucking things back into place, zipping one garment bag, smoothing another, a choreography that Lauryn remembered well. They'd shared closet space until she'd gone away to college and her parents bought this house. In the years where her parents lived overseas and Lauryn was minding the family home, she'd had this closet to herself, but now her mother had taken it over.

As they stepped back into the guest room, her mother brushed invisible lint from the duvet. "How's everything else? How's work?"

"It's going well. Busy," Lauryn said. She hesitated, then went for it. "So, Mom, I'm thinking about starting something of my own. A luxury bath line."

Francine's eyes flicked to her, then toward the hallway like she was tracking the contractor. "Well, baby, there are so many already," she said lightly. "You sure you want to start with that much competition?"

The words landed exactly where Lauryn expected them to. She took a breath anyway. "The market is saturated," she admitted, steady as she continued. "But I have ideas for how to differentiate. How to make it feel special and unique.."

They walked toward the stairs together. Saw dust settling in the air, despite the plastic sheeting. Downstairs, Francine floated into the kitchen and paused to watch the progress on her doors.

Lauryn felt herself start to drift, this felt like one of those conversations she might as well have kept to herself. However, her mother spoke again without looking back at her.

"Is it a bath line or a ritual?" Francine asked, eyes on the men fitting the hinges. "If it's a ritual, you'll need a promise. Not lavender because everybody's tired, not cashmere because everybody wants to be soft. What happens to a woman in her body after she uses it? Does she sleep? Does she forgive herself? Does she feel like she got her time back?"

Lauryn blinked. It took her a second to catch up. "I–actually, yeah. I've been thinking about that. Making it about the moment, not just the product. Curating the mix so the scent and the texture and even the way you light the match changes how you feel." Her voice gathered. "I want different kits. Some that smell like...a specific memory or a place. Not generic spa."

Francine hummed, still staring at the doorway. "Then don't launch too many things," she said, almost to herself. "Start with one or two things done perfectly. Your hero products. And start thinking about small sizes. People love something they can throw in their carry-on."

A laugh caught in Lauryn's throat, surprised and a little raw. "Travel sizes would be...really smart," she said. "And unique. A way to keep up with a bath ritual even when away from home." Her mind was already spinning with ideas: concentrated oil, a very fine polish in a secure tin, a coordinated travel bag with zippers that looked like jewelry.

Her mother nodded slowly, the way she did when one of her event decorations came together. Then, like the spell broke, "Marcus!" she called, stepping toward the opening in the dining room wall, "please make sure that paint matches the doors. I don't want mismatched trim!"

"Yes, ma'am," the contractor said, and the men got back to it.

Francine was already leaning into the light, discussing thresholds and moldings, her hand floating through the air to show where she wanted something to land. The conversation with Lauryn was clearly over, as if it had been folded and put away like her clothes in the closet above them.

Lauryn stood in the kitchen for a beat, tea cooling in her mug. She was still surprised by her mother's recommendations. She hadn't been looking for her mother's approval, exactly. Faith, maybe? But interest, genuine interest in something she was trying to build for herself, was something she hadn't expected all. Still, it was nice.

She watched her mother orchestrate. The frame for the new doors was in, and despite the dust and the dismantled deck it did look beautiful. Bringing in the outside, indeed. Her father would grumble, but she could already see him standing out there puffing away at his cigar proudly, while his friends admired the new design.

As she watched, the image of her and Joe's backyard in Memphis flashed in her mind. She thought of the retro kidney bean shaped pool that had convinced them to buy the home. They'd had so many plans for the house, including an outdoor kitchen and a sauna. Out of nowhere she remembered the pool needed a new filtration system and the trees near the back fence needed trimming. There was so much work to do before that yard would look anything remotely close to what her mother had here. Reeling from the memory, Lauryn slapped a hand down onto the counter to steady herself.

What a joke.

That house had been the furthest thing from her mind for months now and that's where it needed to stay. Still, flashes of their lives pressed in, the way they'd bickered in front of contractors, or how a paint color they'd chosen together one day could ignite a fight the next when Joe suddenly decided he hated it. When Lauryn learned Joe had cheated for a second time, it was like the whole house became a symbol of her poor judgement. Every curtain panel and every piece of furniture is a testament to her incredibly poor choice in a partner.

Lauryn took a few steps forward, into the dining room where the table and moved out, away from the construction. The Memphis house was usually a sore spot and would set off a familiar wave of shame. However, today it passed through her mind without landing.

Day by day Lauryn was learning to live with the decisions of her past that had felt like mistakes, assured she would not be making them again. Sooner or later, she and Joe would have to come to an agreement about the house, which she had left without establishing how they would handle the half she'd invested in it. For now, she dismissed the thought. Regret was loosening its hold on her, and in its place, a clear vision of her future self was starting to form. Her job wasn't an end-all-be-all, but her one year contract offered the perfect timeline to march along. Each day she found herself more inspired, lifted by nights out and gym dates with Deonna and the girls, by her mother's unexpected recommendations, and the ordinary moments in between. Even her brief time with Terrance added a lightness where everything with Perry just felt so intense. For once, her past felt smaller than the choices laid out ahead of her.

Finding her mood unshaken, she set her mug of cold tea aside and stepped out into the cool air to join her mother in the garden.

Chapter 22

Lauryn

Lauryn woke slowly, smiling before her eyes were even open. The day stretched ahead of her, bright with possibility. A quick glance at the clock told her there was more than enough time before Vivienne's launch party. Time for a run on the treadmill, a quick trip to the dry cleaners and the carwash. After that she needed to box up Vivienne's gift, a prototype bath kit she could not wait to show her. Before any of that, she needed tea.

She filled the kettle and slid open the balcony door, stepping barefoot onto the concrete, toasty warm from the sun. She shielded her eyes and sank into one of the new chairs she'd dragged found at a home goods store. They were perfect for the space, totally worth the two-hour fight spent wrangling them into her SUV, up the elevator, and through her balcony door because now she had her own little perch in the sky.

The sage bundle from Deonna still sat abandoned in the corner, charred and forgotten. Below her the condominium's shared garden level was vibrant green, breaking up the building's steel and glass facade. She kicked her feet up on the railing, watching traffic stream toward the city, and marveled at how calm she felt.

A table and a few plants were all the balcony needed now. Something for her mother to fuss about besides Joe. Lauryn closed her eyes, imagining evenings with a book and a glass of prosecco, the sunset catching against the skyline. For the first time in a while, her spirit felt settled.

She'd been looking forward to celebrating Vivienne, but she could just as easily stay rooted to the spot, whiling the day away on her own terms.

The tea kettle clicked off and she ventured back inside to fix herself a cup of tea. Deonna was out of town and Lauryn's mother hadn't emailed all week. For once there was plenty of time and she took her time with herself, running down to the gym before diving into a sinful chocolate croissant at a new café near her dry cleaners. Slowly, morning yielded to the afternoon. She had her music up loud as she bathed and set out her outfit. Things were going well. Work was smooth, she was making progress on *Of Scent & Skin,* and she was sleeping better. Less doubt creeping in every day.

She danced in and out of her closet. With no precipitation in sight, she selected a pair of satin shoes, slipping them on before she'd even gotten dressed. Terrance would be at the launch party too and he'd offered to take her out after. Since their first meeting, she'd seen him once more. Spending time with him was low pressure, light enough that she didn't feel like she was getting ahead of herself. After picking her hair out as big as she could, she ventured out, setting Vivienne's gift into the passenger side and speeding south toward Hyde Park, a historical neighborhood nestled between the University of Chicago and the lakefront.

The neighborhood was bustling. There were more shops than she remembered, but a few familiar spots remained. Like the Promontory club, where they'd all gone out after yet another wedding back in the day. The bride and groom had been determined to keep partying after their reception, calling everyone out to the club for an afterset. She remembered having such a good time, sandwiched between friends on the dance floor. Perry had been there that night too. She replayed the memory of him, having quite a bit of luck with the ladies from what she could remember. They'd all been so close back then.

She and Perry hadn't spoken lately, not even a funny reel or meme exchanged since the bachelor party. Lauryn knew she should call him. He hadn't been the one to put up that stupid post at the bachelor party.

The venue, a beautiful gallery space, was wrapped wall to wall in curved windows, letting the afternoon light stream in. Sculpted lawns and a Japanese garden wrapped the exterior of the space and Lauryn found herself drawn in. There were balloon sculptures and signage all decked out in Vivienne's colors. Lauryn recognized the logo projected onto the floor– the same logo at the bottom of every email she received from Vivienne. Unsurprisingly, the decor was absolutely on point and the DJ had already gotten to work.

"Oh, my goodness, Lauryn! Thank you for coming. This hair is fabulous!"

"Thank you. You know I had to come correct."

"Yes ma'am. You understood the assignment! And what is this?"

"Just something fun to say congratulations and thank you," she handed Vivienne the box.

Vivienne pouted for a moment, then reached out to embrace Lauryn. Suddenly she pulled back, "Wait, is this what I think it is, Lauryn?"

"It might be," Lauryn said slyly.

"Oh my god, I cannot wait to get into this!" She hugged Lauryn again. "Plus, after all this planning I'm gon' need some self care."

"Everything looks amazing. You really outdid yourself."

"Isn't it stunning? I've been up for four days straight, blowing up my coordinator about every little thing, but she fuckin' snapped! She literally listened to every single thing I said. Every de-tail. I'll refer you to her when you're ready for your launch."

Lauryn laughed as Vivienne's earring nearly took her eye out. Moving to a safe distance, she said, "I will definitely let you know."

"So, there's warm bites over here. Cold bites this way and my signature cocktails are coming out soon–oh, Toni!" she shouted suddenly as another woman approached. Lauryn took another step back, waving to let Vivienne know she would catch up with her later. "I'll come find you!" Vivienne called over her shoulder.

Lauryn knew she probably wouldn't, if the crowd was any indication. She tried a few hors d'oeuvres. *Oh my god,* she touched her chest. The food was next-level delicious. She tried the salmon dip, but took too big of a bite. The thick dip coated the back of teeth and she was struggling to sweep it off with her tongue.

"Hey there," a voice from beside her.

Surprised, she turned to see Terrance. "Hey!" she mumbled, bringing a hand to her mouth.

He moved in for a hug, "You look incredible, Lauryn. Have you been here long?"

"Not at all. Just saw Viv."

"Yeah, me too. I'm getting the feeling that we're going to be put on display as her current WIPs."

"It's very possible."

"Dragon Fruit margarita?" A waiter paused near them, lowering a gold tray of pink drinks. Grateful to have something to wash the dip down with, Lauryn took a glass. Terrance chose the aptly named "Moore Mule" and they moved into the next room. They spotted the DJ, a beautiful petite woman in a black halter dress. Despite her girly-girl aesthetic, she swayed, dancing hard over her turntables.

Her energy was infectious; soon Lauryn was bobbing her head too. Terrance touched her arm gently, "I made reservations, if you're still free after?"

She paused, taking a moment to find the words. The truth was, she was enjoying his company, but she wasn't eager to jump into any routine dates. She'd been careful not to lead him on.

He turned to her then, tracing his free hand down her arm. "I'm really enjoying getting to know you."

Although she appreciated that he felt that way, there was no way she was prepared for the conversation he wanted to have. She pressed her hand into his gently, "Hold that thought?"

Lauryn excused herself, heading past the DJ and making a beeline for the ladies room. It was fragrant with eucalyptus and she approached the vanity slowly, eyeing her reflection with a raised brow. "Well, that escalated quickly," she said aloud and popped open her bag to fish out her phone.

Terrance just needed a few moments to simmer down and she could return without having to actually respond to the question he hadn't actually asked, but was clearly hanging in the air. After a few minutes of fixing her lipstick after the dip debacle, she made her way back out.

Somehow in the few minutes she'd been hiding in the bathroom, the party had swelled. She cautiously made her way back to the gallery where she'd left Terrance. As she navigated through the crowd, she spotted a familiar face.

Perry was crossing the room, his long legs carrying him in confident strides through the crowd. Something fluttered in her stomach and she wished she'd messaged him when she thought of him earlier. She wondered what he was doing there. The whole night she hadn't seen many of their mutual friends. In fact, the only other person she knew besides Terrance was Vivienne.

She joined Terrance, but kept her eyes on Perry.

"You alright?" Terrance asked.

"Yes," she smiled up at him in a practiced smile, one that she'd used on Joe many times. "All good."

At that moment, the music softened and the DJ spoke into the microphone. In a soft voice and accent, she announced, *"Ladies and gentlemen, can I have your attention for a moment?"*

"Tonight, we're celebrating a bold new chapter for someone who has helped so many shine. She's a creative powerhouse, a branding visionary, and now officially stepping into her own spotlight as an independent branding coach. Please join me in welcoming the incredible Vivienne Moore!"

The room erupted in applause as Vivienne took center stage where the gallery halls met in front of the windows. "Thank you, Mischa!" Vivienne had a wide smile on her face as she waved to the DJ. "Misha was one of my first clients. Make sure you all follow her socials and book her for your next event."

Everyone laughed. "Always plugging!" a few people around them teased.

"You know I have to take care of my people!" Vivienne responded, smoothing her dress. "Oh, my goodness, look at all of you–you actually came! I mean, I knew you would, but seeing your beautiful faces here tonight fills my heart more than I can say. Truly, it means the world."

Lauryn could feel Vivienne's joy from where she stood, and beamed as she thanked the curator, the catering company, and plugged a few other businesses for the flowers and decorations. "OK, ok everyone, if you don't have a cocktail, now is the time. As it is the golden hour, the staff will be coming around with one of our featured cocktails, the Golden Hour Spritz!"

The crowd shifted as more servers weaved through with their golden trays, topped with fizzing flutes. Without realizing it, she scanned the crowd for Perry, but couldn't find him. Terrance handed her a Golden Hour Spritz. "Madam."

"Thank you," she smiled, shifting her focus back to Vivienne's speech.

"To my clients–past, present, and future–you are the reason I do what I do. Watching your visions come to life has been an honor. To my friends and family, thank you for tolerating my, ehem, strong opinions and endless brainstorming sessions."

At that moment, she spotted Perry just a few feet away from where Vivienne spoke. He stood alone, arms crossed, but a smile reaching his eyes. He looked *proud* watching Vivienne. It was clear they knew each other well. *Is he a client too?* She wracked her brain trying to remember if he'd ever mentioned anything about it.

"So, let's raise a glass to bold moves, big dreams, and surrounding yourself with people who uplift and inspire you. I could not do this without you all. Cheers, my loves!" Vivienne raised her own champagne flute, before adding, "Twerk somethin', Mischa!"

The music came crashing back in, louder than it had been before with everyone's praise and applause. The crowd surged around Vivienne, pushing to wish her congratulations and take pictures. Terrance turned to look back at her over his shoulder, "Want to get a shot with the belle of the ball?"

"Let's!" She followed, but kept scanning for Perry. In all the commotion, she'd lost him again. And she was about to lose Terrance, if she didn't keep up. They'd nearly reached the stage and he turned back for her, touching her elbow lightly to guide her forward. As they approached, the crowd around Vivienne thinned. The videographer stepped out of the way and there was Perry again, standing next to Vivienne, his arm around her waist as they posed for a picture.

And then Vivienne kissed him.

Dumbfounded, Lauryn watched as Vivienne's full lips pressed into Perry's. She pulled back, looking coyishly up at Perry, whose expression was tight, like the sudden public display had surprised him. Vivienne stroked his face and as she leaned in for another kiss, Lauryn turned away.

"The fuck," she mouthed, trying to process what she'd just seen. So, they *really* knew each other. That kiss had been slow and familiar.

"Lauryn, love!" Vivienne suddenly called from behind her.

Lauryn made an effort to fix her expression before turning back around. "Great speech!"

"Thank you, I wrote it this morning while they were curling this wig." She stepped forward and pressed a kiss on Lauryn's cheek. "So glad you're here. And with Mr. Boyd!"

Of course, she'd had to say "*with*". The last thing Terrance needed was encouragement. The two of them hugged and started catching up, standing directly between Lauryn and Perry. Through their chatter, she met his eyes. It was clear he was just as surprised to see her as she was to see him. He lifted his glass to take a sip, his expression giving nothing else away. "Oh, my god, I'm being rude. Terrance, Lauryn, this is Perry Mitchell. Perry, these are two of my favorite clients, Terrance Boyd and Lauryn Lindsey."

Terrance held his hand out to shake up with Perry. "Hey. How you doin', man?"

"Nice to meet you." Lauryn watched as the two men pulled back from one another and Perry turned his attention back on her. A prickle of heat started behind her ears, but she let him take the lead, watching until he spoke again. "Hey, Lauryn. Good to see you."

She was just about speechless.

"Y'all know each other?" Vivienne exclaimed, delighted by the coincidence.

"We do. We went to college together," Perry supplied, smiling.

Lauryn still hadn't found the words and barely managed to say, "We did!"

Perry looked from Vivienne to Lauryn, "How do you two know each other?"

"My old job," Vivienne laughed. "Lauryn's one of the new directors and truthfully the last good thing to come out of that gig."

Perry nodded slowly and smiled as if it was all making sense now.

"Small world. Shit, I love this party," Vivienne cooed, downing the contents of her glass. Being on her third signature cocktail, she didn't seem to notice the tension. However, Terrance was observing the three of them, a mix of wonder and amusement in his eyes.

"How have you been?" Perry asked earnestly, breaking the tension.

He looked right past Vivienne and Terrance, holding Lauryn's gaze. She chewed the inside of her cheek, fighting the urge to roll her eyes. He knew exactly how she was doing; they'd only been hanging out every couple of weeks since she'd moved back into town! They'd practically just seen each other.

"I'm well. And how have you been doing?"

"Things are good. Work, getting ready for this bachelor trip, you know?"

Lauryn chanced a glance over at Vivienne, who was swaying to Misha's mix. She didn't seem to be catching onto the recentness of their familiarity, and even though nothing had happened between Lauryn and Perry, she felt like they'd been found out. Rather, like *she* had been found out. Her mind drifted back to when she'd been fantasizing about Perry just a few weeks before. And when she'd invited him in for a night cap all those months ago! Lauryn cringed inwardly, wishing the ground would just open up and swallow her whole.

"Wait, bachelor party-," Terrance looked back and forth from Perry to Vivienne. "Are you two gettin' married?"

Vivienne was in the middle of detaching herself from their quartet, but whipped her head around. "Me and Perry? No, no, no. We are not engaged." She wasted no time setting the record straight and only paused long enough to give Perry a look.

Lauryn watched his jaw visibly tighten, but he said nothing as Vivienne floated away to greet another group of friends. Suddenly, Lauryn recalled some of Vivienne's comments. The casual manner she'd spoken about her "as needed" situation.

As she connected the dots, Lauryn's heart went out to Perry. Did he know? Or was Vivienne playing him? And although she did feel for him, part of her wondered why the hell he had never mentioned he was seeing someone. *What exactly is Perry on?* Perhaps there was a reason why Vivienne was being so indifferent with him and quote, "keeping her options open".

Terrance caught her eye, eased closer. "Lauryn-"

However, Lauryn could see Perry making his way over. "Terrance, I think I see them bringing out more of that grilled shrimp you wanted."

"Oh yeah? Would you like me to bring you some too?"

"Oh, yes, please. Thank you," she smiled dreamily at him, and squeezed his arm as he headed toward the food tables. She watched until he was a good distance from them, thinking how grateful she was that he was here.

No sooner had Terrance stepped away, Perry reached her. "Hey, Lauryn-"

She cut him off before he could say whatever it was he was about to say. "You didn't tell me." There was no bite in her voice, but her words came steady and firm.

He shook his head, taking a step closer to her, "This isn't that."

"Perry we've been galivanting all over this city since January. Hanging out all kinds of hours. You just forgot to mention your girlfriend?" Lauryn arched an eyebrow.

"Lauryn-

"And how is that normal? We've spent hours talking. And not once did you say anything.."

"I don't remember you mentioning ole' boy, but yet he's here fetching you shrimp."

Narrowing her eyes and tilting her head. "Seriously? Not even the same thing. I've known him for five minutes. However, you managed to never mention Vivienne, who you've been with for how long?"

Perry met her eyes, his voice dropping low when he asked, "Would it have made a difference?"

She opened her mouth, then hesitated. She couldn't answer without revealing herself. Lauryn had been carrying it quietly for weeks–the way he stayed on her mind, the way her here heart lifted whenever he messaged, and the steadiness in his eyes as he listened to her ramble.

Even so she could not admit something to him she was barely ready to admit to herself. Lauryn inhaled and stood a little taller, "I would've known how to conduct myself."

He just watched her, his gaze still searching. "Lauryn, we're not together. We did date, but that was two years ago. We... stand in for one another when-"

"As needed," She finished for him.

"Yeah, you could say that. Look Lauryn-"

"It's fine," She interrupted, shaking her head and forcing a smile. "And it's Vivienne's night. We should be celebrating her."

Perry's dark eyes flashed, as if he wanted to challenge the way she'd dismissed his explanation. He sipped his drink instead, "Yeah, we should."

Lauryn looked back over her shoulder, hoping to catch a glimpse of Terrance. "I'm gonna get some shrimp. Because it was *fire*. You should find Vivienne."

Her voice was even, but the weight of the words settled between them.

Then, before he could respond, she turned and walked away, disappearing into the crowd without looking back.

Chapter 23

Perry

P erry eased the car to a stop in front of Vivienne's building, the late-night quiet of the block settling around them. Streetlights spilled a pale amber glow across the hood, catching the faint smile on her face as she dug in her purse for her keys.

"That is so crazy," Vivienne said, leaning back against the seat with a content sigh.

Perry glanced over, brow lifted. "What's crazy?"

"That you and Lauryn know each other. Six degrees of separation is real in this city."

He kept his eyes forward, speaking softly. "Yeah, we go way back."

She turned toward him, curious. "Was she the same in undergrad? She's been a tough one for me to crack–she's so private."

Perry let a beat pass, deciding how much to give her. Vivienne was still tipsy, but he was ninety-nine percent sure she was genuinely curious about their mutual acquaintance. "Lauryn was always cool."

"She is!" Vivienne agreed quickly, her words carrying a little too much volume for the quiet street. "I mean I get it. Apparently her guy really put her through it."

Perry kept his expression neutral, though his mind pulled back to Lauryn moving to a whole other state with Joe, and without so much as a text message. And here she was, feeling some kind of way because he hadn't shared his dating history.

He shifted the car into park and glanced at Vivienne. "So, you want to tell me what that kiss was about?"

Her brow arched, a sly smile tugging at her lips. "What do you mean?"

He studied her for a moment. "You know what I mean. Why the stunt? We're not in a relationship anymore."

Vivienne gave a light laugh, brushing him off with a flick of her hand. "Please. I was just having fun."

"At my expense," he added, watching her sober up a little when he said it. "I know we had a certain dynamic for a while, but we discussed this. We're not there anymore—"

She sat quietly, her lips pursing as he spoke. Then, in a flourish, she gathered her things and turned to open the passenger door. "Oh my god, I'm so glad that shit is over," she announced, hopping out onto the sidewalk, effectively ignoring what he was trying to say.

Exasperated, he got out to walk her to her door. This probably wasn't the best time to have the conversation he wanted to have, but based on the day's events, namely her kissing him in front of a room full of people and cameras, it was overdue. "You mean your party?"

"Yes! Don't get me wrong, it was amazing. Everything came together so well, but I don't need that kinda stress again for a while." She checked her phone once more before slipping it into her purse, the building's lobby light catching on her jewelry as she moved toward the entrance.

Perry followed her inside, waiting as she unlocked her apartment door and flicked on the light. She kicked off her heels, letting each one clatter to the hardwood. Barefoot, her petite frame seemed even smaller. Gripping the door frame, she leaned into the hall towards him, striking the pose of a siren at the bow of a ship, casting out a line she had to know he wouldn't take. "Thank you so much for being there today. And the ride home."

He nodded, "Today was a big day. You made it happen. I'm proud of you."

She lingered, eyeing him curiously, interpreting his words perfectly. *Today was a big day for you. You made the impression you wanted to make. This is done.* "Perry I'm so—"

"Make sure you drink some water before you go to bed, alright?" He advised, gently interrupting. He didn't want her apologies. He wanted her understanding. What happened at the party couldn't happen again. And worst of all because Lauryn, of all people, had been right there to see it. "Goodnight."

Disappointed, she lifted her hand in a small wave and slowly closed the door. He started back down the hall, listened until the deadbolt turned before heading back out into the night, eager for a quiet drive home.

Less than an hour later, he was home, freshly showered and stretched out on his king size bed. The house was quiet, save for the fan circling overhead. It had been a very long day. He unlocked his phone, scrolling past pending messages to get to the text thread with Lauryn.

He could message her, try to explain again that there was nothing going on between him and Vivienne, hadn't been for months. And that *display* she'd put on in front of everyone today had been just that. Still, Lauryn hadn't been trying to hear it.

He noted the dates of their last messages. The last one, from her, after she'd met him at the Gwen. After that mess at Ricki's bachelor party. After chasing Lauryn to the elevator, he'd come back to find a couple of the guys laughing about it, like it was funniest fucking thing in the world. Perry had checked the hell out of Ricki's cousin, damn near snatching the phone out of the fool's hand and tossing it off the roof.

Perry slept soundly for a few hours, so deeply he barely remembered dreaming, but awoke before sunrise unable to fall back to sleep. He lay in bed, mulling over the previous day's events and the presentation he needed to finish before Monday. In the morning silence, he tried to work out how the world was so damn small that the *girl that got away* worked at the same place as his... past entanglement.

With his hands clasped behind his head, he replayed his conversations with Lauryn. Without even closing his eyes, he remembered her face, her smile, the shape of her walking ahead of him, and her infectious laughter as they leaned in over their drinks, cracking jokes and retelling decade-old secrets. Save for the one secret about him and Vivienne, which really wasn't a secret at all.

From the moment he'd laid eyes on Lauryn at the holiday party, he'd been inventing ways to see her again. Seeing her that night set off a bomb inside of him, blowing open doors he'd shut long ago. It barely felt real, having her back in his life. Whatever reservations he might still have from Lauryn leaving all those years ago, he'd still allowed himself to indulge. For the first time in a while, he wasn't just looking forward to his next assignment at work or the next country to visit. Instead, he was looking forward to her. The way she overthought every damn thing and still managed to move him without trying. There was something about her energy, so unruly, honest, and beautiful that it drew him in every time.

He could lose himself in it.

The slightest blue light seeped through the curtains, gradually unveiling more of his bedroom as the hours ticked by. Perry shifted under the sheets. That night after the speakeasy, when she'd invited him in, there had been a restrained, yet undeniable gratification as he registered the irony and let himself feel the quiet satisfaction of it. He was ashamed to admit, but it had felt like a small win. Proof he wasn't the love-sick nice guy she'd left in that hotel room.

Then he remembered clearly how tempted he'd been to cross that threshold, follow her right back down Nice Guy Lane. Nearly two decades had passed and that girl still had him transfixed. The more of her he'd seen, the more he wanted.

Perry flung the sheets off, the fabric practically cracking as it fell back in a wave as he rose from the bed. He tugged open his dresser drawers, plucking out a pair of shorts and socks. As he dressed, he tried to clear his mind. He wasn't used to this, one woman preoccupying his thoughts to the point where he had to get up and do something about it.

After the pandemic, it was easier to just keep working out at home. Slowly but surely, he was fixing up the basement, starting with the gym equipment, now painting and eventually he'd put in a wet bar. Downstairs, he pushed past the plastic sheeting that was supposed to be protecting all of the weight machines from drywall and paint debris.

With every weight he lifted, her face was still there. The set of her mouth, the blaze in those dark eyes when she'd cut him off, saying, *"You didn't tell me"*.

The words rang louder than the clank of the weights. His shoulders flexed, sweat running in slow lines down the center of his back, but the sting of her words stuck, burrowing deeper with each rep. He dropped to the mat, palms spread wide against the concrete as his body moved through pushups, chest brushing close to the floor with each controlled descent. His shoulders broadened and contracted, each push burning a little more than the last.

How the hell could she question him about anything when she'd shown up with someone? After swearing up and down she was taking time for herself. He speculated on how she could be so upset, lost in thought until his sister's voice cut through.

She'd been calling his name, but the music in his headphones drowned her out. Through the exposed wall studs of the stairwell, he caught her frowning, arms crossed as she waited for him to tug the headphones back. "Hey, good morning. Did you just get here?"

"Good morning to you too, damn." She was clearly annoyed that she had to come all the way downstairs to get his attention. "And no, I've been here. I messaged to let you know I was spending the night."

Perry's brows furrowed. He hadn't even realized. "Simone…"

He wanted to tell her she should've called to make sure, especially when she hadn't heard back. Fortunately, he'd been alone last night. Up all night. But alone.

"Never mind. You staying for breakfast?" he asked, just because.

"No, I'm headed to Milwaukee for the concert, remember? What are you doing today?"

Perry nodded, setting up for his next set. "Meeting the guys at the course."

Simone nodded right back, unimpressed, "Mm. Black Excellence Saturday? OK, well, I guess I won't see you." She was already turning on her heel to head back up the stairs.

Perry called after her, "Let me know when you get there. And be safe!"

"You too," she practically sang it as she disappeared up the steps.

Perry finished working out, showered, and made himself a quick bite before grabbing his clubs and setting off for the golf course. Most of the guys were already there when he arrived and they piled into two golf carts to head out onto the green.

The morning air was cool, but with that hint of the heat to come as Perry adjusted his stance at the tee box. The sun cast a golden hue over the course, but his friends were already wide awake, cracking jokes between lazy stretches and practice swings.

"Can we all just take a moment?" Rashad called out, a grin spreading on his face as he lifted his coffee in a mock toast. "In a few months, our boy Ricky will officially be a married man."

The group cheered in unison, crowding in to congratulate him, a mix of teasing and genuine disbelief.

"Man, I'm so glad the proposal is over. Brittney is impossible to surprise. Me and her sisters had to pull off all kinds of shit to keep her in the dark." Ricky rolled his shoulders and took another practice swing.

"And when you look back on it, you'll remember how geeked you were to sign away your bachelorhood." Rashad clapped him on the shoulder.

"Y'all act like I'm about to be sentenced instead of getting married."

"Same thing," Amon muttered under his breath, earning a round of laughter.

Perry smirked, but remained quiet, rolling a golf ball between his fingers before bending to set it on the tee. Normally, he'd be right there with the guys, getting a wise-crack in, but his mind was elsewhere. He was stuck on Lauryn and it was beginning to annoy him.

"Perry, man, you hitting that ball today or just staring at it?" Amon called out, pulling Perry from his thoughts.

Perry cracked a smile, shaking his head and adjusting his grip. "Just waiting for you to stop running your mouth long enough to observe some skill," he teased before taking a swing. The satisfying crack of the driver meeting the ball sent it soaring down the fairway. Not bad, but not his best.

"Nice shot," Ricky leaned a little, watching until the ball touched down again. "A little tight, though."

"Like your wedding budget 'bout to be?" Rashad shot back.

The group sounded off again in peals of laughter, but Perry was already lost back in his thoughts. Seeing Lauryn standing there next to Vivienne, her expression unreadable, had unsettled him. Had she really thought he was the type of man to keep a relationship under wraps? He was also intrigued. Lauryn had walked away without answering his question. Had he told her, would it have made a difference?

"Alright, let's go, *Romeo*," Rashad nudged him as they walked to the next hole. "You zoning out like that, has to be woman trouble."

Perry scoffed. "You got jokes this morning."

"Always," Rashad grinned. "But seriously—you good?"

Perry glanced at his phone one last time before slipping it back into his pocket. "Yeah," he said, more to himself than to Rashad. "I'm good, man."

Rashad side-eyed him but let it go, and Perry was grateful. The last thing he needed was to give the guys any ammunition. They'd have a field day if they knew he was thrown off his game over Lauryn. They'd surely be asking how he hadn't learned his lesson the first time.

She hadn't been interested then, but now she seemed... bothered? Perry exhaled sharply, giving his head a small shake before gripping his club again. He needed to focus on the game, on anything other than Lauryn. At least for as long as his mind would let him.

Rashad's voice cut through his thoughts. "You going to Sam's birthday party at the end of the month? That nigga invited everybody."

Perry's grip tightened around his club as the wheels in his mind started turning. Sam Amsley was another mutual friend of theirs from college, an exceptionally likeable who knew just about everyone in their graduation class. Everyone included Ricky; and if Ricky was going, his fiancée Brittney would most definitely be there. Perry considered this; if Brittney was there, chances were high he'd run into a certain woman who was currently ignoring him.

Lining up his shot, he took his time. "Yeah," he said, setting his stance. "I might slide through."

With a smooth, powerful swing, his 4-iron connected with another sharp *crack*, and the ball sailed down the fairway.

Chapter 24

Perry

Perry left town with the guys that following week, flying out to the Dominican Republic for Ricky's official bachelor party. Four days of carefully orchestrated debauchery that would remain a secret until their dying days. There'd been plenty of golf and scuba diving to keep them out of any real trouble. The hotel, with its immaculate grounds and glistening pools, had been a much-needed respite after Perry's spring travel schedule. The wildlife and beaches were something he was looking forward to seeing again very soon.

Still, none of it kept him from looking forward to tonight. He'd arrived at Pilsen Yards, a bar on Chicago's lower west side, for another one of their alumni, Sam Amsley's, birthday party.

In the last few years, Perry had taken a step back from some of the gatherings. There were just too many birthdays, fundraisers, and bar-beques to keep up with. His friend circle from college was tight, even after a decade and a half since they'd all met. After graduation, they all stayed close, meeting for parties and long nights at the club. Although their preferred scene was a little different now, they were still one mob, constantly revolving around each other. Expanding and contracting, as people moved away and came back.

Even with their busy lives and family challenges, someone was always there to reach out or roll out the welcome mat for an impromptu get-to-gether.

As Perry inched his way inside the crowded bar, he thought about the pandemic. The shelter-in-place order had done nothing to slow things down. Leave it to Rashad to use Zoom for a virtual game night. Every Thursday, for nearly two months Perry had logged on for spades or battle of the sexes. And although most game nights ended in full-on roast sessions, it'd been amazing to see all the faces that popped up on the screen. All that laughter and reminiscing carried them through such a bizarre and humbling time.

He grinned, thinking about it.

But one face in particular hadn't appeared on those game nights. The one he was glimpsing right now through another sea of swaying bodies. Lauryn was dead center, seated with Deonna amongst the core members of their shared friend group, on dark chesterfield couches, a massive portrait of James Baldwin lit up behind them.

Cross-legged, Lauryn leaned into the conversation, laughing as Sam held court. Swathed in a strapless denim jumpsuit, shoulders and arms out, she seemed to be far more relaxed than the last time he'd seen her.

She was glowing.

Perry pulled his gaze away, turning into the crowd and following the current of people towards the bar. The place was packed shoulder to shoulder, the low thump of bass rattling the glassware while bartenders hustled to keep up.

He was ordering his drink, when a booming voice sounded from over his shoulder. "Man, the baddie in the jumpsuit can get this work."

Perry leaned back, only to find Rashad standing over his shoulder grinning. He shook his head, "Don't start."

Rashad laughed, clapping his hands together. "Ah, so I hit a nerve! You seem to be a little sensitive about a certain young lady."

"I have no idea what you mean, friend," Perry replied, tone light, playing innocent.

"Mm-hmm." Rashad smirked. "Then why you jump just now, like you saw a ghost?"

"Maybe I'm just wondering why you're so close to me?"

"Naw man, you seem a little distracted," Rashad diagnosed, amusement in his eyes. "You got that far off, contemplative look about you." Rashad leaned in, lowering his voice. "You gonna say something to her, or you gonna keep dropping the ball like you used to do on campus?"

Perry cut him a glance. "Damn, man, you keep whispering your hot ass breath in my ear. Don't worry about me."

Rashad grinned, satisfied. "Alright, alright. Just don't wait another decade, my guy." He raised his glass to Perry before disappearing back inside, leaving Perry shaking his head.

Perry exhaled, leaning an elbow onto the bar, scanning the crowd again. He wasn't about to give Rashad the satisfaction of knowing he was right, but the truth was undeniable. He had fumbled things with her in the past. Perhaps that's why it'd been so easy for her to leave. Still, something about her reaction to Vivienne was telling and tonight he planned to test his theory.

The bartender set his drink in front of him, the heavy glass catching the light. He wrapped his hand around it just as the crowd shifted. The bodies parted in just the right way, and there she was, headed in his direction with a few other ladies.

He could see the full line of her now, the indigo denim hugging her waistline beautifully. But those hips–those hips were something else. Her hair, freshly done in thick shining box braids, exposed the elegant line of her neck and swung behind her temptingly as she walked. She startled when her gaze landed on him, smoky eyes locking with his.

She slowed, wary. "Hey Perry, what's up?"

He shifted his glass in his hand, studying her face. "How are you doing? Having a good time?"

"We are. Just said hi to the birthday boy and we're waiting on our food. You?"

"Just got here not too long ago. Haven't had a chance to say hi to Sam yet." Lauryn nodded, looking everywhere but at Perry. A pause, and he let it hang there for a beat before his mouth curved into a half smile. "You look thrilled to see me."

Lauryn gave a short laugh, "I don't know what you want me to say." Her words weren't flippant, just weary, like she'd been afraid he might ask for more than she was ready to give.

"Maybe just clear something up for me?" His voice was even, but he pressed her with his gaze.

Her brows drew together the slightest bit, "Okay."

"You still seem... upset since the last time I saw you."

Lauryn sighed, "Perry, I just really wish you'd told me you were seeing someone. It's perfectly reasonable that you might be seeing someone."

"See that's just it. I tried to tell you, there's nothing going on between me and Vivienne. She'll tell you the same. We stopped talking *like that* before you even moved back home. I was only there to support her and her launch. She caught me off guard with that kiss. I don't know what she was trying to prove. She had an audience I guess."

"You didn't stop her."

"What should I have done? Embarrass her in front of a room full of her people?" He lifted his chin to watch her for a moment, resisting a sudden urge to smile. "Why are you upset about this?" She didn't immediately respond, just kept avoiding his eyes. Perry dropped his head towards her, pressing her with his proximity. He wanted to hear her say it. "*Are* you upset about this?"

"No! Viv has become a good friend, and I just wouldn't want anything to be misconstrued or for her to hear anything out of context."

"Hear *what* out of context, exactly?" his tone lifted with playful interest. He wanted to hear this explanation.

"I don't know, just..."

"Lauryn, is there something that you think happened between us? Or might it happen?" *Something you want to happen?* He thought to himself, watching her lips part to form an objection. When she said nothing, Perry smirked. "We should dance."

A half objection, "I'm not dancing with you."

"Oh, so we're still not cool?"

She tilted her head, lips curving as her tone dipped lower, "I wasn't aware we'd stopped being cool."

Perry stood straight, towering over her again. "I don't know man, you not returning GIFs-"

"Oh, you cannot be serious!" her face brightened in a wide smile as she laughed at him.

He finished his drink, "Left a boy hanging. Once again."

"Wow! Says the man who left me in the dark! Do you know how awkward it was standing there with you and Vivienne, trying to pretend I didn't already know you?"

Perry pulled out his wallet to pay the bartender, he turned and caught her elbow, "Let's dance."

He moved them through the crowd quickly, before she could say anything. The song was all too familiar, and all he could think about was how badly he'd wanted to dance with her to it their senior year of college. Tonight, he would take the opportunity to pull her in close. He led her away from the bar before turning to face her. Playfully, he mouthed the words as he started to dance. He held her gaze, daring her to join him, and he slid a hand around her waist. She eyed him, her expression giving nothing away. Just as he was worrying she might not let go of this Vivienne mix-up, she started singing the chorus with the rest of the crowd, "...In this club!"

She started to move to the music, closing the gap between them. Her perfume was something warm and floral, layered with spice. It clung to her skin, stirred with every sway of her hips. The music pulsed through the room, thick and low, and Perry found himself matching its rhythm as he pulled her just a little closer.

She felt so good in his arms and he noted the denim between him and her perfect shape. He nestled in close to her ear as she moved expertly against him. All apprehension from their earlier discussion seemed to have faded and he traced the length of her arm as the song changed. When she turned his lips accidently grazed her ear lobe, where a delicate hoop of gold dangled down to her shoulder. He barely resisted the urge to kiss her there, the soft skin beneath her ear beckoning.

It felt like the last several years hadn't happened and he was twenty-four again, walking down Wacker Drive with the girl of his dreams. He remembered the feel of her that night, her figure in silhouette before the hotel room windows as she gazed out at the lake. The memory faded as the last verse of Usher's *Good Kisser sounded*.

Lauryn slowed their dancing, her body stiffening before she turned in his arms. With a breathless smile, she pulled back from him. "I'm gonna head back to the girls. They're probably wondering where I am,"

Perry's heartbeat stumbled at the shift, though part of him had seen it coming. She was in her head again. He could tell by the way she gripped his arms, holding him at bay like she was afraid of what might happen if they got any closer. He watched the joy cloud over in her eyes.

"Okay," he accepted, watching her closely. His eyes traced the curve of her neck again. He could still feel the heat from her, could still taste the tension hanging between them like a promise.

Lauryn looked at him, her lips parting like she was about to say something more, but swallowed her words. "I'll see you later," she said softly, something about her tone telling him she wouldn't.

Perry stood there, in the winding crowd, watching her retreat. There was definitely something going on there and he smirked a little, realizing it. He could feel it in the way she'd moved with him and how she'd retreated just now.

Shaking his head, he couldn't believe how long it had taken them to get to this point. Always something between them, always jumping a step back just when things started getting real. His desire for Lauryn was equally matched by his growing frustration with her.

The night felt unfinished, like they were on the edge of something that could go either way. She'd basically left him hanging in the middle of the dance floor, echoing the way she'd slipped out of bed and left his hotel room so long ago. Though, he wasn't angry that she was walking away from him again now. After all this time, Lauryn Lindsey had finally revealed her hand.

Something was shifting between the two of them and Perry knew it was more than just a little nostalgia getting the better of them.

Chapter 25

Lauryn

The light was changing. That late spring brightness lingered just a little longer than expected, stretching golden rays across the tops of trees and the garden beds Lauryn had just finished tending. The clouds above were restless, shifting quickly, but the breeze was steady and cool against her skin, despite the warmth the sun had left behind.

Summer hadn't arrived yet, but it was close enough to taste.

When her mother asked if she could help with the garden, Lauryn said yes without hesitation. She hadn't cared what needed doing–pulling weeds, hauling bags of soil, pruning roses. Manual labor was better than being inside her own head. Anything was better than thinking about that stunt Perry pulled the other night.

She had a week's worth of work she needed to catch up on, deadlines approaching fast, but she already knew if she stayed home she wouldn't do a damn thing. Her focus was shot. Her thoughts too loud. Her body too restless.

So, she'd sped over to her folks' place and allowed her mother to delegate one task after another. It felt like old times–her mother directing, Lauryn falling right in step, the rhythm between them easy and familiar.

And now, hours later, Lauryn sat back against the rod iron garden bench, breathing in the clean, damp scent of earth and flowers. Her arms ached in that satisfying way that came from effort, her gloves still streaked with soil.

Across from her, her mother sat with a glass of iced tea, her gloved fingers tapping lightly against the side of the cup as Frankie Beverly's voice floated out through the kitchen windows.

For once, Lauryn felt like they were in a good place, able to just exist in the same space without tension stretching between them. She'd helped plant the Annabelle hydrangeas her mother wanted, gotten the garden beds in order, and now they were finally here. Talking.

Francine took a slow sip of her tea, then looked at her over the rim of her cup. "So, what happened, baby? You two had such a beautiful thing going."

Apparently her mother wasn't going to waste any time tip-toeing around and Lauryn knew exactly who she was talking about.

She exhaled, weary of the subject already and wiped the dirt from her hands. "It was beautiful, until it wasn't, Mom. Beautiful, intense, and exhausting. Always managing him, his moods, his pride."

"Relationships are work, Lauryn Michelle." Francine's mouth set in a firm line, her expression tightening as she looked away. "Especially marriage."

Lauryn started to remind her mother that Joe had never actually asked her to marry him. Instead, he spoke in hypotheticals–sweet ideas that once distracted her from the fact that nothing was changing. Imagery that kept her hopeful, but amounted to nothing in the end. However, something about her mother's tone just now gave her pause.

"I was *willing* to do the work. I mean, I knew what I was getting myself into. The type of life we would have with his career, but when someone keeps twisting things on you, making you doubt what you saw, what you felt, it chips away at you. I kept feeling like I was redrawing my boundaries, giving up more and more each time. I forgave him so many times, Mom..." She trailed off with a wry laugh.

Francine's mouth set in a firm line, her expression tightening. She didn't say anything right away, just let out a slow breath, shaking her head. "Hm. I hate to hear that," she said softly. "Why'd you stay, baby?"

Lauryn shrugged. "Every time I got close to leaving before, he'd ... change. Be the best version of himself for a while. I tried too. Things would get better, but they wouldn't last. It got old."

"Mm. That's what people like him do, baby. They give you just enough to keep you hoping. But you found your way out, and that's what matters.

Lauryn stared at her, stunned. She'd expected deflection, for her mother to suggest she must have done something to push him away. But there was no blaming, no dismissal. Just understanding.

She had not expected that. Recovering, Lauryn stepped closer to her mother. "Okay, so you got your tea. Now let me get mine." She set her cup down carefully. "What's going on with you and Dad?"

Francine tilted her head. "Nothing. What do you mean?"

Lauryn raised an eyebrow, unconvinced, and set down the small shovel she'd been using. "You two have been weird since I touched back down in Illinois. You're almost never in the same room together. Every time I turn around, you're headed somewhere–some event, some trip. And never with Dad anymore. He's discombobulated as hell without you, but won't admit it, and ..." she hesitated. "Alicia called me."

Francine's lips pursed. "This is not a conversation I'm trying to have with my daughter."

Lauryn scoffed. "Are you kidding? Who else are you going to have it with?" She tossed the shovel onto the dirt. "Mom, just tell me."

Francine's gaze flickered to the house for a moment and she exhaled. "Thirty-seven years we've been married, and I come home to hear that woman's voice on my voicemail?"

Lauryn frowned. "What woman?"

Francine's eyes met hers. "Pat. Alicia's mother."

Lauryn blinked. "Oh. She called you?"

Francine's jaw tensed. "Yes, she did. Called my house, speaking directly to your father on the voice message, like I don't live here."

Lauryn shifted uncomfortably. "Well, Mom, you know she's been very ill."

"Yes, yes, I know that! And it's awful. She's always been so healthy and active. I just don't understand how cancer gets people like that." Her voice softened for just a second before she straightened. "Even so, it was odd coming in and hearing that message on the machine with no context."

"Well, what did she say–"

Francine shook her head. "It wasn't what she said," she sighed and finally sat down on one of the garden chairs. Lauryn remained quiet, waiting, willing her mother to keep talking.

Francine licked her lips, staring at her hands. "When I met your father, he and Pat were still together."

Lauryn sat up straighter. "Oh."

The realization hit her all at once.

Francine continued. "He'd bought her that house in California. Alicia must've been five or six? They were supposed to move back here together. Get married. But your father met me, and he had an opportunity to go overseas. Pat didn't want to leave California. I believed it was fate. I thought if they were meant to be together, they *would* have been, and your father and I would have never had anything to begin with."

Her mother sighed, leaning down over her knees as she spoke. "Honestly, Lauryn, at the time I didn't care about that woman. Or her little girl. I saw your father's uniform and that rank, and all I cared about was getting the hell out of Illinois."

Lauryn sat down next to her, careful not to move too quickly. She knew her mother, if she felt pressured, she'd shut down, and Lauryn would never learn the full story. "Mom, you were young–"

Francine let out a dry chuckle. "You know what they say about how you get a man?"

"That's how you lose them," Lauryn murmured in unison with her. Francine looked at her, a sad sort of amusement in her eyes. "But Mom, Dad loves you. He would never step out on you–"

"God bless him, he never has." Francine gave a small smile. "Your father is not a cheater. I think if that lady had been willing to go overseas, I would've never stood a chance. And that bothers me almost as much as the thought of them having something behind my back. The thought that he *might* have stayed with her. And I wouldn't have had this life."

Lauryn shook her head. "Mom, you don't know that. And you can't take on the responsibility of Dad's decisions. He made his choice."

Francine sighed. "Perhaps. But I was selfish at the time. He was my escape, and I don't know that I would've made it easy for him to go back had she changed her mind. I'm not built like you, Lauryn."

Lauryn frowned. "What do you mean?"

Francine turned to her fully now. "I didn't have faith that I could do it on my own. He was my ticket, and that's all there was to it. What you're doing now, starting over fresh? After spending how long with that man? And you've always had your own life. Amongst all his craziness, you're still whole."

Lauryn swallowed hard. Her mother had never acknowledged her like this before.

Francine leaned back, shaking her head. "All this–you moving back, hearing that voicemail, this retirement –it's just dredging up how I feel about *me*. It's not your father. Although I don't appreciate him keeping it from me."

"I don't think his intention was to conceal it from you." She reached for her mother's gloved hands, squeezing them lightly. "I think we forget that they are his family too. A family that came before us. There's probably a lot more to him leaving than we'll ever know, Mom."

Francine nodded, leaning in, resting her forehead against Lauryn's. Her eyes were watery when she whispered, "Can we stop sharing now?"

Lauryn burst out laughing, throwing an arm around her mother's shoulders. "Yes, Mom, I know how vulnerability makes you uncomfortable."

Francine giggled through her tears. "I think I'm good for the rest of the year after that. Or until your wedding day."

Lauryn groaned dramatically. "Oh God, I just got rid of a man, and you're trying to marry me off?"

They laughed together, the tension lifting into the tree branches above.

By the time Lauryn got home that evening, she felt drained but lighter, as if something she hadn't even realized she was carrying had finally been put down.

She dropped her purse onto the entryway table and kicked off her shoes, sighing as she made her way into the bathroom. The conversation with her mother had been, in a word, unexpected. Francine had never been one for deep personal reflections, especially not where she took accountability for her own choices. For a moment there, it almost felt like talking to another woman.

But even with her mother's confessions and her family's complex history on the table, walking back into her condo had been like pulling the plug on a vacuum, the noise of her family life quickly giving way to her own quieter thoughts.

What if she was a fool for leaving Joe? As her mother said, all relationships were hard work. And according to NPR's Tiny Desk, *No Saints Left* was getting some serious notoriety. Lauryn had unfollowed the band's social media pages before she'd even left Memphis. And despite blocking Joe's personal accounts, an update always slipped into her feed.

Their latest album had just gone double platinum. She could've just quit her job and started a fragrance line, like he'd wanted her to.

"Free to join him on every tour!" Lauryn spoke the words aloud, her voice featherlight and laced with sarcasm. She rubbed her sore shoulder and went to start the bathwater running. Her mother had given her a run for her money today. That hadn't been gardening–*that* was full-on landscaping, she thought, laughing. It would be a while before she signed up for that again. And she was definitely skipping leg day.

Watching the tub fill, she added generous amounts of her favorite bath oils: bergamot, vanilla, and amber, the steamy vapor soothing her muscles before she'd even gotten in. She undressed quickly, fingers moving on autopilot, peeling off her clothes and stepping in, letting the heat swallow her whole.

But her mind didn't settle.

As soon as she leaned back against the porcelain tub, her thoughts went straight back to the dance floor with Perry. She'd flirted. Let him hold her close, let the warmth of his breath brush against her skin, let his hands settle on her waist, stirring a million butterflies. She shivered in the tub just remembering.

She squeezed her eyes shut, breathing through a wave of arousal.

Usher was to blame for this! The songs that played that night would have to be avoided at all costs. That kind of nostalgia was dangerous.

Frustrated, she wondered when everything had become so intense with Perry? Why did they have so many damn mutual friends and overlapping social calendars? She'd been glad to see him, especially after the way her stomach dropped watching Vivienne kiss him. Really, it was the douse of cold water she needed. Lusting after her friend—a friend she'd already crossed a line with once already was not the move. No matter how good his arms felt around her.

She needed to reel herself in quickly, switch the light off on these men. If he called again, she wouldn't answer.

It was for the best.

Chapter 26

Summer

Lauryn

L auryn tightened her grip on the handle of the second beach bag.
Earlier that morning, she and Deonna had giggled like school girls
as they loaded it up with Prosecco and snacks. After making their way
down the dock and a long walk from the parking garage, Lauryn wished
they'd brought a cart.

Deonna and another one of her cousins, Ashley Ellis, the owner of
the boat and their host for the day, sashayed side by side ahead of her,
catching up on some family drama. Lauryn read the names of each boat
as they passed, noting the especially clever ones.

Seas the Day

Knot on Call

Vitamin Sea

As they drew closer to the end of the dock, the subtle lapping of waves
and buoys knocking together gave way to some soulful music. "Is that
Chaka Khan?" Donna asked as the music grew louder. "Alright, now."
She started dancing her way down the dock.

Ashley, seeming to know the source of the music, grinned and edged
her way over, stopping at the back of one boat. The good ship *Pier
Pressure* was aptly named, as it was one of the larger boats they'd seen
that morning. Shielding her eyes, Lauryn took in the sight of it rising and
falling softly in its slip as the waves picked up. It was certainly impressive,

with a deep cranberry candy-coating hull and stark white leather seats gleaming in the sunshine.

Equally impressive was the man who appeared from the front of the boat, greeting Ashley with a smile as he stepped down onto the swim deck. Deonna practically about-faced and blinked at Lauryn rapidly, whispering, "So this is where all the fine men are at?"

"Apparently the tall ones," Lauryn sang back quietly, taking the opportunity to set the heavy bag down.

"And, I feel like he's channeling Tupac and Kofi Siriboe at the same time."

Lauryn peeked back at the man who was chatting away with Ashley. "I can see it," she acknowledged after a minute.

"Right?" Deonna turned back around just as Ashley was introducing the two of them.

"How you doing ladies?"

"Good," they sang in unison, Deonna shamelessly looking him up and down. Lauryn could barely stifle the laughter bubbling up out of her chest. Leave it to Deonna to spot her weekend conquest before they even got on the damn lake.

"You're certainly setting the vibe this morning," Deonna cooed, stepping closer to the edge of the slip and nodding toward the obvious sound system on the boat.

"Oh, you like that? My brother is getting the playlist together." He turned to look back over his shoulder. "Ain't that right, man?"

Another man appeared behind him, his linen shirt unbuttoned and revealing entirely too much chest for ten a.m. Lauryn did her best to avert her eyes, but not before she noticed the man's beard and dark skin. Even in her peripheral he was a dead-ringer for Perry and that too, was more than she wanted to think about this morning. She caught Deonna looking back at her in earnest *silent* communication.

Safe behind the tint of her sunglasses, Lauryn put on her best poker face and picked the heavy beach bag back up.

Reading the situation, Ashley smiled. "Well, guys, I'm sure we'll see you out there." They resumed their walk down the dock toward Ashley's boat. *Ebb and Flow* was 56 feet of cream and white leather luxury. After a quick safety run-through and a grand tour below deck, Ashley put them to work, setting up the drinks and food.

Back on the main deck, reclined in the u-shaped bank of seats at the rear of the boat, Lauryn slipped her chrome sandals from her feet. She stretched her legs out to enjoy more of the sun and watched as a few boats eased out of their slips and made their way out of the harbor. Wiggling her toes, Lauryn closed her eyes and inhaled. As far as she was concerned, they could stay right here and she would still have a good time. She leaned back comfortably as Ashley got the music started, the sunshine creeping up her legs and thighs until it warmed the skin through her knit dress.

"Sunning, darling?" Deonna's sweet voice carried over the music.

Lauryn opened her eyes to a rosy, icy drink in front of her face. Accepting it, she pulled her legs underneath herself. "This is amazing, friend. Thank you for inviting me. I really needed this. Shit's been really *real* lately."

"Of course! And you know we had to get the girlies out to the playpen. This weekend is going to be Summertime-Chi at its finest. Speaking of finest! So... I think I need to spend more time at the harbor, girl. I feel like I need a man with a boat."

Lauryn closed her eyes again and leaned back. "Yeah, I saw you sizing up that situation."

"Girl! And his brother?"

"What about him?" Lauryn kept her eyes closed, hoping to play things off.

"Lauryn, I am not blind and neither are you!" She kicked back on the seats as well, sliding her own shoes off and taking a sip of her cocktail. "If they're any indication of how this summer is going to go, bitch, I'm ready."

Lauryn had to laugh at that. "They were pretty handsome."

"Yeah, I saw you pretending not to stare through your shades. I know you have a type."

Eyes widening, Lauryn sat up, "'Scuse me?"

"I *said* you have a type! Chocolate, beard, crazy nice arms, pretty teeth-"

"Those are all good things. That's a lot of people's type."

Deonna gave her an incredulous look. "Have you spoken to him?"

"No. And please tell me he is not going to be on this boat. For the last six months, all I have done is run into that man all over this damn city. Three million people and I've had one bad run-in after another."

"Yeah, the six degrees of separation in our friend group is ridiculous."

Lauryn scooted closer to her. "Just please tell me I'm not going to see him this weekend."

Deonna placed a hand over Lauryn's. "You're not going to see him. This is a girls weekend! We are going to have fun in this limited-time only Chicago sun. As a matter of fact, I think you should exercise some flirtation on someone else. How are things with-what's his name again?"

Lauryn snorted. "The man's name is Terrance. And things with him are ... cool."

"You sound really enthused about that," Deonna said sarcastically with a grin and crossed her legs. "Just stay away from your type, boo. That man earlier was a friggin carbon copy of Perry."

"He really was!" Lauryn agreed and they toasted their clear plastic cups together before cracking up.

An hour later, they pushed off from the dock. Esme and several other ladies made it aboard before the 11AM departure and now they were gliding out of the harbor, toward downtown.

Their destination, *The PlayPen*, was a popular boating area just off-shore from downtown. With panoramic views of the skyline and an endless horizon, the area was pretty much the Cannes of the Midwest. They picked up speed, and as the spray tickled Lauryn's skin she really started to enjoy herself and be present in the moment.

Most of the other women were taking videos as they cruised up the shoreline, or posting live stories. She sipped her rosé and tried not to think of anything that might ruin the view. Since dancing with him at Sam's birthday party, it'd been hard not to think of Perry. She recalled the firmness of him behind her as she pressed against him. The way he'd matched her move for move. Even now she bit her lip, vividly recalling the feel of his hands on her hips. Lauryn shook her and fixated on the horizon. That mess was a problem for another day. The sky and water were too beautiful to be wrapped up in her thoughts.

"Alright, I want pictures of all of us on the bow before we start sweating in this heat." The boat slowed and most of the ladies ventured to the lower deck to change. One by one, they re-emerged and took turns taking more pictures and videos. The skyline and Lake Shore drive glinted behind them and Lauryn took the opportunity to change as well. Swapping her knit dress for a visor, she fiddled with her bathing suit in the mirror. Flattening her hand against her stomach which was starting to resemble the one she had in undergrad. How free she'd felt then, and happy.

Calling on her twenty-something year old spirit, she climbed the stairs back to the main deck. The breeze was sweet and she paused, taken aback by the perfect weather and the laughter from her friends.

"Lauryn, stop striking a pose behind the camera. Get over here!" Esme called, raising an eyebrow behind her mirror aviators.

Smiling, she made her way over to where all the women were gathered at the back of the boat. Cheerily she found her place among them, turning her back to the Chicago skyline splayed out behind them. At Ashley's request, they all pressed in closer to get the perfect shot. Lauryn beamed, smiling wide for the camera and breathing in the fragrance of all the women around her. The heat from the sun on them created a luscious mix of perfume, hair oil and shea butter. She felt Esme and the others arms around her waist and at her shoulders as they changed poses, each of them turning an ankle out to proudly show off their ample hips and thighs.

Although she wasn't used to it, the comradery wasn't lost on Lauryn. She was impressed by the ease with which they all came together for dinner, brunch, or a day on the water. This was her first time meeting most of these women. Yet, there hadn't been a single sideways glance or hesitation from any of them.

She hadn't felt this kind of community in a long time and she hadn't realized how much she missed it until now. The laughter, shared looks, the simple comfort of being around women who weren't afraid to celebrate each other.

After moving to Memphis with Joe, those things had slipped away. California friendships thinned and the phone calls slowed. She thought of the women she'd managed to make friends with. Many of them wheeling and dealing in so much drama that Lauryn had distanced herself. After a while, she had pulled back, convincing herself peace was easier than people. And maybe it was. She'd always been private, good at keeping things to herself. But standing here now, surrounded by genuine warmth, she could finally admit how lonely that peace had been.

In the early years of their relationship, Joe had been a solace. A best friend, as well as lover. After the incident with her sisters, Lauryn had leaned all the way into him, his circle of friends, his career, and their relationship. Over time she even lost touch with college friends, everyone moving on with their careers, marriages, and babies. By the time she realized how isolated she was, Joe had already been unfaithful.

As the sun climbed higher in the sky, more boats appeared. Ashley's playlist was a perfect mix of new and old, with Megan Thee Stallion drowning out any negative thoughts. Lauryn closed her eyes, turning her face up towards the sun. Mouthing the words, she soaked in the joy of the moment, old memories blending with new ones as she twerked playfully to the applause and teasing of the women around her.

The boat bobbed on the current and they all floated between decks, refreshing their drinks and plucking snacks from the galley. Lauryn was working on a small plate of olives and chicken wings when Deonna called her up to the front of the boat. Carefully they hoisted themselves up, inching their way towards the bow, gripping the side rails as they went. They lay towels down and spread themselves out for some quality sunbathing.

They lay back comfortably, arms and coverups tucked behind their heads like makeshift pillows, and their tummies stretched convincingly flat. Their brown legs fanned out toward the horizon like sun rays, toenails gleaming in the light.

It seemed like the whole city was out on the water. She could make out the laughter, whoops and shouts from other people playing in the sun. If she turned her head, she could see the traffic on Lake Shore drive while drones circled overhead, probably capturing more than anyone had bargained for.

Her ears perked at the sound of Frankie Beverly & Maze, that smooth, familiar intro that always marked the start of summer. Nearby, a single boat's playlist was setting the tone for their entire corner of the Play Pen. Bodies swayed, lips moving in sync with lyrics everyone had probably known since childhood. Lauryn grinned and she bobbed her head, so glad she hadn't declined Deonna's invitation to a weekend in the city.

Somewhere behind them, they heard Ashley call out to another boat.

"Girl check this out. This bitch is flirting across the water." Deonna observed, rolling over on her side and shading her eyes to see.

Lauryn moved up onto her knees to catch a glimpse. A larger charter with a navy hull floated closer, Kendrick Lamar booming from its interior. Ashley, stood at the edge of the deck, her blue and ivory designer head scarf blowing in the breeze as she waved. The men aboard were quick to respond, waving back and calling out compliments over the sound of water sloshing against the hulls. From where Lauryn sat, she could see the people dotted around the two decks. Men and women, scantily clad, having a great time. It seemed like a good party.

She shook her head, half-amused and about to lay back down, when she noticed him.

Perry.

What had been a gentle sway of the boat, suddenly felt like the whole thing might capsize, and Lauryn's heart thudded. Perry stood near the stern of the other boat, laughing with one of the men beside him. The sound of it carried over the water, warm and achingly familiar. He was shirtless and his board shorts sat low on his hips, the line of his abs drawing her gaze down until she had to part her lips to breathe. His smooth skin gleamed under the sun, and his full beard framed what she knew now was the most incredible smile she'd ever seen.

Chicago was massive. Millions of people. Endless festivals and places to go. Yet here he was again, like they were locked in each other's orbit. She hated how her stomach tightened at the sight of him, the way her body betrayed her rational mind. She resisted the urge to slide her sunglasses down for a better look. "The fuck," she whispered, but Deonna heard, glancing at Lauryn with a questioning expression, before following her line of sight back to the other boat.

Deonna bit her lip and averted her eyes, mumbling, "Damn, friend."

"Unbelievable."

In that moment, Perry turned, his eyes lazily scanning the scene before eventually freezing on her. Like every other time she'd seen him, the world shrank away around them. The stern of his boat floated even closer and her body hummed under his gaze. She saw him grin, slow and mischievous, as if he knew the unspoken things she couldn't allow herself to say.

Lauryn watched, grateful for the small blessing of her sunglasses that created the slightest barrier, a hint of concealment. He lifted his hand in a small wave and she waved back stiffly in response. She hoped he couldn't see the panic, or the pleasure, on her face.

Deonna's voice broke the "Um.., did you know he looked like that under his clothes?"

"Hush," Lauryn moved to lay back down, turning her back to the other boat and Perry's gaze.

"I'm just saying, I don't think you knew because, honey, you are catatonic," Deonna managed to keep her teasing quiet, but fell into peals of laughter.

Over the rim of her shades, Lauryn watched as Perry's boat drifted away, doing her best to look unbothered. Their music grew fainter, but her heart thundered against her ribcage at having seen him again, here in the middle of the damn lake. Lifting her butt, she ran two fingers along her bikini bottoms to pull the material from between her ample cheeks. She had to get a handle on her reactions to Perry.

Especially if she was going to keep seeing him everywhere.

She traced her lip, watching as the other boat slipped further away. Frowning, she whipped her head to look over at Deonna who had settled down onto her stomach to finish sunbathing. She playfully poked the crest of her friend's booty, making her shout with laughter.

"So much for not seeing him!"

Chapter 27

Perry

L ater that evening Perry stepped off the elevator doors into a wash of rotating color. Soft blues and lavenders slid across the walls, while flashes of red and fuchsia pulsed slow against the ceiling. He'd been to this hotel before for a private event or two, but the party rooftop boasted a very different scene tonight. As he looked around, sizing up the considerable crowd, it felt like the start of a good night. The sun was setting, but the heat still hung in the air. The night felt fresh, alive, charged with people showing up in their best, moving slow, joyously, like the world could wait.

The DJ was playing no games, priming everyone with summer classics and ebbing beats. Showing his QR code, he moved past the host stand. He weaved through the crowd easily enough, deciding what to check out first. Most of the tables were taken and the small terrace was already crowded. Rashad and the guys were supposedly on their way, but he wouldn't be surprised if they didn't show. After hours on the water under the high sun, he'd almost stayed in himself. As he pressed further into the crowd, he considered what he was about to do. The main reason he'd even come to this event.

Since seeing her last, his frustration with Lauryn had mellowed into a kind of knowing; an understanding that Lauryn wasn't simply avoiding him because of the mix up with Vivienne, the bachelor party, or anything else. She was hiding, using each situation as an excuse to throw up another wall. While he could excuse Lauryn's mild hypocrisy–getting mad at him for omitting his dating history, when she'd done worse by concealing Joe–he could not excuse the way she was still pretending nothing existed between them. Not now when, for once, the timing was finally right.

He'd seen the look on her face earlier that morning, even though she'd been wearing those enormous shades. Past the mirrored aviator sunglasses, he recognized the nervous set of her mouth as their boats bobbed on the waves, how she hadn't been able to look away. That had not been the look of a woman who didn't have some feelings, even if she wouldn't admit to them.

When he drove down to the harbor on 31st Street that morning, he had no idea he would run into her, but he had hoped. The Juneteenth weekend brought friends and family out in droves, some people flying in to get a taste of *Summertime Chi*. There'd been a solid chance he would see her somewhere over the course of the holiday weekend, but he'd still been surprised to find her in the middle of the lake.

The way she'd been looking in that bikini had him thinking all kinds of nonsense now. Her mane of hair that normally draped down, often concealing her true thoughts from him, was pulled up in a regal bun showing off elegant shoulders that caught the sunlight. Every luscious curve of her body had been on display on that boat—more than he'd seen in years. There'd been so much ass on the water that morning it was almost background noise, women moving to the music and the swell of the lake, pressing close to him whether he wanted it or not. None of it held him the way she did.

He replayed the sight of her dark skin set against the blue sky. She'd looked unreal out there, almost unearthly beautiful. It had taken every-thing in him to just stand there. Though he'd played it pretty cool as their boats drifted apart, he made up in his mind that he would find her again before the weekend was out. Sit her down and have a real conversation about what was happening between them.

It was happening again, the same pull, the same fire he'd felt every day of their last summer. Only this time he wasn't interested in letting it go.

Perry made his way to the bar, dodging sequins, shoulder bumps, and greetings from familiar faces. The bartender spotted him, wiping a spot clean for him as he approached. One of those girls who smiled like she already had a story in mind about him.

"What can I get you?"

He smiled, leaning over so she could hear. "Toki on the rocks?"

She nodded, spinning around to grab the bottle. "Want to open a tab?"

"Naw, thanks," he wasn't planning on staying through the evening. Just long enough to find Lauryn and figure out what was going on in that pretty head of hers.

The bartender set his drink down, eyeing him flirtatiously. "If you need anything else, I'm right here."

Before he could respond, another woman to his left slid in close enough to graze his arm. "I was just telling my friend–Chicago is *finally* looking good again."

He laughed appreciatively and turned to scan the crowd behind them. "I have to agree," he replied, giving her a polite smile before he stepped away, drink in hand. His eyes scanned the room again. No sign of the guys. No sign of Lauryn either.

He moved on from the bar, making his way closer to the windows so he could look out over the skyline. Through the glass he could see a floor of offices in the next building, chairs and cubicles abandoned until Monday. He thought of his own job, a company he'd been with since he'd turned thirty. The big-boy job he'd been grinding towards all through his twenties. After seven years, and his birthday right around the corner, it might be time to explore new opportunities. He thought back to Lauryn's birthday, when she'd asked him if he would ever leave Chicago. Looking out on the view in front of him, feeling the pulse of his people behind him, he knew he never could.

"Aye! Look who finally stepped outside!" a voice called from behind him, cutting through his thoughts.

Perry turned, spotting some old coworkers grinning wide, already a few drinks in. "Perry Mitchell. What's up, man!"

"You see this man?" another of the guys added, lifting his glass. "Always clean–taking away any chance we had with these women."

Perry laughed, making his way over as they shook up. "Hey, Anthony, what's up man?"

"Just out her enjoying all the black and brown lusciousness. Oh wait, you still cuffed?" one of them asked, squinting like he couldn't quite remember. "You still with, uh, Viv?"

Perry shook his head. "Vivienne. And nah, man. That ended."

"Oh, say less!" Anthony clapped him on the back like he'd just been drafted to the league. "Welcome back, my boy. You picked the right night. Summer's up. We hittin' Puerto Rico, LA, maybe Houston–if you locked in, you *locked in*."

Perry chuckled, but his eyes had already drifted past them. "I just got back from one of my boys' bachelor trips. Got another trip around the corner-"

He saw her.

It wasn't just that she walked into the room, but how the light seemed to catch her first. Like the room itself made space for her.

Lauryn was gliding through the crowd, flanked by Deonna and another woman he didn't recognize, all of them glowing deep after a morning in the sun. This woman never missed. She wore a white dress shirt, not unlike the ones he had in his closet. She'd tucked into a silver sequins mini skirt that shimmered and showed off her thick thighs, catching the light with every step. Her shoes and toes gleamed.

The music switched and the crowd tightened around him. Taking everyone by surprise, the DJ mixed in a chopped version of "Right Here" by SWV and the whole room started to move as one. The Michael Jackson sample had everyone lip singing and dancing, if they hadn't been already. Lauryn was already having a good time and her steps were graceful, even though she was dancing full out with her friends— she held nothing back. He almost didn't want to interrupt.

Her skin was radiant. And her face— eyelids dusted with gunmetal shimmer, those full lashes accentuating the sweet shape of her eyes as she swayed to the music. She was exquisite.

And he was completely gone over her. Again.

After a moment, as if she'd felt him watching, she looked up. Recognition flashed in her expression, softening instantly. Not displeased. Not surprised, but something else.

And that alone told him everything he needed to know.

Chapter 28

Lauryn

L auryn wasn't even surprised, but she was still frozen, quite unable to move as she gazed at him across the room.

At this point, it was getting ridiculous. She could've flown to another country and somehow still ended up running into Perry Mitchell on the damn jet bridge. This "girl's weekend" was supposed to be simple–drinks, dancing, distraction. But apparently he'd been invited to everything they had. Boat party? There. Rooftop afterset? There. Random trip to the museum? There! She would've had better luck avoiding him by standing in front of his house waving a sparkler.

He really had the nerve to show up everywhere she wasn't ready to see him.

But everything about the way he was looking at her softened her exasperation. She tried to place his expression, to put a name to the look in his eyes. There was a mix of emotions there–both heat and amusement– daring her to protest. Lauryn slowed her dancing, taking in the sight of him. The lights, shifting indigo and lavender, pinks and red, rippled over him like frames on a film screen. She touched her stomach, recognizing exactly what that look was about.

He was closing the distance between them, stepping effortlessly in his own rhythm around groups of people dancing. Despite her recent determination to avoid this man, she felt a prickle of impatience. The anticipation of being close to him again. He didn't break stride as he approached, and she held his gaze across the darkening party. She loved the way this man walked up on her, the way she damn near had to arch her back to look up into his face. He was immaculate as always, in a black and cream woven shirt, his golden chain glinting from behind the unfastened buttons. If he hadn't looked like a seventies album cover before, he certainly did now.

Dammit Deonna. Out of the corner of her eye, Lauryn saw her friends moving off, grinning and making "Oh Shit!" faces as they recognized Perry.

Bravely, she looked back up at him. "How is it possible that out of all the three million people in Chicago, I keep running into you?"

"If I recall correctly, you're the one who keeps coming back to my city." His chocolate eyes challenged her.

Lauryn's wit failed her and she changed the subject. "You solo tonight? I didn't see Rashad or anyone."

"On the way. Moving slow after being on the water this morning."

Lauryn nodded, looking everywhere but him. "Yeah, we had to get a second wind too. We booked rooms here for the night." *Why the hell did I say that?* Weeks of dodging him and now she was volunteering unnecessary information. *I must have sun poisoning.*

"Yeah, I see you changed." He only dropped his gaze for a second, before meeting her eyes again. "You look good on that boat."

She wanted to say, *yeah you did too,* but she managed to catch herself. The sight of him that morning replayed in her mind like a music video. She heard Esme in her head. Perry was indeed *nineties*-fine. Hell, seventies-fine. Fifties-crooner kind of fine. Being around him was starting to become a problem. "Well, thank you! It was a good to spend time with the girls. Speaking of, I should catch up with them. I hope you enjoy-"

Out of nowhere, she felt him touch her elbow, slide his fingers down the back of her forearm and take her right hand in his. Without breaking their gaze, he pulled her into him, turning his head just so as if he might kiss her.

But he didn't.

Instead, he wove his fingers in between hers, turned back in the direction he came, and she followed, any protests dying on her tongue as soon as he'd touched her. He held their locked hands at his back, keeping her close as he navigated, parting the crowd and leading her past the host stand. When they reached the elevator, he pressed the button and stood at attention, watching for the floor numbers to change.

She stopped short behind him. "Perry what—where are you taking me?"

He turned, looking over at her gently. "Somewhere we can talk," he explained, tenderly squeezing her hand.

"About what?" she asked even though she knew full well. Looking at him now, she felt the point of no return barreling toward them and instantly she realized what was happening.

"About why you're avoiding me."

"I'm not avoiding you," she said quickly, her voice pitching higher than she meant it to. She swallowed hard, trying to steady herself before going on. "I'm not avoiding you. I'm just... trying not to confuse things between us."

For a moment his eyes bore into her and he seemed to consider what she'd said. When he turned suddenly to check the elevator, Lauryn looked too. It was still moving slow, stopped at the tenth floor. She felt his hand at the small of her back and let him guide her around the corner to the emergency exit. They slipped into the stairwell, where the light was cool and the light was stark white, an abrupt contrast to the low-lit rooftop. The music dulled to a distant thrumming, replaced by the quiet echo of their footsteps.

As soon as the door clicked closed he turned, his expression interested. "You were saying?"

Just by stepping through the emergency door they were closer, close enough for her to catch the faint hint of his beard oil in the narrow stairwell. The landing suddenly felt too small for her to keep her distance. He looked taller than he had a minute ago, broader somehow, as if the space wasn't big enough for the conversation he was insisting on having.

"I was saying..." she started, her annoyance melting into something like desperation. Just by having this conversation they were completely proving her point. "I don't want to confuse things again."

Perry's eyebrows furrowed, his chin dropping as he studied her. "I don't remember being confused. I remember us having the time of our lives. Back-to-back weekends. Festivals. Shows."

His voice dropped lower, full of memory.

"Just like now," he continued softly. "Hangin' out. Running into each other everywhere. Never wanting the night to end."

He stepped in closer, close enough for Lauryn to feel his warmth in the coolness of the stairwell and he grasped her right hand again. His touch was grounding, drawing her out of her thoughts and into the present moment. For once, her analytical brain was silent.

His eyes moved over her face, slow and searching. "Do you remember?"

"Yes," she whispered, voice catching on the truth of it. Even though she'd been thinking about him, remembering him all year. Every time she saw him over the last few months, he'd pulled her a little further off course, loosening all the discipline she was trying to build. She wasn't just suddenly attracted to her friend–it was deeper than that. Every look, every small moment or laugh between them carried the weight of years, each exchange reminding her of who she'd been before she left.

He reached for her then and leaned down to cup her face in his hands, his thumbs tracing the line of her jaw.

"You've been living in my memory, Lauryn," he said, his words brushing against her lips. "You being back is doing things to me. When I see you, I don't want to pretend that I don't want to hold you, that I don't want kiss you."

"Perry..."

He tilted his head, his voice dropping even lower. "I'm just wondering when you're gonna stop running."

Her skin tingled beneath his palms, her heart stumbling in her chest as he pressed a kiss to her temple, then one along her cheekbone, soft and slow. Lauryn leaned into him, her eyes fluttering closed and she kissed the pad of his thumb as it swept over her mouth. "I missed you," she whispered, the words catching halfway out.

His kissed her, slow and deliberate, as if to make her feel every second he'd been holding back. Lauryn gripped the front of his shirt and she couldn't help the whimper that escaped her throat.

He pulled back just enough to breathe, his forehead resting against hers. "Me too," he murmured. Then his mouth was on hers again, slower and deeper, until the world fell away.

They didn't talk. Not as the elevator doors closed and they made their way down from the rooftop. Not when they stepped out into the warm night and Perry led her across the wide street. They passed idling traffic waiting for the lights to change, his long strides patient with hers. However, when they reached his car, he stopped short and reeled her in to face him.

His kiss came with no warning, deep and hungry, nothing like the cautious touch he'd had in their younger days. His reserve seemed to be replaced with intention and an assuredness she'd seen in him since the moment she spotted him at the holiday party. His mouth moved over hers, slow and certain, tasting her like he was making up for every year she'd been gone.

When they were settled in the car and he pulled away from the curb, she did not ask where they were going. It was enough that they were going together and she was quite sure she wouldn't have to say good-bye—not tonight. She concentrated on his hand resting on the center console, stroking his open palm and tracing the veins of his forearm.

She tried not to think about it too much. Not about whether Deonna or Esme had seen her leave with him, or the looks she would surely get from them later. After months of denying everything they'd said about this man, here she was doing the exact opposite.

They were passing the winery before Lauryn realized where he was taking her. She held her breath as they turned into the alley behind his house and pulled into the garage. He held her hand as he led her through his backyard, their ankles brushing past hostas lining the walkway. She trailed him, watching his frame silhouetted against the bright security lights, her mind racing as she followed him up the steps, waited patiently as he unlocked the backdoor and stepped aside. Taking the queue, she stepped through into the kitchen.

She ventured further into the space, getting her bearings as Perry closed the door behind them. From where she stood, she could see clear through the house, past the dining room, through the living room, to a stunning bay of windows at the front. Curious, her eyes roamed the sleek cabinets and quartz countertops, but she could still feel their last kiss burning on her lips.

All that time spent avoiding him, afraid she might give herself away with one glance. Afraid he could read her thoughts. Yet, whenever she got within ten feet of the man, she forgot all of it.

She heard his unhurried footsteps as he stopped behind her, his hands warm as they brushed over her arms. He dipped his head, pressing a slow, deliberate kiss to the skin just behind her ear. Lauryn's eyes fluttered closed as he turned her around to face him. He caught her mouth in another deep kiss, a slow and steady pull, until she was arched back completely, nearly suspended in his arms.

For a moment she hesitated, her pulse beginning to pound in her ears, but she couldn't resist slipping her tongue between his lips. A low sound rumbled in his throat and he leaned in, guiding her back against the kitchen island. With her hands braced on the counter, she arched toward him and savored his taste. She felt his fingers slide up her sides, a current spreading through her as he found the curve of her breasts and squeezed, the warmth of his touch emanating through her blouse and into her skin.

He released her mouth, nuzzling his way toward her ear. It was too late to stop anything, but as his lips burned into her she couldn't convince herself she even wanted to try. His voice came low and a little rough as he asked, "May I?"

She turned, catching his eye in the dim light and nodded. Then she kissed him. A kiss to reassure them both.

He gripped her shirt then, tugging it out from her skirt so that it fell open, exposing her bra and bare stomach. He drew in a breath, his gaze dragging over her slowly before his hand found her waist again.

With an expert hand, he slipped two fingers beneath the waistband, tracing around until he found the zipper. The sensation tightened low in her belly and she sighed as he eased the skirt down, planting feather light, loving kisses on her mouth, nose, and chin until the skirt began to fall. He caught it, the sequined fabric rattling softly as he knelt before her to guide it down her legs. Lauryn drew in a sharp breath, stepping out of it, one foot at a time, until she was standing over him in nothing but her underwear and favorite silver heels. The satin straps practically glowed in the dark.

"This is nice," Perry raised an eyebrow and her breath caught when he tossed her mini skirt over his shoulder, leaning in to kiss the inside of her knee. Her joints went soft; she had to steady herself as his hands caressed the back of her calves and he kissed his way back up the center line of her body.

With every caress and every kiss she was losing the battle of logic against herself. She had no reason not to give into this, to let herself have it. Have him.

Making up her mind, she pressed in close as her hands moved up his chest, freeing each button until his shirt fell away. She bit her lip, feeling the urge to grip and squeeze the muscles corded beneath his skin.

He was cut, solid and thick in all the right places.

Lauryn recalled the sight of him on the boat again, his bare chest and pretty-ass smile beckoning her from across the water. She'd wanted to

touch him the way she was touching him now. When she lifted her
head to kiss him, he stopped short, holding himself just out of reach.
She stood on her toes, but found him rigid, standing at his full height,
holding her in his gaze. She stretched but no matter how she coaxed him,
he didn't yield to her urgency.

Then she realized—he was making her come to him. After everything,
it was only fair.

Impatiently, and with both hands, she reached up for him, palming
the back of his head and stretching just enough to catch his bottom lip
with her tongue. Something else she'd thought about doing a hundred
times over the last few months. Lauryn wanted this. She'd been wanting
it, with him, for months and when he finally dipped his head to kiss her,
she put every unspoken feeling and every ache she had into it. Pressing,
tasting and sucking until she was sure he had to know.

He lifted her easily, her legs tightening around his waist as he carried
her into the living room. His movements were steady, unhurried as they
always were, like he refused to rush it. He laid her down on his velvet
couch, the fabric cool against her skin, and he kissed her with the same
deliberateness that had taken her off guard from the start.

Perry settled down over her, caressing the length of her body. Lauryn
shivered when he gripped her knee, drawing her leg up beside him, taking
kiss, after kiss from her until time slowed. She could feel him against her,
the length of him warm and growing longer with every second and she
understood, instantly, that he was savoring it. The final moment before
they couldn't just simply go back to being friends.

The idea hitched in her mind for a second, but she let it go, leaning up
for another kiss.

His thumb swept over her shoulder, taking her bra strap with it, and
he lowered his head to kiss where it had been. She closed her eyes, letting
his movements surprise her. He reached between them, undressing her,
kissing each swath of newly revealed skin as he unhooked and tugged,
inch by inch, until she was completely bare beneath him. She thought
she saw him pause, taking all of her in before finding her eyes again. For
a moment she saw reverence, but it burned away, replaced by something
raw and intense.

Without breaking their gaze, he pressed a kiss onto her sternum,
another into the supple inside of her breast, and then he claimed her
entire nipple in his mouth, sending pleasure searing through her. Lauryn
reached for him, but he was already moving lower, kissing down her

stomach until he settled between her legs. He kissed down the inside of her thigh, pushing her knee higher to grant him better access. Lightly, he swept a finger over her sex, stroking her tenderly until her moan pierced the silence. She couldn't help shifting, even with him holding her knee in place, his mouth so close her walls started to pulse.

Seconds stretched and Perry finally pressed his lips against the fullness of her labia. When he inhaled, breathing her in, Lauryn thought she might lose her mind. With his tongue, he opened her up, nudging past her folds, gentle and teasing. Tasting her resolve.

She rolled her head back, letting the whispers float up from her mouth. Whispering his name and *"Yes, please"* as he flattened his tongue to drag it over her flesh. He kept going, lapping at her entrance until she was arching against the couch cushions and all the while he held her leg in place, ensuring she got no relief unless he decided to grant it.

She got lost in the feeling, squeezing her eyes tight one moment then watching satisfyingly in the next. This couldn't be the same reserved, sweet guy from her past. The same man who'd taken weeks just to start a conversation with her in lecture hall? He couldn't be the same person, not with the way he was touching her, devouring her right now. Lauryn felt the waves passing over her, the pleasure pooling in her belly and she struggled to prolong it. It'd been so long since she'd felt a pang this deep, and this was just the beginning...

"Perry-" she whined as his tongue slowed, fluttering over her clit with ridiculous precision. With some final wet kisses he stopped, moving back up her body and she felt him again. His dick was warm and heavy against her. Before she could stop herself she reached between them, claiming it gently. She stroked his velvet skin, leaning up to bite his lip as she memorized every inch. She squeezed, pulling gently in a come-hither motion until he sighed, a deep sound that she felt in her core.

Breaking their kiss, Perry reached for an alabaster box on the coffee table. Lauryn was surprised to see him lift the lid and retrieve a condom. Giggling, she caressed his face. "Is that one of your mother's decorative suggestions?"

He shushed her with a kiss and managed a sheepish grin, even though he was lying between her legs rock hard. "We are not talking about my mom right now."

Breathing out a laugh, Lauryn watched, a little mesmerized when he sat back on his knees to tear open the wrapper and rolled the rubber down over himself. She felt her walls contract again at the sight of him.

"Come here," he reached for her, gathering her up onto his lap so she straddled him. It was almost exactly where they'd left off eleven years ago, traversing together into unchartered territory. Impossibly close after years spent in each other's orbit, hovering close but never colliding. She wasn't the same girl caught between a new love and something she couldn't name with Perry. In this moment, all of her wanted this. Not a single part of her was conflicted.

Lauryn met his eyes, lifting herself high enough to take him inside.

"Fuck..." he breathed, and she moaned when the head of his dick slipped passed her entrance. The delicious pop as their bodies joined for the very first time. They stilled, breathing each other in as she sank down onto him.

She started to move, rolling her hips gradually at first, letting her body lead. Perry leaned back, giving her space to take as much or as little as she wanted, but after years of wondering and regretting, she wanted to feel him completely. Goosebumps rippled across her skin as the cool air brushed over her, the tips of her breasts hardening, responding before she even realized. They ached for his hands, his mouth, anything. It felt incredible to be so exposed for him. Every part of her that had once held back now reached for him instead, wanting to be seen and known. To be claimed by him.

With her eyes closed, she listened for him, loving the sound of his breathing and all the profanity that meant she was having the same effect on him as he'd had on her. She picked up her pace, gliding along his length, each rise and fall plunging them below the surface of reason. Perry leaned up to grip her thighs and hips, kissing her, guiding her until their rhythm grew urgent, like he couldn't get close enough.

Perry slid a hand up her back, slowing her just long enough to lay her back onto the couch. The change was sudden, but smooth and his strength caught her off guard. One second she was moving with him, and the next, she was beneath him, breathless, as he anchored himself deep, claiming more of her.

Lauryn felt herself melting, liquefying as he moved inside her, rolling each thrust into her like he wanted her completely undone. She arched into him, damn near wanting to sing because he felt so good. She reveled in the sounds of her own ecstasy, turning herself on even more with each whimper or groan. The pressure and the weight of him was exquisite and Lauryn couldn't think of anything else.

"Oh, my goodness..." she huffed out quietly, reaching for him.

He smiled down at her, barely slowing down as he caressed her cheek and repeated her words. "My goodness," he whispered teasingly, licking into her mouth for another kiss that made her heart skip. His kiss deepened, hungry in that way she was starting to love, and she held him close, taking everything he was giving.

It carried her higher and as she felt her pleasure start to give way, she let go.

Chapter 29

Lauryn

Lauryn's gaze lingered on him, admiring the coffee-grounds hue of his perfect skin. The slope at the small of his back leading to the expanse of his incredible shoulders. How beautiful and how handsome he was, sleeping next to her, undisturbed since the early morning hours. She felt small next to him, wound tight in the sheets and tucked onto the safe side of the bed, away from the door.

The sun was beaming through the curtains they'd forgotten to close in their haste. Her lips pressed into a line as she blushed, thinking of the night before. There was no going back now-whatever limits of friendship there had been between them were blown to smithereens.

With that realization and a careful hand, she reached out towards his sleeping form. It was as if she was compelled to touch him, unable to resist the contrast between the smoothness of his dark skin and the buttery ivory sheets that were quite wrinkled now.

He didn't stir as she caressed him with the back of her fingers. He was a belly sleeper. She lifted a brow, trying to remember if she'd ever known that, or if it was just one of those little details she'd been too distracted to notice all those years ago. Lazily, she ran her hand back down his torso and tried to recall every moment of that night at the hotel. That morning when she'd woken up in Perry's arms, his dress shirt creased and smeared with her makeup. She'd felt nearly as bad about the makeup stains as she did about spending the night with someone other than Joe.

The Jefferson wedding had been the most elaborate of all the weddings they'd attended that year. It had been an especially good time, and like always, she and Perry had been seated at the same reception table. They'd laughed over the awkward guest seating and the overzealous MC who seemed determined to keep everyone–young and old–on the dance floor all night.

Perry had gently rescued her from the clumsy advances of other single members of the wedding party, and when the DJ started playing oldies, he'd danced with her to every single song. Somewhere in the midst of it all, they'd started moving through the reception like a couple. Arm in arm, never far from each other's side.

Just before midnight, they'd slipped out of the ballroom. Lauryn remembered the ache in the balls of her feet as they wandered down Wacker Drive towards her hotel. Her five-inch satin Bakers heels were, in hindsight, a terrible choice. However, the warm summer air had seduced them both, and they kept walking, carried by something electric and unspoken.

She could still picture the steps down to the Riverwalk, the twinkling lights trailing past the harbor lock and out toward the inky, blue-black night stretched over Lake Michigan. She hadn't known what she was thinking when she asked Perry to stay that night, when she stepped off the elevator and led him back to her room. Maybe she hadn't been thinking at all. The reality was Lauryn's own feelings had steered the course of that evening.

Lying next to him now, she remembered it again; the way he'd kissed her, soft and deliberate, as if she were something rare to be unwrapped with gratitude. He'd waited, even after she'd leaned in. Like he wanted to be sure she was sure.

The truth was, she had encouraged what had been building between them all summer. She'd let herself enjoy his attention, their ease, the quiet intimacy of their friendship shifting into something new. She hadn't told him about Joe, but she hadn't done it to be cruel. At the time, she convinced herself there wasn't much to tell. With Joe starting to travel for gigs and Lauryn finishing up grad school, things with him weren't exactly solid.

Although, she could admit now that it had been so much more than that.

Lauryn withheld the truth because Perry had become important to her. She knew telling him about Joe wouldn't erase their connection, but it would have complicated it. It would have been harder to pretend there wasn't something more lingering in every glance, every inside joke, and brush of his hand.

She hadn't been ready to part with their friendship, even if it was blurry and undefined. Some part of her, maybe the most honest part, had tried to protect it. Protect *him*.

They hadn't gotten any further than a few passionate kisses and the straps of her dress coming down. Still, the next morning, she'd slipped from his arms and left him sleeping. When he'd called, she was already on the train home, the city blurring past the window as she tried to convince both herself and Perry that everything between them was still fine.

Lying beside him now felt surreal, and yet somehow exactly right. For a moment she let herself imagine how different things might have been if she hadn't panicked and left, or run off with Joe. If she'd simply explained when Perry called. Maybe it wouldn't have taken them so long to get here, to this place where she felt so much peace and appreciation.

Reminding herself to keep her mind in the present, she inched her way to the edge of Perry's massive king-sized bed, glancing back to ensure she hadn't woken him. His face, half buried in the pillows, remained still and his shoulders rose and fell with the same steady breaths.

The refinished hardwood floors didn't make a sound as she tip-toed across the room, on a mission to find her phone. She slowed, half-amused as she stood completely naked in the middle of someone else's bedroom, trying to retrace her steps from the night before. Finding Perry's robe on the back of his bathroom door, she pulled it on, loving that it smelled of him, and bundled up, she ventured down to the kitchen.

The stairs gave way to warmth. It moved through the soles of her feet, radiating up from the polished wood. On the main floor, she caught the scent of brewed coffee, fresh paint, and the faintest trace of cologne hanging in the air.

She pulled Perry's robe a little tighter around herself and walked softly, taking her time as she moved through his space. This was his home; a home he was building with his hands. A life he was living without apology.

Lauryn drifted into the living room and slowed. Every detail of the space revealing itself in its own time. The room was exquisite, almost curated; masculine and warm, with deep textures and clean lines. A pair of mocha-toned armchairs flanked a vintage credenza that ran low across the far wall, topped with his record player and a heavy sculptural lamp.

She stepped closer, eyes tracing the grooves of the wood grain, the delicate way the light caught on the curve of a ceramic bowl, the records

stacked neatly below. There were *hundreds* of them. She crouched
slightly, tilting her head as she read a few of the spines. Mostly pristine,
but a few old crumbling soul pressings, albums she hadn't seen outside
of her father's collection.

It was easy to picture: Perry, barefoot and quiet, a lowball glass in his
hand as he scanned his collection until he found just the right one to suit
his mood.

Lauryn's gaze took in the art covering the walls, two striking pieces in
particular, hung side by side, bold in color but restrained in composition.
Suddenly she knew he'd chosen them for just that reason. The space
was a reflection of him unapologetic and rooted. It was the kind of
self-assurance that she personally rarely experienced, and it made her
stomach tighten.

She turned and caught sight of one of his plants by the window,
massive and sculptural, deep green leaves with maroon-tipped points. It
looked prehistoric, like something sacred. Even the shadows it cast were
beautiful.

There was no surprise here. Not really. Perry had always been someone remarkable. Yet, seeing it laid out like this, room by room, it stirred
something in her. Something deeper than admiration.

He'd grown into a man who knew how to take care–of his space, of
himself. A man who, unlike Joe, didn't try to fill the room with noise,
but offered peace and stillness. How had she not noticed that before?

Lauryn moved to the back window, watching the light play across the
yard. There was a small deck with a grill tucked into one corner and the
edges of a garden starting to bloom. From where she stood she could see
tomato plants and other vines curling through.

She turned back, slowly absorbing the extent of the house again, and
spotted her phone and purse resting on the kitchen island. And then the
basement door caught her eye, the thick plastic sheeting draped behind it
and taped at the corners. Smiling, she imagined him down there, shirtless
hopefully, elbows caked in drywall, rapping along to a Larry June track.

Balancing on one foot, she leaned her hip against the island staring
down at her phone. She was thinking of texting Deonna when she heard
the creak of the top stair. The sound of his steps was slow, unhurried as
usual. The quiet rhythm of a man who was just waking up. Her body
responded before her mind could catch up, the memory of their night,
rippling over her.

In a matter of seconds, he was behind her. His arms slipped around her waist like the night before, and he pulled her close, his mouth grazing the top of her shoulder where the robe had slipped slightly.

"That plastic downstairs..." she murmured; her voice ragged with sleep. "It's giving serial killer."

His laugh was a soft rumble against her back. "Just trying to keep the drywall dust down."

Lauryn studied him then, the sleep still in his eyes, and he was holding her like she might disappear. She wondered, truly wondered, what could've grown between them if she'd ever allowed herself to *see* him like this. Back then.

"Your house is amazing," she said, pushing away her thoughts. "How old is it?"

He pulled her close, "Well thank you, ma'am, it's almost a hundred years old. Still a lot to be done though. Can I put you to work?"

"Yeah if you want it to be a disaster." Perry shook his head, smiling at her as he leaned down to kiss her. She didn't even worry about her morning breath. Not after all they'd shared a few hours before. She ran her hands along his arms, loving that she was allowed to touch him like this now. "You have a vegetable garden."

"Is that an accusation?"

She shook her head, "You can't have a garden and dick people down like that."

Perry broke with a loud laugh, a burst of joy that she was glad she caused. "Is that a rule somewhere?"

Lauryn beamed at him, stroking his shoulder as she decided how truthful she was going to be this morning. "I don't think I appreciated it," her voice cracked a little as she tried to find the words. "How incredible you are."

He tilted his head. "You sayin' that now because you're standing in my robe?"

She rolled her eyes at him. "No! I think I've been saying it to myself for months. I just didn't want to mess things up any more than I already had. We picked right back up as friends, and then me thinking the wrong thing about you and Vivian-"

"Lo?"

"Yes?" She answered right away, hoping he was going to stop her from rambling.

Perry pressed his lips to hers, a slow lazy kiss like they had all the time in the world. His hands slid around and dropped low on her back, securing her against him. Lauryn tilted her head, tasting the edges of whatever this new thing that was blooming between them.

When he finally pulled away, his voice was low. "You okay?"

She nodded, biting her bottom lip, suddenly aware of how exposed she felt—even wrapped in his robe, even after last night. "I'm good," she said. "A little shook perhaps."

He smirked, stepping back to the counter and searching for coffee pods. "That's fair. I'm not exactly at full brain function either."

Lauryn laughed under her breath and leaned forward on the island, watching him as he reached for two mugs and fidgeted with a fancy espresso machine that was not unlike Hema's. The sight of him, bare-chested, relaxed, and completely at ease in his own space, made something flutter in her chest. He looked good here. *Too* good. Like he already belonged to this hundred-year-old space, and maybe she wanted to as well. That thought alone startled her.

"Hungry?" he asked, catching her attention

Her lips curled, but her shoulders slumped with conflict. "Actually... I need to get back to the hotel before checkout. I kind of disappeared on the girls last night."

"Left in such a hurry you forgot to tell them?"

"You know I did!" She cut her eyes at him. "You and your... voice and your mouth and you snatching me off the dance floor last night! I barely remembered my name."

That made him grin. He set the mugs down and walked back toward her, coffee forgotten for now. "How about this," he said, gripping her waist, tugging her closer. "We have some coffee. Shower. Then we'll head over to your hotel, pick up your bags, because I *know* you have multiple bags, and you can change, and... Let's spend the day"

Lauryn looked up at him, surprised. "The whole day?"

He kissed her cheek, then her jaw, murmuring against her skin. "Unless you're planning on running away again?"

"No," she whispered, breath catching as his lips traced the line below her ear. "No running."

"Ok then."

He pulled her closer, heat sparking between them again. His mouth was on hers, coaxing and patient. She kissed him back like she meant it, because she did. And it scared her a little.

The moment deepened with their kisses and hurried breaths. When his hands found the tie of the robe, her body leaned in. She was ready to go back to not thinking again. Thinking was dangerous. Thinking would mean overanalyzing why this felt so natural, why it felt like it had always been there between them, and she'd missed it. Left it behind.

Perry led her back upstairs, Lauryn's anticipation mounting with every step. The bathroom was filled with steam and he handed her one of his sister's shower caps. She stepped in the shower after him, his hands sliding over her with the same care and intention he'd shown her all night. Like he already knew her body, but wanted to relearn it anyway.

She closed her eyes, enjoying the stream of water flowing down between them and she kissed him like she'd never get to again. When he entered her, she gasped into his mouth, holding on to the rush and fullness of him. She clung to his shoulders as they found their rhythm, his words in her ear, whispering praise and all the nasty things she wanted to hear.

Lauryn cleared her mind, letting herself be overwhelmed again by his touch and the way he said her name like it meant everything. She stayed in it. Let it all wash over her like the water spraying down.

Because if she tried to name it, to ask herself what this was, or if the timing was made sense, she might break whatever spell was holding it all together.

Chapter 30

Lauryn

L auryn had not planned to see him this much. After their first night together and the quiet morning that followed, she told herself to slow down. Give it space. Breathe. That plan lasted exactly one day.

With Perry, everything felt easy. Her mood lifted without effort. She caught herself laughing more. She slept better. The parts of her that had gone quiet started to come back. It surprised her how natural it felt to let him in.

A few times now, Lauryn had joined Perry, in the vegetable garden behind his house, slipping on the gloves he handed her and following his lead. He put her to work, helping him plant bush beans, collards, kale, and carrots. They pulled others that were ready for harvest. The work was cathartic, and she found comfort in their closeness, the two of them side by side in the dirt.

"This isn't just mine," Perry clarified when she'd asked, pressing seeds into the soil with steady fingers. "It's the family garden. My parents come through sometimes to help. Mom's real quick with it. Dad... he lingers. We end up listening to records, watching the game, cuttin' up until he starts to nod."

He explained that the family garden had started decades earlier with his grandmother, Geneva Ray, who kept a garden behind her 1930's bungalow. When Perry bought his greystone, his father helped him establish a new garden in her honor.

"Some of this came from her. Seeds she saved, even some of her cuttings," Lauryn watched him, hands resting on his hips as he surveyed the plot, proudly.

She loved the way he spoke about his family. Every word was thick with closeness, with tradition and a legacy he carried like a second nature. It pulled at her, made her think of her mother's garden back home. Rows of flowers, all color and fragrance but nothing to actually sustain you the way his garden did.

Perry had crouched next to her, elbows resting on his knees as he supervised. "Ah, you look like you know what you're doin." His eyes had a hint of a smile as he watched her carefully tucking soil around the fragile seedlings.

She'd pressed the soil a little tighter, a smile tugging at her mouth. "My mom's been making me help in her garden for years, but hers is nothing like this. Lilac bushes, lavender, hydrangea, the perfect backdrop for her parties." She'd glanced up at him, amused. "I'm just the free labor."

Perry had shown her his grandmother's secret to a good crop. Lettuce with the broccoli, dill with cucumbers, parsley next to the carrots. *Companion planting*, he explained. The way one plant could help another grow. She'd teased him, called him "Plant Daddy" all afternoon, but she secretly loved how much care he put into everything.

When she tucked her assigned seeds into the ground, he leaned in close over her shoulder and gently adjusted her hand. "Not too much dirt. They do better when they have room to breathe."

Lately her schedule was full. Work during the week, then evenings and weekends with Perry that felt like little escapes. The Bud Billiken Parade. Date nights at Japanese restaurants, bistros, or the arcade, talking shit over *Mortal Kombat II*. A gallery event where they made eyes across the room as the owner talked her into a purchase. The weeks filled themselves like that, one night spilling into the next.

Lauryn sank into the bath, the blissfully hot, steam crawling up the mirror above the sink. She let her head fall back, the heat seeping into her bones. A sweet recovery, after the ripping and running they'd been doing over the last few weeks. She smiled to herself– how had they gotten here?

She could clearly remember sitting in her tub trying to convince herself to steer clear of Perry, that the risk wasn't worth taking. Tiptoeing around the edge of possibilities with him and that slightly sick feeling when she thought he and Vivienne were together. All of that felt very far away now.

Perry had a thorough method of reassurance. Those deep kisses that were so intense they lingered long after he was gone. And hands that made her feel like a goddess whenever he touched her. She was developing a bad habit of thinking about him at the most inopportune times—work, the gym, or the nights they spent apart. Recalling the feel of his deep stroke during meetings or at the nail salon, her walls contracting with the memory.

Lauryn hugged herself under the milky surface of the water. Jasmine buds bobbed in swirls around her—a new combination she was trying. She'd been at Perry's so often, she'd fallen off from her regular bath routine.

When she stepped out of the tub, the whole hallway carried the faint, sweet trace of jasmine. Her skin was warm from the soak, but she cinched her robe tight against the air conditioning as she padded down the hall. He was reading intently, his brow set, eyes moving steadily across each page.

She peered at the title, something her analytical mind might have followed on another night, but not tonight. He glanced up when she walked in. That slow smile spread across his face, unhurried, before returning back to his book.

She headed into the kitchen and as she passed him, the contrast struck her. There was none of the impatience or resentment that she'd seen with Joe. Instead, Perry was lounging, completely unattended and thoroughly engrossed in his book. He knew how to give her space and she was touched by his contentment.

Lauryn took her time preparing her evening tea, deciding on an indulgent rooibos tea latte. She steeped chamomile, rooibos, and honey with vanilla extract until the kitchen was fragrant with a calm mellow sweetness.

"Smells good," Perry called from the couch without looking up from his book.

Lauryn was fishing her milk frother out of her tea drawer, "Would you like some?"

"No thank you, I've got mine right here." She looked up just in time to see him lift one of her crystal glasses above his head. Two fingers of golden liquid swirled slowly as he lowered it back down to set it on the coffee table.

Carefully, she poured the steaming tea into one of her favorite mugs, then poured the frothy milk over it until it rose just above the rim like a glossy mushroom cap. She topped it with a dusting of cinnamon before joining Perry on the couch.

She sipped gingerly, stretching her legs out until they nearly reached Perry's thigh.

His fingers found her bare ankle, the gentle stroke instantly reminding her of being stretched out before him on his bed. Perry easing in and out of her with exquisite precision. He'd lifted her right leg to rest on his shoulder, creating a new sensation for both of them, and turned his head down to kiss the inside of her ankle.

Even now she could feel the soft brush of his beard, the heat from his mouth on her sensitive skin. She looked over at Perry, tempted to snatch that book right out of his hands and take their quiet evening in another direction. However, this was nice. Sitting together in the quiet without having to be all over each other. It pleased her that they could share the same space without one of them needing reassurance or validation.

Best not to compare, she thought, casting aside any lingering thoughts of relationships passed.

She sipped more of her tea. He'd always been there, but she wasn't sure she'd always been there for him. Aside from being gone a decade, she couldn't recall anything she'd ever really done for him. Maybe, a cup of coffee while they studied. Festival tickets once or twice.

Lauryn blinked, unable to think of anything significant she might have done for Perry as easily as she could remember all that he'd done for her. Her mind was wired, despite the chamomile and milk doing its best to lull her to sleep. And just as her eyes grew heavy, it occurred to her that Perry's birthday was just around the corner. "P?"

"Hm?"

"What are you doing for your birthday? Plans out of town?"

He stretched and turned to face her, "Oh, I was supposed to be, but between Ricky's bachelor party and my travel schedule at work, it just didn't work out this year."

She thought of that thirst-trap photo he'd sent her all those months ago. "Yeah I saw your posts from the last couple of years."

Perry pressed his book down, licking his lips as he gazed down the length of the couch at her. "You stalking my page, Lauryn Lindsey?"

"Yep." Lauryn said it matter of factly, claiming it, her eyes full of laughter. "Your page is like National Geographic meets GQ. And I just want to know who's taking these pictures? You're pretty hands-free in some of these and the angles... Rashad must be a great friend."

"Hilarious!" He wrapped his hand around her ankle, playfully threatening to tug her towards him. "I take a tripod on most trips, thank you very much. And I take pictures of me looking out, that way when I'm old, I can remember what I was blessed enough to lay my eyes on."

"I get it," she smiled coyishly at him over the rim of her mug. "But you gotta have your back and shoulders out in every shot? Does your older self need to know how cut he was?"

That did it, he dropped his book and crawled over her, plucking the tea from her hands and gently setting it down next to his drink.

"For someone complaining so much, you sure seem to enjoy stalking my page." He drew close, his eyes, focused solely on her mouth

"Ain't nobody stalking your page. I just noticed... a pattern."

"Mmhm." Perry pressed in close to kiss her, coaxing her lips apart with his tongue. The honey and vanilla from her latte mingled with what she now knew was bourbon on his lips and she let out a soft moan.

Her tea cooled and his drink sat forgotten as the contentment she'd been so pleased with burned away with each kiss. In his arms, there was no pretense and none of the doubt she'd become so accustomed to feeling. With a start Lauryn realized she wasn't performing, wasn't guarding herself.

She felt the calm of being in her natural state, a quiet joy that vibrated through her more and more since she'd been home. She could simply be herself, and Perry would meet her there without hesitation. He didn't require her to adjust or shrink. With him she didn't have to craft explanations or accommodate him. The simplicity of that felt peaceful and familiar.

It felt like home.

Chapter 31

Perry

E sme didn't throw casual cookouts. Out in the west suburbs of the city, her Saturday night cookouts looked like something off a Pinterest page. Her backyard wasn't for growing vegetables or grilling the occasional steak. It was purposely designed for entertaining, with hidden speakers tucked beneath sculpted hedges, oversized lanterns glowing from every corner, and low seating arranged like some of the magazine spreads Perry flipped through on long flights.

The suburbs had their advantages, he had to admit. The yard was deep and wide, edged by thick shrubbery and dense trees, tall enough to swallow the neighboring houses whole. You'd never know there was a cul-de-sac just beyond the line of vegetation.

He and Lauryn made the drive out before sunset, windows down, the city slowly giving way to the quiet sprawl of neighborhoods with names that sounded like they came with HOA fees. The air smelled cleaner out here. He noticed it when they pulled in. The kind of place made for kids on bikes and parents with matching patio sets.

But right now, it was grown folks only. Drinks were flowing, music was vibeing, and Perry was posted up with the guys near Esme's "rock garden", laughing at Rashad's commentary over someone's choice of sandal. The mood was light, the teasing relentless.

He didn't see Lauryn approaching at first. He felt her presence, catching a trace of her perfume in the air. That subtle warmth floated in first, vanilla or perhaps praline? Lauryn always kept him guessing, but somehow no matter what perfume she chose to wear, her scent hit home, like a memory.

When he turned, she was there. She walked up with that quiet confidence that always made him pause, like if the earth suddenly gave way
beneath her, she'd just keep stepping like nothing happened.

Her twist-out was full and soft, fanning out in beautiful dense waves
from her center part, catching the last of the evening sun. She wore
another long dress, vibrant red and sleeveless, showing off those toned
arms. The weightless fabric skimmed over the curves of her figure and
kicked up at her ankles as she moved. Gold earrings, a dainty ankle
bracelet, and slides on her feet.

Simple looked so damn good on this woman.

"Hey," she said, her voice low and easy. "Foods ready, I'm gonna fix
your plate."

He reached out for her hand. "Thank you, Miss. Lindsey, but you
don't have to do that."

She smiled, a little coy, a little amused. "I got it. I won't be offended."

She squeezed his hand before turning back toward the house, the
hem of her dress catching the breeze as she stepped off the patio and
disappeared inside. Perry watched her until someone said his name
again. Laughter erupted around him, pulling him back.

"So, this is an interesting development," one of the guys said, smirking. "How long has this been percolating?"

"Longer than you wanna know," Rashad answered for him from a
nearby lounge chair, pursing his lips. Perry smiled at his oldest friend
lounging comfortably in his seat. Rashad was casual in chinos and a linen
shirt, sipping his beer like he knew the whole story.

Perry smirked, as he sipped a grown-up Kool-Aid. "We're good."

"Don't get excited that she's fixing your plate, bruh," another one of
their friends joked. "This is just phase one."

"Man, Perry closed out nicely before the end of the season. Girl ain't
even been back a year," Rashad said, tipping his beer in Perry's direction.

Another guy sitting nearby squinted. "Wait—didn't y'all go to school
with her? Wasn't she with that one dude? A white guy? He got famous,
right? What's his name-"

The air changed. Perry angled his head, his jaw working and he
realized he recognized the motherfucker. A tagalong, a bad acquaintance, and unfortunately, a cousin of Luis, Esme's husband. A few silent
glances passed between the other men, quick and cutting. No one said a
word, but the shift in energy was more than enough to shut his curiosity
down.

Rashad dropped his legs from the ottoman, standing abruptly. "These niggas gossip more than women at the shop."

He motioned for Perry to follow, and they stepped off to the side, claiming a quieter corner of the yard near the raised garden beds. They settled into two chairs, the sky now a burning orange and blue above them, strings of café lights buzzing overhead.

"Real talk though," Rashad said, cracking open another beer. "That's a good look, man. Took long enough."

Perry shook his head, amused. "You gon' start too?"

"I'm just sayin', you look... Settled. Like it's easy. Like it fits."

"Yeah, well," Perry exhaled, looking back toward the house in search of Lauryn. "I wouldn't say easy."

He found her again through the open patio doors, holding court at the kitchen island, laughing with Esme and a few of the aunties, plating his food with intention. He watched her using the tongs to maneuver and select the best beef rib for him, arranging his plate so that the meat and pasta didn't end up swimming in juice from the greens.

Whatever her relationship with her mother was, she must've picked up something about the ritual. The care. Those portions looked pretty healthy too. She finally turned, meeting his eyes as if she already knew he'd been watching.

Amused, she smiled at him before turning back to her conversation.

Later that evening, after the elders of Esme's family packed up and said their goodbyes, the atmosphere changed. The backyard softened under the lantern glow, the string lights casting everyone in a warm glow.

What was left of the evening belonged to the usual crew—friends who had become something like family over the years. Conversations picked up again, looser now, with a little more profanity and a little more bite, the laughter louder and familiar. It felt like they'd spent the whole summer this way: piled in at a lounge or somebody's house, swapping stories and inside jokes that got funnier each time they were told. Private jokes that were older than some of the degrees they'd earned.

Lauryn stood between Perry's legs as he sat in one of the high boy chairs, her back against his chest, his hand resting casually at her waist. They were folded into each other like they'd been doing this forever. Laughing, reminiscing, cutting up until tears streamed down Lauryn's cheeks and she gripped his knees to stabilize herself, shaking with laughter. Something gave way in his chest and he replayed Rashad's words.

There was something almost surreal about how easily they fit, how natural it felt to fall into rhythm with her like this.

He remembered standing on the other side of rooms like this, watching her with someone else. Cool on the outside, always the shy guy, convincing himself she was one of those girls who would always be out of reach. Yet, holding out hope every time they met up to study or grab Harold's chicken.

Now here she was, not across the room, but right here leaned into him, warm and laughing like they hadn't missed a beat. Things had turned out different than he'd pictured at the start of the year. He was grateful.

When the night had stretched long enough and folks began trickling out, Perry stood and stretched, jiggling his keys in his pocket. Lauryn looked at him with a small smile, nodding knowingly and started making her rounds. They exchanged unhurried goodbyes, thanking Esme and Luis. They left through the back yard gate and followed the solar path lights toward Perry's car.

On the road heading back east, they rolled the windows down and let the night air rush in. Perry turned up the music, and Lauryn started singing along to the Jackson 5's *"Never Can Say Goodbye,"* her voice cracking sweetly as she tried to match young Michael's pitch. Her features glowed from the dash lights and he almost couldn't look away.

It had been another full weekend for them, working from her place on Friday, waking early on Saturday morning to work out together then "work out" again against the bathroom vanity.

Perry tried not to grin, remembering the day's earlier events. After watching her squat routine with those kettlebells, Perry had nearly started something right there in the weight room. He'd managed to keep it together until they returned to her apartment, kissing on the way to her bathroom so they could shower and get ready for Esme's party.

The bathroom mirror was starting to fog when he bent her over the counter, her black briefs tugged down just enough to make him lose his mind.

The way she'd locked eyes with him in the mirror as he slipped the briefs over her hips and down her thighs, leaving her completely exposed, standing in nothing but her sports bra and powder blue Nike socks.

Lauryn's eyes had snapped shut when he stroked between her thighs, guiding his erection in slow loops up and down her folds. Her entire body shuddering, trembling with impatience until he finally slipped inside. Even now, he swore he could hear her moans echoing in his ears.

He thought about what it meant to be that close to her. To touch what she trusted him with and feel her let go. It was more than desire. More like a high, a rush in knowing he could move her and be moved by her in the same breath. He'd cared for her longer than he ever admitted, never allowing himself to think of her that way. Now, having her so close, it felt like finally exhaling after holding his breath for too damn long.

Perry shifted in the driver's seat and tried to focus on the road. The image of how she'd arched her back so perfectly and met him with everything she had still replayed in his mind.

They'd elected to shower alone, lest they get any further behind schedule. Esme and Luis lived nearly an hour outside the city, out in Aurora, a suburb with great schools, and everything someone might want if they were looking to settle down and raise a family. He could see the appeal, but didn't imagine himself leaving his greystone any time soon.

He wondered for a moment what Lauryn's idea of settling down was. Having grown up overseas and done so much traveling, he did wonder what type of life she wanted to carve out. Even though he knew he was getting ahead of himself, he was starting to love this; the everydayness of being with her. When they'd stopped by the store to get drinks and dessert to bring to Esme's, walking through the aisles together and deciding on the perfect cake, he'd felt something settle in him. Like this was what it could be.

He could get used to it.

At the same time, he wondered, is this how it might have been had she not disappeared on him back in the day, if he hadn't botched things so badly that he'd let her run away with someone else? He was starting to brood over the topic when he felt her hand slip over his, instantly quieting his thoughts. She was the only one who could shake his calm and somehow be the only thing to restore it.

He turned his palm up to let her lace her fingers with his. It felt wonderful to have full days with her, to wake next to her in the morning and lay down with her the same night, scrolling through Netflix until they found something to watch.

He had no idea what was coming next, but he wanted it to be with her. She squeezed his hand and he realized she must've been speaking to him.

"Hmm?"

"You okay?" She asked, her voice melodic and light.

He glanced over at her. "Yeah."

Her expression was soft as she observed him. "You've been in your head the last few miles."

He lifted their hands, watching the road as he kissed her knuckles lightly. "This feels... Normal."

"Normal is not a bad thing," she said, gently.

"Nah. It's not."

They rode in silence for a minute. It felt good. Comfortable. Like neither was in a rush to explain it all away.

How could something so hard-won feel so right?

"You know," she said, turning to him, "Randomly, I don't think I ever felt this grown before."

He smiled at the sound of her laughter.

Neither had he.

Chapter 32

Lauryn

L auryn leaned back on her Sophia Webster heels and sipped her glass of rosé, half-hidden behind a flower arrangement taller than she was. She eyed the elaborate table settings, crisp linens, convention hall staff dressed elegantly in black and white, and the growing crowd.

This was the first personal day Lauryn had taken since starting her job in January. Had she taken it to decorate her incredibly bland condo? A spa day after the incredibly stressful membership launch at work? Nope, today wasn't about rest or about Lauryn for that matter. It was about survival.

Her mother's annual summer luncheon with her sorority sisters, part fundraiser-part fashion show-part social ceremony, was the kind of event that could easily run five hours. It was a marathon of hugs, speeches, and pearls. And if Lauryn had come alone, she might have had to stay until the final plate was cleared and the last raffle prize was handed out.

Fortunately, she and her father had an unspoken agreement. Show up. Smile. Stay for the table photos and the salad course. Then make a gracious, early exit under the guise of "prior commitments." A tactical team effort and although her mother was fully aware, Francine usually let it slide.

Through the shifting crowd, she watched more of her mother's sorority sisters arrive–familiar brown and caramel faces, and glinting pearls. Women kissed each other's cheeks and men exchanged shoulder squeezes, everyone sliding easily into the practiced rhythm of the afternoon.

She spied her mother, moving through it all like a current, smiling and greeting, delegating and orchestrating without appearing to lift a finger.

She gazed at her mother's silver hair, pinned up so elegantly and barely moving as she directed people into action. She wore a pastel sheath dress, classic and severe at first glance. But that was her mother. Always poised and always put together. With a smile, Lauryn remembered all the events she'd been dragged to as a young girl, recitals, fundraisers and luncheons just like this one.

Still watching, Lauryn tipped her glass to her lips, taking a slow sip. The scent of florals wafted up, filling her nostrils and reminding her instantly of her mother's garden and the conversation they'd had only a few weeks back. She paused, silently comparing some of the blooms to those growing along the sides of her parents' home. The sweet fragrance tempered her annoyance and endeared her to her mother.

She made her way across the room toward her mother, officially ready to show face.

Her mother was delegating when she approached, intimidating the hell out of the hotel staff without even raising her voice. She was taking a breath to issue more instructions, when she caught Lauryn approaching out of her peripheral. Pausing, she turned to take Lauryn in. A flicker of something a little warmer than just approval flashed in her mother's eyes.

"You like?" Lauryn, fanning her hands out at her sides like a ballerina as she closed the distance between them.

Francine grasped her hand, leaning in to kiss her cheek hard. "You clean up good, baby. Ah-" Her gaze dropped to Lauryn's neckline. "I haven't seen that in a long time."

Realizing, Lauryn reached up to touch the jade necklace at the base of her throat. "I found it tucked away in one of my old jewelry boxes. Hid it from myself."

Francine met her eyes, a broader smile tugging at one corner of her mouth. She said nothing, only stroking her thumb over the back of Lauryn's hand. Prepared for a battle of wits, Lauryn found herself a little disarmed by her mother's affection. She was grateful she'd taken the day off to attend the event. Her mother seemed to be making a real effort. Perhaps she should too. "Everything looks beautiful Mom, you killed it."

"Well, you know, I'm leading the board now. Had to set the tone." Her mother raised a delicate eyebrow at her, smiling cheekily.

They both laughed and Lauryn gave her mother's hand one last squeeze. "I'm going to find Dad; I'll see you later?"

"Yes, thank you for coming, baby. I know this isn't your thing."

"Of course, Mom," she started to say more, but another wave of sorrors and guests was surging towards them and her mother was already back in chair-mode.

Spotting her father, she wove her way around the decorated banquet tables until she reached their designated table. He was seated with several other husbands, consoling each other through the day's festivities.

"Excuse me gentlemen, may I join you?" She spoke eloquently and they all looked up, smiling.

Her father, the last to turn around, laughed in surprise and stood to greet her. "Lauryn–you made it!"

"Hi Dad," she beamed as he squeezed her and proudly introduced her to the other men at the table, all of them adjusting their gaze now that they knew whose daughter she was.

"My girl. Sharp enough to cut glass!" he said proudly, pulling out a chair for her as the room was settling down for the luncheon to begin.

The two of them slipped out after the salad course, excusing themselves with practiced ease, and made their way to the valet. It had been a good day, but her mind was already wandering home. After asking Perry about his birthday plans, she'd decided to prepare a full dinner at her house for him, even though she'd barely been cooking for herself lately. If she wasn't out with Perry or the girls, Lauryn was usually content to fix herself some tea and *girl-dinner*: charcuterie made from vegetables and restaurant leftovers.

As they waited for the car, a breeze lifted Lauryn's blazer and swept a few strands of hair across her cheek. She turned just enough to find her father's gaze waiting on her.

"You handled that well," he teased. "You even laughed at your mother's jokes."

"Had to. You know she seated us where she could see us," Lauryn laughed lightly as the valet pulled up in her father's glossy sedan. "You don't think she'll be too mad that we left early?"

He shook his head as he walked around to the driver's side of the car, unbuttoning his suit jacket and sliding the valet a tip. "She's in her element now."

They slid into his car, and for a while the drive was quiet. Traffic hummed along as the city architecture grew smaller behind them.

Eventually, he spoke. "You seem... happier lately."

She turned to look at him, raising an eyebrow, much like her mother would have. "You do too."

He laughed lightly, "We're getting there, but you were glowing in there. You're glowing now."

Lauryn bit back another smile and looked out the window. "Things are good."

He nodded, eyes on the road. "I've been meaning to ask, and you don't have to answer, but what really happened? With Joe?"

She hadn't been expecting that turn in conversation. The morning had been so pleasant, and for several weeks now, Joe hadn't made his way into her thoughts as often as he used to. Lauryn felt the rumble of the car accelerating up the highway. Surprisingly, it felt like the right time to share. "We just stopped working, Dad."

She chewed her lip, deciding how to continue. "I stayed longer than I should have. I kept adding more time to let things level out, kept trying to manage it. Manage his moods. But in the end, I just... disappeared."

Her father glanced at her, concern etched in the creases of his forehead.

"I mean, from myself. I stopped thinking about what I needed. I was steadily making space for him, and eventually there was none for me."

Her father gripped the wheel a little tighter. "You said his moods?"

Lauryn frowned, understanding flickering slowly in her mind. She shifted abruptly, realizing her father must be thinking the worst, "Oh–not like that Dad. Joe *is* a piece of work, and definitely unfaithful, but he never put his hands on me."

Nodding, her father focused on the road and grew quiet again. "I hated that you got so quiet. We barely heard from you. I didn't know if you were happy or just tired of explaining."

Lauryn blinked at the road ahead, throat tightening. "I *was* happy in the beginning. It was truly an adventure, but I let someone else's dreams obliterate mine and I'm about to be thirty-seven years old and I have to deal with that."

"You just turned thirty-six," he reminded her, voice gentler now. "I just want you to make sure you're happy. I worry I missed something or that I wasn't paying enough attention."

"I didn't need you to fix it. I just needed to know I could come back home. And I did." Lauryn did her best to hold the tears back as she reassured him. "You didn't miss anything, Dad. I was doing a really good job of pretending that's all my life was supposed to be."

They didn't say much after that and she couldn't tell if he was relieved or more concerned than ever. She thought of her sister then and wondered what bombshells she might have dropped on the old man.

The sun was starting to shift, hanging low and soft above the treeline as they pulled up to her building. "Thank you for the ride," Lauryn gave his arm a small squeeze before leaning over to kiss his cheek.

"Never a problem," he turned. "Oh–don't forget this!"

She turned back to see him reaching in the back, lifting a brown paper sleeve off the back seat. Lauryn blew out a breath, "I completely forgot." He'd remembered her request, tracking down a special album a few weeks before. She'd nearly forgotten until he sent her a text with a photo of his find. It was in pristine condition, still sealed, and the perfect record to add to Perry's collection. Quite a challenge, considering Perry already owned some pretty rare recordings. Carefully, she accepted the flat package from her father, beaming at him. "Thank you, Dad."

"You're lucky I convinced Gabe to let that one go. At any price. When did you get into this anyway?"

She cradled the package to her chest. "It's a gift for someone."

Her father raised an eyebrow, "Nice gift. Someone who deserves it, I hope?"

"Love you, Dad," she said, confirming nothing. She beamed at him before slipping out of the car and heading up to her place, feeling every bit like her father's little girl as her heels clicked softly on the concrete. Inside, she watched until he pulled away, the quiet of the lobby allowing her thoughts to churn.

She wasn't used to feeling so... seen. Not just by her father. By Perry too. The way he looked at her, his eyes searching hers, then drifting to her mouth as she spoke, as if he was drinking in every word, reading into things she hadn't realized she was revealing. The way he moved through a room and still clocked where she was, always within reach but without crowding or clinging to her.

Speaking of Joe in the car just now felt foreign, as if her heartbreak had been a lifetime ago. Lately, her mornings were busy with meetings, inspiring brainstorming sessions with Hema and her team. Most evenings she spent with Perry, and even on the off nights they spent in their own homes, she no longer battled the stream of regrets that came before sleep. In its place, wonder and joy had settled in.

Back in her place, she pulled off the suit on her way into her closet. Her eyes swept across hangers until she landed on the copper dress she'd been saving for the right occasion, the one that melted against skin and felt like she was wearing nothing at all. She held it up against her body, then smoothed it across the bed before heading to the kitchen to make a cup of tea.

The roasted chicken she selected for Perry's birthday dinner had been marinating since that morning–citrus, garlic, and a generous amount of the herbs. She'd found the recipe on Pinterest, proud of the even crisp on the skin as she pulled it out of the oven, juices pooling beneath. Alongside it, lemony farro with caramelized shallots, and honey-glazed carrots roasted just long enough to wrinkle at the edges.

She sprinkled the herbs into the pan, stirring slowly as the sauce bubbled. The aroma hit her immediately and she grinned. Not long ago, she thought she'd never cook for a man again. The kitchen was growing warm and she felt the edges of her hair start to prickle as she stood on her tiptoes, pulling down her best plates and wine glasses.

The doorbell rang–a delivery of balloons she'd nearly forgotten about. "Thank you," she sang, signing for them as the delivery guy helped her wrangle the gigantic bag of balloons and string through her front door.

Turning off the oven, she checked the time. Perry would be landing in another hour or so, then maybe twenty minutes before he was off the plane and headed to pick up his car. Just enough time to set the dining table and take a quick bath.

She set out a white linen runner and gold flatware, but as she struggled to center the matte black balloons above the centerpiece, her nerves began to creep in.

For a moment, she worried she might be doing too much. It was his birthday, but should she be making such a fuss when they'd only just started to figure things out? Not even a full year since she moved back, and somehow Perry had slipped past all the safeguards she'd put in place. None of this was part of the plan, and for once, she didn't want to overthink it all.

Tonight, she just wanted to celebrate Perry; make him feel as good as he made her feel. She'd come to see how often he'd been there for her over the years, quietly, without asking for much in return. He'd always carried more of their history than she had, but tonight she was determined to start giving some of that back.

After her bath, she smoothed body butter and sparkling body oil into every inch of her skin. She got dressed slowly, pulling the gauzy dress onto her arms before carefully slipping it over her head. The off-the-shoulder dress left her collarbones bare, the fabric hugging her curves and matching her skin so closely it looked like she wasn't wearing anything at all. She felt soft in it. Romantic.

She tapped her fingers along the tops of her fragrances–selecting the same one she'd worn the night of the holiday party and recalling the extra time he'd taken to let her go when they first embraced.

She pulled a glistening pair of Giuseppe heels from its dust bag and slipped them on her feet, wishing she'd applied just a little less oil.

She surveyed the scene as she dimmed the lights and finally hit play on the music. Everything was ready. From the steaming platter of roasted chicken and vegetables, to the balloons that drifted back and forth along the ceiling, it was all as perfect as she'd imagined.

Save for the missing servingware. Something about the motion as she swung around the counter to fish through her utensil drawer, felt familiar. All the special nights she'd planned for Joe, only for him to show up late, with an attitude, or a group of friends he'd forgotten to mention were stopping by.

And just as her thoughts began to race, wondering again if she'd overplayed her hand, she heard a knock.

Any misgivings she had gave way to the downright girlish excitement she felt.

Opening the door, she found him standing there, casual yet somehow not so casual, in joggers and a matching zip front, the small carry-on of a seasoned traveler beside him. She caught the slightest travel weariness in his eyes, even as it gave way to surprise, then something a little darker.

"Damn," he murmured as he reached for her, his eyebrows furrowing in that way that let her know he liked the dress.

"Happy Birthday," she cooed, leaning over the threshold to place the lightest kiss she could manage on his lips. He was still a little dumbfounded as she reached for his carryon and wheeled it inside for him.

"How was your flight-" she was barely able to finish the sentence, as Perry, who'd been holding her hand lightly, suddenly tightened his grip, pulling her back into his arms. She was grinning as he embraced her and ran her hands up over his biceps as he leaned in to give her a proper kiss. "That bad huh?" she asked breathily when he finally let her up for air.

"Now you know we're not talking about the flight." He moved in again, claiming her mouth in one hungry kiss after another until she thought she might fall right out of her shoes.

"Brother man..." she pleaded as his kisses slowed. "Could you let me finish my surprise, please?"

"Mm, is the rest of it like this?" His joggers were betraying him, she could feel his arousal as she tried to turn in his arms.

"Why don't you come see?" She led him toward the dining room, nearly melting at the expression that took over his face when he noticed the table.

He took in the table setting, the food and the balloons towering and squeaking lightly overhead. He turned back to her, "Lo, this is ... amazing. You didn't have to do this."

"I wanted to."

He reached for her again, pulling her tight against him so that her back arched and she found herself being backed into the kitchen island. "Thank you so much."

Without warning and with hardly any effort, he lifted her onto the counter, plopping her down and spreading his fingers wide so he could feel her ass bounce as she landed. She let him claim her mouth again and welcomed him between her legs. The copper dress drew up high on her thighs, the delicate gauzy fabric close to tearing, but Lauryn could care less. Her mind had been swimming in anticipation of this moment all day–all week as she planned his surprise.

She felt him leaning into her, his strength silently guiding her to lay back. She followed his lead, leaning back until her elbows met the cold marble. Perry pressed his thumbs up the inside of her thighs, smiling that incredible, horribly irresistible smile. His gaze dropped to the spot where her dress was scrunched up between them, then back up at her and she felt a pulse low in her abdomen. She watched as he bent down, guiding her legs over his shoulders as he went.

Lauryn closed her eyes. Dinner be damned.

Chapter 33

Perry

Perry hauled three more boxes up the narrow attic stairs, careful not to clip the banister. The vinyl flooring he'd specially ordered for the attic had been sitting in his garage for weeks, waiting for him to stop traveling long enough to get it upstairs. Between client trips and weekends with Lauryn, the house had been patiently waiting for him to resume renovations. Now it was time to catch up.

"Yeah, Dad?" Perry exhaled heavily, standing straight and fishing his phone out of his pocket.

"Why can't I hear you properly?" His father's muffled voice sounded from the back pocket of his joggers.

"You're on speakerphone. I'm bringing the flooring in." He was headed back down the stairs to grab another load.

"Ah! You're finally getting to that attic, huh? You know your sister said she was gonna help you with the design up there. Said something about creating the ultimate guest suite. "

Perry rolled his eyes, stacking three boxes and hoisting them onto his shoulder. "Mighty funny, I don't ever see her here when it's time to work on the house, but she's got recommendations?"

"You know your sister. Whenever the weekend comes we can't catch her. Always some event or a party to go to."

"She's twenty-three, Dad. We should expect nothing less. I just don't know why she thinks she's getting an ounce of input."

His father chuckled softly, "It's your decision, son. Besides, after the way you finished the main floor, I have no doubt everything will look great. Or maybe you've got a woman up in there giving you design tips?"

"I'm offended. You think I can't decorate my own house? I'll have you know I spent a significant number of Saturdays finding the perfect pieces for this place. Shoot, some are from your old bachelor pad days."

He glanced toward the corner of the attic where an old teak bookcase waited to be sanded and stained, still solid after decades of use. Downstairs in his office sat his father's old record player, along with the heavy speakers that could still flood a room with sound like nothing modern ever quite matched. Perry had rescued them from one of his mother's garage sales, determined to get them working again. He liked the idea of hearing the music the way his parents had, filling his own walls with the same sound that once filled theirs.

"I know! Your mother's always purging. Says it clears the energy and balances the aura. Mighty funny, she's only ever purging my stuff."

Perry cracked up, "Well everything has a good home over here, if you need it. I guess I took after your style–everything mom has given me just works."

"It should! My old place was hooked up! And you think your record collection is good? Shoot..." His dad was really getting started now.

"Yup–hey Dad? You mind if I give you a call back? I just need to bring up the rest of this flooring."

"Ah! I'll let you go–oh wait, how are my tomatoes looking boy?"

"Taking over the yard," Perry grumbled. He needed to get back there and harvest anything ripe enough before he left today. Another thing to get done.

His father laughed pridefully, "See, I told you they'd like that spot near the fence. Don't let my vegetables rot on the vine now."

"I won't, I'll grab everything just as soon as I'm finished with this."

"Good man. Alright I'll let you go, but when are you going to get a woman over there?"

"Dad!" All Perry could do was laugh, hunched over, he'd been ready to hang up and resume with the boxes. "Where is this coming from?"

"Nowhere in particular! Can a brother inquire?"

Perry rubbed his head. "Not *a brother*... Dad, I really have to go."

"I'm just saying we haven't seen that young woman you were dating a couple years ago. Tiny thing. Redbone?"

"Vivienne," he supplied, his voice neutral as he wiped his hands down the front of his joggers.

"Yes, Vivienne! How's she doing?"

"I imagine she is just fine." Perry stooped down to hoist up another carton of flooring.

"You imagine? I know what that means. Well, I give you this, you don't string them along, son. And I don't mean to press, I just want to see you happy."

Perry exhaled, lowering the box into place with a dull thud. "There is someone."

"Is that right?" He could practically hear his father grinning on the other end. "Will your mother and I be meeting her any time soon?"

Another pause. "I'm not sure yet," he admitted because he wasn't sure. Lauryn wasn't the kind of woman to be introduced casually, not when she already carried so much weight in his life. Perry wanted to believe that what they had could stand up to the daylight. The truth was, he *could* imagine them meeting her. He wanted them to know the version of her he hadn't been able to shake since college, but he also knew Lauryn. He knew how her mind could get the better of her. Of him.

"And how did you two come to know each other?" His father was beyond twenty questions today.

"Uh, school actually. U of I," Perry stumbled, wondering just how much information he would have to reveal before his father released him from this conversation.

"Ah–small world! What's her name?"

"Lauryn." A smile tugged at his mouth as he said it.

"Ah okay, well are you taking Miss Lauryn out tonight? That why you working so hard to get me off the phone?"

"Yes, sir, it is."

His father's hardy laugh sounded through the phone speaker, "Alright, have a good time."

"Thank you! I'll catch up with you later, Pop." Finally off the phone, and thoroughly interrogated, he finished bringing up all the flooring and paint cans from the garage. As he did, he wondered again what brought on his father's line of questioning. He didn't bring women home often, but he had brought Vivienne by when Chicago's shelter-in-place orders finally lifted.

They'd both used the isolation of the pandemic for reflection, to get focused and that had been a turn on. Vivienne's energy was infectious and at the time her drive had matched his. He'd gotten ahead of himself with the introductions, but that didn't matter now.

He made quick work in the garden, twisting off tomatoes and jalapeños with an expert hand. He resisted the urge to investigate a few leaves with bite marks. Something was getting into the strawberries, but it was way too hot and far too late in the day to start tracking down pests. Whatever critters were nibbling had one more night to get it in.

He brought everything inside, including a jasmine plant he'd found when he'd gone to pick up the flooring. Something small for Lauryn to try her green thumb with or make some tea one day from the flowers. If she could keep it alive. After scrubbing the vegetables and drying them, he headed to his bathroom for a hot shower. For the last few weeks, he hadn't been able to shower without thinking of Lauryn, her murmurings over the spray of the shower, the water pooling and sliding down between them. Her hands bracing against the tile he'd installed last year, while his hand palmed between her legs, his thumb gently working on her clit.

He told himself to stop reminiscing or he'd be late for the real thing.

With the towel tucked tightly around his waist, he pulled out his clothes for the evening and chose his cologne carefully, a scent he only wore for very special occasions. Dressed in a lightweight suit and loafers, he gave the house a once over before heading out. Most days Lauryn came into the city, but this time he wanted to pick her up. The last few weeks had unfolded better than he could have imagined, effortless really, but it was high time he took Lauryn on a real date.

Especially after all the effort she'd gone through for his birthday. The rich smell of something incredible cooking when he'd reached her apartment, the sight of her when she'd open the door, absolutely radiant in that dress. Even without the extravagant dinner and the cloud of thirty-seven balloons to match his age–coming home to her had been exactly what he needed.

With the summer closing, his travel schedule would be picking up soon. The senior leaders of his company would be returning from vacations or settling their kids away at college. Client visits would soon resume. The anticipation he usually felt about his job felt tempered now and he was afraid to say why.

Perry stopped for flowers when he reached Lauryn's neighborhood, though the jasmine plant was waiting for her back at his place. If this was a real date then he was going all out. Twenty minutes later he eased his car into the circle drive of her condominium and pulled his phone out to call her.

"Miss Lindsey," he crooned, addressing her in his favorite way. "I'm here to escort you to dinner."

Her reply came through the speakers, melodic enough to make him smile. "I'm ready, just putting on my shoes. See you in a minute."

He was still smiling as they hung up and the music resumed as soon as the call disconnected. He felt good about his plans tonight, it was sure to top the places they'd gone together so far. He got out to check the passenger seat before she came down.

When he glanced up again, there she was. Through the glass of the lobby, he could see Lauryn gliding from the elevator bay. Even with her weekend bag in one hand her stride was smooth and deliberate. The sight of her shimmered and fractured through the glass as she crossed the polished floor. When she stepped through the double set of automatic doors, Perry felt the moment catch in his chest. With a start, he realized this woman had been taking his breath away for years.

Her black and gold heels clicked softly as she made her way toward him and Perry closed the distance, one hand sliding to the small of her back as they greeted each other with a kiss.

It wasn't a polite PDA; not even close. Warmth flooded through him as the kiss gave way to something that left no room for their old boundaries. Any pretense of friendships was gone, replaced by an affection that was familiar and new all at once. When he finally pulled back, Lauryn was smiling, a coy tilt to her lips that made him want to dive right back in.

"Hi," she teased, her voice low, eyes bright.

"Hi," Perry grinned, taking her bag and handing her the bouquet he'd brought. "These are for you."

Her smile grew wider, "Aw, Perry! Thank you." She held the flowers to her nose for a moment before letting him help her into his car.

As he slid her bag into the trunk, she called out, "You know, you didn't have to come all the way out here to get me. I could've come to your place."

Perry eased back in on the driver's side and reached across the console, touching her fingers with his. "You've done enough of that. I wanted to pick you up at your door. Plus, today I'm thanking you for the birthday dinner. Sorry, everything got cold."

Lauryn pressed her lips together, trying to suppress another grin. "Speaking of, I forgot to give you your actual gift."

"Oh?" he leaned towards her, curious.

"Yeah, I was taken *quite* off guard by someone that night."

"Is that right?" Perry looked straight ahead at the road, trying not to laugh.

As he navigated toward the highway, cruising down the entrance ramp, toward the city, his father's question bounced around in his head. *"And will your mother and I be meeting her?"*

In the past few weeks, their rhythm had only deepened. She slipped into his days as if she had always belonged there, her presence at his side feeling natural and less surreal each day. They worked side by side, cooked together, and spent long mornings tangled in the sheets. He hadn't questioned any of it.

Now, sitting with his father's voice still in his head, he felt something shift. A small, growing belief that it might be safe to imagine something more between them. The thought came quietly. Somewhere between her midday text messages and watching her tie on her scarf at the end of the night, he considered what lay ahead with Lauryn.

From the passenger seat, Lauryn reached over to cover his hand with hers. "P?"

"Hm?" He turned his hand to grasp hers, his thoughts trailing off again.

She leaned over the console, "I think that's the second old lady to pass you."

"Oh! You in a rush, my dear?"

"I mean you said dinner reservations..." she toyed with a coil of her hair. "Just wondering if you meant dinner *tonight* or tomorrow."

"I can't believe this. I try to do something nice, got you some flowers, letting you enjoy this beautiful afternoon-"

"Whatever! You've always driven like this. Even back in college. Crawling through every turn like we had nowhere to be."

He laughed softly. "You complaining or reminiscing right now?"

"Both," she said. "Like the night of the rooftop party? You come snatch me off the dance floor, get me all *bothered*, and then proceed to drive slow as hell! I thought you were doing it on purpose. It was excruciating."

He smiled, eyes still on the road. "Maybe I was."

Chapter 34

Perry

They caught a little traffic as they drew closer to downtown, but Perry had planned for it. Afternoons like this–eighty degrees, sun high, everyone heading somewhere–always slowed the drive.

He didn't mind. They had plenty of time to get to dinner, and even with Lauryn sighing beside him like she might take the wheel herself, he wasn't about to rush. As they edged closer to the restaurant he'd booked for them, they passed the same hotel where the last wedding they'd attended took place. To his left, out to the driver's side window, the river was a jade grey green, growing choppy as the wind picking up. The area was teeming with pedestrians, crossing the iron drawbridges, posing for pictures and generally slowing down traffic with their poor judgement.

Out of the corner of his eye, he saw Lauryn toying with her purse as she gazed out of the window. Had it not been for the way her beautiful hands clutched the bag, she would have seemed completely cool, just watching the skyscrapers pass by. He knew she recognized where they were, and that she was probably all in her head about the last time they'd been around here together.

Perry merged over to the right, letting the car glide until finally stopping in front of one of his favorite hotels in the city. The valet stepped forward, giving a quick nod as Perry cut the engine. He eased out of his seat, pulling his suit jacket back on. The temperature had barely dropped, but his fit was too good not to rock in its entirety. He and the valet exchanged keys and a claim ticket, before Perry strode around the car, signaling to a second valet who was just about to open the passenger side door.

"Thanks man, I got it."

The man stepped back, giving a quick nod and an understanding smile as Perry reached for the passenger door. Lauryn stepped down, accepting his hand. She smiled, meeting his eyes as he led her inside. The doorman greeted them and they stepped through the lobby to catch the elevator. They stood side by side, facing the mirrored elevator doors and he saw Lauryn's reflection smirk.

"Do you have concerns about the size of my purse today?" she asked out of nowhere, and he broke out laughing just as the doors opened.

"This one seems reasonably sized," he replied as they approached the rooftop restaurant.

The host welcomed them, finding their reservation quickly and she escorted them through.

Inside, the restaurant was vibrant and lively, even for an early dinner crowd. The light fixtures glowed in amber light, but the afternoon sun poured in brightly from the two-story windows that overlooked the river. They followed the host across the dining room, Perry trailing a few steps behind Lauryn. He blinked as he took in the sight of her from behind. Her dress that was so unassuming from the front, was open in the back, showing off her shoulder blades and spine down to her waistline.

How did I miss that?

He adjusted his jacket, noting the way the dress flowed smoothly over her hips and gorgeous behind, flaring out slightly at her ankles.

He noticed the other diners as they passed. Eyes flicked in their direction, men and women pretending not to stare. Perry allowed himself one smile–Lauryn was a bad. Had always been bad. Even more so when their server led them to a booth near the windows and she grinned wined, delighted, as she took in the incredible view the restaurant was so famous for.

It was the whole reason he'd chosen this place. It had one of the best views of the river, only slightly better than the one they'd seen from her hotel room eleven years before. He'd hoped they could reset; pin a new memory to this cityscape.

So far his plan seemed to be working: he saw her eyes sparkling as they followed the boats speeding toward the harbor lock. He chuckled silently, watching the delight in her eyes as she slid into the green booth gracefully, but kept gazing out. A tourist in her own damn city. Like she'd never seen anything better.

Their server, just as suited as Perry, welcomed them again and walked them through the menu and took their drink orders.

With all the talk of *antipasti, primi, and carne*, Perry's stomach reminded him he'd only had a banana and black coffee before hauling all that flooring up the stairs. He hadn't wanted to be late picking her up, nor had he wanted to rush the afternoon with her. Since deciding to arrange a real, certifiable, non-platonic date night, he'd been looking forward to this; seeing the current expression on her face.

"This is beautiful, Perry," she stopped looking around and zeroed in on him.

"Yeah?" He set his menu down. "You look right at home in this."

"Are you saying I blend in?" She eyed some of the tables around them curiously.

"I'm saying you elevate the view." He leaned back, as their server reappeared. Lauryn had never been a woman to command attention, but she shifted the energy without trying. Everything and everyone around her adjusted, drawn in, wanting to be close. Another stream of college memories hit him, but he let them pass, wanting to remain in the present where she wasn't so unreachable.

Seeing her face always set off music in his head–old Kanye, Lupe, Sam Cooke.

It might have been the whole *One-that-got-away* aspect that had him feeling like something was missing with every other woman. However, Perry knew there was no other woman he laughed harder with, no one he enjoyed talking shop with more, no one more frustratingly evasive, and not a single woman that made his heart so full.

The server placed their drinks on the table; a tall, bubbling glass for Lauryn, and a darker pour for him, fragrant with citrus and smoke. He thanked the server before poking fun at Lauryn, "You and your bubbles. Let me find out you're not a whiskey girl anymore."

Lauryn laughed, shrugging her shoulders. "I hate to break it to you, but before I came back here and started spending time with a certain someone... it'd been quite a while since I had anything dark."

Her tone was playful and she lifted her glass to take a sip.

"Oh my, that's good," she almost purred, setting it down on the table again.

Lauryn had a similar reaction to the tiramisu they shared after finishing their dinner of house made pasta. He'd barely had any room left, but sharing in her sweet tooth was enticing.

The cityscape shimmered behind her and the table candles reflected off the giant windows. Something in her eyes was a little dreamy, and he hoped it wasn't just the dessert.

It was still early evening when Perry paid the bill and they headed back downstairs, meandering back through the lobby which was busier than it had been. For a minute, Perry forgot about everything else: the upcoming Monday, project deadlines, the constant stretch of being "on" in front of clients. It was just them. A summer night, the feel of the city around them, and her hand reaching for his every few steps.

When they reached the entrance, Perry stepped out to give the valet his ticket for the car. The sky was streaked in violet and blood orange as the sun began to set. All around him, the architecture was glittering with glowing windows and bridge lights.

He turned to return to Lauryn inside, but found her stepping through the revolving doors. Her skin glowed under the entrance lights and the wind made her dress flutter forward, highlighting her curves.

Perry pulled her to him. With one hand, he pushed back a few coils of her hair against the wind, and secured her fluttering dress with the other. He resisted the urge to caress her the way the dress had been beckoning him to do all night. She let her hands rest on his arms and lifted her head to face him.

"You're beautiful, Lauryn."

She dropped her gaze and her eyelashes splayed out over her cheeks, making her eyes appear like half-moons. Every now and then, since they'd finally started seeing each other, he would feel a tug of the old ache. When she was the cool girl in his economics class. Back then, he'd never known where to start with her. He'd always waited too long and as a result she'd slipped through his fingers again and again.

Her eyes fluttered up again and captured his as she slowly eased up to kiss him. Her lips puckered fully and the kiss popped softly before she went in for another kiss. Absently, he stroked her hip and he felt himself falling in for a third kiss. *Every time I think I'm getting used to you, you go and show me that I haven't.*

He considered how free she seemed around him lately, and natural, like they'd been together for years. Out of all the years he'd harbored feelings for her, this was the first time he could envision something lasting between them. He could almost see it in the shine of her dark eyes. Still there was still something surreal about where they were now. Not on the street, Lauryn kissing on him like she hadn't just been denying her feelings a few weeks ago. No, it was the way things seemed to be falling into place.

After everything, maybe there had been some reason for her leaving. If it meant they'd finally caught up to each other now, then so be it. He could forgive their old insecurities. He could even forgive Time for the cruel trick it had played on them.

Back at his place, they fell into what was becoming their evening routine. They entered through the back door, Perry turning on lights as they went. He presented her with the jasmine plant, earning himself another kiss and a hilarious round of questions on how to take care of it. Lauryn pulled her slippers out from her weekend bag before Perry carried it upstairs and started to take off her jewelry. Outside the windows, the sky was deep and dotted with stars; the city was just getting started while they were already calling it a night.

Perry padded back downstairs in joggers and a t-shirt. "Lo, you want tea?"

She was crouched down in front of his albums, her dress puddled around her like a paint spill. Turning to look over her shoulder she sucked her bottom lip between her teeth, "Mm. Bourbon? Neat."

He raised his eyebrows, his lips parting in surprise. Lauryn giggled before turning back to her album search and Perry spun on his heel and headed into the kitchen. He fixed their drinks in two crystal glasses that had mysteriously appeared in his cabinets. No doubt, something his mother planted. He heard the record player start and smiled when he heard Lauryn's selection. Yet another reason they got along; their musical tastes complimented one another's.

When he stepped back into the living room, he found Lauryn perched in his arm chair, her jewelry set in a neat pile atop his stone drink table. He handed her one of the glasses, easing down onto the floor in front of her.

"How them knees treating you?" she asked coyly, watching as he got down on the ground.

"You got jokes! And you in my chair."

She couldn't even keep a straight face, her shoulders shaking with laughter. "I'm just saying, you did turn thirty-seven the other day."

"Yeah, yeah, yeah. Hush your fuss," he drew his voice out like an old man, leaning back between her legs like she was getting ready to braid his hair. "Speaking of old jokes... you see this?" He pulled his phone out, scrolling through a few messages to find one from Rashad and turned the screen toward her.

Lauryn leaned down over his shoulder to get a better look. Rashad had posted a throwback, a moment some years after graduation, all of them crammed onto a couch in someone's basement. The photo had captured Perry mid-laugh, Rashad and all the guys, younger, their beards barely filled in, red Solo cups in hand.

"Wow," she breathed. "Seems like a million years ago."

"Man. This is the night before Eddie's wedding. Twenty-fifteen I think." He inspected the photo more closely. "You were still in Cali, right?" he asked carefully, without turning his head. He gazed at the photo, recalling the noticeable vacancy they'd all felt when Lauryn left. The speculations of why, and with who. Before they learned about the famous boyfriend, Joseph Gray.

She nodded, then paused. "Yeah. I was."

Her voice dropped, and Perry felt her shift slightly behind him. After a beat she asked, "Did I tell you I connected with Alicia recently? One of my sisters."

Perry turned enough to look at her. "Yeah?" He offered a small smile. "That's good right?."

She nodded, just a hint of a smile reaching her eyes.

"I remember you all weren't close growing up," he added, keeping his tone gentle. "I'm glad to hear that's no longer the case."

"We're not close-close or anything," she clarified, looking down at the glass cradled in her hands. "But we've talked a couple times. It's slow, and awkward, but I think we both want something better than what we had."

Perry reached up for one of her knees and squeezed.

"I've also been seeing my folks more," she continued. "Trying to be around. There was so much tension between them when I got home, but things are starting to feel a little lighter. Like we might start acting like a family again."

He nodded, watching her carefully. "You're doing the work. Being present and there for them. It'll be worth it."

She smiled faintly, but her eyes grew distant again before too long. That hesitancy was back. After a moment, she squeezed his shoulders with her knees. "Anyway. Let's change the subject. What about you, how's your week looking, P?"

He leaned back against her with a deep sigh. "Busy. Mostly status meetings. Got another trip to L.A. at the end of the month."

She made a sound of understanding, fingers lightly trailing along the collar of his shirt as she sipped her bourbon.

"I'm taking a few days off after. A few of us are going to Napa for the Jazz Festival. Rashad booked this ridiculous Airbnb." He hesitated, then added, "You should come."

She leaned down over his shoulder to look at him, surprised.

"I'll handle the details," he assured her casually, glancing at her out of the corner of his eye. "Flights, car... Just a little end of summer reset. We both deserve that, right?"

For a second, she said nothing, her gaze unreadable. Then she smiled, that soft, deliberate smile that always made his chest feel too full.

"Yeah," she said simply, "I'd like that."

Despite his asking, he hadn't exactly expected her to say yes. She seemed to sense this and kissed him for good measure. Her "yes" landed deep. The pieces were indeed falling into place with them. Maybe timing had truly stopped working against them.

Chapter 35

Lauryn

The office had taken on a rare stillness that week. With most of the team out on end-of-summer vacations, the usual daytime hum gave way to something quieter, more serene.

From her desk, Lauryn watched the skyline smoldering through the windows. Streaks of orange, lavender, and soft pink casting a warm glow across the room as afternoon slipped toward evening. She clicked through the final pages of a quarterly campaign report, the quiet tap of her mouse the only sound left.

The few people that had come in were already gone for the day, but she didn't mind. She liked these late moments; the calm, stillness, and the faint trace of eucalyptus drifting from the diffuser near reception. Everything felt a little more manageable after hours.

She didn't hear Hema until she was already leaning against the doorway, arms crossed, wearing another immaculate blazer.

"You planning to spend the night," Hema said, "or can I steal five minutes before we both turn into pumpkins?"

Lauryn smiled, saving the report. "Of course. What's on your mind?"

They moved to one of the glass-walled conference rooms. Hema took a seat across from her, posture regal even now, her expression unreadable.

"I won't draw this out," she said. "We want you to stay. Full-time. Director title. Permanent role."

Lauryn blinked. She hadn't expected the conversation tonight. Things had been clicking with the team over the past few weeks, and leadership was pleased. She'd sensed something was coming, but Hema's directness still caught her off guard.

"That's... I mean, wow," Lauryn said. "Thank you. That means a lot."

Hema raised an eyebrow. "But?"

Lauryn hesitated, fingers threading together in her lap. "I'm grateful. I just... when I came back to Chicago, I promised myself I'd take a year. To reset. Then invest in something of my own."

Hema's gaze didn't waver. "What kind of something?"

"It's still taking shape," Lauryn said, her tone careful but certain. "Something in the beauty and wellness space, more ritual-based. Slower, more intentional. I'm not trying to chase trends. I want to help people slow down, care for themselves. Especially Black women. We pour so much into everything else. I want to create something that pours back."

There was a beat of silence. Then Hema leaned forward, eyes steady.

"I don't doubt your vision," she said, folding her hands lightly in her lap. Her tone never changed—still calm and pleasant, but Lauryn could feel a shift. "But just out of curiosity," Hema leaned in slightly, voice as smooth as ever, "have you secured investors?"

Lauryn blinked. "No. Not yet."

"Have you registered your LLC?"

She shook her head. "No."

"Do you have a launch timeline? Trademark? Your sources? Early operating budget?"

Each question was gently put, measured without bite or edge. However, somehow that made it worse. They didn't feel like criticisms. They felt like a mirror. Lauryn's shoulders pulled back instinctively, her spine straightening even as something inside her wilted.

"I've been focused here," she offered, bristling. "I want to do it right, when the time is right."

Hema didn't miss a beat. "That's the thing about brilliant women," she said, almost matter-of-fact. "You can't wait for the right time. The timing is never *right*."

Lauryn stayed still. She didn't know what to say to that—because it was true.

"I'm not trying to talk you out of your dream, Lauryn," Hema continued. "If anything, I want you to do it. Fully. Not halfway. You're not the kind of woman who can stay half-committed. Not to this, not to anything."

The words landed softly, but Lauryn felt them settle deep.

"So, decide what you're building," Hema said, rising. "And if you're going to build it, be bold. Do it right. But if there's any version of the future where you're staying..."

She met Lauryn's eyes.

"Don't make me fight for you too late."

Lauryn nodded slowly, her chest tight, heart beating faster than she'd realized. "Thank you, Hema."

Hema walked to the door, then paused, looking back over her shoulder. "Promise me something else."

Lauryn looked up.

"Don't talk yourself out of the best parts of your life just because they didn't arrive exactly when, or however you planned them."

Then she was gone, heels soft against the polished floor.

Lauryn didn't move right away. She sat there for a moment, hands still folded in her lap, the hum of the city just beyond the glass. She hadn't expected to feel so small. Not shamed, just suddenly aware of how far she still had to go.

In truth was she'd done more than she let on. The brand name was trademarked. The domain was hers. She'd sketched out product ideas, outlined a subscription plan for potential customers, even started sourcing fragrances and materials that felt true to her vision. She wasn't ready to say it out loud yet, but she *was* building it.

However, the website wasn't live. She had no plan for investors. Most of the planning Vivienne had helped her with hinged on an actual *launch*, which Lauryn couldn't even define a date for yet. Her concept, although fully formed in her mind and in her heart, was still just a concept. She wasn't networking, wasn't building a following. Hadn't sent a single pitch.

The last few months had gone by fast—too fast. *What have I been doing?* She paused, thinking back. An image of Perry's handsome face filled her mind's eye and she almost cringed. For the past few weeks, she'd been completely wrapped up in spending time with him. She liked going out with him, doing nothing with him. Looked forward to the evenings when he spent the night or driving to his house on Thursday nights so they could work from home together the next day.

With that thought she actually did cringe. Not one of those things were part of the plan. Lauryn pressed her fingers to her temples and rubbed. A quiet laugh slipped out, equal parts self-aware and slightly ashamed.

Hema read her right.

She couldn't be halfway in. Not after packing up her shit and moving all the way back home. If her dream was going to happen she had to show up for it. Fully.

No more waiting for the perfect moment, and absolutely no more distractions.

Chapter 36

Lauryn

Lauryn spent the rest of the week trying to make good on her proclamation to Hema.

Her focus renewed, she ordered in for dinner and turned her dining room table into a full-blown command center. Easing herself past garment bags and shoe boxes, she hauled out clippings and printouts she'd been hoarding for years–corners curled, pages faded, ideas scribbled in the margins. There were Post-it's from old ideas, screenshots printed from old google searches, and a dusty manila envelope she hadn't opened since grad school. She sifted through it all– notes, market research, even a quote she'd once scrawled on a napkin from a conference: *Build the thing that won't let you go.*

A few old photos of Joe and their life together surfaced too, her hand reflexively pulling them aside, setting them face down without letting her eyes linger. That chapter needed to stay closed. What mattered now was following through.

Each night, after working out, she lit a candle and sat with herself. No distractions. She didn't even play music. Just the hum of her refrigerator, a cup of tea steaming atop a stack of thick magazines, and the growing thrill of choosing herself.

She took a few days to return her mother's and Deonna's calls. By Friday, she'd drafted her pitch deck and typed out a client outreach email. She hadn't sent it yet, but she was close. She was closer to making her dream a reality, certainly closer than she'd been a week ago while sitting with Hema, sounding like an idiot for turning down a sure thing without even having set her business plan in motion.

She was stiff from long nights at her dining room table. She needed to buy a desk and chair–finish furnishing her second bedroom so she had a decent place to work at home again. It felt like those late nights in school again, when the future was wide open and she was still figuring out who she wanted to be.

Still when Perry texted that Saturday morning, asking "Meet me at the gym?" she didn't hesitate. She replied, "Yes," with a peaceful looking emoji and meant it.

They met at a sleek looking studio in West Loop, one of those boutique gyms with exposed brick, matte black kettlebells, and eucalyptus towels stacked in perfect rolls. The kind of place that made you feel stronger just by walking in. It was quiet because the weather outside was beautiful–just a few regulars and a bootcamp class off to the side, their instructor shouting like someone owed her money.

Lauryn unzipped her hoodie, revealing a fitted black tank that cinched just right at the waist. Her patterned leggings hugged in all the right places, and her bun was high, sweatband secure to salvage her edges if possible. She was looking forward to getting a good sweat in, lean into something physical after a week of cramming and staring at her laptop. Unfortunately, she noticed every time Perry looked her way. And he was definitely looking.

They fell into a rhythm–trading machines, tossing playful jabs and innuendos between reps. She caught him watching her during split squats, his gaze lingering just long enough to make her slow down, tighten her form, lift her chin. She wasn't about to fumble through a workout in front of this man. Not today.

At one point, they met eyes across the mat, each mid-stretch. The corner of Perry's mouth lifted, with all the suggestion in the world behind his eyes. She held his gaze for half a beat longer than she meant to. Then dropped it. Smiled. Moved on with her stretches.

After an hour, they were both stretching near the mats, when Lauryn shifted into a seated position, moving slow as she tried to get into a proper quad stretch.

Perry glanced over, towel draped across his shoulder, amusement tugging at his mouth.

"May I help you with those thighs, ma'am?" he asked, his tone pleasant and professional.

Lauryn snorted. "You offering physical therapy now?"

"Something like that," he murmured, crouching beside her.

Before she could protest, his hands were already on her–steady, warm, gliding along her leg as he guided it into a better position. One hand braced the top of her knee, the other cradled her shin, and the space between them narrowed as he leaned in, pressing just enough weight to hold her still while her muscles opened beneath his touch.

"You've been cheating in your stretches," he added, voice calm but close to her ear.

"I was doing just fine," she objected.

"Mmhmm," Perry hummed, not bothering to argue. He moved her into a deeper hold, hands firm but precise, full of the quiet knowledge of someone who had already memorized her body. Where she tensed and all the places she softened. "Lie down," his command was soft and she did as she was told.

He moved to her feet, positioning himself at an angle that felt entirely too familiar. Gently, he reached for her right leg, his touch smooth. One hand steadied her calf while the other slid behind her knee, guiding it upward until her thigh was angled back towards her torso. He leaned against the back of her leg, applying just enough pressure, his weight controlled and deliberate.

A rush of heat rose over Lauryn's torso and she felt a familiar thud in her abdomen. Trying to stave off the desire blooming in her belly, she quipped, "I love how partner stretching is basically dry sex. I'm a thousand percent sure you've had me in this position before."

Perry didn't respond, only smiled as he shifted to the other leg. His chain swayed forward as he moved, catching the light, dangling between them like it had on so many nights. Lauryn clocked it immediately, her eyes trailing from the golden necklace to his face. *God, this man.* She rolled her eyes. It was completely unreasonable for him to have this type of impact on her.

Perry continued, his eyes low and steady, and he eased her left leg back down without a word. His huge hands never rushed, just shifted her smoothly into the next pose, even taking the time to realign her foot. She didn't rush the moment and neither did he. Still, she felt the familiar heat building between them, not urgent like before they'd gotten together, but still there. Simmering and inevitable.

When he finally stood, he offered her a hand.

"You should be good to go now," he said, voice even, like he hadn't just bent her wide open with the same confidence he used to make her come undone in the bedroom.

Lauryn took his hand, rising slowly. "Appreciate the... service?"
He just shook his head, chuckling under his breath as they gathered their things.

They ordered smoothies from a place across from the gym and wandered down the sidewalk until they found a shaded bench. It was a sweltering summer afternoon where everything moved a little slower. The concrete radiated heat, the air clung to their skin, and even the breeze–when it came–felt warm and heavy, like it needed a cool drink.

Across the street a restaurant bustled, a curbside patio crowded with people in linen and sunglasses, forks clinking against ceramic. Music pulsed faintly from a nearby rooftop bar. Lauryn sipped her smoothie and let her legs stretch out, sore and satisfied from the workout, sweat still drying at the back of her sports bra.

Everything shimmered slightly in the light around them and Lauryn felt a swell of gratitude in her heart. Where might she be otherwise, if she hadn't stopped making excuses and left Memphis? The last few months had gone nothing like she'd imagined, but she finally felt like she might salvage her thirties; make up for all the lost time bobbing around like a buoy in Joe's wake.

On a day like this, with her body humming from the work out and Perry sitting just inches away, it almost felt like she might actually figure everything out. She was surprised at this, having felt panicked since Hema had called her out.

"How's work?" Perry's question was timely.

She gave a small laugh. "Kind of wild, actually."

His brow lifted, waiting.

"I've been working on my own idea for a brand," she said. "Like, really working. I finally dusted off all my old notes I used to scribble when I thought I'd be some genius strategist-slash-founder-slash-everything."

Perry smiled. "That sounds about right."

"Hema called me out earlier this week," she added. "Told me to stop playing small. She's not wrong. I've been sitting on this for years."

He nodded, not interrupting.

"I don't know," she continued. "I guess I'm finally taking it seriously. It feels... Good. Scary, but good."

"Scary *is* good. My Dad tells us that all the time. If your dreams don't scare you, they're not big enough," his voice dropped in a light impersonation of his father. "May I ask what the idea is?"

"It's called *Of Scent and Skin*." Her voice was quiet at first, like saying it aloud made it more real. "It's a health and beauty subscription concept, still in the works, but the goal is to create bath and self-care kits. Not just products in a box, but curated rituals with fragrance, oils, bath teas... small touches that make slowing down feel luxurious. I want it to be the kind of thing women actually look forward to at the end of the day, something that makes them feel cared for."

She glanced over at him, feeling braver the more she shared. "I finally pulled together the deck. It's rough, but I think I'm onto something."

A pause, biting her lip before she continued. "Would you mind looking it over? I know it's not your lane exactly, but you're good at cutting through fluff, and I'd love your take. Just, let me know if I'm rambling or if it actually makes sense."

Perry leaned back slightly, studying her with that quiet, focused look she was starting to love. Like he was already solving for something. "Of Scent and Skin?" he repeated, nodding slowly. "I like that a lot. Memorable."

He smiled warmly and it reassured her. "Of course, I'll take a look, it sounds like a killer concept. Whatever you need. Send it to me when you're ready. And just so you know..." He lifted his smoothie, pausing before he took a sip. "You don't ramble. You think deeply. That's different. That's the good kind, baby."

Lauryn felt something soften in her chest. She was grateful for him; for his steadiness. She'd never experienced this kind of support in a relationship before. Hell, she'd only dated three people before Joe. She nearly dropped her own smoothie with realization that this was becoming a relationship—and maybe the first healthy one.

She met Perry's eyes, remembering how he'd been during the early years of their friendship, how he always showed up when it mattered. Maybe he hadn't admitted his feelings back then, but he'd always been in her corner. That hadn't changed.

She smirked, "Thanks."

They sat with that for a moment. The buzz of the city blurred around them.

"I talked to Rashad," Perry said breezily, sucking down the last of his lumpy green smoothie as if it was the most delicious thing in the world. "Our Airbnb is confirmed. Private tasting on Sunday. That same vineyard I told you about–the one with the sliding glass walls and the insane view."

Lauryn's heart dropped. *Shit.* She'd forgotten about Napa. His invitation to join him had been swept away with her urgency to make good on her business plan, prove she could make it happen. The idea of the trip was romantic. A fantasy and an indulgence that now felt like a detour she could not afford.

Lauryn shifted slightly on the bench, setting her cup down on the hot sidewalk. "Perry... I'm not sure I can go."

His brow furrowed slightly, but he didn't immediately speak.

"I've just got so much going on right now," she added. "Planning. Research for this brand. I'm trying to stay in this headspace, or I'll be working for someone else forever."

He looked down at his cup, gave it a light shake before tossing the rest into a nearby trash can. The sound of ice cubes hitting the bin felt louder than it should have.

"I get it," he said.

"I wanted to," she added quickly. "I really did."

His eyes met hers for a beat. "You said yes last week."

"I know and at the time, I meant it. But I've got some momentum right now. I need to hold onto it."

Perry nodded, slow and thoughtful. The lightness between them had shifted. He stood, brushing his palms on his joggers.

"Alright," he said. "I'll let you get back to it then. Be safe on the road getting back."

Lauryn stood too, instinctively. "Perry–"

He offered her a small, courteous smile, a polished version that didn't reach his eyes. "All good. We'll talk soon."

He leaned down, nudging a small kiss into her temple, but he didn't linger as he usually did.

Lauryn watched as he turned, adjusted his sunglasses and calmly walked off back towards where he'd parked his car. But she could feel the space that had just opened up between them, wide and unresolved. She sat back down on the bench, wrapping her arms around herself as if to gather the pieces of the conversation. He hadn't said much. But he didn't have to. And somehow that was worse.

Chapter 37

Lauryn

There's a particular kind of silence that settles in when someone pulls back–not out of anger, but restraint. It's not loud. It doesn't echo. It just lives there, quietly, in the space where intimacy used to be.

Lauryn didn't see Perry the entire following week.

She rationalized the silence between them. They were both busy. He had client work. She had work and a research to do for *Of Scent & Skin*. Still, each day ticked by with a quiet unease. Despite how busy she tried to keep herself, it settled into her chest and refused to subside.

By Thursday, she cracked and called him.

He answered, but his voice was clipped, not overly short, but distant in a way it had never been.

"I was gonna see if you wanted a ride to the airport," she offered, trying to keep her tone breezy. "I know you've got that early flight–"

"It's all good," he said, cutting her off gently. "Already scheduled the Uber. But thanks."

She paused, unsure what else to say. "Okay. Safe travels, then. Have a good flight- have a good time." She might as well throw *Bon Voyage* in there for all the muttering she was doing.

"Appreciate it." And that was it.

He texted the next morning:

> *Boarding now.*

Then again later that afternoon:

> *Landed.*

Nothing more.

Lauryn stared at the final message longer than she would ever admit. No emojis. No warmth or humor. Just the facts. He was in San Francisco for work, and then he'd be on his way to Napa for the Jazz Fest. They didn't talk, even as the work week melted into the weekend.

At first, she told herself she was fine with that. After all, she needed the space, didn't she? She'd made the right call. She was finally focused, finally following through on something that was hers, and just when she found her stride, Perry wanted to sweep her off to wine country for a sun-drenched weekend getaway.

It was hard not to see the parallels—to look past the resemblance this moment had to another time in her past. Joe had done the same thing in his own way. Romantic gestures and impromptu trips that blurred the lines between companionship and control. Perry wasn't like that, was absolutely nothing like Joe. Yet the feeling of being tugged away just as she found her balance? That felt entirely too familiar. She resented it.

By Saturday, she'd just about convinced herself she was right to say no, but by Sunday, her conviction was beginning to wane.

Their silence had stretched too long. When she opened Instagram and saw him smiling, fully in his element, it landed like a gut punch. Annoyed, she closed the app, mentally coaching herself not to open again.

After much prodding from Deonna, she joined the girls for breakfast at a spot in Logan Square, a historic neighborhood, known for its artisanal coffee and terrible parking. The four women found a table near the front of the breakfast spot, indulging themselves on iced lattes and cardamom buns. Brittney was passing around floral ideas for her ceremony and Esme had shared that she and Luis were finally ready to start trying for a baby.

Lauryn should've been engaged in the conversation. Sharing her own good news about *Of Scent & Skin* and where she, honestly, could use their help. Instead, she was concentrating on not checking his page every ten minutes— and failing.

Perry looked unreasonably good. One post at a time, he was living a moment she had said no to. Sleeveless linen vest showing off his sculpted arms, tortoiseshell sunglasses, pearl-white smile, beard glinting like polished obsidian under the damn California sunshine.

She rolled her eyes as regret settled into a headache over the bridge of her nose.

Of course, he looks this good right now. "Of course," she muttered under her breath.

Brittney, almost always within earshot of anything juicy, glanced over her shoulder. "Is that the jazz festival in Napa Valley? Ricky and I wanted to go, but it was way too much with the wedding coming up."

Lauryn locked her phone quickly, forcing a smile. "Yeah?"

Brittney tilted her head. "Wait–isn't Perry there? You didn't go with him?"

Lauryn shrugged, casually reaching for her latte. "We talked about it, but I had a lot going on this month. The timing didn't line up."

Esme and Deonna exchanged a quick glance but didn't jump in. Brittney, ever the curious one, kept going. "Damn, I thought you two were locked in."

Lauryn gave a clipped smile. "We're fine."

But the truth was echoing in her head louder than she wanted to admit. *Why the hell didn't I just go with him?*

It wasn't like she hadn't wanted to. Now he was there, in sunlight and sleeveless linen, living out a weekend that could have been hers too. She thought of the wide brimmed hat currently boxed in her closet that would have been perfect for the occasion. Her resolve faltering, she imagined them swaying in the crowd as they watched the performances. She could see herself pressing into him when an especially good song came on, and imagined him sliding one of his big hands around her, down over her ass and squeezing.

She bit the inside of her cheek, blinked down at her saucer, bits of flaky pastry in the center. Another pastry was in order if she had to deal with this shit.

Lauryn headed home afterward, passing on the antique shopping Deonna suggested to the group. With one hand on the steering wheel, Lauryn sped north on the highway. It felt good to get home early, with so much of the day still left, but the air felt stickier than usual, her mood matching it completely.

When she got back to her place, she didn't even try to open her laptop. The pitch deck she'd been obsessing over suddenly felt like a reminder of Perry. How kindly he'd offered to look it over and share his feedback. She tried not to scroll, but couldn't help herself. She and Perry's mutual friends were posting now too, and her feed wouldn't let her avoid it. Tossing the phone onto the bed, she turned on the bath water.

She cleaned, scrubbing surfaces that were already spotless, rearranging the chaos on her dining room table, and loaded the dishwasher. It was the only thing she could control. She avoided the balcony and the jasmine plant blooming all over the place, even though it probably needed water. The weather had been no less than eighty degrees for the past four days.

Eventually, she brewed some ashwagandha tea, hoping to achieve some clarity by the time she reached the bottom of the cup. She took a first sip then simply stared down at it.

The earthy, somewhat bitter taste coated her tongue. "Actually, no."

She walked back to the kitchen, poured it out, suddenly craving something stronger. She had just pierced a bottle of Cava with a corkscrew when she heard it—a knock at the door.

She jumped, turning towards the sound. *Perry?*

Her whole body softened, as she set the chilled wine bottle back on the counter, staring at the door. Another knock. Perry wasn't due back until the following day, but he must have changed his flight. *And he came straight here?*

Lauryn made her way to the door, feeling more and more lifted with each step. He was coming to talk and put an end to this stupid spat of theirs. Or maybe their little spat hadn't even been that deep and he'd just been respecting her wishes to give her space.

Lauryn fluffed her hair, padded barefoot to the door, exhaling out all of the angst she'd allowed to build up over the last few days. She reached for the door.

And there he was.

Joe.

Chapter 38

Lauryn

For a full three seconds, Lauryn forgot how to blink.

Her mind worked to make sense of what her eyes refused to accept. Joseph Matthew Gray was standing at her door. Not on a screen, not in a memory, but on her actual damn welcome mat, looking as if he belonged there.

"What are you doing here?" her voice didn't break, but it was quiet as she realized Perry wasn't coming and the man in front of her really was Joe. She wasn't surprised by his audacity–he'd always had that in endless supply. What she hadn't expected was for him to actually find her.

He smiled, casual as ever in a wide brimmed fedora, his hands shoved into the pockets of a lightweight denim jacket. "Nice to see you, too." He pointed at her through the pockets of the jacket.

Lauryn did not return the smile. "How are you here? How did you find my address?"

Joe shifted his weight. "Your mom gave it to me."

"What?" Lauryn shouted, eyebrows pinching together in frustration.

"She called a couple months ago. Said you were doing okay but... different. She didn't say much else, just mentioned you'd moved back home and gave me your address. Told me I needed to come fix things. I've had it since Spring."

Lauryn paused trying to think. Before this moment, she'd started to feel like she and her mother had taken some great strides. Even so, her mother had neglected to mention this.

Joe stood awkwardly, giving her a look that was half-apology, half-accusation. "I wasn't going to use it. I didn't think it was my place-"

"Then why are you here now?"

He rocked back on his heels, scanning the hallway like he had all the time in the world. "I'm in town for a couple shows. Promoting the album. You might've heard of it," he said, half-smiling, *Smoke Signals? No?*"

Lauryn was losing her patience, but still felt bewildered and wondered what the hell could have possibly brought him all the way to her door. Joe hated nothing more than to be inconvenienced and taking a chance on an apartment door seemed unlike him. "I saw the release."

He nodded once. "Yeah. Well, that. I was rehearsing at a friend's studio not far from here. Figured I'd check in. See how you're doing."

"Check in?" she repeated, almost laughing.

He shrugged. "You left, Lauryn. You packed up, cut things off, moved across the country—"

"Across the country? Chicago is a ninety-minute flight from Memphis, at best!"

"Fine," he allowed. "But you left. And we never really talked. You just... walked away."

Lauryn's expression didn't change. "You made it very easy to walk."

For a moment, Joe looked like he had some retort, but he let it pass. "I'm not here to fight with you," he said instead. "But we should talk. About the house. The artwork. Your stuff. I'm moving again."

Lauryn took a breath, swallowing the next thing she'd been about to say, and instead asked, "You're moving?"

He nodded, brightening a little. "Yeah. There's an opportunity in Japan. Tokyo. A residency. It's short-term to start, but if it goes well, it could open things up for us. The band's got quite a following there, and I'd be helping launch something unique. It's a good move."

He was animated now, the way he used to get when he was dreaming something into existence. Eyes lit up, hands moving as if he could sculpt the future right in front of her. It was the version of Joe that had always pulled people in, his kinetic charm and tireless ambition.

Once upon a time, that had moved her. Inspired her.

She had watched him hustle for years. Had been beside him during the highs, when the band got national attention and things finally seemed to click, and she'd held him after the lows, when early deals fell through and the weight of disappointment nearly broke him. Underneath the years of scar tissue, despite everything, she'd always been in his corner.

Even now, she was truly happy for him, but she wasn't invested anymore. The part of her that used to build around his dreams, the part that mapped her own future around him was gone. She recognized that she could wish him well without wishing for a seat beside him. The realization was startlingly clear.

Lauryn's mouth tightened. "We are not going to do this here. You need to go. We can find another time to talk about the house. Wait, did you already put it on the market?"

He held up his hands. "Why don't you come meet me later? Just dinner. Somewhere neutral. There's a mall up the road, I'm pretty sure I saw a sign for Cheesecake Factory—"

"We cannot go to the Cheesecake Factory," she deadpanned.

She didn't explain why, but they both knew. Joe wasn't just some guy anymore. He couldn't blend in with the booths and laminated menus. She couldn't risk being seen at a table across from Zara and Forever 21, trying to have a breakup postmortem while fans hovered nearby with their phones half-raised.

Joe smirked, reading her expression. "Fair. Somewhere else, then." He reached into his back pocket and pulled out a hotel key card, then held it out to her. "I'm at the Robey. I'll be around for the next few days. If you want to talk."

Lauryn didn't take the card.

"I don't need the keycard," she said. "But I really need you to go."

Joe's smile faded. "I know I handled things badly. And I said many things I shouldn't have. I've been thinking about it a lot."

She started to close the door, already tired.

"I know better now," he added, voice gentler. "But I still want to square things away with you. However, we can."

Lauryn held the door, but said nothing.

"I'll text you the show details," he said. "No pressure. Just... if you want. For fun. Like a last goodbye."

When Lauryn remained silent, Joe nodded once, then turned and walked back toward the elevator, slow and unbothered, like he already knew this wouldn't be the last time he saw her.

She didn't wait to hear the elevator arrive, just closed the door softly, leaning against it as she tried to process what had just happened. There had been a time when she would've given anything for him to show up out of nowhere, make things right.

But that time had passed.

Chapter 39

Perry

T he first thing Perry did when he got home was strip the sheets.

Not just the bed, but everything. Towels, blankets, pillowcases, even the extra duvet from the linen closet. Anything soft enough to hold a fragrant memory. The house didn't exactly smell like her anymore, but it didn't *not* smell like her either. That warm, faint scent she wore–fig and something creamy beneath it–still lingered in the cotton, the air, the back of his bathroom door where his bathrobe, that she often borrowed, hung lifelessly.

It might have been a little excessive, but he needed to clear the space.

Coming home usually felt grounding. The hundred-year-old greystone was his reprieve. Cool air, quiet rooms, and the rhythm of his own footsteps on old hardwood. But coming back this time, it felt off and unsettling.

His guest bathroom renovation had stalled weeks ago. He kept telling himself it was because of work, the back-to-back travel, the fatigue from too many flights in too short a span. But really, he hadn't been thinking about any of it.

Instead, he'd spent the entire summer chasing after the same woman he'd been chasing since he was nineteen. He resented the fact that after weeks of spending time together, getting to know each other in the most insanely intimate way possible, he might actually *still* be chasing this girl after all these years.

While unpacking his carry-on, he thought about the last time he'd seen Lauryn, the way she'd reneged on their trip after agreeing to it so easily just a few days before. He couldn't stop wondering what had changed in those last few days.

Lauryn hadn't disappeared entirely. She'd called before his trip and offered to see him off. He'd declined. It didn't feel right to linger, to hold onto something that was already pulling away.

When he'd landed, he sent her a message out of habit, almost forgetting for a moment that they weren't in the same place they had been. Her reply came soon after.

> Glad you made it safely! Hope the week goes quickly so you can enjoy the festival.

It was thoughtful— like she always was. Warm, even. But the tone was unmistakably measured. Like she was trying to sound thoughtful without giving too much away. It was familiar, frustratingly similar to how she'd sounded the morning she'd tried to let him down easy so long ago.

He read it twice, but did not respond. What was he supposed to say? *Wish you were here? I can't stop thinking about you?* All that went without saying.

And anyway, she'd asked for space. So that's what he gave her.

Unable to shake the thought, he set about trying to distract himself from thinking about her. With music playing loudly from his living room sound system, he started his laundry. Next he emptied the dishwasher, cleaned out the fridge, and wiped down the counters. He tossed the bread that had gone stale while he was gone and a box of assorted teas toppled over from behind it.

He reached for it, tucking the bags back into the wax paper and froze.

He instantly saw Lauryn sitting at his kitchen island, one of his heavy coffee mugs in her hand as she peered at her laptop screen. He'd gotten the box so that she'd have tea whenever she worked from his place.

He set the box back in its place.

Shaking his head, he stepped outside and got to work in the yard. It was already almost too hot, but he watered everything down anyway, getting lost in his thoughts again.

He worked out in the basement gym until the sweat ran down his back and pooled at his collar. Pushed through three circuits, arms burning, music blaring.

Still, she lingered.

He toweled off, pulled on a shirt, and looked down the hall toward the unfinished trim and half-installed light fixture near the stairs.

Fine. If she needed space, she'd have it. And he'd finish the house. The hallway. The damn fixtures. Everything he'd been putting off while falling for her. Again.

He had another day off and a life to keep building.

By the next day, the house was spotless. The garden was trimmed and meals prepped. The light fixture in the upstairs hallway was finally hung, casting the moody glow he'd hoped for, lifting his mood every time he reached the landing at the top of the stairs. He'd worked through every line on his to-do list like it might keep his thoughts from circling back to her, but that was only so effective.

So, when Rashad messaged and asked if he wanted to go out on his boat for an evening cruise—just cigars, cognac, and some music—Perry said yes. Not for the company, but because he needed air. He needed a change of scene.

The water was calm that evening, all blue sky and glassy lake, with the city unfolding behind them in sparkling silence. They were out for over an hour, gliding slowly through the harbor, passing other late rides lit with string lights and thumping slow jams. Perry mostly let Rashad steer while he leaned against the side rail, arms folded, watching the horizon shift from violet to indigo.

They didn't talk much at first. Rashad smoked and Perry stretched his legs, letting the wind scatter his thoughts.

When they finally docked, the sun was gone. The marina was quieter now, but a few folks lingered on their boats enjoying the warm evening while their boats bobbed in their slips

"I still haven't recovered from the festival," Rashad said, swirling his drink. "Your behavior didn't help."

Perry raised an eyebrow.

"I mean, you showed up solo but didn't look twice at half the women who were clearly tryna shoot their shot. You barely drank, didn't dance with anyone—you were putting off married energy all weekend."

Perry gave a quiet laugh, kept his eyes on the water. "Guess I was focused on the music."

"Focused?" Rashad cut him a look. "So, this doesn't have anything to do with a certain young lady?"

Perry didn't answer right away. Just looked out across the still water.

Rashad softened. "You haven't mentioned her once. Not since we got back. Wasn't she supposed to come with us?"

"She changed her mind," Perry said and cleared his throat.

Rashad looked surprised. "She say why?"

"She wanted space," Perry said. "I figured I should respect that."

Rashad nodded slowly. "And after that?"

"She messaged when I was on the plane. Something polite, but... distant."

"Yeah," Rashad said, taking a slow sip. "Those texts hit different."

The city skyline glowed behind them, and the boat rocked gently in its slip, nudged by the occasional ripple. Perry leaned forward, an elbow on his knee as he stroked his beard. He still felt unsettled, especially with the turn in conversation.

"I thought we were getting somewhere," he admitted suddenly. "But now... I have no idea. It's like she flinched, and I'm not going to force it."

Rashad was quiet for a second, then tapped the side of his glass. "Yeah, I'm just gonna stay out of your business, man."

Perry rolled his eyes, smiling over at his friend. Then, slowly, he reached for his phone, thumb hovering over her name. He stared at the screen for a beat, then hit dial.

The call connected and started to ring.

He sat with the sound, the soft drone in his ear anchoring him to the moment.

He had missed her—fully, deeply—in a way he hadn't let himself admit out loud. Not just the unattainable version of her that he'd fallen for in school, but the version that was in progress right now. She was trying hard with her family, killing it in her career, and trying to make some peace with herself. He knew all that.

He'd wanted that version with him in California. Not just for the festival, or the photos or even the physical. He'd wanted them to have time together out of the context of their lives; without their past hovering over them like a cloud. Another new memory that belonged to them alone.

When she changed her mind, it shook him more than he'd let on. Maybe if they just talked, they could reset and get back to the amazing thing that was starting to bloom between them.

"Damn," Rashad muttered from behind him, staring at his phone. Perry didn't look over. "What?"

Rashad stood and sauntered over, turning this phone toward Perry. A bold Instagram ad read *Joe Gray–Live at House of Blues. This Weekend.*

Perry frowned. "Joe?"

Rashad nodded, reading more of the post details. "Yep. Apparently sold out. Three nights. You said Lauryn changed her mind at the last minute?"

Perry didn't respond but Rashad's words started to take root. Lauryn had changed her mind and she had not mentioned Joe being in town. He considered the timing, and how suddenly she'd decided not to take the trip. It didn't take much to do the math.

He ended the call, locking his screen and sliding the phone back into his pocket. The boat rose and fell, slow and quiet. He was over it, weary of Lauryn's indecisiveness, the way she'd folded, just when things were starting to feel real.

Perry had let himself believe this round would be different. That they were moving toward something. Instead, she'd pulled back just as he revealed his hand. It smacked with familiarity.

In a flash he saw himself at twenty-four years old, sitting on the edge of the bed, wondering how badly he'd blown it with the girl he'd been in love with since freshman year, that she'd had to sneak out of the hotel in the middle of the night. Not to be seen for another decade.

And there was Joe in the wings again. No mention of him. No heads-up and too much of a damn coincidence to ignore.

Perry sat still, cup resting on his knee, the boat still rocking beneath the weight of early evening. Lake Shore Drive shimmered with headlights in the dusk light, cool and distant.

He'd seen this all play out before. He'd be damned if he played the fool twice.

Chapter 40

Lauryn

The weather was perfect with the kind of warmth that made you slow down. Five degrees in either direction and it wouldn't have felt the same. After weeks of sticky heat, the air was soft again. Above her, the sky was streaked in navy and lavender wisps, the last light folding behind the skyscrapers. Her head ached after a long day at the office and sitting in traffic trying to get across town. She'd wanted to take the train, but Joe had chosen an out of the way place. His restaurant of choice was less about being inconspicuous, and more about the history and experience–steaks the size of his head, and owners that remembered him year after year.

By the time the steakhouse came into view, she started to question herself. Her mother would have called it closure, and before she'd left work, Lauryn ran through a mental list of things left unresolved when she left Memphis. There was plenty they needed to iron out if he was moving to Japan, but she was unsettled. After the last conversation with Perry, sitting down to dinner with another man felt disloyal.

Although this wasn't just some man. This was Joe, the man she'd shared a bed with since a bed was the only piece of furniture they owned.

He was the person who'd introduced her to what was now her favorite tea. Always remembered to hold the onions which she hated, told the server before she ever had to. He knew she disliked antique shopping, but loved vintage clothing. He'd held her all night after her first layoff, was her surrogate family when her true family pulled away. He'd been her first real love. Then later, he'd looked her in the eyes and lied. More than once.

Inside, the restaurant hummed with low conversation and the metallic clink of glass. She was hit with the heavy aroma of seared butter, garlic, and charred meat. Candlelight flickered across mahogany tables and mirrored walls, shadows stretching long across worn leather booths. A Dean Martin song wove through the dining room, swallowed now and then by laughter rising from the bar.

She spotted him near the back, already seated in a big booth, scrolling through his phone. He looked thinner than she remembered. Sharper in the face with darkness shadowing his green-grey eyes. The kind of exhaustion that success didn't quite cover up.

He stood when he saw her, slipping his phone into his jacket pocket. "You look good, hon," he said, and had the nerve to be checking her out. For a moment he looked like he might actually try to hug her.

"You look tired," she said bluntly, stepping past him and easing into the booth.

"Nice to see you too." He sat again, leaning forward, elbows braced on the edge of the table. "Thanks for coming. I wasn't sure you would."

Lauryn set her purse down next to her. "Neither was I."

She was about to jump right in, get straight into talking about the house, but their server appeared out of nowhere, bending politely to tell them about the specials. Joe gave him a pleasant nod of recognition, as if they were already old friends. "We'll start with the Chateau Margaux...," he said without checking with her, "and oysters for the table."

Their server was kind enough to turn to Lauryn, despite Joe's attempt to order for her. "And would the lady care for anything else to start?"

Lauryn smiled at him appreciatively, letting a little warmth into her eyes. "No, thank you."

After a few minutes he returned, presenting the bottle before uncorking it and pouring a small amount into Joe's glass. Tipping the wine glass to his nose, Joe sipped carefully, his eyes set on the tablecloth as he considered the taste. With a smile, he said, "That's perfect, thank you."

They ordered quickly, a ribeye for Joe and the sole for Lauryn. Silence fell between them as the bread and oysters arrived, but it wasn't awkward. They handed back their menus and sipped the wine. Moving with muscle memory, having dined like this a thousand times.

When they finally spoke, they talked about the easy things first. His rehearsals, the success of the new album and everything going wrong on the tour. Lauryn nodded when she was supposed to, but her mind drifted.

She wasn't really there to catch up.

"I hear you're a director now," he said, drawing her back into the conversation. "Your mom mentioned it when I talked to her. Big promotion, right? I'm proud of you."

Lauryn stilled at the mention of her job. It sounded like he was fishing for more information, when apparently the details of her life were already being reported to him.

He dipped a piece of bread into the steaming white wine oyster broth. "She said you've got a whole new set up here. Condo. New friends. Sounds like you're making it work."

"Yeah, I am," she said matter-of-factly and reached for her water. As he rambled, she thought back on the past year– the quiet mornings alone, the brand she was building from scratch, her family finally starting to heal, and everything that had unfolded with Perry. Then she thought back to her life with Joe–long workdays, hiding in her routine, just like now, friends that had lost her trust, and a man she couldn't trust either. Then there was the house they'd bought for a life they would never have together, a love story that was long since gone. The thought made her shudder and she was so grateful she'd finally let go.

Joe speared an oyster with his fork, squeezing lemon over it before popping it into his mouth. "So, how's this been?" he asked, like this was small talk.

Lauryn arched her brow. "How's what been?"

"This..." he gestured vaguely with the shell, setting it down against the plate. "This exploration thing you're doing."

Her jaw tightened. "Exploration?"

"Yeah," he said lightly, tearing into a piece of bread and dragging it around the oyster shells. "Personally, I think moving all the way to Chicago was a little extreme. You could've just taken some time off work. We could've gone on a trip. But I get it. Sometimes a change of scene is important. Actually, I'm doing the same thing with Japan-"

"Joe, why did you come to my apartment?" She didn't want to dance around this anymore.

He looked up as if he'd expected the question, but hoped it wouldn't have come so soon. He rolled his glass between his palms before answering. "Because I wasn't ready to let you go."

"I already left." Lauryn did not break her stance. If he thought he was going to win her over with some *Please-baby-please-Chris-Sta-*

pleton-I-Was-Wrong-ass-shit, he was in for a surprise. "What were you thinking?"

He blew out a laugh, "I don't know, Lauryn. You left a ton of your things behind. I figured you just needed space, some time with your folks, work some shit out. I didn't think it was final."

"Because my *folks* are the only people I needed to work some shit out with?" She blinked, tilting her head as if daring him to contest it.

"Hey, hey–" he held his palms up, mock-placating. "That's why I'm here. You've been dodging my calls, not answering my emails. Everybody else seems to know more about this move than I do. And they barely know anything. People finding out where you are through Instagram, asking me questions I can't answer..."

Lauryn swallowed, sitting back in the booth. Having to explain wasn't the only reason she hadn't told anyone she was leaving. In truth, she didn't want to risk losing her nerve. From the moment she received her offer letter from Amara Labs, she hadn't stopped, determined to give herself a fresh start. There'd been no actual break up conversation, no sit down to let him down easy, or a speech to say she was leaving for good.

She hadn't told him anything.

When her car arrived that morning to take her to the airport, he'd been reading on the couch, his round eyeglasses making a rare appearance. She'd rolled her bags to the front door, catching his eye. For a moment, they'd just looked at each other, his expression questioning. Then he'd jumped over the back of the couch, racing to follow her through the door. He'd stood in the driveway, in nothing but sweatpants and socks, calling her name in disbelief.

Was I wrong? She considered whether or not it was fair, after so many years, to just pack up and go without saying anything. By then she'd forgiven him so many times, made peace with his shortcomings, and they kept trying.

Sitting across from her now, Joe tore off another piece of bread and spread it with butter. The sharp clink of his knife against the plate jarred her from her thoughts.

He took a bite, but spoke anyway. "You know it brings me no joy to say this, but you weren't the easiest person to live with either. Sometimes, you'd just get this... vibe. Like you wanted to be somewhere else. From one day to the next, I didn't know what I was going to get from you. And it was like nothing I did made you happy."

Lauryn tilted her head at his words. Just when she'd started to feel bad for how she'd left, he tried to put the whole thing on her.

"I thought you'd forgiven me," he said, swirling his wine glass. "I was trying so hard to fix things and balance everything. I mean you know what this life is like for me. The pressure. The pace."

She saw him look around, checking for anyone who might overhear.

"Yeah, I messed up, but we both did. You were buried in work all the time, I was chasing my music and we just let things go. Then one morning I wake up, and you're packing your bags. No conversation. I mean, what the hell, Lauryn. We're supposed to be a team."

Lauryn crossed her legs and sighed; her headache fully blown now. She'd almost slipped—old instincts kicking in. That urge to reason with someone who couldn't be reasoned with. To defend herself against a story that wasn't even real. The way he said things, like he was fault-less and she'd somehow wronged him. There'd been a time when she would've consoled him, maybe even apologized.

But now was not that time.

"Do you remember what you said to me? When I tried to talk to you? You said I was 'adding pressure' when I was 'supposed to be your peace'. It's like because everything else in your life was so monumental and stressful, I wasn't allowed to question you. Ever!"

He opened his mouth to object, but she didn't give him a chance to interrupt.

"You cheated on me and lied about it for a year. Then when you did it again, you tried to explain it like it was some inevitable thing that happened *to* you. And you want to talk about being a team?"

"But you stayed." He actually shrugged when he said it, his tone quizzical, like he genuinely couldn't grasp why she'd had enough.

She sighed hard. "Yeah I did. Too long."

They sat in silence for a long time, the sounds of the kitchen filling the space between them.

"I'm sorry." His words were soft, like he'd only just realized how sorry he was.

Lauryn didn't say anything. She hadn't come for an apology. He'd never really apologized in the past. Now that he had she wasn't sure it mattered.

"I didn't really know how to show up for you back then," he contin-ued. "You always had it together, and I was all over the place. Everything was happening fast– the shows, the contracts, all of it. I thought I had time to get it together. I thought we had time."

Lauryn let out a slow breath, her eyes fixed on one of the vintage photographs mounted on the wall next to them. *Time wasn't really our problem, Joe.*

He reached across the table for her hand. "You were the only real thing I had. You were the best thing I had, always in my corner. You get me. And I miss you. If you come back, I promise you, it will be different."

Lauryn raised an eyebrow. "How, Joe? How would it be different?"

He blinked at her, caught.

"You have one of the most successful albums this year. You've been working your ass off for this moment. You're going overseas. You're finally building the thing you've always wanted. Tell me, how would it be different?"

"I could finally give you more when I got back. I could slow down."

"There's no way you're slowing down now," she said, knowingly. "And by the way, I never asked you to do that. I never asked you to take a break from your dreams. The only things I asked for were consistency and honesty."

Joe looked away from her. "I know."

Seconds ticked by and the air between them softened just enough. He leaned back, lifting his wine to his lips. "You should come to the show tomorrow. I know the guys would love to see you."

Lauryn didn't respond. She thought of his band mates, Ezra and James, both of them frequent witnesses to every time she forgave Joe. Possibly co-conspirators too.

When she still said nothing, Joe nodded once and pushed his empty wine glass to the center of the table. After another long beat, he lifted his head, meeting her eyes. "I really messed us up, didn't I?"

She nodded once, mirroring him and watched as the realization sunk in. Standing, she spoke as gently as she could, "Joe, I'm gonna go. Cancel my order?"

Joe looked up at her, his eyes full of a remorse. "We didn't talk about the house-"

She reached for her purse. "We don't need to talk about the house. Sell it, send me my half. Have someone pack up the rest of my things, or I'll have them picked up."

While Joe had been confessing, it dawned on Lauryn that they didn't need to draw this out. There were people they could pay to wrap this mess. In reality this was simple and for the hundredth time she wondered why she'd even come this far. Perhaps she wasn't as unaffected by him as she liked to think.

A little more healing to do, she admitted silently.

"Goodbye, Joseph." She pressed a hand to his shoulder as she moved to leave. Felt him lean into it before she pulled away. After twelve years, it was over.

Lauryn felt raw and exhausted when she got home, drained from the past few days' events. All she wanted to do was sink into a hot bath and find something sweet to eat, but she couldn't bring herself to get out of the car. She sank deep in the driver's seat. Pulling her phone out of the cup holder to call Perry, she noticed a missed call from him.

Clearing her throat, she pressed the phone icon to call him back. It rang and rang until his voicemail sounded, his professional greeting offering her little comfort. And maybe that was for the best. Her mind was already too full. She didn't want to accidentally offload this onto Perry, or throw things even more off between them.

Her phone buzzed in her hands. A message from Vivienne, of all people:

> *Girl, that reel you did about having a candle lighting ceremony when you get home to decompress...*

> *Brilliant!! I can't wait until your bath kits drop!*

Lauryn smiled, surprised by how much she needed that. Without overthinking it, she called her.

Vivienne picked up right away. "Okay influencer! That candle shot with you stepping into the steaming tub? You better sell luxury."

Lauryn laughed, easing her car seat back into a recline. "You told me to use the socials to build a community."

"I didn't mean softcore boudoir in a marble tub, but I'm not mad at it," Vivienne teased. "I was like, 'let me find out Lauryn had an Onlyfans this whole time'!'"

Lauryn snorted. "Naw, I missed that boat."

The warmth was still there between them. Familiar, but a little fragile. Vivienne's voice softened. "I'm glad you called, girl, Texas is crazy."

"Yeah?" Lauryn's tone dropped. "Here is crazy too."

They caught up on everything and nothing. Vivienne's official move to Dallas, her viral branding workshop that sold out in two hours, and her new roommate who was apparently training for a triathlon and ate like a teenage boy.

"You still doing HIIT classes at sunrise?" Lauryn asked.

"Absolutely not. I'm a Twerk & Tone girl now. You?"

Lauryn shook her head. "More like... gym when I remember I'm aging."

Vivienne cackled. "Wow. We really let our thirties humble us."

The conversation drifted into their usual rhythm casual shade, encouragements, even some nostalgia about their old office days. There was a little distance between them, but it was softening with every update, every laugh.

The call stretched longer than Lauryn expected and she was glad for it. She paused, drawing in a breath. "I should tell you something."

"What's up?" she heard Vivienne clattering away with something in the background.

Biting her lip, she tried to think of the best way to approach the subject, but ended up just blurting it out. "It's Perry."

There was a pause. Then Vivienne exhaled, seemingly amused. "Of course it's Perry."

Lauryn blinked. "You're not... surprised?"

"No, not really. He's moisturized, handsome, emotionally intelligent, and he has a fricken garden with vegetables and butterflies. I would've fallen harder if I hadn't been so busy being unimpressed."

Lauryn laughed, covering her eyes. "Oh, my goodness, I have been stressing on how to tell you."

"I wasn't in love with him when we dated," Vivienne said, more gently now. "I was just tired of the wrong kind of attention. But I guess I'm still in my fuck-boy phase."

She continued, "And I probably talked slick about him because it was easier to pretend he was boring. But he wasn't. Perry's consistent."

Lauryn wasn't sure how to respond. Yet another conversation this week that almost rendered her speechless. "And if its deep for you," Vivienne added. "Don't run from it."

"Vivienne, I know this is weird-"

"Just give us some time, okay? We'll be fine. And as for the brand? I can already tell, you've got this."

The two of them stayed on the phone a little longer–enough to promise another call soon, although Lauryn wasn't exactly sure they would.

After hanging up, she finally made her way upstairs, her heels sounding as she made her way across the parking garage and into the elevator.

She checked her phone one last time before setting it down on the kitchen counter. Still no return call from Perry, although it was late now. She stripped on the way to the bedroom, found her robe and wrapped it tight around herself like armor.

Joe had said all the right things. Just way too late.

Vivienne had said the one thing that mattered.

Don't run from it.

Lauryn settled onto the couch and closed her eyes, too tired for a bath. She curled into the cushions, letting the day's heaviness dissipate.

She just wanted to sleep, shut it all off, and retreat into herself the way she always did when things got too tangled. No more replaying or analyzing. Just her breath, and sleep coming to claim her.

That was the only thing she had to do tonight. Tomorrow was another day.

Chapter 41

Lauryn

Lauryn woke early Friday morning and, for the first time in weeks, felt calm. Maybe it was the relief of finally closing the door on something that had been unraveling for far too long. Maybe it was the quiet that comes after telling the truth out loud. But as she lay in bed staring at the soft light filtering through the window, she realized something. Formally ending things with Joe had given her back a piece of herself.

It had finally severed what had been a very long tether.

She took a personal day, sending a note directly to Hema that she hoped was gracious enough while still being direct. She thanked her for the opportunity to lead the strategy team, expressed gratitude for the board's confidence in her, and reiterated her commitment to completing her one-year contract.

Hitting send felt a little like pressing 'play' on *Of Scent & Skin*.

She took her time undoing the loose braids she'd plaited into her hair the night before to preserve her style. It was day three, when the volume and wave pattern were just right–her favorite point in the cycle of her hair between washes.

Later that morning, she sat out on her balcony with a cup of masala chai, sipping from a blue and gold cup and matching saucer. The highway whooshed faintly below her, but up on her balcony, surrounded by her jasmine and a few new plants, she felt still. The solitude brought the peace she'd been seeking.

For the first time in a long time, she felt genuinely hopeful about what she could build for herself, by herself.

She'd tried calling Perry again, but he hadn't answered.

Why is it always all or nothing with these men? She wondered, turning the phone upside down on the little glass table next to her.

Just then, her phone buzzed. Her mother. On FaceTime.

She debated declining, eager to maintain the morning's peace just a little while longer. Pursing her lips, she remembered she had a bone to pick with one Francine Lindsey.

"Lauryn Michelle! You never called me back," her mother hollered at the phone when Lauryn answered. "I'm still waiting to hear about the other night, but first let me tell you–I am so tired of these women. You would think after all these years they could coordinate one damn fundraiser without turning it into an ego contest."

Lauryn sat patiently, smiling faintly, waiting for her mother to finish her rant. "Mom. Why did you give Joe my address?"

Her mother blinked, speechless for the first time in about twenty years. Then she sighed. "Did he actually show up?"

"Yes he did."

Her mother winced, but a small laugh slipped. "Well shit, honey, I am sorry. But honestly, I didn't think he would. It was more of a challenge than anything."

It was Lauryn's turn to blink, first at her mother's language, then at the older woman's reasoning. "Well, your challenge was accepted. Goodness, Mom, sometimes I think you hate me."

Francine laughed again, more openly this time. "Don't be dramatic. I had no idea at the time how bad things had gotten between you two! I thought you were upset because he hadn't proposed, and you were creating some distance to make him step up–"

Her mother's comments echoed Joe's so closely, she questioned how much her mother really didn't know about him popping up. "Seriously. Mom I can't believe–?"

"But I see now that it was more than that," Francine finished, her voice rising slightly over her daughter's to finish her point. "Plus, you're not like me. The cold shoulder isn't your style."

Lauryn said nothing.

"Besides," her mom added, leaning closer to the screen, "you're clearly seeing someone else. Don't tell me it's not serious. I can see it all over your face. I love this FaceTime thing."

Lauryn swallowed as her objections lodged in her throat. She bit back a smile. "Goodbye, Mom."

She waited just long enough to see her mother wave at the phone screen before ending the call. Surprised, she found she wasn't so upset with her mother. The betrayal she'd felt after hearing she and Joe were in cahoots had softened to a mild annoyance. Ironically, in keeping with how she normally felt towards her mother.

Still barefoot and wrapped in a blush silk robe, Lauryn shifted in her chair and took a long sip of chai, the ceramic mug warm against her palms.

Her mother's words replayed in her mind. She stared out at the distant city skyline, the Sears tower unmistakable, even from here. She inhaled deeply, thinking of all the versions of herself that had skipped all over that city. Everything felt quieter now as if something had truly turned over in her mind. Her mother's commentary, and her own fears, the years of regrets—none of it felt as heavy anymore.

Lauryn exhaled, reaching for her phone and pulled up her message thread with Perry:

> I'd like to see you. Are you around?

She was a little disappointed when no response came, not even the little gray dots.

It was probably silly to expect an immediate response after days of not speaking, but staring at the sparse chat window, she couldn't help feeling a pinch of doubt behind her ribs.

"I'm being ridiculous," she said aloud, pushing off from her deck chair and heading back into the house. More than an hour passed—long enough for her to get dressed—and Perry had not responded.

Suddenly annoyed, she snatched up her purse and keys, heading out the door and hitting it down the hallway towards the elevator. She wasn't being ridiculous—this *silence* between them was ridiculous.

She had to double back to her apartment in order to retrieve Perry's birthday gift that she still hadn't managed to give him. She knew he worked from home on Fridays. Normally she would've been working from home right along with him, both of them settled into his couch, legs propped up on the edge of his coffee table. Then tossing her laptop to the side, crawling across the cushions to get closer to him. Catching the lobe of his ear in her teeth, kissing along the line of his beard until she finally broke his concentration...

Traffic was terrible. It didn't help that she had to get past downtown just to get to Perry's neighborhood. And just as she was merging off the highway, his text reply finally came:

> I'm around. Where?

Her thumbs froze mid-response. She'd been bold enough to start driving to his house anyway, but now she felt self-conscious. How crazy would she sound saying, *I'm outside*–when she practically was, idling at the light by the winery just a few blocks from his place.

Instead, she sent a quick reply, softening the truth with a small lie about already being in the neighborhood. She took her time parking, half-convinced he might spot her the second she pulled up. *Well, you drove all the way down here,* she chided herself, snatching up her purse and his gift from the passenger seat.

Climbing the front steps, she pressed the doorbell and waited. A long, uncomfortable minute dragged by, and she wondered if she'd really driven all this way just to be left standing on the stoop.

Finally, there was a cracking sound as Perry opened the door. He stood in the frame for a beat, like he wasn't sure whether or not to let her in. There was something unreadable in his gaze, probably wondering how the hell she'd gotten there so quickly.

"Come in."

He stepped aside to let her in, but the foyer felt tight as she passed through, trying not to brush his arm as she stepped inside. As it had when she first moved home, it felt too soon for contact. As if he wasn't hers to touch anymore.

The house smelled clean and the hardwood beneath her feet gleamed like it had been freshly buffed. The afternoon light pouring through the front windows hit every surface, highlighting the vastness of the space. Even the small runner rug was perfectly straight. He'd been busy.

They orbited around each other awkwardly, Lauryn struggling to find the ease that had always been there between them. She took in the changes, noticing new light fixtures, the plastic sheeting that once covered the basement door was gone, the drop cloths too. The renovations he'd started months ago had apparently resumed.

"The house looks great," she tried to lift her voice.

"Thank you," he was pleasant enough, standing there looking fine as ever in a gray t-shirt and jeans. Before he'd left for California–before Lauryn had reneged on him–they were just getting to the point where she started to recognize pieces of his wardrobe. This T-shirt in particular had become one of her favorites–the thick fabric soft against her skin when he pulled her close, carrying his warmth and the faintest trace of him after he took it off.

"How are you?" she added gently. "How was the festival?"

"It was good," he said. "Good time."

She nodded, fiddling with her fingers. This was going to be tough if he was only going to give two-word responses. She realized he'd been caught off guard by her changing her mind, but right now he was guarded and it felt misplaced. "I brought you something. It's late, but–happy birthday."

She handed him the envelope. He opened it carefully, sliding out the Donny Hathaway album.

His eyes lit up as he read the title, then flipped it over, fingers grazing the edges like something sacred. The moment swelled with the kind of softness that had once lived so easily between them.

"Original pressing?"

She nodded.

"Damn. I've been looking for a clean one for years."

"I know. You mentioned it back in school. My Dad helped me track it down."

He looked up then. And for a moment, the old warmth returned, flickering across his face like he might reach for her.

But he didn't.

Carefully, he set the album and it's wrapping down on the entryway table, nodding. "Thank you. This really means a lot."

She hesitated, searching his face. "P, I wanted to explain why I didn't go to California."

Perry leaned against the edge of the table; arms crossed. "You don't need to do that."

"I want to," she said, keeping her voice even. "I needed to make some real progress on the business plan. Clear some space in my mind for what I really want to do when this year is up. And... reconciling some things."

"I'm glad you had some time."

"For the first time in years, I feel like myself. Not someone's girlfriend, or someone's daughter, or someone trying to pretend. Just me."

Perry watched her, his expression still unreadable.

"I'm finally making decisions based on my own reasons," she continued. "It's the first time I've done that since I was twenty years old."

"And what?" he asked, voice low. "That meant not telling me any-thing? Just disappearing from something we were building?"

"I wasn't disappearing," she said, frustrated. "I was trying to be honest with myself. I was trying to stay focused."

He shook his head slowly. "Lauryn, I wasn't trying to get in your way."

"I know you weren't," she assured him. "But I might've let you. That's the part I'm still working on. I finally feel like I'm starting to figure things out, but I'm not even sure if I'm staying in Illinois. I just can't afford to be distracted right now."

Perry dropped his head, watching her for a moment. His brow fur-rowed in confusion and she realized she'd shared too much.

"I'm a distraction now?" he asked, clearly taken aback. "And what do you mean you don't know if you're staying?"

"I haven't decided, yet. And I didn't mean you're–Perry, I wasn't saying that you are the problem. I'm saying I'm just now starting to forgive myself. For everything I let slide. For how much time I wasted. For not trusting my own instincts. Ignoring what I knew I needed."

When he didn't say anything, she continued, because she needed to say it out loud. "I no longer feel like my regrets have me in a chokehold. And I don't want to apologize for finally being free of that."

He stood still for a moment, the silence growing heavier with each passing second. "I saw that you called the other day. I meant to get back to you, I just..."

An olive branch? Lauryn thought, smiling weakly. "Yeah. I wanted to see you."

He gave her a half smile. "I wanted to see you too. Last week."

She winced. "Perry–"

He stepped closer to her, his voice calm but carrying weight. "Let me say this, please. Before you start explaining. I was looking forward to that trip. Not just because of the festival. I wanted you there with me. Us, away from everything else." He shook his head slightly. "And you pulled out at the last minute. Again."

Her lips parted to respond, but he sighed, seemingly already weary of the conversation.

"I am glad that you're finding your way with your brand. Your idea is *smart,* it's timely. There isn't a doubt in my mind that it'll be a success. But you didn't even share it with me until you had to."

"What do you mean?"

"Your business plans. The perfect excuse to back out. Then I get back home, and I hear–*through somebody else*–that Joseph Gray's in town. What am I supposed to think?"

"Perry, that was nothing. It isn't like that."

"Then what is it like, Lauryn? From where I'm standing, it feels like every time it comes to me, there's a line you won't cross. And I'm wondering, do you keep that boundary because you think I'll never push back, or because you're still leaving room for him?"

She blinked hard, stunned by his bluntness. "That's not fair. I didn't even know he was in town until after I'd already decided not to go on the trip with you."

Perry exhaled, shaking his head. "I can't believe I'm here again with you. This just feels so familiar. You didn't tell me you were seeing Joe back in grad school either. I just had to find that out on my own, through the socials. Kinda like I found out this time." He motioned his hands in a circle between them, further demonstrating his point. "And then, you get mad at me because I didn't tell you about Vivienne?"

Lauryn straightened, her jaw tense. "I understand how it looks," she spoke slowly but firmly. "But me deciding not to go with you to Napa had nothing to do with him. It was about me. I just–" She blew out a sharp breath, shaking her head. "I needed space, and I didn't know how to ask for it without messing things up between us."

His gaze didn't waver, his dark eyes boring into her. "Yeah well, your approach needs work."

Lauryn threw up her hands, exasperated. "You act like I planned this. Joe showed up out of nowhere, because my mother gave him my address! He tells me we have to sell the house because he's moving to fucking Japan for however long–look, it doesn't even matter. I met with him, it's over."

"You met with him?"

His question hit Lauryn like a blow. Stricken, she watched as emotion settled in his eyes, not anger, not disbelief, but disappointment.

"Just to talk iron things out, but it's done. I didn't even stay–" Her tone lifted as she tried to reassure him.

"I thought you two were already done."

"We are, but..."

"What, now you're not done?"

For a moment, Lauryn pressed her eyes closed, heat rushing to her face. He was focusing on the wrong things, oversimplifying it all too, and she felt ridiculous trying to explain away something when nothing had happened with Joe.

"Look, I know I don't have the greatest track record here, but there is nothing going on between me and Joe. And by the way, twelve years is a long time. It's like trying to stop a freight train on a dime. I *wanted* it to be done last year, that's why I came home. But there was still shit to unravel and I'm trying my best."

Silence surged back in again, so deep she could hear the house breathe.

She hung her head, her thoughts spilling out before she could catch them. "This is why I didn't want to do this with you." As soon as she said it, she regretted it. "Perry, I didn't mean..."

His eyes were fixed on the floor between them, his hands sunk deep in his pockets. She saw him nod slowly, like he was letting her words settle. When he finally looked up at her, the warmth and even that disappointment was gone from his face.

His voice was flat, almost professional, "Thank you for the album."

Lauryn's stomach dropped and suddenly she couldn't find her voice. How had they gotten here and why hadn't she told him all the things she'd meant to before walking in his front door? The conversation had unraveled so spectacularly she wasn't sure how to backtrack.

The hardwood floors creaked beneath her shifting weight as her thoughts raced.

Perry's eyes flicked away, his voice even, stripped of anything soft. "I need to meet the guys."

The conversation was over. She wanted to argue, to stay long enough for him to understand where she was coming from, but no amount of talking would get them anywhere tonight.

"Okay," she spoke softly, gripping the leather straps of her bag. "We'll talk later I guess."

She crossed the room quickly, ready to put some distance between herself and the disaster that had unfolded in Perry's front room. She'd stepped through the front door and was pulling it closed behind her, when Perry caught the door.

She paused, looking back to find Perry. "I'll walk you to your car."

He followed her silently down the steps. The evening air had cooled with the fading light, as if the whole neighborhood had heard their conversation. Each step toward her car dragged with it the weight of it.

At her car, Perry pulled the door open for her, waiting. She slid inside, but looked back up at him. "I didn't mean—"

He cut her off, voice low and final, eyes unreadable. "For the record, I didn't want *this* with you again either."

He shut the door with a muted thud and turned back toward the steps. Lauryn stayed still, watching Perry's retreating form through the windshield. Her chest burned with frustration—at Perry, who couldn't see how much she was carrying or how hard she was trying to reconcile it all. At herself, for letting Joe crash back into her life and wreck the little peace she'd managed to build. And most of all at herself for this—hurting Perry, her oldest friend, a second time. When she knew better. When she'd promised herself she'd stay away.

She started the car, the seatbelt chime cutting through Perry's words already looping in her head. *I didn't want to do this with you again either.* She understood what he meant. He hadn't wanted to find himself here again, caught in the same ache, standing in the same place as he had before. She hadn't wanted to renege on him again either. In her mind, she retraced her steps, but she couldn't figure out how to undo it all.

Somehow, in trying to make things right, she managed to recreate the past.

Chapter 42

Lauryn

"I 'll have the... Very Berry?" Lauryn read from the menu above the cashier's head as she ordered. After their work out this morning, Deonna had insisted on a new smoothie bowl place, and although the shop was adorable, with its black and white bistro chairs and muted botanical wall paper, there wasn't a single part of her that wanted a smoothie.

Despite their early morning walk and Pilates class that morning, all she wanted was a flaky, golden croissant and a matcha latte to wash it down with.

"Lauryn! You want to sit outside?" Deonna called over the roar of commercial blenders all running simultaneously.

"Let's," Lauryn nodded eagerly. When her smoothie was finally ready they headed outside, Deonna claiming the only table left with an umbrella.

"Oooh girl, I'm going to sleep so good tonight," Deonna eased down into her chair, obviously feeling the effects of their Hot Girl Pilates class.

"It's not even noon and you're already thinking about sleep?"

Deonna shook her head, puckering her lips together and frowning like she had a brain freeze. "Mm-mn! My bed and I have a wonderful relationship. He's always there when I need him and he always knows I'm coming home."

Lauryn laughed, taking a cautious sip of her smoothie. It was good, but it was no croissant. Not to mention the texture instantly reminded her of the smoothie she'd shared with Perry before he left for California. She'd lost her appetite after he left, and the frozen blend of greens melted into a terrible tasting sludge.

"Plus, my pillows whisper the nastiest things in my ear. *'Come on girl, you know you want to lay down'. 'Wear them panties I like'. 'Just get under the covers, it'll be so good for you, baby'*..."

"Oh, my goodness. Not your pillows trying to seduce you–"

"Girl, every night. Snatch my bonnet off and everything." She ran a hand over her smoothed bun.

Frozen smoothie juice nearly came up through Lauryn's nose. She took a moment to swallow, trying to not choke on the laughter she could barely control. "Deonna, shut up!"

Her friend just flashed her a grin, giggling as she went back to sipping her own drink. They settled down, enjoying the season as it changed around them. The heat of summer had broken into a string of thunderstorms, and even now that the rain had cleared, a telling breeze was working its way through town. Lauryn watched a patch of trees across the street, their leaves still holding their green color in the bright morning sun. It had been years since she'd seen fall unfold in her hometown, and she was surprised by how much she was looking forward to it. The light shifting. The air crisping. That slow, deliberate pause before winter wrapped everything in stillness. Not to mention all of her boots.

The summer had been a beautiful kind of chaos, hot, full of memories and laughter that had nearly swept her away. She was looking forward to the quiet and getting back to a routine she could rely on.

There was an ad for a soap making class on her refrigerator door and Deonna already had two ramen shops lined up for their next girl's night–if Brittney ever let them off the hook. With her wedding barely 8 weeks away, Brittney had transformed into the lovable tyrant, armed with her tablet, a color-coded Google doc, and absolutely zero chill. Deonna, as maid of honor, was often caught in the crossfire while Esme received a new list of bridesmaid duties via email every Thursday afternoon.

Lauryn was gloriously untitled, secure in the *New Friend* bucket. No fittings, no speeches. Just a beautiful dress and a Nespresso machine that was already giftwrapped and on its way to Brittney's apartment.

Maybe she'd take a few days off once the weather turned cooler, drive north and rent a quiet cabin in Door County. She imagined watching the leaves turn gold and scarlet. Pulling on a wool sweater and shuffling around with no pants while she tried new recipes.

But she hadn't even finished that thought when Deonna exhaled dramatically, setting her smoothie down like she needed both hands for what was coming.

"Lauryn, I have a confession."

Lauryn blinked, slowly turning toward her friend. "Shoot."

"I listened to Joe's new album."

Lauryn closed her eyes and smiled, exhaling through her nose. "Any good?" she asked, lifting her mug. "Don't lie. I know it is."

Deonna leaned back, the bistro chair creaking slightly as she shifted, "It is, actually. And it's about you."

Lauryn turned her head slowly, one brow arched. "What?"

"Every track on here is: *Baby, why'd you go. Baby, please come back... Baby I was wrong*–you get the picture, girl."

Lauryn smirked, barely looking up. "Oh yeah? Let me know when you get to the track where he blames me."

Deonna's laugh came easy, but there was something softer behind it now. "Have you heard from him?"

"Since dinner? Fortunately, no." She'd already filled Deonna in on the disaster of a dinner.

A few long moments passed before Deonna asked the question Lauryn already knew was coming. "And Perry?"

She chewed the inside of her cheek, focusing on a lone ant making its way across the table.

"Did you reach out?" Deonna pressed carefully.

Lauryn didn't answer right away, but pulled in a deep breath while she debated how much she wanted to share. So much of what she had with Perry was layered, complicated, and so much messier than she'd ever wanted to admit. She'd shared pieces of their saga with Deonna over the last few months, but it was always surface level. Never her full feelings.

But now, sitting on this adorable main street with the late summer light shining on them, and the last of her Very Berry smoothie melting into a swirl of deep pink, it felt dishonest not to say more.

"Look Lauryn," Deonna started, setting her own cup down. "I know you like to process and figure things out on your own, but if you want to talk, I'm here."

Lauryn gazed at her friend, her face warming with appreciation. "I'm meeting my estranged sister for the first time today."

"Oh shit," Deonna blinked.

"Mm-hm. My Dad had three other girls before me. The oldest two–I don't even want to talk about them–but my middle sister, Alicia, seems... open?"

"Well, that's good."

"It is. My Dad finally convinced her to come visit."

"That's what's up. We love a family reunion."

Lauryn continued, reaching to sweep the ant gently off the table. "Yeah. So, I can't call Perry. I'm in the same place I've always been. There's always something–some part of me I'm still sorting out. It's never the right time and he deserves better than that. Honestly I shouldn't have crossed that line to begin with."

They sat in silence for a moment, traffic passing in the distance, cicadas starting to hum as the morning quickly turned to afternoon.

Then Deonna reached across the table and wrapped her fingers around Lauryn's. "I have an idea," she said very seriously. "Let's just move to Capri. Eat figs and forget everybody."

Two hours later Lauryn was setting fresh towels out in the powder room on her parent's first floor. Outside on the deck, her father was grilling, probably more food than was actually needed for the occasion and her mother was prepping the living room for the third time.

After months of conversation and making amends, her sister had agreed to visit. And she'd brought her girls. They stayed closer to the city so they could explore, but today she was bringing them to meet their grandfather. It would be the first time Neal had seen his middle daughter in years.

Once she'd completed all the chores on her mother's list, Lauryn wandered toward the front door where she'd left her purse and a tote filled with a few gifts for her sister and the girls. She smiled as she retrieved the matching paper gift bags. *Hopefully this goes well,* she hoped silently as a clash of bowls sounded from the kitchen.

When she turned back from the sound, she caught a glimpse of a sedan turning into the driveway. She leaned into the window and called out, "They're here!"

She stepped outside, her linen dress flapping around her ankles as she stepped down off the porch. Her breath hitched a little as they got out of the car.

Alicia was taller, much taller than Lauryn, with fairer skin and cinnamon brown silk pressed hair. The girls were nearly four years apart. The elder, Zora, already carried herself with maturity, helping her little sister out of the backseat of the car, while Alicia waited at the edge of the walkway.

They joined her and they all turned, taking baby steps toward the house.

"You made it!" Lauryn worked to keep her voice from breaking.

Inside, their father hugged Alicia so long they all grew quiet around them, but Lauryn noted how Alicia let him hang on. She didn't pull away.

However late or awkward this family reunion was, they clearly needed it. And when he was introduced to his granddaughters she could see a mix of emotions in his face. Glossy eyed, he shook hands with each of them, telling them how impressed he was with their grip and how nice it was to finally meet them.

Zora smiled politely and responded with a lovely, "It's nice to meet you too, Mr. Lindsey."

The younger of the two spoke up suddenly, "You're our grandfather, right?"

Beaming, Neal stood up straight. "I am."

"Are we supposed to call you Grandpa?"

He stumbled in response, "Only if you want to- er-"

He looked over at Alicia for approval? Guidance? Something was exchanged between the two of them in a split second and with a little more confidence he leaned down toward Angela and said, "Pop-pop is okay too. That's what I called my granddad."

The little girl twisted in her sandals as she looked up at him, squinting against the sun. "Let's get to know each other better first," she said, with all the charm of Rudy Huxtable, then fell into giggles.

They all laughed, some of the tension easing as they shook hands again and her father said, "It's a deal."

It was wonderful to see him like this, surrounded by his girls. He sat at the head of the rod iron patio table, leaning in as Alicia filled them in on their family travels, each of the girls' activities, and good news on her mother's treatment.

Little Angela was a water baby, excelling in her swim classes and music lessons, while Zora was a math whiz, having already been crowned a math Olympiad two years in a row.

"Ah! We've got another math whiz in the family. You know your aunt is a big deal analyst at her company." He squeezed Lauryn's hand.

Zora's interest peaked, but she only smiled at the two of them in response. Angela piped in, swinging her feet and leaning into her mother's arm. "She looks like you mommy," Angela whispered loud enough for the whole table to hear.

Alicia, who'd leaned down to listen, nodded and squeezed the little girl's hand. She looked up at Lauryn, and smiled, with warmth Lauryn hadn't anticipated, "She does."

"You know that's mommy's sister right? Like your auntie Patrice on Daddy's side."

The little girl seemed to delight in the idea of a new aunt now that she had a clear understanding. Alicia continued, "So that makes her... what? What would you call her?"

Angela went sheepish and picked up her corn on the cob while she thought about it.

"Auntie Lauryn," Zora supplied for her sister, catching everyone's attention.

She sipped her iced tea, smiling directly at Lauryn over the rim of her glass and Lauryn thought she might melt.

After growing up an only child with two preoccupied parents, never holding onto girlfriends more than a couple years, she never imagined the concept of being an aunt. Since she and her sisters had no relationship, the thought had never occurred to her.

But now, she winked at her eldest niece, picking up her own glass to take a sip.

The table hummed with new familial air and core memories unlocking. She wasn't sure how things would turn out, but she was fully determined to be a regular part of their lives.

Her mother broke the pleasant silence, when she stood asking "Who wants cake?"

"Yes please," Angela said from behind the corn cob that was nearly as big as she was.

Alicia laughed, "Well finish a little more of your food. When you're done you can ask Mrs. Lindsey for a piece."

Lauryn drew her eyes to the end of the table where her mother smiled pensively, then busied herself gathering up everyone's plates and napkins.

When Alicia offered to help, her mother raised a hand and smiled, "No, no thank you sweetheart, I've got it. I'll put some coffee on too. Unless you'd like some wine?"

Alicia's eyebrow raised, "I may take you up on that."

The universal ice breaker–Rosé. Lauryn thought, nearly snorting. Her mother nodded and headed back into the house.

The table fell silent again, the air less familiar than it had been just a few moments ago. She could tell her father didn't know what to say. This endeared him to her all the more and she set her napkin down on the table. "I'm going to give mom a hand. Dad, did you tell them about your vacation in Belize?"

He seemed grateful for the prompt, his amber eyes round with appreciation.

As he started the story, Lauryn slipped inside and slid the glass door closed behind her. The interior was quiet and cool as compared to the raucous of cicadas and heat outside. "You alright, mom?" Lauryn asked knowingly as she rounded the kitchen island.

Feigning ignorance, her mother looked up from the sink filled with soapy dishwater. "Of course–what do you mean?"

"Just checking on you. I know this ..." she paused. "This is a lot."

"Little girl–I'm fine. *This* is long overdue. I'm just giving you and your father time to bond with them. They're only in town a couple days. They'll be back in California before you know it. I don't know why you're here with me."

Lauryn couldn't help the smirk tugging at her mouth. "Mom."

"Lauryn Michelle, I told you I am fine. Just–when you all were goin' around the table saying Grandpa, Pop-pop and explaining the whole Auntie thing, I started worrying the conversation was going to turn to me. And how am I going to explain who *I* am in this equation to those babies?"

She was laughing, hands still below the soap suds. Lauryn laughed too, "Mom, kids understand more than you think. Just tell them to call you Nana."

Her mother froze in the middle of reaching for another dish, her charm bracelet dripping with bubbles. "Who now?"

Lauryn cracked up. In the end, she was proud of her mom. It seemed whatever rough patch there had been between her parents had begun to ease. And even though she wasn't eager to be anybody's "Nana" she seemed to enjoy teaching the girls how to correctly slice a cake, advising them that the best part about serving the cake is deciding who gets the biggest piece. And licking your fingers.

Later that evening, after the patio table was clear and the sun had begun to set, Alicia joined Lauryn next to the fire pit.

"The girls having fun?" Lauryn asked, pulling her hair up into a bun.

"A ball. They're in the basement playing chess with Dad."

Dad. She'd referred to him as a common entity, something they shared. As if it had been that way all of their lives.

Alicia sighed heavily, sinking down into one of the other three lounge chairs surrounding the fire. "This is beautiful."

"Yeah, Mom doesn't mess around. Her garden is everything." Lauryn crossed her ankles, admiring the hostas that she'd helped her mother put in, they're delicate purple flowers rocking in the breeze. "More wine?"

"Oh no. We're going to be getting on the road soon."

Lauryn felt the bittersweetness of the day winding to a close. She thought of her eight-year-old self, writing those letters. She tried to imagine fourteen-year-old Alicia receiving them, and maybe, *maybe* deciding not to read them. She felt her older sister's eyes on her then.

Alicia took a breath, "I really hope you can meet us for lunch downtown on Sunday." And before Lauryn could confirm, she stumbled into an apology. "I'm sorry, I know we didn't get much of a chance to visit, you and I. And with Mom's treatment, I haven't called..."

Lauryn shook her head. "Alicia, no, you are good. Today was about you and Dad. And yes, I will definitely be there on Sunday."

"Good." Pleased, Alicia leaned back into the cushions of her chair. "So how are you? The last time we spoke you were starting a new job."

"It's great! Although I'm–I'm actually starting something of my own." She spoke with deliberation, still getting used to talking about her dream out loud.

"That's amazing! What's the concept?

"A luxury bath kit subscription. Making Luxuriation normal. Slowing down, self-care..."

"Oh, I love that. Lauryn that is spot on, wellness is very big right now."

"Right! I just want to promote Black women taking time with themselves. I think the subscription works two-fold. On one hand it's a great monthly reminder to slow down and care for yourself, but on the other hand–"

"It keeps those subscription fees coming in!" Alicia finished for her, knowingly and they both laughed.

"Exactly, exactly." They chatted more, Alicia asking questions that Lauryn hadn't fully considered, but felt a boost of confidence finding she had the answers.

"So..." Alicia leaned over, her elegant arms twisting in her lap playfully. "What about romance? Any men?"

Lauryn jumped back playfully, surprised by her sister's frankness. "Alicia!"

"Girl, we are not going to have any time for girl talk tomorrow with my chilluns in tow. I need to get whatever tea I can, right now."

Lauryn beamed into her wine glass, taking another sip as she decided exactly what she was ready to share. "Oh geeze... I don't think you have enough time."

"Oh so there is someone? Wait–are you back with the singer?"

"No! No, that's done. Although he did pop on me last month."

"Not a pop up," Alicia frowned, leaning forward a little as if she wanted to hear more details.

"I know it was crazy, but I actually shut that shit down for good," Lauryn shook her head. "But, uh, there is another guy. From school actually. We reconnected," she was staring into the flames thinking of Perry for the twentieth time that day.

She did her best to paraphrase, punctuating their history and all the times they'd run into each other, how good he made her feel, and how damn sexy his walk was.

"It's a mess, girl," she bent forward, elbows on her knees as she rubbed her forehead.

After a minute, Alicia got up and moved to the lounge chair closest to Lauryn. "Sounds very simple to me actually."

"How so?"

"You like him. A lot based on all this *cringe* you're giving right now," she waved a jeweled hand overhead as if to point out Lauryn's aura.

"Finding someone decent who makes you feel that good is the hard part. Out of all the people in the world you ran back into him. So, what is it, what's stopping you?"

"I have no idea."

"Eh! Stop." Alicia spoke softly, but pointedly. "Yes you do."

"You're really getting deep into your big sister bag right now!"

Alicia erupted into a laugh that was so beautiful and unguarded it almost brought Lauryn to tears. Somehow against all odds, after those unanswered letters they were here and she was getting *advice* from her big sister, even if she wasn't ready to hear it.

"Anyway..." Alicia continued. "As I was saying. You have to know what the problem is because you're the one who stopped the ball rolling. Am I wrong?"

"Nope."

"Okay then. So, what is it? Oh–start with this. Why didn't you go to Napa?"

Lauryn opened her mouth, ready to repeat the same reasons she'd been spouting since she first decided not to meet Perry in California.

"He offered to take care of everything, right? Flight? Hotel??"

"Yes," Lauryn practically groaned.

"And, I'm assuming this man is sexy? Obviously, he's a vibe if he was trying to take you to the Jazz Festival in Napa Valley," she emphasized, clearly aware of the prestige.

"We both like jazz!"

"Lauryn, I like jazz too. And I *live* in California, but even without having to pay plane fare it was *not* in the budget. This man likes you. And you like him. Is the sex bad?"

"No, it is not," Lauryn sighed, painfully recalling their last time together.

"Did you not like the group he was going with?"

"No, everyone is cool," Lauryn sighed.

"So is there someone else-"

"No, I was just afraid I'd be doing the exact same thing I did with Joe. Getting wrapped up in another man and flying back to California, of all places!"

Alicia leaned back, folding her arms neatly in her lap again, "There." Her cross examination was complete.

Lauryn sighed, knowing her sister was right. Having known it all along. She'd been so busy justifying her decision, so busy convincing herself that she was right that she hadn't stopped to examine what had driven her decision. And then the whole mess of Joe being in town and Perry hearing about it. She'd left the door wide open for disaster. Left too many things unsaid.

"What do you do for a living, again?" She whipped around to side-eye her sister.

"I'm a therapist actually," Alicia replied pleasantly and they both fell out laughing.

Chapter 43

Fall

Lauryn

"**B**eautiful dress, Miss. May I ask where you are headed this afternoon?"

Lauryn looked up to find her Uber driver's friendly reflection in the rearview mirror. An older gentleman with grey hair and skin like toffee. "A wedding. My friend is getting married and its black tie." She toyed with the tasseled clutch in her lap, making sure she'd remembered to bring the glow oil Deonna had sent a frantic text about that morning.

"Ah, a wedding," his smile widened. "That is a sacred thing. Two people choosing each other—not just in love, but in patience and forgiveness too. My wife and I... thirty-two years now. And every morning, I still choose her. May it be a joyful one."

Lauryn smiled softly, her gaze lingering out the window. "That's... really lovely. She's very fortunate, your wife."

She turned back to the window, letting the words settle. There was something grounding in them—quiet and true.

The long Cadillac truck slowed to a stop in front of the Chicago Cultural Center—an impressive neoclassical building on the corner of Michigan Ave and Washington Street, directly across from the greenery of Millennium Park and just over a mile from where she'd gone for the holiday party this time last year.

"Have a good evening, ma'am," her uber driver's warm accent drew her attention from admiring the building as he opened the door for her and offered a hand.

"Thank you," she smiled appreciatively, taking his hand and stepping down onto the curb carefully. Her evening gown swept down off the seat and barely grazed the sidewalk as she headed for the brass doors.

Like the year before, the weather was unseasonably warm for November. Probably the only upside to global warming. She'd paired her dress with a velvet bolero to stave off the chill, but it would most likely be draping the back of a chair before the end of the night.

Inside she found herself standing before a grand staircase of creamy Carrera marble. She craned her neck to see more–finding the staircase swept off in two directions at the top. She'd never been in this building. In all of her years cruising up and down Lake Shore Drive with friends and pretending to be a city girl, she had not ever once stepped foot here.

Spinning slowly, she took in the architecture around her. She was tempted to wander around a little, examine the walls and corridors while things were still quiet.

But Deonna had been unusually frantic in her messages that morning, having forgotten the Fenty body lava Brittney had insisted all her bridesmaids wear so that they all glowed in the wedding photos.

Lauryn quickly started up the stairs. After all the fixation, delegation and tears, it seemed Brittney had truly pulled together a beautiful wedding after all. It was early, but even with no guests and the finishing touches still going up, it was stunning.

Seeing all the elements, the bouquets carefully transported in their sturdy boxes, steamed linens folded over the staff's arms as they made their way to the far ballroom, all of it coming together made it more magical somehow.

Lauryn wandered past a gilded doorway, heels clicking against the marble as she searched for signs of the bridal suite.

Her phone buzzed just as she rounded the next corner. Deonna.

Relieved, Lauryn exhaled and answered. "Please tell me you know where I'm going."

Deonna's voice came through, calm and amused. "Describe your surroundings."

Lauryn turned in place, laughing. "Um, marble? More marble... an elevator?"

There was a beat of silence from the other end of the line, and then, "Lauryn."

A door in front of her opened with a soft pull and a rush of air-conditioned calm. Deonna stood framed in the doorway, smirking, the phone pressed to her ear.

She looked *devastating*–draped in a black gown with a velvet bodice and a satin skirt that ruched at the hip like it had been sculpted there. The slight mermaid silhouette cascaded over her curves, catching the light like oil on water and pooled at her feet.

Only Deonna could look that glamorous and still be wearing fuzzy black Puma slides underneath. The unapologetic comfort of the slippers stood in stark contrast to the regency-inspired drama of the dress.

"Well, Brittney did say she wanted Bridgerton vibes. I think we achieved that," Lauryn laughed, nodding toward Deonna's chest.

Deonna laughed, rolling her eyes as she leaned in to hug her, "Girl! She's got us in here gasping for breath. This bodice is so damn tight I can't even sit down. My right booty cheek is killing me from perching on all the damn vintage furniture in here."

Lauryn held up her bag, tassels swinging. "I brought the body lava."

"Oh my god, thank you," Deonna whispered. "My ass was about to be in *trou-ble*."

She pulled Lauryn into the suite. It was warm and fragrant inside, the air laced with perfume and florals. Compared to the ornate masonry just outside, the room was simple, painted in sage green walls finished with box trim molding and soft, cloudy glass sconces that glowed like dusk.

Deonna introduced her to three of the bridesmaids, all of them younger cousins on Deonna's mom's side. The three of them beamed and waved as Deonna spoke their names, looking like triplets in short satin robes.

Lauryn spotted Esme accentuating her eyes with eyeliner and looking equally stunning in a full velvet dress that swept off her shoulders. Another mermaid silhouette that was all drama, and gave her tall frame a candelabra effect. Her natural curly pixie was set in deep shiny finger waves with the faintest hint of silver dust.

"Oh, you understood the assignment!" Brittney squealed, trotting out of the bathroom in a deep chocolate tulle robe, yards of ruffles flowing airily behind her. She pulled Lauryn into as tight of a hug as she could, without messing up their makeup. "Thank you for coming."

She was already a little misty as they pulled away from each other. "Don't you dare," her makeup artist called, appearing out of nowhere. "No, No, No."

Brittney fanned her face, trying to stop the tears. "We did waterproof right? I just know when I see Ricky I'm gonna lose it."

Having finished her eyeliner, Esme shook her head and floated towards them, leaning in to air kiss Lauryn on both cheeks. "A year of planning and she barely let the man pick out his own suit, now she keeps bursting into tears at the mere mention of his name."

"I just love him so much. And I can't believe this day is here..." Brittney whined a little and blew out a slow breath to calm herself. "Besides, my baby loves our theme. He trusts my creative expertise."

The make-up artist chimed in, "The theme is black excellence meets regency. What's not to like?"

"The theme is clearly breasts!" Deonna corrected, and they all laughed, palms resting over their stomachs as they tried their best to breathe.

"You're all going to thank me when these photos come out," Brittney sang as she settled into the makeup chair. Lauryn watched as the artist resumed her work, dusting a final sweep of highlighter across Brittney's already flawless skin. Her hair was perfectly coiffed around her delicate neck, cascading in soft waves over one shoulder. Her arms rested easily at her sides, the sheer sleeves of her tulle robe nearly grazing the floor.

She looked perfect.

Appreciation and affection bloomed in Lauryn's chest as she smiled at her newest friend. In the grand scheme of things, they hadn't known each other very long–just a few months–but Brittney had still thought to include her in her special day.

"You look beautiful, B."

"Thank you so much, girl. But can we *please* talk about all the guys you are going to catch at my reception!" Still the same Brittney, emotionally overwhelmed or not. "Wait, you didn't bring a date, did you?"

"Brittney, dear, you didn't give me a plus one," Lauryn smiled sweetly.

Brittney threw her a side eye, faux lashes making her doe eyes look even more quizzical than usual. "You can't avoid my questions. It's my wedding day."

Deonna chimed in to save Lauryn as usual, "With all the available men you just *insinuated* will be at this reception, it's probably a good thing she's flying solo. Why bring sand to the beach?"

Brittney waved her cousin off with a playful flick of her hand, eyes closed as her makeup artist blended her eye shadow. "You're just mad that you're related to most of the men here."

Even their younger cousins had to laugh at that one.

Lauryn lingered for another hour with them, sipping sparkling water cocktails because Brittney refused to get tipsy too early and wanted everyone hydrated and clear eyed for photos. When the photographer arrived, everyone except the bride was dressed. Like a conductor, he maneuvered them around for bridesmaids' shots. Brittney was handed a small silver envelope– a note from Ricky. She held it delicately, already tearing up as she slipped a finger under the seal.

Lauryn used the fuss as a cover to escape. Back in the corridor, she inhaled deeply and let the cooler air seep into her lungs. The hallway was quiet, its stillness helping her recover from the previous hour. She was grateful to only be a guest, able to observe all the romance from a safe distance and, when the time was right, slip back to the hotel room she'd booked for the weekend.

Her heels clicked softly as she drifted into Preston Bradley Hall, the grand ballroom where the ceremony would be held. Soon she found herself moving through clusters of wedding guests–elders mostly–old school folks who believe in getting to the wedding on time.

It was all breathtaking: lavish sprays of burgundy hydrangea and velvety peonies marked the start of each row, flanked by soft gold candelabras that shimmered in the candlelight. And above it all, a massive Tiffany glass dome arched like a jeweled crown overhead, casting the entire room in a magical haze.

Girl. Lauryn thought to herself, mentally applauding Brittney's choice of venue. Gracefully, she stepped past other guests as they found their seats, choosing a row close enough to see everything, but far enough to leave space for family.

More guests trickled in, drifting past her with curious glances and soft murmurs, wondering who the contemplative woman was sitting alone. This was, after all, a romantic celebration.

She fixed a pleasant expression on her face and adjusted her posture, all the while thinking of her mother who always seemed to know what to do at such formal occasions. Most importantly, how to conceal her thoughts and true feelings.

Lauryn eyed the ornate mosaics scaling up to the ceiling. The dome seemed endless with its halo of soft blues and cyan glass. As she waited for the nuptials to start, she ran the math. Nearly a year had passed since she landed back in Illinois. A full year since she made the decision to leave everything with Joe. At the time, she had no inkling of how things would truly turn out.

She was finally making real progress with *Of Scent & Skin*, having secured new sources for the raw ingredients she'd been searching for. For the past few weeks, her kitchen island had transformed into a makeshift lab. Amber bottles of essential oils, dried botanicals, hair turbans, and porcelain match holders spread out across the surface. Each item sat atop an index card, her handwritten notes scribbled and taped to the counter like evidence in a case she was determined to crack.

A few weeks before, while wandering around in Oak Park she'd stopped into a candle shop, the aroma drawing her in off the street. The interior had been calm and cozy, with chic table displays each focused on a particular fragrance, candles covered in glass domes, and each candle packaged in classy grey boxes with gold lettering.

What started as a "Hi, welcome in" from the owner turned into an hour-long chat about her brand. Somewhere amongst the flickering candles, interest had sparked and she'd walked away with a business card and a lunch on the books to discuss more. Slowly, surely, and little by little she was piecing her dream together.

As good as it felt to be building something of her own, it was nice to step away from all the brainstorming and planning. She'd chosen to stay the night downtown and just uber to the wedding, less chance of wrinkling her gown more than necessary.

Work was going well. Her team had finally accepted that she wouldn't be staying, but Hema's mentorship hadn't wavered. She remained inspiring, generous with her guidance, even knowing Lauryn planned to walk a different path.

The holidays were creeping up again, and Lauryn had recently agreed to spend them somewhere warm with her mother. Probably a bad idea, but she wanted to keep working on the bond developing between them.

Her father would be spending the holidays with Alicia's family and Lauryn had plans to join them for the new year.

Her thoughts drifted back to the ladies in the bridal suite. She had real friends, a sisterhood she could never have imagined would be so supportive.

And then of course, Perry, who she hadn't planned on. Another summer they were never supposed to have was over, but she couldn't shake how much she missed him. How much she wanted him there.

Nearly three months had passed since their last conversation. In some cruel trick, there'd been no more accidental run-ins. As summer wound down, so did the invites. The rooftop birthdays, the late-night cookouts, the impromptu gatherings that once made the city feel so small. Not a single chance encounter –unless, maybe, today.

Lauryn hadn't dared ask if he'd be at the wedding. Brittney, bless her, was far too wrapped up in the details of her own big day to remember his actual name. "The Chocolate One," she always called him, with a dreamy smile and zero shame.

Their entire chapter, it seemed, had lasted only a season. How could that be?

Lauryn looked straight ahead, trying to be grateful for everything that was going well in her life. After years of drifting, moving with the currents and always reacting, she was finally building something true to herself. Moving with some agency for once.

But the cost of finding herself hadn't been small.

She'd fumbled things horribly with Perry. The person who reminded her who she was and wanted to love her for that. Not because he needed her. Perry had come into her life like some mirror, reflecting back all the things she wanted, but wasn't ready to take. He stirred old feelings she'd tried to outrun.

She hadn't been able to meet him where he was.

There was no grand lesson in that. Just the clear understanding that timing isn't always kind.

Chapter 44

Lauryn

The ceremony started late, but ended beautifully. Brittney was breathtaking in a white satin gown with sculptural puff sleeves that swept low off her shoulders. She glowed as her older brother, the man who'd always stood in for her father, walked her down the aisle. Her eyes were locked on her fiancé, like nothing else in the room existed. None of the meticulous planning or grandeur mattered more than that moment.

Their vows had the entire room wrapped around their fingers. Sultry and sweet, their promises to honor and cherish one another pulled the audience in. Lauryn couldn't help but notice the shift in the room as couples inched closer, hands reached across chairs, and someone rested their palm on a partner's knee. And when the newly married couple finally kissed, slow and full of intent, it was enough to raise the temperature in the room.

Cheers erupted, three hundred guests rising to their feet as the couple made their exit to Jay-Z and Beyoncé's "Part II, On the Run", floating back down the aisle like royalty.

Lauryn fell in line behind friends and family, following the bride and groom as they exited the hall. However, as soon as they cleared the doors, she peeled off, slipping to the top of the grand staircase. Most guests filtered toward the cocktail hour, but she hung back, running her hand along the cool marble banister. She needed a moment.

Although usually pragmatic, Lauryn wasn't immune to what she'd just witnessed. She was truly happy for Brittney, but the illustration of love and commitment stirred something inside her. She felt fragile, like every feeling she'd been suppressing was floating to the surface.

As the last few guests exited the ballroom, her eyes settled on the criss-crossing marble staircase and the shimmering mother-of-pearl mosaic beneath the lights. Beyond the massive arched windows, the sun was setting. She'd only meant to check her phone, push down the emotion rising in her throat, but she got lost in the stillness.

Lauryn was gazing out at the architecture, when she felt someone behind her. A faint shift in the air and the sound of footsteps. Out of the corner of her eye, she glimpsed a blurred silhouette approaching, a tall man in a dark suit, followed by the soft touch on the back of her arm.

"Lauryn?"

She turned, the satin of her dress rustling as she pivoted. Her gaze lifted and fell on a familiar face.

"Rashad?" she said, startled. She tried not to let her disappointment show. "It's nice to see you! How are you?" she added, her voice pitching too high.

"Well, I was feeling pretty good about myself until two seconds ago. Thought I was killing it in this tux, but judging by your face..."

She laughed. "No! No, Rashad, you look very handsome. I was just in my head."

He gestured toward the ceiling in a playful flourish, his cufflinks catching the light. "Weddings."

"Weddings," she repeated, forcing a wistful smile.

He watched her for a moment and Lauryn did her best not to look as odd as she felt.

"May I escort you to your table?" he asked, offering his arm.

"Ah, yes, thank you." She took his arm, letting him guide her toward Gar Hall where the cocktail hour had started. Servers moved through with champagne and hors d'oeuvres.

"You know, for a moment, I thought you were expecting someone else," he said lightly.

"Is that right?" she replied coyly, without confirming a damn thing.

"You just had a look about you," He smiled knowingly, but didn't press. "By the way, you are killing it in this dress. Has the bride seen you today?"

She laughed, mostly because she knew he was trying to lighten her mood. "She has. I got full approval from the one and only Brittney Davis-Jackson! Jackson now."

"You better get her married name right."

They laughed as they entered the next hall, the space intricately decorated and warm. The coffered ceiling caught her eye as they approached
the table of place cards. Hundreds of them, lined up in near perfect rows
and adorned with thin velvet bows. She and Rashad separated to search
for their names. Lauryn spotted hers, plucking it from amongst a row
of other *Lindseys* that weren't related to her.

Lauryn Lindsey

8

She smiled, finding her name wasn't printed, but handwritten, the ink
and penmanship crisp on the linen cardstock. Brittney had insisted on
that detail over brunch weeks ago. At the time, Lauryn hadn't thought
much of it. Now, gripping the card, she appreciated her even more.

She turned to find Rashad again, but another place card caught her
eye. Slightly askew and only a few rows over from where hers had been.
Lauryn's breath caught and she drifted toward it before she could stop
herself. She paused in front of it, staring down at the name.

Perry Mitchell

8

So, he had been invited.

She hadn't seen him during the ceremony. She thought about the
rows and rows of gold chairs and wedding guests, some faces familiar,
most not. However, none of them holding her transfixed like this card.

"He couldn't make it," Rashad spoke gently from beside her, his voice
low despite the rising music.

Lauryn exhaled. "Tell me. How much does he hate me?"

"He doesn't hate you," Rashad said, pausing.

She turned to find him struggling to find the words.

"He just—Perry can be a bit of a closed book, you know?"

She nodded, and the bodice of her dress began to feel too tight. But
she was grateful for the boning, for the corseted shapewear that kept her
standing tall when all she wanted to do was find a quiet place to rub her
head which was beginning to ache.

She missed him. And not just because this wedding was so damn beautiful. She missed *him* and his steadiness, his voice and the calm he brought. The absence of all of it sat heavy in her chest.

Rashad shared more details. Even the universe had seen fit to keep them apart, delaying a final flight out, making him miss a crucial connection. She nodded, and murmured, "Thanks, Rashad."

She touched his arm before heading off to her table. She needed to accept it. She'd let Perry down again. A whole decade to learn from her first mistakes, a clean slate, and she'd done the same thing to him all over again.

For the umpteenth time she wished she hadn't gone there. If they had just stayed friends. If she had just stuck to her damn plan, they *would* still be friends.

She remembered the last time she felt like this. In the days after she'd left Perry behind in that hotel room. And although she hadn't wanted to admit it, the ache had lasted a long while after she and Joe first moved to California.

And now she knew what she hadn't allowed herself to admit before: She was in love with Perry Mitchell. And no matter how many times she ran it back in her brain, she couldn't change it.

Distracted, she was headed for the reception area when Deonna spotted her and made a beeline over.

"Hey girl! How's it going?"

Lauryn perked up, "Great! Everything was beautiful."

"It was, but girl, I've been stalking like every server in here. Brittney swore up and down there'd be lamb lollipops. That's the only thing I asked her for when she roped me in to planning and partaking in this wedding foolery. Said it like a promise. With conviction! Now, do you see lollipops?"

Lauryn shook her head, trying not to laugh. "Just stuffed mushrooms and a feta-something so far. I didn't try the mushrooms though-"

"Exactly. *Cute* appetizers. Nothing substantial! Between this dress, and the champagne I should not have had on an empty stomach, I'm about to fall out."

Lauryn grinned. "You're not serious."

"Oh, I'm serious-adjacent," Deonna said, scanning for the next tray. "I've already had to flirt with three servers to get first dibs on the shrimp."

Lauryn laughed, the heaviness in her chest beginning to lift.

"In other news, did you see me walk down with the Best Man? One of Ricki's friends and sexy as hell." They laughed together for a few minutes before Deonna slipped back before Brittney could miss her.

Lauryn continued on her way to the reception hall, her dress rustling as she wound through the round dining tables to Table 8–the "Singles Table".

A few of her tablemates were already seated, some already engaged in conversation, while others used their cocktail or clutch to conceal how awkward they felt. The initial oddness of sitting down for a formal dinner with people you don't know. Lauryn introduced herself before taking her seat, shaking hands with anyone she could reach, waving at those seated on the far side of the table, their faces nearly concealed by the gold and botanical centerpiece.

"I love your dress! How do you know the bride and groom?" One of the women, a red head in a deep green dress, asked.

"Thank you, I um- Deonna introduced me to Brittney earlier this year. And I know Ricky through–" she stopped herself. "Mutual friends. Lots of mutual connections," she finished with an airy laugh and flashed them her best smile. She was certainly channeling her mother now.

At another wedding, Lauryn might have known more people. As it was, Brittney was a few years younger and had gone south for college. She didn't have the same ties to Lauryn as Deonna did.

She did recognize the groomsmen, and a few other guys from that damn bachelor pre-game, whatever it was. In particular, the one who'd posted that photo of her on Instagram. He nodded at her sheepishly as he and his wife passed her on their way out of the wedding hall, then quickly averted his eyes.

And then of course she knew Perry.

She glanced over at the one chair at their table that remained un-claimed, place setting and water glass undisturbed. As if on cue, just as the longing for him began to thud in her chest, the DJ picked up his mic, greeting and welcoming the wedding guests.

The music shifted as he introduced the bridal party, each pair, brides-maid and groomsman, carrying out their own choreographed entrance. Deonna simply strutted out, arm in arm with who was, indeed, quite a good-looking Best Man.

When the lights dimmed, Brittney and Ricky made their entrance, hand in hand, glowing. Their joy, unfiltered and full, they moved into their first dance. And it was magic.

Lauryn danced just enough and ate just enough cake to avoid questions. Throughout the evening, she toasted with Brittney, Deonna and Esme, posing for picture after picture. She'd done her part, faking the funk for as long as she dared, but now it was time to call it. There was no way she was going to make it through the garter belt or, worse, tossing of the bouquet.

More than anything, she wanted to be in bed in the quiet of her hotel room.

She headed back to table 8, sashaying a little as the DJ played a classic by The Dream. She gathered her things, swiping her thumb across her phone screen to wake it up. She'd just booked an uber back to her hotel when her phone started to vibrate in her hand.

She held it up to get a better look at the name. Terrance.

She tried not to let the disappointment leak into her voice when she answered.

"Hey stranger," he said warmly. "Wasn't sure you'd pick up."

"Yeah, it's been a busy few months," she replied and bit her lip. She couldn't remember the last time they'd spoken.

"I figured. I just hadn't heard from you in a while. I wanted to see how you are."

She exhaled. "I'm well, thank you, but I'm sorry for going quiet. You didn't do anything wrong; I just wasn't in the right headspace."

"I get it," he spoke gently. "Would you still want to grab a drink sometime? No pressure. Just something to catch up."

She smiled faintly. "Terrance, we always said we'd tell each other when things changed."

"Yeah, we did."

"Well, they have."

She heard him sigh lightly on the other end. "Take care of you, sweetheart. And if things ever change back-"

"I will let you know," she finished for him warmly.

Lauryn ended the call gently and returned the phone to her clutch. *Time to go.*

She slipped away from the hall and down the grand staircase. The green and creamy white stone glowed in the soft lamplight as she descended. She stepped carefully, her black and white satin gown gathered up in her hands until she reached the bottom.

Outside on side entrance steps, she checked her phone, watching the map for her Uber. The evening air was cool. She was counting down the minutes until she would sink down into the deep pristine tub back in her room.

Today had been... a lot. A violent churn of feelings, memories, and a few new regrets that she had no heart space for.

She moved down another few steps, craning her neck to see if she could spot her ride coming up Washington Street. *Any moment now.*

"Lauryn?"

She turned at the sound of her name.

Perry.

In a tuxedo. Standing at the foot of the building steps.

Lauryn stilled, rooted in place and stunned by the sight of him. The night air thickened between them, pulling at her chest until she finally remembered how to breathe. "I heard you couldn't come."

"I managed to get a flight to Montreal." He took a step, drawing closer. "From there, Pittsburgh."

Another step.

"Then finally, Home."

Lauryn had to swallow before she could speak again. "With a tuxedo in your carry-on obviously." She pinched the skirt of her dress gently, lowering her right heel down one step.

"You know I stay ready," he flashed her a smile, his beard fuller than it had been, the dark line of it striking against the clean white collar of his tux. As he moved in closer, Lauryn lost her words.

She'd just spent the whole night wishing he'd been there but facing him now she couldn't think of what to say next. There was so much she wanted to say. An apology started to form behind her lips, an explanation that she'd been turning around in her mind for weeks.

"How was the wedding?" he asked,

"Beautiful," she answered before he even finished the question. "It was absolutely beautiful."

Perry lifted his arms toward her. "Well, if this dress is any indication-"

"Perry, I'm sorry." She pushed passed the compliment

He looked up at her intently. "I've been listening to the album you gave me."

"What?"

"Donny Hathaway. Such a good album," he shook his head with reverence.

"Perry-" she started again, but he interrupted.

"Lo, I've been in love with you since I was nineteen years old. I looked forward to seeing you every chance I got, but I convinced myself that if I told you how I felt, that you wouldn't feel the same. Then I tried to bury everything that happened when you left with Joe because I couldn't forgive myself for never telling you. I've been in love with you for almost twenty years, and I've never said anything." Perry laughed softly under his breath as he spoke.

Lauryn's fingers lost their grip on her dress and it fell between them, puddling on the stone steps, covering their shoes.

"How could I expect you to take a chance on something I never told you?" His question hung in the air between them.

She felt his hands encircling her waist, where the boning of her dress was the only thing keeping her steady. Her sides burned where he touched her.

"I thought my feelings were obvious. It took a while to understand that they weren't. And when you changed your mind about the trip to Cali, I felt like it was happening all over again. I lost faith in you. You don't owe me an apology."

Speechless, Lauryn's lips parted and closed as the truth threatened to force its way out. "Perry, I'm apologizing because I was afraid. It scared me because I was always so overwhelmed by Joe. I didn't think I was supposed to have anything deeper than that."

She ran cautious hands up the arms of his jacket. "Things with you are so effortless and I didn't trust that. Every single relationship I've ever had has been hard-won. Always having to be what they need."

"And now?" he dipped his head, seemingly searching for the answer on her face.

"I just miss you. I tried to tell myself it was just another summer, but I wonder how you are *all* the time. You make me remember what's important. You make me laugh—you make me think about things I don't want to deal with. It's infuriating," she laughed, exhaling as the confession spilled out. "And nothing about this wedding is helping!"

Perry bowed his head again, "I think you've battled enough. Don't you?"

She nodded, knowing he was right.

"I know you needed time to figure things out. I know how your brain works. You deserve time to heal. I will always have your back, but I need to know I'm not in this alone, woman," he pulled her close and his onyx gaze bore into hers.

"You're *not* alone in this," she assured him, her voice piping up to ensure she was clear. "There's just so much that's happened, and I-"

He stopped her before she could run through all the risks, "You know, I was thinking we could start from scratch. With all our cards on the table, but no baggage."

A smile tugged at her mouth. The idea of them moving past everything sounded wonderful, if perhaps a little optimistic. "What about everything we said at your house? I know I... I hurt you."

"I think we said what we needed to say." His voice was low and assured. "Maybe now we could stop being so damn cryptic all the time. Always leaving each other wondering."

Lauryn pressed closer, "I don't want to wonder. I want to figure this out with you. I do have something to prove to myself, but I want you with me while I'm-"

"Lo," he shook his head. "Tell me how you feel. Don't explain it, just tell me."

She tipped her head back so she could take in his expression. All of the kindness that was always there, his set mouth that was being so direct with her now, and his eyes that challenged her. She breathed deeply, the cool air sailing in and out of her lungs as she finally spoke.

"I love you. I've been in love with you."

She watched as his easy smile returned, "Yeah, that's what I thought."

Cradling her face in his hands, he claimed her mouth in a kiss that was sweet and lingering. Lauryn's eyes fluttered closed, the kiss deepening until she forgot how long she'd waited to feel this sure. Every fear and every hesitation fell away, until all that remained was the simple truth of him and a love that had always been there.

"I love you, Lauryn Lindsey," Perry said against her lips. "But, I have another thought."

"Yes?" she laughed, looking up to meet his steady gaze.

He traced her smile with his thumb. "What if you stayed put this time?"

"What if I wanted to?"

The End

Epilogue

Summer 2024

T he kitchen smells like butter and grilled meat. Lauryn is bent halfway into the cabinet under the counter, reaching for the last sleeve of paper plates. Perry eases in behind her, both arms balancing a heavy foil pan filled with barbequed chicken and beef ribs, the sauce thick and steaming beneath the tightly wrapped foil.

"Alright now girl, you better be careful with that thing," he says, navigating behind her slowly.

She turns her head just enough to catch his meaning.

He nods admiringly toward her backside.

"Boy..." Lauryn rolls her eyes and straightens, bumping him lightly with her hip. "My father is in the next room."

"And he's focused on my records," Perry says with a grin. "I'm safe."

Lauryn shakes her head, but can't stop the smile that's tugging at her mouth. Perry has been on the grill since the early morning hours. She's handled everything else: sides, drinks, set up, and of course, the dessert. They've been moving around each other all day like they've done this a thousand times.

In the living room, their fathers are knee-deep in Perry's vinyl collection, nodding with serious appreciation. Her nieces are giggling out back as they dutifully help Simone set the table. Alicia and her mother are tucked under the patio umbrella, chatting over lemonade. Deonna is posted up near the drink table and has finally debuted her mystery man. Brittney's already talking about her one-year anniversary plans, reminding everyone that there's a dress code. And Esme, glowing and visibly pregnant, is pretending she's not ready to take a nap.

Lauryn hoists the macaroni and cheese out of the oven, sliding the baking dish onto the stove so she can inspect the bubbling cheese and caramelized edges.

"You got it, baby?" Perry asks behind her, already leaning in, pretending to help, but really just trying to sneak a kiss.

"I got it, babe," she calls without turning from her task.

The food table outside is set up near the fence, covered in more baking dishes, foil trays and mismatched serving spoons, everyone's favorites ready and piping hot. Two spaghetti dishes sit side by side, a silent but proud battle between Esme and Perry's mother.

It's the summer after the wedding. After Lauryn and Perry ran into each other on the steps of the cultural center. After long conversations, many slow mornings, and one heated argument over a ceiling fan installation. There's still no agreement on what the install instructions actually said, but they made up twice. On the new hardwood floors.

Lauryn renewed her lease on her place in the suburbs, but spends much of her time at Perry's. Somehow, she's completely taken over the master bathroom with her perfume and shower oils. Perry still acts like it's an outrage, but she knows he doesn't really mind.

They spend evenings together when he's not traveling. He makes green smoothies in the mornings with kale and spinach from the garden, and she drinks them without grimacing now. Progress.

Her company, *Of Scent & Skin*, is really starting to take off. She completed her one-year contract with Amara Labs, just as she promised, and left to pursue her business full time. She has a small circle of investors who believe in her vision, including Hema, who knows exactly what Lauryn is capable of. Lauryn hired her first intern last month.

Perry and Lauryn talk shop while they cook dinner—he asks good questions, listens better. He understands her brain, her rhythm. And he's gotten good at recognizing the exact moment when her thoughts are about to spiral—sometimes before she even notices.

She catches him watching her now, smirking like he knows something she doesn't. And rightly so.

Because tucked away on the top shelf of the closet, in his least used carry-on bag, is a small ring box. He's had it for a few weeks. Thought about asking his father what to say. He's been biding his time, but if there's one thing he knows after all these years, is that he's not keeping quiet about how he feels for Lauryn Lindsey. Not anymore.

He plans to ask her tomorrow morning, when the house is quiet again. When everyone's gone home and it's just them, sitting outside with tea.

The two of them step out into the backyard together; Lauryn balancing the macaroni and cheese and Perry following close behind with the chicken and ribs. Twinkle lights stretch overhead across three long tables. It feels like the whole block is having a cookout. Music drifts over the fence from next door and mingles with the playlist Rashad put together. Laughter echoes from every corner.

Lauryn pauses for a second, taking in the scene. Everyone's here. His parents and sister. Her parents and sister. Her nieces. Friends.

She feels whole.

For the first time in a long time, she's not punishing herself for the years she gave away, for the versions of herself she had to let go. She's creating a life she is proud of, and has finally started to forgive her past decisions.

Perry's steadiness is rubbing off on her. He's always had a way of knowing. Moving calmly, clearly, and still driving slow as hell. He always saw the best in her, even when she couldn't.

The music shifts and Donny Hathaway's *Love, Love Love* sounds. Perry's already in front of her, hand outstretched, his smile soft.

Lauryn doesn't hesitate. She takes his hand and lets him pull her in. They sway together between the tables, the conversation fading around them. He wraps his arms around her waist and she closes her eyes, sinking into him.

They dance, slow and easy as the sun starts to dip low and the whole yard glows. She imagines the rest of it–the life she'll have. More days like this. More summers. More laughter. Maybe more than that, she decides as she gazes up into Perry's handsome face.

For now, this is more than enough.

This is everything.

Acknowledgements

T o my parents, C&P, whose love story inspires me every day and reminds me that true love and fairytales do exist. Thank you for ensuring I always wrote thank you cards and letters to family. Thank you for always telling me I was smart and that I could do absolutely anything if I set my mind to it. Thanks for showing us (giving us) the world so that my imagination might have no limits. I love you both so much. Here's to the first one!

To my sister, April Marie, whose support, encouragement, and faith know no bounds. I can't fail with you in my corner. Thank you for the space and time I needed to make this dream happen. I know it cut into our sister-time. I love you and I am eager to get back on schedule! Also, the soundtrack reveal was lit!

To my Grandaddy, the English teacher, whose typewriter I can hear right now as if I were in the basement sitting next to him. Thank you for summers that went too fast, regular trips to the library, and "frankfurters" for lunch. Thank you for taping every episode of *Fresh Prince* and *A Different World* and mailing them every week while we lived abroad. These are some of the best representations of our culture and of Black Love on screen. I aspire to create stories that resonate as deeply.

To my Nana, who told me the story of her friend losing a ribbon in the butter churn–a story told so well that it inspires me to this day. I often hear you saying in my mind, "Love me and the world is mine." A mantra of yours that I'm quite sure I've adopted.

To my best friends: Autumn Sonee, who kept me sane and grounded through all of this. For the nights you listened to chapter after chapter as I struggled to share this story publicly. Thank you for being you and the best book release weekend ever- Brandy & Monica 2025! Krystle Patricia & Heather Rae, my original writing buddies. I've been thinking back on the stories we crafted at our parents' kitchen tables, and how we passed notebooks between classes, drafting something special, just for us. This feels surreal, but meant to be. I can't wait to see what you both think and thank you for being better friends than I could've ever prayed for. KG: Thank you for always being the first to post, the first to follow, and the first to scream from the mountaintops that this story was on its way. I love you.

To my writing coach and friend, Lebia C., without whom I might still be keeping stories tucked away. In the two years since we reconnected, I have grown so much as a writer and a creator. Thank you for the late-night brainstorming sessions, my first-ever author event, the timely advice I didn't want to hear, and for reminding me that an author is who I always wanted to be.

To Karina, for helping me bring out the best in my writing and make this story shine.

To Jerome, for your unwavering support, advice, and incredible friendship. For being the sounding board when I was afraid to voice my ideas to anyone else. Thank you for reminding me to keep it in perspective and to take care of me first.

To Kenny, for your guidance and insight during the publishing process. Now that my book is done, I'm looking forward to kicking back and diving into one of yours.

To Kira & her father, Robert G, for their help in my research on army life. Kira: Thank you for cheering me on when I was at my most frustrated and overthinking everything. You are a light, you really are.

To my Brothers: Y'all know who you are! It was so important to me that Perry be more than what women imagine a romantic lead to be. I wanted his reactions and emotional arc to feel real–to reflect a man's perspective in all its complexity. Thank you for answering my random questions, for taking it seriously when I interviewed and surveyed you. If nothing else, it was pure fun picking your brains and hearing how you'd handle certain moments with someone you love. I'm so grateful for your honesty, vulnerability, your joy, and the respect you showed for this project.

Stay Connected

T hank you for reading *No Place Like You*. If you enjoyed the story, I'd love for you to stay connected and be part of what's next.

Website
aswrittenbycb.com

Instagram
@aswrittenbycb

TikTok
@aswrittenbycb_

Newsletter
Join my email list for monthly editions of my newsletter, *Coffee & Toast*. aswrittenbycb.com/contact

www.ingramcontent.com/pod-product-compliance
Lightning Source LLC
Chambersburg PA
CBHW050010120726
47903CB00006B/1713